SECRET IDENTITY

SECRET IDENTITY

A NOVEL

ALEX SEGURA

FLATIRON
BOOKS
NEW YORK

This is a work of fiction. All of the characters, organizations,
and events portrayed in this novel are either products of the
author's imagination or are used fictitiously.

www.flatironbooks.com

Designed by Michelle McMillian

Library of Congress Cataloging-in-Publication Data

Names: Segura, Alex, 1980– author.
Title: Secret identity : a novel / Alex Segura.
Description: First edition. | New York : Flatiron Books, 2022.
Identifiers: LCCN 2021041614 | ISBN 9781250801746 (hardcover) |
    ISBN 9781250801753 (ebook)
Subjects: LCSH: Comic books, strips, etc.—Fiction. | LCGFT: Detective and
    mystery fiction. | Novels.
Classification: LCC PS3619.E4155 S43 2022 | DDC 813/.6—dc23/
    eng/20211007
LC record available at https://lccn.loc.gov/2021041614

Our books may be purchased in bulk for promotional, educational, or business use.
Please contact your local bookseller or the Macmillan Corporate and Premium
Sales Department at 1-800-221-7945, extension 5442, or by email at
MacmillanSpecialMarkets@macmillan.com.

First Edition: 2022

10 9 8 7 6 5 4 3 2 1

For my wife and children—true superheroes

Life, at best, is bittersweet.
—Jack Kirby

Obsessions are the only things that matter.
—Patricia Highsmith

SECRET IDENTITY

PROLOGUE

Her eyes fluttered open at the sound.

Carmen Valdez rolled out of her small twin bed with ease, the muscle memory kicking in—even now, in the middle of the night. The shrill scream was familiar, too.

She tiptoed across her small bedroom, avoiding the toys strewn on the floor, as she made her way to the door.

Another scream.

Mami.

The screaming and arguing were routine. Carmen found that she'd become numb to it. She could almost predict it, in the hours before bed. If Mami and Papi were drinking—drinking that stuff—it was a bad sign. It meant they were changing. Becoming meaner. Darker. Something else. She would rush through her routine, rush to get to the relative safety of her room, her closed door, her darkness.

But she also knew the darkness could only shield her from so much. It hid her, but it didn't silence them. She knew the screams would come. Carmen would just pray she could sleep through them.

She took the steps slowly and sat in her usual spot. They lived in a compact three-bedroom house in a suburban slice of Miami. It was worn-out in a lived-in, comfortable way. It was home. Carmen loved it here. Felt safe here. Most of the time.

She held on to the spindles of the thick, faux-wood banister and looked down onto the tiny living room, lit only by a flickering lamp that loomed over her parents. The screaming had stopped for now, replaced by a sound Carmen had never heard. At least not from her father.

Sobbing.

"Por qué? Por qué, Clara? Why? Why are you doing this?"

Her father's stiff, unfamiliar English surprised Carmen. Her parents always spoke to each other in Spanish. It was their language. Their way. English was something else. A chore. A means to an end. To hear her Cuban father force himself to speak English—while crying, no less—gave Carmen a disorienting feeling that made her question if she was even awake.

"Get up, Pepe, párate. Háblame como un hombre, por Dios," Carmen's mother said, her words tight and seething, through gritted teeth.

Her father's sobs continued. Racked, painful cries that amplified Carmen's dizzy, frightened feelings. The ground under her felt uncertain. Her world seemed shaken and malleable. She didn't like that.

She felt her face redden, the tears sliding down her cheeks slowly as she fought back the whimpering sounds she knew would come anyway. What had she done? What had made her parents this way? What could she do to fix it?

Before she could ponder it further, her mother's eyes met hers—pulsing with rage at first, then softening with surprise and shame. The entire spectrum of emotions playing out in less than a second. Carmen tried to push herself back into the shadows, but it was too late. She'd been spotted. She did it anyway. She heard her mother's slow footfalls as she approached the banister, could almost feel her looking up at the spot where Carmen had been.

"Carmencita, qué haces?" her mother asked, her voice mannered and forced, clearly trying to not sound like she'd had too much of that stuff to drink. Trying to sound like she was her usual, daytime Mami. "Es muy tarde, mijita . . ."

Carmen didn't respond. She pivoted her small body away from her crying father and slowly crept back to her room.

Carmen had built defenses for these nights. These dark moments where her life felt unmoored—unsafe. She'd think about better times. Warmer times. Walking to la farmacia with Papi, his big hand in hers, the smell of his sweat and cologne mixing together to create a familiar, comforting feeling. His worn features shifting into a tired smile as he held the door open for her, his "princesa."

They wouldn't go far. They didn't come to the pharmacy for medicine, usually. They'd make a beeline for the magazine aisle, past the glossies and paperback books to a wire-frame spinner rack loaded with pictures so colorful and welcoming that they practically whispered Carmen's name as she approached. The red, white, and yellow of the Flash. The patriotic gear of Captain America. The muted green-and-yellow insectoid costume of the Fly. The gray, red, and black of the Dusk.

It was their ritual. Their special routine. Papi would walk with her, she'd step back and watch him spin the rack, his fingers gently touching the stacks of comics as it went around and around. He'd grab one or two, show them to Carmen, and then recite a brief description.

"Batman tiene mucha fuerza, pero es muy inteligente, también, Carmencita" or "Captain America—un hombre bueno. Decente."

Then they'd walk to the cash register, and, like clockwork, her father would tell her how, as a newly arrived Cuban immigrant with a wife and baby daughter, he'd learned to read English with comics. Learned about this country they now called home from the adventures of people like Superman, the Blue Beetle, Martian Manhunter, or the Freedom Alliance. Carmen would nod and smile. She knew the story by heart. But she loved it. She loved this man—good-hearted and strong. Fallible but always striving to be better.

Carmen thought back to those moments as she climbed the stairs on all fours, like a cat trying to wiggle through a fence without making a sound. She needed to go back to her safe place. She needed to cover herself, hide herself, with a cloak of her own creation. Only then—in her cramped room, loaded with boxes of comics and drawings, and ideas—would she be safe.

She had to become someone else to survive.

PART I

ORIGIN STORY

Excerpt from 1975's *The Legendary Lynx #1, "Behold—The Lynx!"—Story: Harvey Stern, Art: Doug Detmer, Letters: Todd Morelli, Editor: Rich Berger, President/CEO: Jeffrey Carlyle.
Published by Triumph Comics.*

CHAPTER ONE

A **scream tore through the office.** It was barely eleven and Carmen Valdez already wanted to die.

"Carmen? Where are you?"

Her smile tightened a bit as she turned from the large, noisy copier in the small, overcrowded Triumph Comics office on Eighteenth Street in the Flatiron District. The usual workday bustle seemed to grind to a halt as her boss, Triumph Comics owner and editor-in-chief Jeffrey Carlyle, walked across the space—hands flailing like a young bird desperately trying to stay airborne, nothing but asphalt below. He cut a quick path to where Carmen stood, her expression still calm, eyes wide and expectant. This was their schtick, Carmen had come to accept. Carlyle would hiss and whine about some inane thing—misplaced original artwork, an appointment he hadn't been told was happening, or just because he felt like it—and Carmen would calmly explain to him why the world was this way. It'd been like this for as long as Carmen had worked as Carlyle's secretary. Almost a year. It was the dance.

"Right here, boss," she said, her tone clear and alert. "Copying Maynard's new script. Just takes a minute with this new machine. Kind of amazing."

"I asked you to do that hours ago," he said, his tone somewhat muted. A tiny, fruitless victory.

Carmen caught a glimpse of the two beleaguered bullpen employees, looking down at their pasteup stations at the first sign of conflict. They were probably making a last-minute correction to the art on a book that was running hot. The sounds of Carlyle sniping at someone were a welcome and entertaining distraction.

Carmen raised an eyebrow at them before turning to face her boss.

"That was for *Gray Wolf*—the one where he battles the Interloper, remember?" she said, handing him a stack of just-copied pages, the fresh ink smearing on her hands. "This is his new *Avatar* one. Issue fifteen."

"Right, right," Carlyle mumbled to himself as he grabbed the pages, his shrug of surrender almost imperceptible as his tiny eyes scanned the top sheet of the script. The book was hot. Len Maynard was Triumph's top writer, but that didn't mean he was their best. Or their fastest. Fans loved him for his bouncy, philosophical dialogue and innate, almost instinctual ability to create characters who felt otherworldly. Carlyle hated him for his spaced-out, trippy plots that clearly stemmed from Len's fondness for mushrooms, acid, and White Russians. Not so much because of Maynard's literary aspirations, but because in Carlyle's twisted view, Len's attempts to elevate his work were seen as an affront to Carlyle, a man with his own lofty literary dreams of writing the Great American Novel.

"Let's see what kind of cool vibe we get tapped into this time," he said, spitting out "cool vibe" with unbridled disdain.

Carlyle swiveled away toward his office and Carmen was left alone by the copier again. A brief respite. She took a moment to tie back her shoulder-length black hair in a hasty ponytail. In about an hour, he'd want his lunch—pastrami on rye, lots of mustard, no pickles—laid out on his desk, maybe with a bottle of Coke. Secretarial work was a slog, but Carmen was good at her job. When Carlyle complained, it was never about her. It was *at* her—usually about the staff or his own family. She kept her boss on a schedule, kept him focused, and, if she wasn't being modest, kept the Triumph Comics machinery humming. She invoiced talent for work, she made sure artists had script pages to draw, and she co-ordinated staff time off and the holiday party. Usually for meager thanks and plenty of quibbles and complaints. She did it all with a knowing grin, too. She wanted to be here, and she wasn't going to let anyone shake her. Working for Jeffrey Carlyle was a dream. Working in comics was *the* dream—the dream that brought twenty-eight-year-old Carmen to New York from Miami. To snowy winters, air-conditioning units, moldy studio apartments, skyrocketing murder rates, and smoky streets. The New York of 1975 was fraught, menacing, and hopped up on paranoia—where muggings were commonplace and home break-ins a rite of passage. You didn't wear your nice jewelry, and you looked over your shoulder as often as you could. This was in stark contrast to the tropical suburbia that Carmen still thought of as home. She was worlds away from Mami's arroz con pollo and one single warm-weather wardrobe.

Away from Katherine.

She shook her head and grabbed the original script from the copier. Before Carmen could make her way back to her own tiny desk—stationed outside Carlyle's large, glass-walled alcove—she felt a tap on her shoulder.

"Need a break?"

The nasal voice gave it away. Carmen turned around, unsurprised to find Harvey Stern, his lanky figure leaning on the doorway that led to the main elevators, a warm grin on his long, mischievous face. His overgrown brown hair flopping onto his forehead. Harvey was a junior editor at Triumph. He also had cigarettes.

"God, yes," she said, dropping the script back onto the copier and following him out. "Can we smoke outside, though? I need to feel some kind of air."

Harvey nodded and they moved in unison toward the elevator bank. Carmen gently swatted his wandering arm away from the small of her back. Harvey was sweet. Too sweet. And sweet on her. Carmen wasn't dense. She saw how men looked at her. More importantly, she understood how men looked at her—trim and fit, with sleek, dark brown hair that fell to her shoulders and a pair of feral eyes that seemed to amplify a sharp, sly grin. The kind of cool, distant beauty and presence that could be both mysterious and warm at once. She'd heard variations on the theme from too many dudes, and it never ceased to bore her.

Harvey was a nice kid, maybe not even a kid—she honestly couldn't tell how old he was, but there was no way he was a day over twenty-five. Carmen was closer to thirty than he'd ever get.

He played off the gesture and tapped his feet as they waited for the elevator.

"So what was he bitching about now?" he said, his words sounding awkward and stilted.

"Oh, he forgot what he asked me to copy," she said, not meeting his gaze. "You know, the usual."

Harvey was, as far as these things went, one of her only friends at work. But being a nice guy among a squad of over-the-hill assholes didn't really mean much. She didn't grade on a curve when it came to friends, which was probably a big reason why she'd spent a lot of time on her own since moving to New York. Carmen hadn't figured out if Harvey was being nice to her because he genuinely wanted to be friends, or if he wanted to be friends because he hoped it'd mean more. Carmen was certain he'd sleep with her if she let him. Most men would fall into that category. But he was nice, and that was fine, at least when it came to passing the time at work.

They cut through the vacant lobby and made it out onto the street. It was a chilly, gray March day, the clouds threatening rain as the entire city struggled to figure out if they needed to cling to their winter coats or if it was okay to saunter outside in a lighter jacket. The past week had felt colder than any March should, and the city seemed particularly unhinged. New York was a nexus point for young people looking for work, but the city itself seemed to be ripping apart. Vacant buildings. Rampant crime. The most beloved city in the country was disintegrating, and all they could do was watch from the inside. Carmen shivered as she reached for Harvey's outstretched pack of Parliaments. Not just from the cold, but from everything. He lit her cigarette before his and they slumped into their midday smoking positions.

"How's the new Len script?" Harvey asked, probably spasming internally at the brief silence between them.

"It's good," Carmen responded, blowing a quick cloud of smoke out into the street. She watched the people walk by the building, all hypnotized by their own to-do lists and problems. An overburdened mother dragging a toddler behind. A leather-clad man wearing visor sunglasses nodding to a beat only he could hear. An elderly couple looking like a pair of Rip Van Winkles, awakening to a world they didn't recognize. The flurry of people seemed to blend into the gray, polluted skies of the kinetic city Carmen now called home, creating an energy she still hadn't found a way to channel or understand. Carmen wasn't new to New York, not really. But it felt like it'd taken her a year just to learn to survive. The rest of her time here had been spent trudging along with a bit more confidence.

"I love his stuff," Carmen continued, turning to look at Harvey. His eyes seemed to widen upon contact, hungry for some kind of connection. "It feels more alive, you know? Less paint-by-numbers than what he did at Marvel. It just feels like he's trying to do more with it—give these characters a reason for being."

"Yeah, yeah, totally," he said, nodding his head. "Have you read Starlin's *Warlock*?"

She felt offended by his question but didn't let on.

"C'mon, Harvey. Of course I have. But I liked his stuff on *Captain Marvel* more," she said.

Harvey nodded once more before turning away, taking a long drag from his cigarette.

"I feel like that's what Maynard's doing with *Avatar*," he said, almost to himself. "I mean, that idea was pretty lame before he came onto the book."

"It was dull," Carmen said. "It read like a bad *Superman* knockoff, and Superman's pretty boring as is."

Harvey chuckled.

"Yeah, yeah, exactly," he said. She caught him mouthing *boring* to himself. It was almost cute.

Carlyle would be slithering around the office soon, probably looking for something to complain about, but she didn't want to get back upstairs just yet.

"You think we're in trouble?" Harvey asked.

It took her a minute to figure out what he meant.

"The company?" she asked, playing it coy. Harvey knew Carmen was privy to a lot more than the average employee. She sorted Carlyle's mail. She took his calls. She often heard at least one side of those conversations through the thin wall that separated her from their boss. It was the oldest trick in the office politics playbook. Pick the secretary's brain.

The exertion of asking the question made Harvey lose his nerve. He stammered a bit and let it drop. She was fine with that. Carmen looked at her watch.

"I have to get back," she said. "Thanks for the smoke. Any big plans for the weekend?"

Harvey shrugged. It was cute this time. She wanted to like him more. She could use a real friend, she thought.

"I might catch a show at CBGB on Sunday," he said, trying to play it off. Carmen rolled her eyes at the attempted cool.

"I didn't think you were into the hip new sounds, Harvey," she said with a tilt of her head.

"Well, no, but I—"

She patted his arm with a quick double tap.

"Relax," Carmen said. "That seems fun. Who's playing? Patti Smith and Television?"

"Yeah, I think so," he said. *Shit,* Carmen thought. *I got his hopes up.*

"Have a good time, if I don't see you," she said as she turned toward the building.

She tried to offer up a warm smile, but Harvey was looking at his feet.

CHAPTER TWO

Rich Berger's office door was open as Carmen walked by, a stack of makereadies in her hands.

"Hey, Carmen," she heard him mutter, almost to himself. "How are you?"

Carmen backpedaled and peered into Berger's office. Berger was Triumph Comics' most senior editor, an industry veteran who'd made pit stops at Charlton, Quality, and—briefly—DC. He was about Carlyle's age, perhaps a handful of years younger. Where Carlyle was gruff and exuded "blowhard," Berger was mild-mannered and sharp. Over Carmen's time at Triumph, they'd bonded over their shared love for the medium. She found him charming, in an odd, doddering-uncle way. But she knew beneath the bookish exterior was someone with a great passion for the art of comics if not the trivial, fan-driven aspects of it. She appreciated that more than she could really comprehend.

"Rich, I'm doing okay," she said, stepping into his office and taking a seat across from him. "How're you?"

Rich had been a "big get" when Carlyle lured him from DC, and one of the perks was this office—slightly smaller than Carlyle's and packed from floor to ceiling with comics from every era. It felt like a museum to Carmen, and the musty smell of aging paper always welcomed her as she walked in. But she could tell Triumph was not what Berger had expected. After a brief stint in editorial at DC, he'd envisioned the jump to Triumph as a chance to shape something, to provide guidance to a smaller fish in the same pond. Instead, as he'd told her a few times, when he was feeling a bit uninhibited, "I was hired to do the part of Carlyle's job he didn't like."

That included the bulk of the company's editorial duties—rejecting ideas and firing freelancers, placing calls to late writers or artists, reading scripts that weren't first issues or important turning points, and generally making sure the trains ran on time. It was a job that Rich would have certainly savored if he was the one actually making the decisions. But it's less fun to tell someone their work is shit when you don't necessarily agree.

"Fine, fine, just toiling away," he said with a humorless smile. "How is our fearless leader today?"

Carmen shrugged.

"Standard Carlyle," she said. "Alert level yellow, I'd say. His usual gripes—Maynard, our competitors, how he doesn't get the credit he deserves—you know the drill."

Berger pushed his glasses up the bridge of his nose. "Don't I ever," he said. "Anyway, that's not why I stopped you."

She watched as he opened a side desk drawer.

"Got another one for your consideration," he said, pulling out a comic book and handing it to her, facedown. It was part of his routine when he did this—maintaining the suspense. She thought it was somewhat lovable.

Every week or so they'd take a few minutes from the workday and he'd hand her an issue or two from his collection—books he'd picked up over his years in the industry or as a fan. Carmen enjoyed the lending library because Berger never treated it like some kind of education, or an aging professor bestowing a slice of his own wisdom to a young student.

He talked to her like a fellow traveler or fan, someone who shared his passion for comics and the people who make them.

She flipped over the comic. It was an issue of DC's flagship series, *Detective Comics*. The cover featured the Dark Knight stepping down a spooky flight of castle stairs, a woman standing over him and exclaiming, "*I offer you IMMORTALITY . . . or instant death!*"

She'd seen the cover before, she could have sworn, but she'd certainly never read it. Though Batman was one of her earliest comic book memories, she often took the vigilante's adventures for granted. He was ever-present—with his sidekick, Robin—protecting the streets of Gotham. She could always find him if she wanted to. Still, the cover beckoned to her with something new and different. Her curiosity was piqued.

"Batman, eh? How mainstream, Rich," she said with a raised eyebrow as she opened the book and flipped through the pages. That's when she noticed the credits—writer Dennis O'Neil and artist Neal Adams. Though the book she held was at most five years old, the two names carried a lot of weight. O'Neil's journalistic writing often paired with Adams's stark, realistic art to create stories that brought fantastical characters like Green Lantern into our real lives, making the worlds they inhabited feel a bit more believable. She looked up at Rich, who was smiling under his bushy mustache. "Why this, though?"

"I know Denny and Neal a bit," Berger said a bit sheepishly, not one to name-drop. "As good as they are, as beloved as their work is, I still feel like they don't get enough credit. Everyone wants the sexier book. The hot title. But I really think people are going to look back on these stories"—he pointed at the comic Carmen was holding—"as truly definitive. I mean, before Julie brought them on, and put them together, Batman was this happy-go-lucky guy, just skipping around town. But Denny and Neal made him a dark avenger. This creepy vigilante that's as much Sherlock Holmes as he is a superhero, with a nice dose of the supernatural. It starts with this one, if I'm not mistaken. They're really quite fabulous. I know you want to learn the craft, to write your own stories someday. This shows you how it's done—and done well."

Carmen smiled as she carefully closed the comic and placed it atop the stack of makereadies. The printed-out color copies of comics reminded her that she was at work. She glanced at her watch.

"Gotta go, Rich," she said, standing and scooping up her stuff. She felt her face redden. She was embarrassed but also grateful for the gift. "But thank you. I mean, just glancing at it, I know I'll enjoy it. I appreciate you thinking of me."

"I'm just happy you haven't read it," Berger said. "You're an expert, Carmen. It's nice to have another one here."

"Hardly," she said with a playful shrug. She motioned toward Berger's crowded bookshelf. "I could read these all day. It's the dream, I guess."

Carmen realized she'd let her words drift a bit, distracted by the stacks of books and comics Berger had accumulated over the years in the industry. Why, though? Why, when at every other point in her day her defenses were up, was she at ease in this room? She knew a big part of it was Berger, this kindly older man who just enjoyed talking comics. There was no agenda here. She didn't have to suck up to him, and it reminded Carmen of a simpler time—when her biggest problem was whether she liked the new issue of *House of Mystery* or *Showcase*. The comfort that brought her was impossible to quantify, she realized.

Berger cleared his throat.

Carmen turned to look at him. "Think your boss might be beckoning you," he said, a tinge of regret in his voice. Maybe he enjoyed these chats, too, she thought.

"Probably," she said, heading out of his door. "See you later, Rich."

He gave her a slight wave as she turned left toward Carlyle's office.

She waved at the production staffers huddled in the center of the bullpen, marking up xeroxed copies of an upcoming issue of *The Black Ghost* as lettering guides before sending them by messenger to letterers around town. She could smell the rubber cement and Dr. Martin's dyes that were left half-open at a nearby table, the hues hastily painted over tattered color guides, notations scribbled on the margins that only insiders could understand. The comics business was messy—a slapdash sprint to meet immovable deadlines, a blur of pages flowing from production to editorial and back before being jettisoned out the door to the printer. Carmen loved it.

"Valdez? Where's my lunch?"

Carmen could hear Carlyle's practiced complaint—he liked to rehearse his petty requests before storming out into the main office—as she approached her desk. She grabbed the brown bag the delivery boy had left on her desk and walked in. Carlyle stopped himself as he was getting up from his chair, his brow furrowed and back slouched, like a bear preparing to flop onto an unsuspecting animal. His expression softened when he saw her delivery.

"Oh, I was about to check on you," he said.

"What for?" Carmen said, trying to keep it more sweet than sharp. "When have I ever been late, boss?"

Carlyle slumped back into his seat as Carmen turned for the door.

"Wait, Carmen, stick around," he said, motioning for her to take one of the two empty seats in front of his brown desk.

Carlyle's bookshelves were a who's who of English Literature 101: Hemingway, Faulkner, Fitzgerald, Orwell, and Austen. A nod to his own literary aspirations, but not much else. The sheen of dust that covered the copies of the classics were a sign that the display was just that—a show for visitors, not a collection of well-worn reading copies. The surface of his desk was more workmanlike, littered with comics in various stages— proofs, finished books, character designs, scripts, makereadies, marked-up pages. You could cobble together a few issues of something just with the materials Carlyle was too lazy to throw out. Carmen scanned it hungrily, trying not to betray her excitement.

Carlyle tapped two fingers on a stack of papers. Len Maynard's script. *Here we go.*

"You read this yet?"

"I did," she said, her tone confident and clear.

"What did you think?"

"It was good, but you know where I stand," Carmen said. She tried to stamp out any hesitation in her voice. She knew she wasn't on stable ground. Whenever Carlyle asked her for notes on something, the conversation was certain to be fraught with land mines. But she hadn't gotten this far to mince words or defer. She knew Carlyle well. Some days, he just wanted someone to agree with him. Other days, maybe when his wife decided to pay attention to him or he'd just come back from a boozy lunch with a new writer he was desperate to hire, he'd be open to criticism or pushback. Carmen couldn't predict his mood. But she knew what she thought—and Len Maynard was a good writer, maybe the best one working for Triumph.

A low, whiny sound escaped Carlyle's mouth. He was older, well into his fifties, and in pretty good shape, all things considered—his face a bit too puffy and coarse, more gray than brown in his overgrown mustache, and a potbelly that was expanding at an alarming rate. Beneath the demanding, particular exterior was a heart, though Carmen wasn't totally sold on whether it worked regularly. His bursts of kindness—flowers, a minuscule raise, and the occasional free lunch—were overshadowed by more frequent bouts of cutting cruelty, a general dismissiveness, creepy compliments, and a dense, impossible-to-penetrate belief that only he and his cronies could do what he and his cronies did. Which made his increasingly regular habit of picking her brain about how to do his own job more bitter than sweet.

"It's weird, but it feels forced," he said, more to himself than to her. "I mean, what is he trying to say, you know?"

His question didn't land in either of the two buckets she was used to. Did he want her to agree with him, or did he want something . . . new?

She doubled down.

"He's trying something different, I think, something more like the comic books at Mar—"

Wrong choice.

"Marvel? Please, no. I'm so burnt out on Stan and Jack," he said, waving his hand dismissively. "We're our own place, all right? We do things differently here. I'm a story guy—I like tall tales that take people somewhere else. But what Len's doing, it's—it's not clear, it's muddy and confusing. There's no action, no sex appeal, no drama. I mean, we're in the comic book business. It's just this guy, who we're supposed to think is a hero, all his deepest . . . I dunno, feelings, I guess? It's too dense. I feel like I just sat through a literature class when I read his scripts. He aims high, but it doesn't land."

Carlyle let out a long sigh as his thick fingers rapped on his forgettable, bland desk with a slow, plodding rhythm. He was looking at Carmen, his head shaking almost imperceptibly. His brain still processing her comment.

It'd taken a few months for Carmen to realize that Triumph Comics survived on defiance, spite, and resentment. Carlyle wasn't a comics connoisseur. He was, however, a snob with literary aspirations, who also wanted to make money. Carlyle's professional life had been spent in advertising, wheeling and dealing with clients to create a narrative that would hook customers with ease. Carlyle's character was a toxic blend of salesman, lukewarm Hubert Humphrey liberalism, and hubris—a door-to-door guy who had finally decided he knew enough about the product he was selling to create his own. An avid follower of literary circles—if not a reader—Carlyle longed for a place in publishing, not just in comics but in "real books," as he often put it. He didn't write. That was too much work. But he'd love to tell you how to make something better. He'd also love to hear about how much you enjoyed work he had a hand in producing.

The son of Theodore Carlyle, owner of Silver Claw Publishing, a company built on nudie mags, gambling advice books, whoopee cushions, and dime-store pulp novels, Jeffrey Carlyle got his current job the old-fashioned, easy way—by being the boss's son. While Silver Claw's pulps were floundering, his father's tchotchke business seemed to keep everything else afloat. He cobbled together modest financing and bought his father out, keeping the Silver Claw subsidiaries and relaunching the company's comic book branch under a new name—Triumph Comics, cannily using his advertising skills to keep the lights on. Barely.

Carmen saw Triumph for what it was just a few weeks into her job—an exercise in ego. Carlyle knew what should sell, what people should read, and if they didn't buy or consume what he produced, they were wrong. It was the height of entitled hubris. It was also a means to an end. Carlyle hadn't been shy about telling Carmen—or anyone, really—that his true desire wasn't to run a comic book company, but to publish literature. Novels. "The kind of stories that'd last," he'd told her more than once.

But for all the headaches and money woes Triumph Comics brought down upon her boss, Jeffrey Carlyle could never imagine a scenario in which he'd sell the company. Was he just that interested in proving to the world that he could do what no other company had in decades? A burning desire to keep going in the face of the huge, overwhelming success of Marvel Comics? To persevere despite the seemingly permanent, titanic presence of DC Comics and characters like Superman and Batman?

Carmen cleared her throat. Carlyle didn't respond. Her cue to continue.

"It's good—it feels different, textured, literary," Carmen said, her eyes on Carlyle's. "It's different. We need different. Avatar always felt, I dunno, so bland before," she said. Carmen was taking a big risk here, considering Avatar was Triumph's flagship character and title. If there was such a thing.

If you'd asked her after a glass of wine, Carmen would've labeled Avatar a poor man's Superman. In his earliest appearances, Avatar told the tale of teen sports hero Charles Veitch, a square-jawed, all-American kid who's injured on the football field and sees his dreams turn to dust. Visited in the hospital by an otherworldly being who imbues him with super strength and flight and a vague connection to "the planet itself," Veitch decides to adopt a superhero persona to protect his hometown of Triumph City, their company's fictional nexus point.

All of that changed when Len Maynard, a twentysomething self-proclaimed rock aficionado with a long black beard and thick glasses, stepped in. Maynard subverted the very idea of *Avatar*—revealing that the being that granted Veitch his powers was actually a fraud created by the US government to allow them to test a super-being serum on him, in the hopes of creating an army of warriors to crush the "East Asian" rebellion that was as veiled a reference to the Vietnam War as Maynard could muster. At first blush, it all felt very Captain America to Carmen, but as she—and everyone in the office, jaws on the floor—read on, things began to coalesce into a bigger meta-commentary on "might is right." Soon, Avatar was exploring his connections to the Earth, becoming a shamanistic wanderer, speaking out on environmental causes and decrying US imperialism. By the time Carlyle noticed what the hell was going on, it was too late: The book was a hit, Maynard was as close to a star as Triumph had, and there was no looking back.

Carlyle shook his head, yanking Carmen back to the present.

"It's too much," he muttered, a slight lilt to his voice. "Now he has Veitch renouncing his identity—revealing himself to the world. For what? You have to read all the issues to have any idea what's going on. There's got to be a better way to do it."

"But that's how comics work," she said with a shrug.

"Oh, really?" he said, raising an eyebrow. "Now you're the expert?"

"You asked me what I thought, right?"

"Fair," Carlyle said, his voice a low, defensive gurgle. "Okay, that's all. You can go back to your desk."

"Did you read my script?"

Carlyle stiffened. He had known this was coming. Had been dreading it, apparently.

Carmen felt her mind race in the second before Carlyle spoke—scenarios playing out in her head, some good, some bad, some mundane. She'd been handing in spec scripts to Carlyle for months, each one fraught in its own way. She needed closure. Carmen wanted this conversation to happen, whatever the outcome. Of that she was sure.

"Look, Carmen . . ." Carlyle said, straining for the next word. "Yes, I read it."

"And?"

"It was fine," he said, nodding, trying to be soft. "It was competent. It needs work, but you know I can't use it. I don't, well, look—"

She stayed silent. Not giving an inch.

He let out a long, meandering sigh.

"Do I have to spell it out?"

Carmen didn't respond.

"I have a line of guys outside my office who would kill, literally murder someone, to write a comic here, to be in business with us," he said, motioning toward his window. "Writers with actual credits, either here, or Charlton, or Harris, or Warren; some even have Marvel or DC issues under their belt. I can't just hand an assignment to my *secretary*. How do you think that'd look? Everyone outside my door would think—would get the wrong idea, about you, or us. It's just bad form. I can't do it. I have enough gossip swirling around as it is. No way. Is that how you want people to think about you?"

"Think what about me?" Carmen said, a touch of heat in her response. "God forbid people discover a woman knows how you like your sandwiches, huh?"

Carlyle raised his hands in surrender.

"Calm down, all right?" he said. "Don't go all women's lib on me. You know I'm proud to have you on staff. It's important to have women in the workplace and all that. It helps us all. But writing? No. I have other plans for you, okay? I think with some—I dunno—seasoning, you could have a real shot at being an editor here. Down the line. Doing more than just cranking out this hack crap. You could really help me pick the right people and run this place. But I can't do that right now. You need to be more patient—"

"I want to write. That's why I took this job. I don't want to be groomed to be your sidekick," she said, instantly regretting it. But Carmen couldn't let Carlyle off the hook with such a feeble defense. She wasn't built that way.

His face scrunched up and she knew she'd lost whatever chance she'd had of winning this argument.

"Huh. Well, I'm going to pretend I didn't hear that," he spat. "I don't know what you think should happen, but here in the real world we grant jobs based on experience and merit, all right?"

Said the guy who inherited this very company, she thought.

"So, how would that even happen? How am I supposed to—"

Carlyle sliced his hand over his desk. This conversation was over.

"Go, get to work," he said, not meeting her eyes. "We're done here."

CHAPTER THREE

He is such a fucking asshole."

The words wafted out of Molly's mouth, mingling with a cloud of cigarette smoke as she leaned back into the rickety barstool. They were between sets at the Village Gate, a nightclub on the corner of Thompson and Bleecker. The place had been known mostly as a jazz club, featuring performances by the likes of Coltrane, Bill Evans, Dexter Gordon, and Miles Davis—but of late it seemed to be hosting more rock and avant-garde acts. Carmen liked the laid-back vibe and relatively affordable drinks. The lighting was dim and smoke seemed to fill every corner of the bar, which was growing louder and more crowded as the night progressed. Conversations buzzed around them, creating a cushion of sound that Carmen found soothing, no matter how loud things got. She'd never find a place like this in Miami, she'd thought when Molly first brought her. Dark, cramped, old, and musty. Miami was tropical and new, air-conditioned and bright. This felt like old New York, and Carmen could get lost in it forever.

A rare lull had kicked in. People were leaving, people were coming in, and—most important—people were making their way to the bar.

The familiar sounds of amplifiers being disconnected and mics being checked blended with the crowd chatter to create a staccato backbeat to the boisterous sounds bursting from the venue.

Carmen took a quick pull from her beer as she watched Molly's long brown hair fall over her shoulder as she turned. Molly's dark skin seemed to get lost in the bar's foggy atmosphere. They'd done this once or twice over the last few months. They'd convene at the Gate, recap their day, share some drinks, pay a few bucks for some new music, then part ways. It felt very Wolf and Sheepdog to Carmen. The kind of routine she craved.

Molly was Carmen's roommate. They shared a tiny Upper East Side studio they'd managed to split into two rooms, a flimsy divider erected between their beds for a bit of privacy. Carmen had met Molly her first day in New York as she'd wandered the streets of Manhattan, dizzy and homesick, her head buried in a listings book, desperate to find somewhere to call home. She'd taken a bus from DC, after visiting a college friend, to New York—the drab, claustrophobic walls of the Port Authority giving her the most honest first impression of New York she could expect. As she wandered the cavernous transport hub, a concrete behemoth at the tail end of the Lincoln Tunnel, she got a heavy dose of what she'd only imagined. A city in disrepair, boiled down into this one sprawling bus terminal. Leaky ceilings, shadowy conversations, blaring horns, and unidentifiable smells all coalesced into an unbridled fear that gripped Carmen as she stepped out into the New York sunlight. She raced for a phone booth.

One of the few numbers she had was for Molly, whom Carmen's Miami friend Sandra had known when they were younger. Carmen gave her a ring, explained who she was, and a few hours later they were having a drink. Turned out Molly needed a roommate, and the rest fell into place in the magical way that seems to only happen in New York. She was in an apartment she couldn't afford, playing gigs downtown, and Carmen was about to interview for a few publishing jobs. Eventually, she figured, one of them would be able to pay the rent—so why not pool their chances?

Molly played bass and sometimes sang in a group that had sported more names than Carmen could keep track of. Dakota, Ms. Manhattan, the Faraway Nearby, the Shockers, Black-Tie Affair. The latest, Magna Carta, seemed to have stuck. But Carmen wasn't holding her breath. Molly's lyrics were punchy, and she talked about things in a way Carmen wasn't used to—harsh, honest, angry. Carmen loved Molly's band. She was so-so on Molly as a person, but they got along well enough. There was just something about her. Carmen found her fascinating, but not in the usual post-college-lecture coffeehouse way. She just liked to look at her, to study her reactions. She was so different from anyone she'd ever met. Carmen felt a rush of gratitude for having found at least one person she could count on. Their occasional meetups were the closest thing to couplehood she could handle at the moment.

"He *is* an asshole," Carmen said. "And now I'm stuck."

"What do you mean?"

Carmen took a long sip of her beer.

"He won't buy my scripts, and because I pushed it, I have no way of coming back to this," she said, shaking her head. "And it's not like I can write for someone else."

"Not unless you grow yourself a dick."

They both laughed.

The crackle of a cable being plugged into an amp distracted them. They both looked toward the bar's tiny, makeshift stage. Carmen couldn't recognize the band, which didn't mean much, but she also didn't see any flicker of awareness from Molly, who was the expert. It was a five-piece—a sleek-looking blond woman on piano, a short-haired lady on bass, two dudes on guitars, and a distant drummer. One of the guitarists, a frumpy-looking guy closer to forty than thirty, stepped up to the mic.

"Uh, hey, we're the Faulkner Detectives," he said nervously. "You might not recognize this tune, but we love it."

Carmen almost scoffed.

But before she could, the guitarist turned around and the drummer counted off with his sticks. The piano player slid into an opening riff that felt urgent and also constant, leading the rest of the band into a rock shuffle that belied their generic appearance. Carmen kept watching, until a slight squeal from Molly pulled her back.

"Oh my God, talk about a choice," she said, nodding her head at the band in approval. They wouldn't notice, of course, but it was equal to shaking a band member's hand after a gig and whispering, "Good show, man." Rock music etiquette, Carmen assumed.

"You know this song?"

Molly was on her feet now, dancing to the number, which to Carmen seemed to just be about a loser guy wondering why he wasn't good enough for an evil-sounding woman.

"It's Springsteen—you know him?" Molly asked.

Carmen winced playfully. Molly poked her in response.

"C'mon, Carm. Don't be such a weirdo," she said. "He's playing the Bottom Line next month. We have to go. My treat."

Before Carmen could answer, Molly was grabbing Carmen's hands. "I almost forgot this song existed. C'mon, dance with me?"

Carmen laughed but shook her head, waving Molly off.

"You're crazy," she said.

Molly stuck her tongue out at Carmen and dropped back into her seat.

"You gotta learn to have some fun, girl," Molly said. "Life's too short to be so damn serious."

The song wound down with a raucous chorus of guitars and banging piano chords. A smattering of applause followed, back-ended by Molly's enthusiastic hooting and hollering. As the cheers wound down, she looked at Carmen.

"Wanna go?"

Carmen nodded. Molly motioned to the bartender for the check.

By the time she turned back, there was another person standing nearby. Carmen and Molly looked up to see a tall, statuesque blond woman, more Nico than Farrah Fawcett. Carmen had just figured she was looking for the bathroom, but now realized she was looking at her—an easy smile on her face.

"Are you leaving now?" she asked Carmen.

"I don't know . . . maybe?" Carmen said. She was telling the truth. She could go for another round. But she could also feel Molly's confused, *Do you know this woman?* stare.

The woman chuckled dryly and rested a hand on the back of Carmen's stool. She leaned in slightly.

"Let me rephrase that," she said more quietly, her attention on Carmen, as if Molly didn't exist. "Can I buy you a drink?"

Carmen stiffened, more from surprise than anything else. She smiled slyly and motioned to Molly with her chin.

"I'm just chatting with my friend here," Carmen said. "So, I'm okay. Thank you, though."

The woman straightened and nodded, taking the hint. She slapped her hand gently on Carmen's chair and started on her way.

"Sounds fine," she said, turning her gaze to Molly. "Lucky friend."

Carmen nodded as the woman disappeared into the crowd. When she looked at Molly, her roommate was biting back a laugh.

"That was . . . something," Molly said, eyes widening. "Talk about fearless."

"New York City, huh?" Carmen said, eyebrows raised.

Molly started to laugh, but her expression changed suddenly—as if she'd just remembered she'd left the oven on, concern flickering across her face.

"Hey, I meant to tell you—your dad called again."

Molly's words hung in the air like a loud chord fading into silence. Carmen brought her beer up to her lips and paused. The bartender returned and signaled to Molly with his hands: five bucks to settle up their drinks for the night.

"What'd he say?"

"Just to call him, you know," Molly said. "He seemed annoyed but also worried, so maybe we're a minute or two closer to the end of days on the Doomsday Clock."

"That's a song lyric if I ever heard one," Carmen said, trying to smile.

"You ever gonna tell me what the deal is?" Molly asked. "Or do I have to keep wondering?"

"About what?"

Molly bounced up to her feet from the barstool. She dropped a few bills on the bar.

"That answers that, I guess," she said with a slight shrug. "Hey, I'm gonna pick up my gear at our place and head to our gig in Brooklyn. Wanna walk me? Maybe we'll see your admirer on the way out."

Molly was right, even if she didn't say it out loud. Carmen didn't want to talk about her dad. She didn't want to talk *to* him, either. But Carmen wasn't going to unburden her heart to someone she barely knew. It just wasn't in her blood.

"But of course," Carmen said, before taking a long, lazy pull from her beer. She placed the bottle on the bar. They shared a smile as Carmen got down from the seat and followed Molly's weaving path through the crowded bar. Like most places this time of night, it reeked of stale beer and secondhand smoke and seemed to pulse with that same electric energy Carmen had never experienced before coming to New York. A dark sense of pulsing danger—a feeling that around any corner, something might pop out and surprise you.

"Think you'll get a decent crowd tonight?" Carmen said as they stepped out into the chilly New York evening, the wind slapping their faces as the sounds of the bar were muted by the closing door. Carmen felt herself lean into Molly, smelling her tangy perfume. She was drunker than she'd thought, Carmen realized. She'd needed to blow off some steam.

"We'll play the same chords to an empty bar," Molly said, not looking at Carmen. "Eventually a band either falls apart after doing that forever, or you get stronger. I've never made it that far."

Molly helped Carmen keep her balance but stepped back as soon as she had righted herself. They walked down Bleecker toward Sixth Avenue, where they'd start their trek uptown. Carmen scanned their surroundings as they shuffled by closed stores, damaged signs that read PASTRY SHOP, MEAT, or VEGETABLE GARDEN, muted and dark. It all still felt new to Carmen—the dirt-caked sidewalks, the garbage littering the streets. A chipped beauty Carmen couldn't look away from—the faded brick of the apartments above the myriad bodegas and butchers, the winding black fire escapes that ran up and down the buildings, and the rainbow of faces and expressions on the people she'd see—all the people—at any hour of the night.

She knew New York City was dangerous. Yet she felt a strange, probably false, sense of security—because she was surrounded by so many people of so many different stripes and shapes and sizes, she would be okay. It made her feel alive.

As they turned onto Sixth Avenue, the streets took on an eerie, desolate quality that surprised Carmen. One minute, New York City would be bustling with thousands of people vying for purchase, but other times—later in the evening—you'd strain to see anyone else, the night covering the street like a velvet cloak. And if you did see anyone, you'd wonder why they were out this late, too.

Even now, months into her new life, Carmen felt like an alien. Miami was so different—a wide swath of small municipalities cobbled together under the Florida heat. Pedestrians were unicorns and any local worth their salt would either be indoors, basking in the air-conditioning, or in a car—on their way somewhere else, over myriad highways and roads. Sidewalks were perfunctory and often nonexistent. Not New York. The city was a living, moving organism—a concrete tapestry that seemed to change its mood depending on who was around. And right now, in the late evening—as she walked her roommate back to their apartment uptown—it seemed very grumpy.

"She seemed to like you," Molly said, breaking a lengthy silence. It took Carmen a second to register who she was talking about.

"I guess," Carmen said. She let the words dangle for a few beats. She liked Molly, of course. They got along, in the way complete strangers thrust together into an intimate living arrangement had to. But if Carmen had learned one thing in her brief time in the city, it was that you always kept your shields up—until you were absolutely certain you could bring them down. She wasn't there yet with Molly. Might never be.

They made the irresponsible decision to splurge on a cab, once Molly realized what time it was—and did the math on how long it'd take to get uptown and then back to Brooklyn for the band's set. By the time they reached their cramped studio, Molly was on edge, furiously zipping from one corner of the space to the other, gathering her belongings like some kind of hopped-up scavenger. Carmen couldn't fight off the smirk that formed on her face.

"Okay, gotta run, CV," Molly said, propelling herself toward the door. "Stay breezy."

"Break a leg," Carmen said. Molly nodded, her used Fender case hanging over her shoulder. She didn't look at Carmen as she headed out.

Carmen waited for the comforting click of the front door, followed by the *clack-clack-clack* of their "backup" locks. After a few moments, she slid down to the floor, angling her head to look under her tiny bed. It was there. She reached under and pulled it out. The box was nothing special—the kind you'd find on the side of the road. It's what was inside that mattered. The tattered, beat-up remnants of her childhood. And, she hoped, the road map to her adulthood. She sat down on the floor, legs crisscrossed, and dove in.

Atop the pile of comics was a battered issue of *Detective Comics*—the words "FEATURING THE BAT-WOMAN!" emblazoned above the title logo. It was Carmen's first comic book—the first one she could remember her father buying for her at the pharmacy newsstand. But it wasn't just the words that had beckoned to her. The entire image was intriguing—featuring a yellow-and-red-clad heroine, her lithe body speeding along on a motorcycle—well ahead of series stars Batman and Robin. The kicker? Her playful grin, as if beating the boys was commonplace for this female vigilante. Even then, Carmen felt a crackle of excitement when looking at the character. Robin's pleading word balloon had just been icing on the cake for her: HURRY, BATMAN—THE BAT-WOMAN IS BEATING US ON THIS MISSION!

When her father had picked up the comic for her, the first one she'd ever considered her very own, she had no idea who the Bat-Woman was. She'd barely known who Batman was. She certainly had no idea why these men and women would wear these tight costumes and jump around. But her father loved them so, was wide-eyed and amused by this American craze, these superheroes. "Mira éste, Carmencita—que locura, eh?"

She flipped past the book to another powerful image, this one mostly black—with bold red letters across the top that read THE FLASH. At the center of the cover was a zoomed-in shot of the titular hero, a man in a full red bodysuit, only the lower half of his face and eyes visible. His hand was held up, as if to command the reader. The word balloon that dominated the left side of the image was one of the most ominous, and compelling, things Carmen had ever seen: STOP! DON'T PASS UP THIS ISSUE! MY LIFE DEPENDS ON IT. It had felt so potent then, Carmen recalled, to love the Flash. His power was pure childhood fantasy—to be the *fastest*. But had Carmen wanted to be fast, or did she dream of running away?

She didn't spend too much time on the thought before flipping to the next comic—a haunted, red-purple sky providing the backdrop to five figures in the foreground. One an alien-looking bald man, pointing to the sky. The other four more familiar—brave, logical Reed Richards. Demure, blond Susan Storm. Young, hotheaded Johnny. The monstrous, jagged Ben Grimm. The Fantastic Four. Explorers of the undiscovered. Scientist heroes. The greatest product of the fertile Stan Lee / Jack Kirby partnership. Like the Flash cover, the text was the first thing her eyes gravitated to, even now, years later: THE COMING OF GALACTUS!

The boys in Carmen's hometown of Westchester had always gravitated to Batman and Spider-Man, but she had always been stuck on the thinkers. The police scientist who happened to be the Fastest Man Alive. A sharp guy who seemed to like what he was doing. The four family members who were one part superteam, another part Kennedy clan all-American, and as New Frontier as you could hope for.

Bzzt!

The doorbell. She groaned. Molly must have forgotten something— one of her stupid pedals or the hat she'd been planning to wear onstage— and didn't have her keys. Again.

Bzzt! Bzzt!

Molly had ruined a special moment. A connection to a time when comics were a dream—an intangible thing that got her through her own day-to-day. Now working in comics *was* her day-to-day. She saw how the sausage was made. She got the nasty calls from creepy freelancers looking for work, who managed to also awkwardly flirt with her. She dealt with the desperate freelancers showing up at first light on Friday, hoping to get their check to pay off their alimony, child support, or loan sharks. She saw how creative efforts got smooshed and squeezed into generic shapes only to become something else—something bad. She watched as the older generation got shoved aside, nothing made or earned from decades of creative labor, just because their style was no longer de rigueur. Carmen saw it all from her small perch outside Carlyle's office. She was no longer a fan, but she was barely a professional—and that stung in a way Carmen had not fully realized, but felt. It was even worse because she was helpless, pounding her fists against a window that let her see beyond. But the glass was so strong there was no way she could break through. *Fuck.*

Carmen swung the door open, her annoyance powering her every action.

"Harvey? What the hell?"

Carmen blurted the words out before she fully registered Harvey Stern at her door. Before she started to wonder about how Harvey knew where she lived. Why he was here worried Carmen most. She'd tried her best to be gentle with his clumsy advances, but even the mildest puppy can learn to bite when scorned too often. He spoke, his voice slurring and his stance wobbly.

"Sorry, sorry, Carmen," he said, reaching out his hands, more to balance himself than to make any kind of physical contact. He was drunk. Sloppy drunk. "I—uh, I hate that I did this, you know—"

"What do you want, Harvey?" Her voice was calm now, her tone flat, like someone who'd just had a gun pulled on them, desperate to keep the maniac waving the weapon cool.

"I need to talk to you," he said. He was leveling out a bit, trying to get his shit together. "About work."

Carmen almost let out a sigh of relief, but she wasn't out of the woods yet. Work could be a springboard to anything—how he'd noticed she was the one from across the cramped office, for instance. No. She wasn't in the clear yet.

"What about work?" she asked carefully.

"I know about you," he said.

She didn't respond. The words could mean so much. Carmen felt a shiver shoot through her. Had she—

"About the scripts," he said, a skip in his voice. He wanted to move things along. "The ones you've written, for Carlyle."

This time Carmen did sigh, because, of all the things he could know or uncover, this was the one she would love for more people to see, to know and share. The rest of her secrets could burn in hell for all she cared.

"How?"

"Can I come inside?"

Carmen hesitated, but her curiosity won out.

The front door slammed shut behind Harvey, the sound echoing down the musty, grimy hallway.

CHAPTER FOUR

Harvey, are you out of your mind?"

He seemed to wilt as Carmen spit out the words, but she didn't care. He must be nuts. Or much drunker than she'd thought when she'd let him in. Like, blackout drunk. Because what he was asking her to do was insane.

"No, Carmen, just—well, hear me out?"

She jumped to her feet from the bed on which she'd warily sat, already feeling weird about having let him into her apartment. Doubly strange because there wasn't much real estate between him, Carmen, and her bed. She felt hot and suddenly hyperaware of the fact that she was alone in her tiny, cluttered apartment with a half-in-the-bag guy she barely knew.

"Let me make you a cup of coffee," Carmen said as she walked toward the kitchen area, hoping she actually had some coffee.

"Sure, yeah, I could use a cup."

It was late. Harvey was unsteady on his feet and smelled of spilled beer and secondhand smoke. Normally that wouldn't faze Carmen, but it added to the anxiety of the moment. *Why is he here? How did he find me?*

She got the coffee going and wheeled around, leaning back on the counter.

"Tell me again," she said. "This time, very slowly."

Harvey took in a long breath, as if steeling himself for a job interview or acceptance speech. It would've been cute under different circumstances. But if he repeated anything close to what he'd told Carmen a few moments ago, she was going to be very upset.

"I want to pitch something. To Carlyle. He's promised me writing work before, but I've never tried to take him up on it," he said, the words coming out slowly, a byproduct of Harvey's buzz and his own deliberate nature. "But I know the window is closing fast. I want to put something on his desk that will wow him."

This was news to Carmen, and she felt a wave of frustration. Why had he offered Harvey work and stonewalled her? And last she'd heard, Carlyle had closed the door on new pitches—unwilling to take on additional books in a volatile market. She was supposed to be the source of all the good intel in the office. How the hell did lowest-assistant-editor-on-the-totem-pole Harvey get the goods? Carmen played the only card she had.

"Does this have to do with that guy Jensen?" Carmen asked. She'd heard rumblings that Carlyle was in talks with the freelance writer for . . . something. But she couldn't pin down what, exactly. She waited to see if the bluff shook Harvey enough to talk. "I know he did some writing for us, but—"

"Well, no—I dunno. This would be different, just something else. Not related to Jensen," Harvey interjected. "I mean, last I heard, Jensen's not doing anything for us—I think he was writing a fill-in for *The Freedom Alliance,* according to Trunick in production—"

Jensen was a hack, Carmen thought. A washed-up never-was who hadn't recovered from the horror comics purge twenty years ago. Carlyle liked him because he was fast and reliable, and could sometimes put something together that felt "more than" comics—almost literary. It was catnip to a climber like Carlyle. But it was smoke and mirrors as far as Carmen could tell. The guy could pull quotes from classic literature and sprinkle them into a script, but his characters were cutouts and his women made June Cleaver look like a militant feminist. Worst of all? Carmen had heard he was handsy, a violent drunk, and there was nothing to be done about it—he was Carlyle's lifelong chum, which granted him virtual immunity. A reality that, Carmen had learned, was not uncommon in comics.

"He was also doing the *Ms. Frightful* annual, I think," Carmen said, unable to stop herself from correcting poor Harvey. "But continue."

"Anyway, I happened to run into Carlyle at the office tonight, while he was leaving, and he mentioned I hadn't pitched him anything yet. That I'd been with the company awhile and he was surprised I hadn't thrown my hat in the ring," he said. "So, I—I lied. I told him I had something great, something he'd love. I figured he'd brush me off, but instead he said he wanted to read it immediately. So now I'm in a bind— not only do I have to write something for him to consider, but it has to be something good, because he's already waiting for it."

"Do you have any idea what he wants?" Carmen asked.

Harvey smiled. He'd caught the curiosity coating her flatly delivered question. Blood in the water.

Dammit, why am I even entertaining this?

"Not exactly," Harvey said. "He just kind of blurted it out, that he wanted a female hero, something—what did he say?—'something sexy and risqué—not too much like a wank rag, but still hot enough to give our readers a stiffy.'"

"Jesus Christ," Carmen said, shaking her head. Had her conversations with Carlyle pushed him in this direction—to create a woman hero who wasn't just meant to titillate? At least his own twisted perception of what that could be? She didn't want to spend too much time on the irony of that. Carmen turned around and poured Harvey some mediocre coffee. She walked it over to him and he sipped it cautiously.

"Thanks," Harvey said. "Yeah, I mean, you know Carlyle. He wanted something—but he didn't know exactly what. 'Make it great, like film noir or something,' he said. Like that's going to pull the kids reading Spider-Man and Justice League away, I guess."

"Isn't that Carlyle?" Carmen asked, raising an eyebrow to encourage him to get going. "He's always trying to figure out a cheap, fast magic bullet to beat out his competition and take the credit. But can we speed this along?"

"I know, I know, it's late," he said. "So I'm in a bind. I need to write something and it has to be great. If he likes it, I think Carlyle will put some real ammo behind it. I mean, a big part of this is I just want to avoid being embarrassed, you know? This is a big opportunity. It's what got Maynard and the other regulars in the door. I can't screw it up."

"Get to the point, Harvey."

Carmen watched as his shoulders slumped. She should feel bad, she thought. But she didn't. She was tired and she knew what he was getting at. But she wanted to hear him say it.

"Carlyle wants me to write this pitch, for this series," Harvey said, still looking at his feet. "He wants me to create this character." He hesitated. "And I want you to help me. I need you to help me."

Harvey's gaze moved up, meeting Carmen's expectant eyes.

Carmen felt confused—and worried. She felt off-balance. One minute, Carlyle was basically slamming a door on her career. The next, Harvey was presenting her with a way around it. She tried to temper the anger bubbling inside her with logic. She had to see this through, she thought.

"All right, I'll listen," she said. "Let's talk."

*Excerpt from 1975's **The Legendary Lynx #2**, "Fatal Fallout!"*—Story: Harvey Stern, Art: Doug Detmer, Letters: Todd Morelli, Editor: Rich Berger, President/CEO: Jeffrey Carlyle.
Published by Triumph Comics.

CHAPTER FIVE

s this a trick?" **Carmen** asked, pacing around Harvey like some kind of interrogating officer. "Is this a weird, mean joke? Because that doesn't seem like you."

Harvey was seated on the edge of Molly's bed, his eyes looking up at Carmen, wide and desperate. She could see his hand was shaking slightly. He was eager and scared all at once. Carmen realized that was Harvey in a nutshell—a curious but frightened bird.

"I'm dead serious," he said, standing up abruptly. "I know you want to write."

"Yeah? Who told you that?"

Harvey squirmed as Carmen walked over to the sink and poured herself a glass of water.

"I've heard it, that's all," he said. "And, c'mon, Carm—how often do you critique other guys' scripts to me at lunch or while we're smoking? It's no secret."

He was trying to be kind, she could tell, and that made her angrier. Nothing pissed Carmen off more than pity. And here was this guy she barely knew feeling bad for her. She wanted to strangle him.

"What's in it for me?" Carmen asked.

Harvey stammered. She pressed.

"Seriously—what do I get?" she asked. "I help you write this, don't even get my name on it . . . then what? It's not like I can use it on my résumé or anything, right?"

Harvey frowned. He took a beat before responding.

"It's a start for you, I guess," he said, his head tilting slightly, as if he were analyzing his own words as he said them. "And if it becomes popular, well, then we sit Carlyle down and let him know what's going on. Then he'll have to put your name on there."

"So we trick him, you mean?"

"No, no, not like that," Harvey said. "Look, this is an opportunity—a way to get in the game. We can figure out the logistics later—"

"An opportunity? Wait, do you feel bad for me or something?" she said, her tone hot and defensive.

"Why are you so . . . *ugh* . . . so difficult?" he asked, his voice quavering.

Hmm, she'd even broken sweet Harvey. Oh well.

"Do you want to do this or not? I can just go home and—"

"Yeah?" she asked, pushing her luck, her body leaning forward. "Then why are you here, Harvey?"

He didn't respond. Carmen knew why he was here. She'd grappled with the doe-eyed boy-children of the world her entire adult life. Scratch that, her entire life. You have one mildly polite conversation with a guy, throw him a casual smile or laugh at his joke, and suddenly he's waiting outside your door with flowers, wondering about seating arrangements at the wedding. Harvey wasn't a bad guy—that's what made it harder to lash out at him—but he was still a guy.

Carmen shrugged and turned to place her glass on the small wooden table by her bed. By the time she'd turned back around, Harvey was putting on his coat and heading toward the door.

"What? You're leaving?"

He looked at her, confused.

"Don't be such a baby," she said. "Let's get to work."

"Maybe it's, like, an animal totem or something that gives her powers," he said. "Like a hidden artifact."

Harvey was pacing around Carmen's small apartment, his hair out of place and his glasses slightly askew. They'd been going back and forth for hours. Take-out containers littered the small table in the kitchen nook. The apartment smelled of General Tso's chicken and dumplings. All on Harvey's dime. But even if he was being generous with dinner, she wasn't going to let what was left of the night go off the rails.

"Why does she need powers?" Carmen asked, finishing a last forkful of fried rice. "Why does she need to be empowered by something else?"

"What do you mean?" Harvey asked. "She's a superhero. She has to have—"

"Batman doesn't have powers. Daredevil barely has powers. Why can't she just be strong and smart? I feel like we're coming at this the wrong way—"

"But the powers explain how she becomes a hero. Like, maybe she's half animal, like a werewolf woman," Harvey said.

"A werewolf woman? Really?" Carmen asked. "Didn't Marvel just do that with the Cat and Tigra?"

"I guess so, but we need something, she needs some kind of powers," Harvey said, shaking his head slightly. He'd seemed exasperated ever since Carmen had asked him to stick around. "That's how you build her origin."

"No, that's a crutch," Carmen said, getting up to toss her fork in the sink. "It's lazy. So, what, she gets bitten by a radioactive cat and suddenly has power and is motivated to fight crime? That's bullshit."

Harvey waited a beat.

"Then what's her motivation?"

Carmen didn't hesitate. "Her character. We need to flesh her out.

Who she is. Why she is," Carmen said. "The powers don't matter if people don't care about her. What spurred her to do this? Think about it."

"I am."

"No, really think about it," she said, moving closer to him, her eyes on his pale face. "Batman's parents were gunned down, and that drove him to put on a bat costume. Spider-Man's uncle was murdered because Peter chose to let a robber get by him. Superman is the American ideal, raised to be the best of us. Wonder Woman was banished from her home to bring her beliefs to a 'man's world.' Where does our character fit? Who is she?"

Harvey rubbed his chin, his gaze distant. Carmen could see the gears slowly churning in his head. She sat back down on her bed and waited.

"Maybe . . . maybe she's a zoologist?" Harvey asked. "She loves big cats and wants to become one."

"She wants to . . . become a big cat?" Carmen said, letting the words hang between them.

He shrugged his shoulders. "So, okay, this—this woman. What was the name you liked? Claudia . . . What did we say her last name was?"

"Calla," Carmen said. "It sounds nice, doesn't feel too WASPy, and it also rolls off the tongue, like Clark Kent or Peter Parker."

"You had this in your back pocket?"

"Hey, I can't say I want to do something and not be ready when I get my shot," she said with a sharp smile. "I've been waiting for this my whole life."

Harvey's eyes seemed to light up.

"Okay, Claudia Calla, and she's a reporter?" Harvey said, shaking his head to himself. "That's fine. But you're right—why?"

"No, she's not a reporter—she works at the paper."

"What's the difference?" Harvey asked. "What, is she a secretary?"

Carmen smiled.

"Huh," Harvey said with a nod. "Nice. Okay, so she works at the paper, but what is she after?"

"She's on the hunt for truth. She wants to be a reporter. She sees it as heroic."

"Truth?"

"I mean, isn't that what reporters are supposed to do?" Carmen said. She could feel her face getting warm. Claudia's story was coming out, and Carmen realized it was close to her own. "Maybe she . . . maybe she's not just curious, but she's after something. About herself. The truth about herself. Who she is."

"Like, she's an alien? Or about her powers?"

"No, no," Carmen said, trying to keep her tone neutral, not frustrated. Harvey meant well, but it was becoming clear to her that he was mired in the past. She wanted more. "Like, her own world. Maybe she was adopted, but she never knew her parents, her biological ones. And she's trying to become a reporter to not only help people find the truth, but to find her own truth. I mean, think about it, Harvey. What's the closest thing we have to a real superhero? Woodward and Bernstein, don't you think? They took down Nixon."

Harvey sat down across from Carmen and took a long sip of his cold coffee. He swallowed slowly.

"I like it," he said, as if convincing himself. "It's different. But it doesn't . . . it doesn't activate her, you know?"

"How so?"

"I mean, look, it sucks to not know where you're from," he said. "I get that. It's so primal and relatable. And that explains why she went into her field—but what made her . . . I mean, what's this lady's superhero name?"

Carmen stretched and stood up. Her body was aching and her eyes were pulsing. She was tired. She'd lost track of time, but she figured Molly would be home soon. Molly might not take kindly to some random guy sitting on her bed. But Carmen also didn't want to stop. This was becoming something. More than just silly brainstorming. It felt like she and Harvey were adding their notes to a song . . . to something bigger and louder.

"She's smart, sharp—I dunno, claws? The Lioness?"

"Eh, it feels too much like it's riffing off the male name . . . the Lion?"

Carmen smiled approvingly. "Good on you, Harv. But I like the feral-cat thing. You?"

"Yeah, it points to guys like Batman or Catwoman, but can be different. What, though? The Leopard Lady?"

Carmen gulped back her coffee, fighting off a spit take.

"Leopard Lady?" she said with a laugh. "Harv, have you ever actually spoken to a woman before me? I think you're on to something, though. She's tough. She's not afraid to claw your eyes out. She's agile and fast. Like a lion or leopard. The Cat?"

"Very taken."

"Cheetah?"

"Also taken," Harvey said. "What about Puma? Or Panther-Woman?"

"Feels too . . . macho?" Carmen said, rubbing the sides of her head.

"Panther . . . ena. Pantherina . . . Panthena!" He jumped up off Molly's bed, excited that he finally got it.

She arched an eyebrow at him and he slumped back down. "Maybe just cat, or lynx, or tiger . . ." she said.

"Lynx, that's it," Harvey said, eyes wild, pointing at Carmen. "That's it! It's perfect."

"Lynx," she said slowly, almost to herself. He was right. It worked. Carmen wasn't sure why yet, but she liked it. "The Lynx. The Lethal Lynx."

Carmen reached under her bed and pulled out a small notepad. She started scribbling inside. The strokes were jagged and haphazard. She wasn't writing anything. She was drawing.

"Didn't know you were an artist," Harvey said, taking a seat again.

"I'm not, really," Carmen said, moving over to Molly's bed and sidling up next to him. "But I always wanted to be, at least when I was a kid, you know? My dad would bring me to . . ."

Her voice trailed off. His chin was close to her shoulder. She could hear his slow breathing. The drawing was crude, rudimentary, but Carmen could see her—Claudia, the Lynx—taking shape. The full-body suit. The yellow-and-black costume. The speckled leopard-like spots hastily drawn in certain areas. The sharp black claws on her fingers. The domino mask with the pupil-less eyes. The things that would become elemental parts of the Lynx were already on the thin piece of notebook paper. And Carmen knew they had something.

Then Harvey leaned over and kissed her square on the mouth.

It lasted less than two seconds, but even in that small window, he managed to try to slide his tongue past Carmen's lips. She pulled back, her face red-hot. *Son of a bitch*, she thought. *Son of a fucking bitch.* She felt her hand close into a fist and had to will her arm back down. She heard the notebook and pencil clatter to the floor.

"What the fuck, Harvey!" she said, sliding back on the bed and away from him. "You've got to go. Right now."

"No, wait, no . . . I'm sorry," he said, wiping at his mouth, clearly angry at himself. Carmen could see how ashamed he was. But she didn't let herself feel bad. She didn't let the anger dissipate.

"Harvey, get out of here," Carmen said. She was standing now, fighting the urge to point at the door like a sitcom wife.

He nodded. He understood. Saying anything now would ruin what little hope he had left. Not at romance, but at anything. Friendship. Collaboration. He'd sunk the whole thing for . . . what? A power move? A half-hearted attempt at getting her into bed? *Typical*, Carmen thought.

He grabbed his notebook and sidestepped her, like a soldier avoiding a land mine. She didn't turn around to watch him leave. She wondered what she'd just sacrificed by making him leave. By spurning his clumsy advance. Carmen looked up. She watched the door for what felt like hours, its yellow paint slowly fading as her vision blurred it away.

CHAPTER SIX

Carmen couldn't sleep.

She wasn't sure if it was anger—at Harvey, at herself—or adrenaline. Before Harvey had tried to kiss her, something had happened. There'd been a spark, just not of the variety that poor, shy Harvey had been hoping for. A creative burst that Carmen had only experienced alone. But this one was different. This wasn't an idea she'd jotted down with no hope of ever seeing come to life, like many she'd had over the years. This had some kind of potential. Some sliver of hope. Maybe, she thought, Harvey would take this heroine—this Lethal Lynx—and place her story in front of Carlyle. Just that alone would put her closer to making her dream a reality. *And what if he decides to publish it?* she wondered.

She let her body flop onto her uncomfortable bed, pretending she didn't feel a puff of dust float up as she landed. The tiny Upper East Side apartment was dark and silent, but no cramped space could dampen the sounds of New York City—the sirens, the screams, the buzz of cars, the rumble of the subway, and everything else blended to make a droning, pulsing rhythm that had at first terrified Carmen, but now helped her sleep. It still didn't feel like home, Carmen realized; the familiar comforts she'd taken for granted in Miami replaced by the inherent anxieties of New York. The smell of burning, uncollected garbage in the street—a byproduct of budget cuts and striking or disgruntled sanitation workers. The heightened sense of danger as she stepped out into the street. The methodical scanning of people on the subway, wondering if this would be the time Carmen faced the wrong end of a mugger's knife. She'd heard rumors people were passing out flyers to travelers arriving at the city's airport that read WELCOME TO FEAR CITY, rattling off reasons for people to fear for their lives just seconds after landing.

Even the apartment itself just felt—well—broken. Old. Beaten-down and worn-out. She wondered who'd lived there before and who might live there when she finally left. Their building, a three-story walk-up with fading white trim and redbrick exterior, was on the corner of Second Avenue and Eighty-Second Street, above a fried chicken restaurant and a locksmith that never seemed to be open. The restaurant, on the other hand, sounded like it was open at all hours—rowdy drunks barreling in for a late-night meal, early-morning bar patrons shuffling in for a coffee before heading to work. It felt alive in a way that Miami, with its long stretches of green parks, palm trees, and wide-laned highways, never had. Miami was a city, too, Carmen knew—but New York was something else. A disease that bubbled and expanded and multiplied and morphed, like some kind of magical, mystical being that seemed from another world.

Carmen's eyes fluttered open. She'd been asleep, she realized, in the clutches of some kind of bombastic, jagged, Kirby-esque creature, like Bombu or one of those other monster characters Stan and Jack had cranked out before the Fantastic Four had inexorably diverted the river that was comic books. She rolled left, her back to the door and to Molly's bed. She didn't want to have to talk. To Molly. To anyone. It wasn't so much that Harvey had surprised her with that kiss. She'd known the moment was coming. Had always known. She'd built up her defenses enough, though. She could tell when a boy—*a man,* she reminded herself—wanted more than her friendship. She could see the wheels turning behind their warm eyes. Could feel the strategies forming as they tried to find a way in, to find a chink in her armor. A shot. She'd let her guard down, was all. She'd be better next time. She had to be.

No, what bothered her was that she'd let her ambition camouflage what she could see all too clearly now. Harvey had dangled something in front of her that was a lifelong goal, a dream. There was no way he could know that. Reading and loving comics were as much a part of her as being from Miami, or being Cuban. Their smell, texture, look, and rhythm were ingrained in her mind. Writing them would literally be a dream come true.

She could feel her father's leathery hand slide into hers, the hot, humid Miami summer enveloping her like a warm towel. Could feel her sandaled feet scraping down Galloway Road as they made their way toward the newsstand, where her father would pick up the *Miami Times* and scan the comic book rack. The titles always changed—the market was volatile then, even more than today. But the barrage of colors and letters always had the same effect. The titles screamed out to her, as if begging to be picked up: *Journey into Mystery. Tales to Astonish. Detective Comics. Tales of Suspense. Strange Tales. Batman. Patsy Walker.* She wasn't picky. She'd ask her father to grab one for her, and he always would—no matter how they were doing, if he was working, or what struggles they might be facing. Pepe knew his only daughter took great joy in flipping through the pages of a comic book, any comic book.

Those short walks—just a few blocks, now that Carmen thought of it, but they'd felt like miles then—covered a lot of ground between them. They'd talk about life, her father's thoughtfully crafted advice giving Carmen small clues as to what might be bothering him. They'd talk politics. The world felt in flux, uncertain—like the basic pillars of society were shaken and cracked. To Carmen, it was all she knew. But to her father, who'd been forced to cobble together an escape plan from the only home he'd ever known for himself and his family, it was almost old hat. Nothing was certain. Life was never calm. And it was up to him to protect his family.

Her mind continued to drift down the well-worn path. She'd been thinking of her father a lot lately, despite her best efforts. She felt a wave of relief wash over her as she heard the scraping sound of Molly's key sliding into the lock, followed by the slightly inebriated, hoarse sound of Molly singing as she walked through the door. She was happy. The gig had been good. Which could mean anything—that the club paid, that there were more than a dozen people there, that she'd seen someone. John Cale, Springsteen, Tom Verlaine. Anyone she thought might be able to propel Magna Carta to a higher stratum. One that didn't involve playing Brooklyn dive bars for peanuts while drunks passed out into their lite beers.

"Carm?" Molly's voice cut through the room. She was trying to whisper, but her ears were probably still recovering from the show. Quiet to her was pretty loud to Carmen. "Carmy, you up?"

Carmen rolled over and smiled. "Now I am."

"Shit, sorry," Molly said as she sat on the edge of Carmen's bed, her hand resting on Carmen's legs. "Asleep long?"

"Can't sleep."

"What now, kid?" Molly asked. "What's bouncing around in that pretty skull of yours?"

Carmen gave her the highlights of the night, and Molly shook her head, a wry smile on her face.

"Predictable boy boner bullshit," Molly said. "Why'd you even let him in? You're lucky he wasn't a complete psycho."

"He's a nice guy," Carmen said, sitting up now. "And I knew he liked me—but I guess I just wanted to talk it out. I've never, I dunno, brainstormed like that. It was fun. Imagine if this character becomes, well, real? Like an actual, true-to-God character?"

"Then why don't you seem happy about it?"

Carmen shrugged.

"It wouldn't be mine," she said. "It could never be mine."

"What do you mean?" Molly asked.

"It'd be a secret," Carmen said, her voice lowered. "If it got published, I'd be ghostwriting it. . . . I mean, I'd get a shot, and if it did well we'd reveal my involvement, but . . ."

"You'd be anonymous at first? Like his secret partner?"

Carmen waited a beat, letting her mind skim over what she already knew to be true. She nodded at Molly, hoping her friend couldn't see her resigned expression in the dark.

"Is that what you want?" Molly asked. "To live your dream—in secret?"

Carmen felt her stomach twist into a painful, aching knot.

CHAPTER SEVEN

Where is he?"

Stephenson's words slurred, the "he" drawing out into an almost musical sound. He leaned over Carmen's desk, the whites of his eyes more pink than anything. She could smell the cheap wine on his breath—tart and strong, as if he'd snuck a long swig before taking the elevator up to the Triumph offices. Carmen thought back to what Harvey and the other young production staffers had told her about the man—that Stephenson, an old friend of Carlyle's with a checkered history as an editor of comics and pulp novels, had hit on hard times. A sloppy drunk who'd lost his way, but one that Carlyle kept around because he loved to have a side of industry gossip with his drinks. It was a little past nine, and Carlyle—the "he" Stephenson was looking for—wasn't in yet.

"Can you hear me, missy?" He was swaying now, his rumpled gray shirt mottled with spots and stains that Carmen didn't really want to think about. He was clutching the edges of her desk. She took a deep breath. He wasn't leaving, which meant she couldn't ignore him anymore.

"Mr. Stephenson, I asked if you needed help," Carmen said, her tone flat, like a phone operator's. She'd learned over the years—in work and life—that the best tactical response to someone coming on strong was to stay calm. It took them off guard. At least at first. "Mr. Carlyle is not here. He may not be in until later today. . . . Can I take a mess—"

"Tell him his ol' pal Stephenson came by, all right?" He was shaking now. Carmen could see him holding on to her desk harder, trying to push back on the tremors. "I don't appreciate him pulling the rug out from under me, okay? Tell him that. Tell him I've served him and his companies and whatever else he's been doing since well before he could drive, all right? He owes me. I don't take kindly to being ignored, okay? Hell, I don't even know who—"

She caught a glimpse of Harvey—walking into the office, his breakfast from the building coffee cart in one hand. He stopped in his tracks, eyes locked on—not her, actually; on the man. On Stephenson. Harvey spun around and left.

"Are you listening to me, young lady?"

That did it.

"Mr. Stephenson, turn around and leave the office right now and I might wait a minute before I call the police." Her eyes were on him, clear and angry. She needed someone to yell at, and this drunk sad sack would have to do. "I felt bad for you a few minutes ago, but that's gone now. This is a place of business, not a bar."

Stephenson straightened. His expression was a mix of anger and resignation. Even a drunk knows when they've hit a wall.

"Well, you're an insolent one, aren't you?"

"I'm calling now."

He blubbered something incomprehensible as he turned around, shuffling toward the elevator bank. He didn't look back.

"Must've really blown it to get fired," she muttered as she turned her chair toward the small file cabinet next to her.

"Was that Stephenson?" a voice asked.

Carmen looked up to see a tall, thin man in front of her desk. She recognized him immediately. Doug Detmer. Veteran comic book artist for any company you could imagine. The large case slung over his shoulder implied he was turning some art pages in, and expecting to be paid. She spun her chair to face him.

"Hello, Mr. Detmer," she said dryly. "Yes, that was Mr. Stephenson, for better or worse."

Detmer gave her a sharp, sly smile.

She was familiar with most of Triumph's major talent, but she couldn't recall if she'd met Detmer before. Though he wasn't Triumph's top freelancer, his art had meant a lot to Carmen. She tried to remind herself not to gush too hard. Part of her job involved overhearing most of Carlyle's rants, and a few had been slung Detmer's way over the last few months. Not because of the work—Detmer's pages were always something to behold. But most creative folk were quirky and combative. Detmer happened to be both, especially if he felt he'd been wronged or misinformed. It added to his mystique, Carmen thought. She could tell he toiled over his pages and that the work mattered. Comics weren't a lesser art to Doug Detmer, and Carmen appreciated that.

"Still a charmer," Detmer said. He placed the case on Carmen's desk and pulled out a stack of original art pages. "Got those *Gray Wolf* pages Jeffrey needed. Early, too, I should note."

Carmen took the proffered art.

"Do you need me to invoice it for you?"

"It's in there, all filled out," Detmer said, pointing to the yellow form affixed to the top page. "Remind him of my rush rate, please, if you can."

Carmen nodded.

"Will do," she said. "I'll just assume you discussed it?"

Detmer sighed.

"We did, but Jeffrey tends to forget that," Detmer said, wincing. "But he can call me and we'll clear it up."

"Consider it done," Carmen said, making a note on a stray piece of paper. She looked up. "Can I help you with anything else?"

Detmer started to step back but stopped himself. His eyes narrowed.

"You type up Carlyle's notes, don't you?" he asked.

It took Carmen a second to respond. She stammered a bit before he continued.

"On scripts and art—his comments," Detmer said. His voice was lower now, conspiratorial. "I ask because they don't sound like him. Like the way he talks. They're good. They're smart."

"Mr. Det—"

"It's nothing to be ashamed of," he said, his tone flat, almost clinical. "You have a good story sense—even your art notes are good. I hope you plan on writing your own stories someday."

Before Carmen could say anything else, Detmer was heading for the elevator bank. She considered getting up and following him, but that felt somehow untoward and awkward. She felt a smile forming on her face. It was a small thing, a crumb, really. An unexpected kindness that briefly numbed her new reality: that she'd been reduced to creating stories in secret because her boss couldn't bring himself to give her the same shot he handed out to people like Harvey without a second thought. She decided to let it be for a few moments as she watched Detmer step onto the elevator.

Carmen didn't notice the shadow spilling across her desk. A throat was cleared. She looked up.

Harvey.

"Carmen, I just—"

She raised a hand and he stopped talking.

"Harvey, you're literally the third guy to appear by my desk in the last ten minutes. This is not the place," she said, her voice soft but not tender. She didn't want to be cruel. She understood it'd taken him a lot to come see her—but he was still in the wrong. He'd violated their trust. What little friendship they'd built. She wasn't going to milk the moment, but she didn't have to accept his whimpering, either. "I'm at work. So are you. We can talk about this later."

She watched Harvey wander back toward his desk, which was face-to-face with the other junior editors in the bullpen area—more frat house than office, she thought. She loved coming to work, most days, but she never felt like she was really part of it all. The practical jokes. The late-night discussions over pizza and beers about which Marvel or DC character they'd want to write. The volleyball games in Central Park. One time, she'd just missed getting pie in the face as a production staffer heaved a steaming cherry pie at a coworker. That was Carmen's role here. Present, but outside. Like the Watcher from *The Fantastic Four*—a powerful being that could do little more than chronicle what goes on, forbidden to interfere.

Well, she was tired of that.

Her conversation with Molly after Harvey departed had had an impact. She couldn't control how she was credited, assuming Carlyle even accepted Harvey's pitch. But she could control the story. The content. It was what she'd always wanted, and it'd be foolish to slip into the passenger seat now.

Unable to sleep the last couple of days, Carmen had sorted through her boxes of files—her ideas, pitches, and spec scripts. All the work she'd fruitlessly handed to Carlyle in varying degrees of completion. She'd discovered something, as she sifted through the pages and reworked them, almost in a trance. There was a theme—of an outsider trying to find justice, trying to reclaim an identity and legacy that had long been denied. After a few hours—time that flew by, dreamlike—she'd woven together a stack of pages. Six full scripts. Not complete—she'd made a point to leave some spaces for Harvey to contribute. But hers. Whether Harvey helped her or not, these would become something.

The rest of the morning puttered on, uneventful—a few late work invoices in the mail, the usual array of cranks on the phone, but nothing else. Carlyle called to say he'd be taking the rest of the day off, which was unlike him, but Carmen didn't give it much thought. She felt more excited by the chance to not have to interact with the man for a few hours.

The phone rang again, cutting through the din of the office—the bellowing laughs, the worried deadline yelps, the frantic sound of paper slapping a desk. She picked it up reflexively.

"Triumph Comics, Jeffrey Carlyle's office—this is Carmen."

"Carmen?"

She froze. She felt as if her heart had stopped mid-beat. Her breathing sped up.

She knew the voice immediately. Of course. How could she forget her?

"Carmen? Is that you? Don't hang up, please," she said. "I just want to talk to you . . . to explain myself, I guess."

Her voice was pleading, tender. So different from the last time they'd spoken. Soft instead of cutting and angry.

A few moments passed. The only sound her breathing on the line. Slow. Labored.

Carmen hung up.

She grabbed her bag and sped toward the elevators, not looking at anyone. She needed some air. She wasn't sure she'd be back.

"You okay?"

Carmen turned to find Harvey behind her. She let her mostly smoked cigarette drop to the sidewalk, then ground her foot into it. She'd made it a few paces from the office before she stalled, confused. Where could she go?

"Not really," Carmen said, not trying to force a smile. Her anger at Harvey seemed like it was almost petty compared to the torment she was feeling now.

Katherine.

How had she found her?

"Carmen?" Harvey asked again. "What happened?"

"Why did you do that, Harvey?"

"What?"

"I thought we were friends," Carmen said, not meeting his gaze—her eyes trailing down the busy New York street, distracted businessmen dodging and sidestepping around her. The air smelled of fried food and wet garbage. The sounds—the cabs honking, the hum of the chattering crowd, the stilted vocal and *chunka-chunka* guitar of John Lennon's cover of "Stand By Me" blaring from a nearby apartment—forced Carmen to almost yell her words. "Partners. It was going so well. . . ."

She stopped herself. Why was she talking about this now, when her head was somewhere else? She knew she was channeling everything—her anger, her surprise, her hurt—at Harvey. But what choice did she have?

"I'm sorry, I messed up," Harvey said. He was reaching into his back pocket. He handed her a few rumpled sheets of yellow notebook paper. "But I did this."

Carmen scanned the top page quickly. Harvey's handwriting was terrible. Like a drunk doctor's. But she caught the gist of it. She'd seen enough first draft plots to know what it was. It didn't fix anything, but it did soften the sting, surprisingly.

"You're trying to win me over with a half-baked plot?" Carmen said, smirking. "Wait until you read my script."

Harvey scoffed. "You wrote one?"

"I wrote six of them. What do you think, that I'd just sit and wait for your genius to lead the way?"

"Six?" he asked, mouth agape. "How is that even possible?"

"You gotta work smarter, not harder, Harvey," Carmen said with a laugh. "I've been trying to do this forever, turning in scripts to Carlyle every chance I saw. So I just tweaked and reworked some ideas and notes I had to build the Lynx's world. If Carlyle likes this character, I want to be ready to deliver. This is my shot. I plan to take it."

"Well, we can pool what we have. Make it stronger. We can combine our ideas," Harvey said, fighting back a sheepish smile. "We have to do this, Carmen. I'm sorry—I fucked up, okay? I don't want to ruin being friends because I . . . misread the situation."

She let his words hover between them for a moment. She wasn't savoring the silence so much as digesting what he'd said. She'd run into a lot of situations like the one with Harvey. Friends, or supposed friends, desperate to become more. Always older men. Always men who had never seemed interested in her or her life before, not until they noticed some kind of opening for romance. But Harvey felt a little different. A bit lost. More genuine. She hoped she wouldn't regret forgiving him. She knew she probably would.

"This is interesting, and I think I can weave it into what I have," she said, flipping through the rest of the pages. "We can make this work. We can make this character ours."

Harvey smiled.

"I won't screw it up," he said. Carmen could tell he was straining to keep the smile off his young face. "You okay?"

The question caught her off guard again. She thought she'd sidestepped Harvey. She realized there might be more to him than she'd first thought. But why did that concern her?

"For now I am," she said before turning around and heading back to the office, unable to shake the lingering feeling that she was falling deeper into something she couldn't fully comprehend.

CHAPTER EIGHT

Carmen first met Katherine Hall in Miami a few years back. It was an introductory creative writing class at Dade Junior College. Carmen had her English Lit degree from the city's fledgling public university, Florida International, but she'd been floundering—her job, as a bookkeeper for a small printer in Hialeah, was tedious and soul-draining on a good day, utterly miserable on a bad one. She'd decided to sneak into the class when her friend Sandra told Carmen about her instructor, Emma Lytton.

"She's amazing, Carm," Sandra had said, her voice rising with each syllable. "Like, so good. She makes me think I can actually be a writer."

"You can," Carmen had said. And Sandra could—she was a capable poet, with a strong voice and style that made her work stand out in a way Carmen wasn't accustomed to. She didn't like seeing her talented friend just defer to some unknown teacher. "You will."

But the conversation had left Carmen intrigued. Sandra wasn't prone to flights of adulation. So she wanted to see for herself. Get a glimpse of this woman who had inspired Sandra—caused her friend's eyes to smile, her expression to brighten.

Which was why she was sitting in the back of the packed classroom on a sweltering Miami day, watching a woman break down writing in a way Carmen had really only imagined—or figured out for herself through her own trial and error.

"If your characters are developed, if you spend enough time with them—really, truly, get to know them," Lytton said, pacing around the front of the class, her eyes jumping from student to student, "then they'll come to life."

A few muttered sounds, perhaps a groan. Carmen shared a knowing glance with another woman seated across the classroom, her soft features framed by blond hair. *Who was that?* Carmen wondered, before turning her attention back to the instructor. Lytton seemed to zero in on a low-key heckler.

"Sounds stupid, right?" she said, a combative smile on her face—as if to say, *Watch this.* "But it's the truth. They'll start pushing and pulling against you—against your plot. They'll start acting out, like impertinent toddlers. Your job, as the writer, is to let that happen. Ride the wave."

She stopped pacing, placed her hands on her hips and looked down at the floor. Carmen wondered what was going on—if she'd lost her way, been offended—but as soon as the thoughts formed in her head, Lytton looked up. For a second, it felt as if she was looking straight at Carmen, straight through her.

"You have to channel this energy—this power—or you will lose it," she said. Carmen's gaze instinctively shifted over to the blond-haired woman, her eyes still on Carmen, a flicker of recognition in them. Or so Carmen thought then. So Carmen thought now. Lytton continued: "You have to create a world, with people in it, so believable that you are just the tool that the world uses to tell the story."

Carmen didn't remember much else from the lecture. She felt shaken, jarred loose. Someone had quantified what she'd been struggling to figure out for months, years. Her half-hearted attempts to write that novel. The labored and overwrought short stories. The poetry that seemed to dance around what she felt but was unable to say. The pages and pages of comic book plots and scripts—an entire universe of characters and powers and subplots—all stored in a drawer in a file cabinet in her parents' utility room. When Sandra had reached out to her about the class, Carmen had basically given up. She just hadn't told anyone but herself. *Why bother?* The words had rung through her head over the last few months as she'd attempted to write. To kick-start that engine again. Instead, she'd felt nothing; a cloud of resignation she was unable to shake loose with an idea. But now she felt something else. Hope?

"You're not part of the class, are you?"

The words ensnared Carmen as she followed Sandra, spinning Carmen around as if someone had grabbed a loose thread from her shirt and pulled. Carmen turned to see the tall blond-haired woman looking at her with placid hazel eyes, calmly keeping pace with the other students as they filed out. She was lithe and pale, her figure nestled comfortably in a light blue blouse and tan slacks. Carmen couldn't break the gaze the woman held on her. And though the bustle of students formed a river of bodies between and around them, Carmen could sense this woman's eyes locked on her—those feline features, her sleepy, soft eyes—sizing her up carefully. Carmen had felt it immediately—this strange, magnetic need to be close to this woman she'd never met. Her hands were clammy. A jolt of electricity went through Carmen as she tried to answer her innocent question.

"No, uh, I'm not," Carmen fumbled. She just wanted to be able to take a few more steps—to make her way out of the classroom and back to her life. "My—my friend . . ."

She glanced toward Sandra, but found an empty space where her friend had been. Carmen looked toward the exit and caught a glimpse of her, shrugging for forgiveness as she backed away from the door. *What the fuck?*

"I'm not going to report you," the woman said. "At least, if you tell me your name . . . ?"

"Valdez, Carmen Valdez," she said. "My friend suggested I come hear your professor speak about writing."

"She's fantastic, isn't she?" the woman said, her eyes widening with sheer awe. But before she continued, she stopped, closed her eyes, and shook her head—as if she'd just realized she'd forgotten to use her turn signal. "Sorry, so rude. I'm Katherine. Katherine Hall."

She extended a hand. Carmen took it. Her palm felt warm and charged. The handshake lingered a bit longer than usual.

"Nice to meet you," Carmen said. "Are you crashing the class, too?"

Katherine smiled knowingly.

"That obvious?"

They laughed.

Carmen watched her movements, smooth, fluid, not calculated or stiff—like someone completely comfortable in her own skin. In that moment, Carmen hated and loved her with equal measure, this strange, almost alien woman she'd just met. What was it about her, she wondered.

"Oh, I enjoyed what she said, I could relate a lot," Carmen said, cursing every word as it dribbled out of her lips. She sounded so young. So awkward. So desperate for approval. But she pressed on. The rush was hard to ignore. "I need to do that more—let my characters pull me along."

"I do, too," Katherine said with an almost imperceptible nod, as if chastising herself. "It's kind of why I came here. I felt like I needed to hear it from someone else—someone with experience, you know?"

Carmen did. But before she could sputter out a response, Katherine looked up and smiled at her as she slid a few files into her own backpack. The smile was genuine and warm. They'd found some unexpected common ground. Suddenly, Carmen didn't care where Sandra had gone. Katherine seemed touched to find a compatriot—someone struggling with the same writing demons. At least that was the story she'd tell Carmen later.

"Yes, a little guidance down the path," Carmen said.

"Exactly. I couldn't have said it better myself," Katherine said, looping her arm through her bag and making toward the door. "What do you write? Walk with me. I want to hear all about it."

Carmen did. She noticed Sandra as they exited the class, her look of surprise as Carmen kept walking, past her friend and toward something else, something different.

She hadn't really needed the cafecito, but it felt good and warm on her throat, and the jolt of caffeine—pure, concentrated Cuban electricity—made the moment feel more alive, loaded with endless possibilities. They'd wandered off campus and found a tiny Cuban place selling coffee through a walk-up window, a ventanita. Taking a seat on a nearby bench, Katherine carefully opened the larger foam cup of coffee and poured a serving into Carmen's tasita.

"Do you have anything with you?" Katherine asked.

At first Carmen thought this woman was asking if she could cop some weed, but she shook the thought out of her brain fast when Katherine looked up at her with an expectant smile. She wanted to read her work, Carmen realized, and that fact seemed almost worse. She kind of did want to smoke a joint with this woman—who appeared to be everything Carmen was not: confident, well-dressed, smooth in appearance and delivery—despite being around the same age. She had it all together, it seemed, and while she fit in perfectly in this messed-up world around them, there was still some gristle to her—a flair of defiance and romance that Carmen wanted to get to know. But no, no—of course she didn't have any writing samples.

She tried to laugh it off, but Katherine stopped her.

"What's funny, though, Carmen?" she asked, an innocent look in her eyes. "I'm sure you have a lot to say. I'd love to read your work. We can trade. I know it's crazy, but we can become partners."

Carmen felt herself stiffen, and Katherine noticed immediately. She placed her hand on Carmen's quickly, her touch warm and tender.

"Writing partners," she said with a chuckle. "We can help each other. I know I need someone to hold me accountable. So I don't keep treating this like a silly hobby, you know? Is that how you feel about it sometimes? Like you're the only person who believes in you? It'd be nice to have someone in my corner."

Carmen nodded slowly.

"Yes, yes," she said, unable to form anything more than monosyllabic. They were looking at each other, their eyes smiling warmly. Carmen could feel her face reddening—but from what, she wondered. "I'd—I'd like that."

"All right then, my new friend Carmen," Katherine said, emphasizing her name, taking her time—as if her mouth were trying it on for size, getting comfortable with the sound. "Then we'll make sure we're both taking this seriously—and treat it like something we really want, not just a passing interest."

Carmen felt herself sag—the prospect of writing more seriously, not just pecking at it and fantasizing about it while more real-world concerns weighed her down—but it was fleeting. She felt something else, too. Katherine's warm hand on her arm.

"It'll be great," she said, patting her gently and pulling back, her muted wedding ring scraping Carmen's skin slightly as Katherine turned her toward the coffee. "I feel like we're both going to really help each other."

Carmen smiled. Their eyes met and lingered for a few seconds longer.

It was in that moment that Carmen knew she was in trouble.

CHAPTER NINE

eads up! Heads up, Carmen! Heads up!"

The volleyball slammed into Carmen's face with a loud *thwack,* sending her flying back, landing hard on her ass. She rubbed the side of her face that had taken the brunt of the impact, already reddening from the hit. She got up fast, doing a quick spot check and dusting off. She was more embarrassed than hurt.

She felt a hand on her arm. It was Harvey, who was flanked by two of her coworkers—Trunick and Hahn from production. She waved them off and walked toward the edge of the court. These games, held on the west side of Central Park, were regular events for Triumph, and for much of New York's comic book industry. A chance for desk-riding comic lifers to work up a sweat outside. Most people didn't take it seriously—well, except the Marvel team—but it guaranteed a few laughs, some exercise, and plenty of fun. Carmen was not a particularly good player.

"You okay?" Harvey asked.

"Stop asking me that. I'm fine," Carmen said, giving him a bland smile and jerking her arm away.

He stepped back. "It happens."

Their plan was still the same—they were going to meet up later to merge some of Harvey's notes with Carmen's scripts, pool their takes on the Lynx—but that didn't mean everything was fine. She still felt hurt by his betrayal, and it didn't help that she also felt unmoored by the phone call she'd received earlier in the week. She just didn't have the headspace for it.

"I'm fine. Please. Just let me be."

He nodded and raised his hands in mock surrender before walking toward the front of the bench area, where a few other Triumph staffers waited for their chance to enter the game. Carmen grabbed her bag and pulled out a cigarette. She dug into her purse, but couldn't find her lighter. Had she left it on her desk?

"Light?"

Carmen turned around. A woman, maybe five years older than Carmen, stood there, offering a lighter. Carmen took it and smiled.

"Thank you," she said, the cigarette still in her mouth as she tried to light it. "Thought I was in the wrong crowd for this."

"You're mostly right," the stranger said. Her red hair stood out in the Central Park sun; her warm smile, too—in contrast to the usual defiant New York glare. "You work at Triumph?"

Carmen nodded, taking a long drag and sneaking a glance at the team, still performing as poorly as when she'd left them. She caught Harvey's eyes—he was watching her. Watching them. A look of concern across his face. *What is he worried about?*

"Yeah, Carmen Valdez," she said, extending her hand. The woman took it, her grip strong but not forced. Confident. Carmen looked at her more closely. She was stunning. It'd taken Carmen a second to notice— the woman carried herself with ease, her entire demeanor smooth and comfortable. Carmen found it jarring at first. It reminded her too much of someone else.

"You work for Carlyle," the woman said, more of a statement than a question.

"I'm his secretary, yeah."

"His assistant," the woman corrected her.

Carmen responded with a raised eyebrow. She wanted out of the conversation already.

"Marion Price," the woman said, her smile lazy but honest. Her green eyes seemed to sparkle in the afternoon sun for a moment. "I just started at Warren. Nice to see another woman here."

Carmen tried her best to return the smile but felt her face straining at the fake gesture. She wasn't warm. She couldn't turn that on. But she'd tried; that would have to be enough. And Marion was right—they were the only women around, aside from Fran, an older lady who worked in the Triumph mail room managing Carlyle's secondary but far more lucrative tchotchke business.

"Warren, huh?" Carmen asked. "What's that like?"

She enjoyed these irregular games not just because they were fun, and a distraction, but because they showed her what life was like at other companies, and how those places contrasted with Triumph—which, from her vantage point, was stuck in the 1950s. While DC was stuffy and buttoned-up, Marvel seemed downright progressive—with a few female staffers and a young, frat-party vibe that was more charming than disturbing. Everyone else landed somewhere in the middle. But no company could match Triumph in terms of being preserved in amber. Her job was a relic; her place in the company forever affected by that. She stole another glance at Harvey.

"It's nice, I guess, as far as full-time gigs go. Our boss is a character, that's for damn sure," Marion said, looking at the ground, as if realizing she didn't have Carmen's full attention. "I'm thankfully not the only woman there. Not sure what I'd do if Louise wasn't around. Anyway, my speed is more West Coast—you know, drawing strips for underground newspapers or low-print-run deals, but I know how to put a magazine together, so I fit the bill."

Marion let out a slow, natural laugh. A few moments of silence followed before she continued.

"How do you like Triumph?" she asked, almost as if she already knew the answer. "I'm friendly with Harvey."

"Oh, yeah?"

"Yeah, we worked together at Bulwark, this tiny outfit that did some comics stuff," Marion said, her eyes on the game now, too, her face slightly flushed. "I guess I was his boss. He didn't last very long, to be honest. I'm sure he'll tell you the sordid details at some point."

Carmen had some passing knowledge when it came to Bulwark. Their line of superheroes was a joke, even to the staff. The books came out sporadically if at all, the rates they paid talent were laughable, and the production values were abysmal. She'd known that Harvey had worked there, but he didn't seem to talk about it much. He'd certainly never mentioned Marion.

"Ah right, yeah, they had some good stuff," Carmen said stiffly, trying to be polite.

"You don't need to sugarcoat it, dear," Marion said with a melodic laugh. "They were shit. Harvey even wrote some of them—books like *Blood Ace* or *The Buzzer*, which was basically a D-list Spider-Man riff. We all knew the books were shit, but we were younger and learning as we went. The people that worked there never talk about it. It's not exactly a shining line on your résumé, you know?"

"I can imagine," Carmen said with a quick nod.

"It's funny," Marion said, her eyes on the game, the Triumph side preparing to serve. "I ran into Harvey a few nights ago—poor sap was drinking alone. I hadn't seen him in, well, years. Since I had to hand him his last paycheck. Talk about awkward. You came up, actually."

Carmen felt herself tense up. Had Harvey seen Marion after he'd come to her place? After he'd tried to force himself on her? Did it matter?

Carmen tried to change the subject.

"Did you always want to work in comics?"

The question tumbled out of Carmen's mouth—as if, deep inside, Carmen was desperate to find someone, anyone like her. A woman in comics who might want to be more than someone's sidekick.

Marion smiled warmly. "I'm a writer, really, at heart," she said, tilting her head—trying to get a better look at Carmen. "I kind of hate all the boy books—the action stuff that everyone seems to want to make. You know, teen boy jack-off newspapers."

Carmen laughed. She felt her eyes water. It was nice. Unexpected.

"I write and draw, when I have time," Marion continued. "I did mostly fringe, weird stuff out west, when I was in San Fran."

Carmen perked up. She wanted to know more. Wanted to share some stories with this person. But before she could ask a question, she caught Marion looking past her—at the crowd of freelancers and staffers congregating around the game. Marion returned her gaze to Carmen, her expression different now—focused and precise.

"Look, just be careful with Harvey, okay?"

"Careful?" Carmen asked. "Why?"

Marion frowned. "I wish we could sit and talk somewhere—like, really talk," she said, glancing past Carmen. "But I'll tell you the one thing I told Harvey when we let him go. 'No one likes to get conned.' It leaves a bad taste in people's mouths. And Harvey, in his heart, is better than that."

"I don't understand why you're—"

"Like I said, watch yourself," Marion said, her voice low and focused. "Harvey's a complicated kid. He painted me into a corner at Bulwark, I'll leave it at that. He acted like a toddler, and my stoner demeanor aside, I'm a grown, professional woman. I probably shouldn't have expected all that much from him to begin with. That's the worst, I suppose. He didn't surprise me in the least."

Carmen felt rattled. Why was this woman telling her this?

"Did Harvey mention anything else to you?" Carmen asked. "About me?"

Marion stepped toward Carmen and gently placed a hand over hers.

"Not a lot, but enough," Marion said. "You're too smart and beautiful to get played like that. Don't get lost in the moment."

Played like that?

"Did I overstep?" Marion asked. "Sorry, I have no filter sometimes—"

"No, nothing, I'm just . . . tired," Carmen said, fake smile in full view now. "I should get going."

Marion nodded. Her smile was fake now, too, as if she felt the need to parry. Why couldn't she just befriend this woman, Carmen wondered. Why did she have to instantly assume the worst—that she was some bitter ex-flame of Harvey's? And what did it matter if she was? Carmen didn't care for Harvey that way. Didn't see him like that. Had it been any other day, Carmen would've jumped for joy at the sight of another woman in her profession, someone she could share experiences with and maybe learn something from. But not today. No. Now she just wanted to go home, to lie in her tiny bed in the dark and stare at the ceiling until it was time to do something else.

"It was nice to meet you," Carmen said, backing away.

As she made her way to the train, Carmen looked back at the game. She caught a glimpse of Harvey making a beeline for Marion, a dark, twisted expression on his face.

She buzzed the bell and waited. Her arm ached. It'd only taken a few blocks for Carmen to regret lugging her old Erika Model S typewriter to Harvey's place in the Village, on the corner of Bleecker and Christopher Streets, above a downtrodden bodega named Fancy Groceries. It wasn't lost on Carmen that Harvey lived down the street from the Stonewall Inn, where just six years before, members of the local gay community had clashed with police in a series of skirmishes that would bring much-needed attention to an intolerable, unfair status quo, and launch a gay liberation movement. Buoyed by the sixties counterculture and the civil rights crusade, the riots served as a flash point to an explosion of seething anger and resentment—and, to Carmen, had more importantly resulted in some substantive change. But there was still a long way to go, she thought.

The exterior wall leading Carmen to the building entrance was plastered with every kind of sign—missing pets, upcoming music gigs, pleas for work, and offers galore. Some were ripped, revealing the faded flyers that had once been at the forefront. A bulletin board for the wanderers.

Harvey had called her a few hours after the volleyball game on Friday and admitted he was broke—something about a hefty bar tab earlier in the week. Carmen had been hesitant, but agreed to meet him at his place. The conversation with Marion had shaken her more than she wanted to admit. Carmen promised herself she'd bolt from Harvey's place at the first sign of anything strange.

Despite Harvey's awkward kiss a few nights before, Carmen didn't find him threatening. She'd felt more betrayed than violated, she realized. He was her friend. She didn't have many of those in New York, and she valued him. Still, Molly didn't think going to his place was the best idea.

"Carmen, guys are creeps, period—you know this as well as I do," Molly had said while checking herself out in the apartment's sole mirror. She had a gig that night and the process of transformation was just beginning. "There are no nice, honest dudes. That's it, case closed, sentencing has commenced. Just because this guy seems like a wuss doesn't—"

"It's not that he's a wimp, all right?" Carmen had said, packing her typewriter in its case. "I just think he's a friend. He screwed up. If he does it again, we're done. Molly, second chances are still allowed, right?"

Molly had shaken her head, still spinning in front of the mirror, her black T-shirt revealing a bare shoulder.

"Your funeral," she'd said, turning to her friend with a smirk. "Oh, your dad called. Again. Like, for the fiftieth time this week. I'm thinking we should just change our number?"

"You think so?"

"Carmen, I'm joking," Molly had said, surprise in her eyes. "What is going on? I don't even know your dad, and I've talked to him more times than I think you have this year. It's starting to get weird."

Carmen had shrugged.

"I have to go."

Papi.

Carmen knew she'd have to deal with it. With her parents. With everything. But now was not the time. Now was the time to be creative and seize this bizarre, unreal opportunity. Harvey's crush on her be damned.

The door swung open to reveal Harvey Stern in a rumpled Batman T-shirt and baggy jeans, his thick glasses slightly askew. If she liked guys like him—if she liked guys, period, she thought—she would find his geek-chic look charming.

"Hey," he said. "Thanks for coming."

She walked past him into the apartment.

"Let's get to work, Harv," she said. "Legends don't create themselves."

Harvey's place stank of old books, cheap cologne, and even cheaper beer, but it was tidy. The kind of tidy that came from frantic, last-minute scrubbing, not routine upkeep. He'd cleaned up before she arrived. There weren't pizza boxes strewn all over the floor, and the bookshelf impressed Carmen more than she'd expected it would. There were comics all over, sure, but it also seemed like Harvey had an affinity for the classics—Eudora Welty, Gertrude Stein, Ernest Hemingway, and F. Scott Fitzgerald all took up a few slots on a banged-up black shelf near his tiny desk. A few pulp novels by Mickey Spillane and Jim Thompson and a Claire Morgan book completed his library.

"*The Price of Salt,*" Carmen said, picking the book up and waving it at Harvey as he walked into the apartment, the door slamming shut behind him. "You surprise me, Harvey Stern. You know she wrote comics, too?"

"Yeah, for Nedor and Timely, I think," Harvey said. "I know good writing when I see it."

"Oh?"

He walked past Carmen, into the living room. It was a medium-sized one-bedroom with the expected amount of single-male clutter. Carmen found herself at ease for some reason.

"You brought your typewriter, nice," he said, plopping down on the small couch opposite his tiny desk, where Carmen had set up shop. "There's half a pizza in the fridge."

"How predictable," she said with a smirk. "Got any beer?"

"A few Schaefers, not much else."

Carmen nodded and slid into the desk chair, spinning it around to face Harvey.

"Okay, let's talk about these scripts," Carmen said.

"Well, there are your pages and my stuff, and we need to figure out how to consol—"

"Yeah, well, the pages you gave me—they need work," Carmen said, trying to stifle a smile. "Major work."

"What do you mean?"

"They just felt . . . I dunno, Harvey—don't take this the wrong way—they just felt . . . stale?" she said, waving her hands around, as if trying to find the words hovering in front of her face. "Like I'd read it before? The long, piecemeal origin story, the damsel in distress . . . we don't have to do it that way."

She pulled out a large stack of pages from her purse—six stacks, to be exact, each one held together by a large black binder clip.

Harvey paused. He hadn't been expecting this, she realized. He hadn't believed her. She was coming on strong, she had opinions, she was prepared. Even though this was exactly as she'd acted in her apartment the first time they talked, he still seemed to think himself the senior partner. She didn't like that. She didn't want that. If she was going to be in this, if she was going to write her dream in secret—as Molly had so aptly put it—she was going all-in.

"This has to be different," she said, handing him the first script. "This has to feel special."

Harvey nodded, a delay tactic as he sized her up and pondered the unexpected complexities this partnership might bring him. Then he spoke.

"I agree," he said as he flipped through the script. "What did you have in mind? Can you walk me through these?"

Now it was her turn to pause. Carmen hadn't expected him to roll over so fast. To accept that this was the best play. Now she had to actually show her cards.

She reached for her purse and pulled out a battered manila file folder. Inside were a few legal pads and loose sheets of paper—Carmen's clear cursive covering most of the pages, some words underlined or circled. The pages looked worn and beat-up. These weren't just scrawled on.

These pages had been with her for a long time. Since Miami. These were the ingredients that made up the scripts. The Lynx's blood.

"Huh," Harvey said, watching as she methodically laid out the pages. The top page of one had *Characters* written across the top. Another had *Motivations* emblazoned over the first page. "You came prepared, Carmen."

"Are you surprised?" Carmen asked.

Of course I'm prepared, she thought. She had already learned the toughest lesson back home—that she'd have to work twice as hard to get the same recognition a male peer got.

"Guess not," Harvey said.

"Okay then, let's get down to it—the best stories start with character, I think. Who is Claudia Calla? Why should we care about her?" Carmen asked. "What makes her want to put on this costume and fight crime? Risk her life?"

She was speaking truth now, because while Carmen didn't have all the answers yet, she knew the only way to get them was by trying. Writing. Brainstorming. Rewriting. What made this character—the Lethal Lynx—any different from the myriad failed heroes and villains whose only legacy was lining birdcages? The lost heroes of Triumph Comics, like Avatar, the Dusk, the Freedom Alliance, and more? Sure—she'd done the work, crafted the first six adventures featuring their hero, but it could always be better. Until it was time to turn it in.

Harvey stood up and began to pace, his eyes on his feet as he made his way around the tiny office area. He stopped and spun around to face Carmen.

"Dead parents?" he said. "Dead boyfriend? Uncle?"

"Boring. Predictable."

"What then?" Harvey asked, a bit of defensiveness in his voice. "Spider-Man has Uncle Ben. Batman has his parents. Superman has an entire planet, for God's sake. What drives this woman? What makes her special? It's got to be something primal, intense—it has to compel her to do it."

"What if it's not that, though?" Carmen asked. "I was thinking something else—that's what I put in those pages. Hear me out. What if . . . I dunno, what if she's just fucking tired?"

Harvey shook his head.

"Tired? She's sleepy? Like—"

"No, no, no, no, no," Carmen said, raising her arms in frustration. "Just . . . tired. Fed up. Tired of the bullshit. Tired of this patriarchal society."

"So she's, like, a women's-lib hero?"

"Don't be so simplistic, Harvey," Carmen said. "I just mean, she's tired of . . . the system. Of criminals going free. Of bad people getting away with things. Of bad things happening to women like her."

"That's fine," Harvey said, nodding. "That's real. But I think you see that with heroes like Daredevil, too—they still need some pathos. Some compelling reason to do it every damn night."

Carmen's voice got quieter. She could see Harvey strain to hear her.

"Maybe . . . maybe it's not just that she lost someone, it's that . . ." she started. "She lost herself."

Carmen could feel his gaze. Could feel her skin running hot. She was trying to do what Katherine had taught her, as much as it hurt her to think about her now—but she needed to. She needed to dig deep and find the heart of this character, or everything else would be lost.

"She was hurt somehow. She was hurt . . . badly," Carmen said. "So . . . she's determined that no one will ever hurt her again. Or hurt anyone else, that way."

Harvey's eyes seemed heavy—as if they carried an unexpected burden. He just stared at her for a few moments, waiting for more. But more didn't come. Not yet.

He cleared his throat.

"So, you don't want to do an origin story?" Harvey asked, letting himself fall back on the couch, still clutching that first script. "Is that what you're saying?"

"I just don't get why we have to spell it all out for people from page one," Carmen said. She felt calmer. "Why not let the reader figure it out eventually?"

"A mystery?"

"Maybe, but at the very least, something more complicated, okay?" she said. "Like, we learn about it as we go—we meet Claudia, we see the Lynx, but maybe we don't know they're one and the same right away?"

Harvey nodded.

"Yeah, yeah, that's great," he said, grabbing a pad from the seat next to him and jotting something down. "I like that. That's good."

Carmen spun the office chair around and began to type, her machine clacking a half-second behind her thoughts. It was a soothing sound, it meant she was doing—instead of thinking about—something for once. Marion's ominous warning pulsed through her mind for a second. Her hint that there was something more to what was going on. But she pushed past it. She had to.

"What does she do?" Harvey asked. "What's her job? You wanted her to be, like, a newspaper secretary—"

"Assistant," Carmen interjected.

"Uh, yeah, okay," Harvey said, scrunching up his nose. "Or not? Or is she rich?"

"No, neither—it's not just about her job," Carmen said, shaking her head, not turning around. "She should feel—different. She can have a day job, but there has to be more to her. She should be like one of us, you know? A creative type. Maybe she doesn't even have a job. Or maybe she hates her job?"

She didn't need to look at Harvey to know she'd stumped him. They were both comic book readers. Fanatics. They knew the medium like some people knew sports or jazz or European history. But Carmen had seen beyond the stapled, four-color stories. She knew there was more to be done in the space. She hadn't realized, until now, that Harvey was happy just to play in the box that already existed. She wouldn't let that slow her down.

"Don't freeze up on me," she said, lifting her hands from the type-writer. "We're on a roll."

"I just feel like we're—this is all so indefinite, you know? Like, she's an artist? She doesn't have a death to avenge?"

"Right, but it's different, Harvey. She can deal with loss, but it's not linear. She doesn't just put on a mask because someone dies," she said, her tone mildly incredulous. "That's the point. Don't you want to push things a bit? Try to make it feel like something new? I do."

Harvey shook his head. He stood up and started to pace again.

"I get it, Carmen, I get why you'd want—"

"Please, tell me why I'd like—"

"No, no, let me finish," he said, gently, not combative. "I just under-stand. This is your moment. But it's my moment, too. You know I've tried to write something like this for years? At Bulwark, I was pitching and pitching, working so hard to get a shot—but they'd only give me garbage assignments. When someone was late, or decided the page rate was too low. 'Oh, here, Harv—can you write the last issue of *Blood Ace* before it ends?' Maybe a fill-in on *Fangtina* if I was lucky—that kind of stuff. Not enough to build a career. Or even, hell, show them anything beyond meeting a deadline. But this is it. For you and for me. This is our shot."

"So why not take it?" she said. She was facing him now, her eyes wide and eager. "Let's hit it out of the park, Harvey. Stop trying to be cautious. That's for those garbage assignments. Showing you can turn something in, you can fill paper. This . . . this is a chance to create some-thing. A piece of mythology."

She leaned forward.

"Think of Spider-Man, Harvey. Stan and Steve Ditko didn't just want to create another grown, tough, perfect hero-man—another steel-jawed Superman. No. They flipped the script. They took the idea of the young sidekick—the teenager, the *reader*—and made him the hero. They gave him problems we could relate to. I'm not saying we can do something like that, but we sure as hell should try. Otherwise, what's the point?"

Their eyes met, wide and excited. They both knew that what came next could change their lives. Perhaps forever.

Harvey smiled. And they got to work.

The brainstorming session slowly morphed into something more concrete, tangible. They got to work integrating some of their shared ideas into the framework Carmen had created with her six scripts. At the same time, Carmen got to see Harvey in action—the work of someone who, for better or worse, had written his fair share of professional comics. Writing a script, in many ways, is like building a puzzle for an artist to piece together. The descriptions, camera angles, and panel layouts of the comic page just float, words on paper, until an artist is able to translate and visualize them. The trick, Carmen would learn over time, was giving the artist—a person they had yet to meet—enough details to use their own skills on the visual side to create something wholly new and different from the initial story. Something greater, she hoped. Something special.

By the time Carmen hit the final *clack* on her typewriter, she'd begun to see the first glimmers of the sun. Had they really been at this that long? Had an entire night flickered away? But Carmen knew one thing—they had it. A debut script introducing a new character, their slashing street vigilante Lynx, and her supporting cast—the dense, potential beau Simon Upton, menacing arch-foe Mr. Void, and hints that point to a compelling, unforgettable origin story—about a sheepish newspaper secretary named Claudia Calla who witnesses the murder of her social debutante twin sister, Lisa, at the hands of an abusive lover. Claudia, enraged and feeling helpless, decides to take on the mantle of an old male pulp hero to ensure that no one loses their life in the same way.

It was sharp, it was fast, it was moody, and it was mysterious. Best of all? It felt pretty damn *great*.

Carmen looked at Harvey. He didn't seem tired. He seemed electrified. Eyes wide, if a bit bloodshot.

"That is really good, I mean, this is fantastic," he said, flipping through the revised stack of script pages Carmen had placed next to her. "This is it. Finally."

"Finally?"

Harvey frowned, regret on his face. "Er, um, yeah, I just mean I'm exhausted."

Before she could respond, the phone rang. It was jarring—and pulled them down from their creative high. Harvey wandered to the kitchen. Carmen could only hear snippets.

"Yes, yes, I understand . . . No, of course not . . . You can't be asking me that, really? . . . Okay, all right, fine . . . Yeah, yeah, bye. You know where to find me."

The *click* of the phone receiver being replaced seemed to ring out for a second too long.

Carmen watched as Harvey stepped back into the office area, his gaze darting around the space.

"Lose something?" she asked.

"No, uh—no," he said, forcing himself to slow down. His expression was dazed, as if he'd just remembered Carmen was there. "I—hey, I need to go, okay? Sorry to cut this short. I just need to handle something."

"Harvey, it's not even seven in the morning," Carmen said. "Is everything okay?"

Harvey waved her off.

"Nothing to worry about, I just need to do something."

"Sure, sure," Carmen said, nodding as she stood up. She heard Marion's voice in her head again, but ignored it. "Let me just get my—"

"No, stay, please, keep going," Harvey said, wincing to himself. "I just need to go, all right? I'll call you later. This was fun. Really great, okay?"

She started to respond, but he was gone. She thought she'd get something—a fleeting goodbye, an apology—but nothing materialized. It felt like an awkward speech someone would give after an unfortunate, inebriated one-night stand.

Instead, Carmen just heard the dull slamming of the front door as Harvey left.

She shrugged. She was grateful for the distraction the project provided, even if the road map was unclear. It helped her focus, and it helped her ignore the other things buzzing around her periphery. Like Katherine. She slid her typewriter back into its case. She patted the various stacks of script pages on his desk.

She stopped for a second, one foot out the door, gripped by a sudden, all-consuming sense of fear. The kind of childlike panic one never forgets. A shiver she hadn't seen coming. It disappeared as quickly as it'd formed. Carmen shook her head and continued on her way.

It was nothing, she thought—no, hoped. Nothing.

IT HITS ME THEN.

AS I SEE MY TWIN SISTER'S BODY PULLED INTO THE DIRT.

ENCASED FOR ETERNITY. HER PHYSICAL FORM GONE.

I AM ALONE.

I CAN NO LONGER RELY ON THE POLICE. ON SOCIETY.

NO ONE WILL AVENGE HER DEATH. MY POOR, SWEET LISA.

IT WAS MORE THAN MUGGERS AND THIEVES. CRIMINALS. IT WAS MEN IN POWER, WHO CHOSE TO EXERT THEIR STRENGTH OVER INNOCENT WOMEN.

THE ONLY WAY TO STOP THEM--THE ONLY WAY TO CHALLENGE THEM WAS BY ABSORBING THE BAD, DEADLY, AND DARK.

TO USE IT FOR GOOD. FOR REVENGE.

WITH MY CLAWS, MY SPEED, MY ANGER--

--I WOULD BECOME SOMETHING ELSE.

I WOULD BECOME THE LYNX.

*Excerpt from 1975's **The Legendary Lynx #3**, "**The Untold Origin of The Lynx!**"—Story: Harvey Stern, Art: Doug Detmer, Letters: Todd Morelli, Editor: Rich Berger, President/CEO: Jeffrey Carlyle. Published by Triumph Comics.*

CHAPTER TEN

Carmen stepped out of the shower and started to dry off, her movements stiff and automated. Her mind was elsewhere—on earlier in the morning, and Harvey's hasty exit. She'd never seen him like that, she realized. Distant and focused on something else. Could there be anything more important than this project? she wondered. Perhaps. She didn't know what his life was like. Barely knew anything about his past. She knew he'd worked at Bulwark—with Marion Price, apparently—and had aspirations to write, but what else was there? She made a mental note to look into it as she started to get dressed. *It's not about you, though,* she thought.

Before she let her mind move on to the more mundane tasks ahead—groceries, bills—she let it veer back to their story. It'd come so naturally, she thought, as if they'd both been waiting for the chance to pour their ideas into something alive and real. Maybe that was it. While the idea for the Lynx, and certainly the name, had come from their conversations together, a lot of her essence had been scribbled on those legal pads by Carmen months and years before. Ideas, fleeting thoughts, names—little scraps she was weaving together into something new and alive, like a team of outcasts: her own personal Doom Patrol.

There was a lot of her in Claudia—in the Lynx. She was strong. Driven. Confident. But also forced to claw and scrape for any purchase. She also felt a deep sense of loss, and a need to protect—

Bzzt!

Carmen almost jumped. She wasn't expecting anyone this early, and aside from Harvey, who somehow got her home address, no one knew where she and Molly lived. She checked her watch. It had to be Molly. She was being paranoid, she told herself.

Carmen sighed and made her way to the door, not bothering to check the peephole. They'd lived here less than a year, and this was probably the fifth time Molly'd done this. Carmen was already visualizing the trip down the street to the locksmith as she opened the door, her words already chiding her roommate in a friendly tone.

"Molly, don't you get tired of losing—"

She stopped. The woman standing outside her apartment door wasn't Molly. But Carmen wished it were. Despite the call a few days prior, Carmen hadn't thought this might happen.

"Hi, Carmen," Katherine Hall said, a nervous, timid smile sneaking onto her face.

Does everyone know where I live?

"Katherine . . ." Carmen said. "What . . . why are you here?"

"Can I come in, Carm? To talk?" Katherine said. "I need to see you."

Carmen gasped before stepping back and slamming the door shut.

A sheen of sweat had replaced the residual drops of water that remained from the shower. Her breathing was quick and shallow. *What is she doing here?*

A slight rap at the door. Hesitant.

"Go. Away," Carmen said, low and focused, straining to hide any fear or anxiety in her voice. She was failing. "I don't know why you came here."

"Please, can you let me in? Can we talk?" Katherine said, her words sounding muffled through the wall. "Just hear me out."

Carmen wanted to open the door and let her in. Sit with her. Feel that kinetic jump of energy as their bodies inched closer. Hear her warm laugh, smell her aromatic perfume. Watch the way her eyes would squint when she smiled. It almost made her forget the other times. The reason Katherine was here to begin with.

Their first cafecito together opened the door to an immediate, warm friendship. They'd meet up for lunch or coffee to swap pages and discuss what they were working on. Their rapport was light and breezy, but also lived-in—like she'd known Katherine her entire life. They talked and talked. Carmen griped about her dead-end job, her love of comics, her visions of Manhattan and moving away from her loving but conservative parents. Katherine wished she could get a break from her overbearing husband, eager to accelerate their lives and get the two-point-five kids and housewife he'd always dreamed of. But Katherine wanted more. She wanted to write. To teach. To be something on her own before she started creating more people or serving someone else. When their exchanges got quieter, when Carmen felt like she was really seeing this woman who'd entered her life like the bolt of lightning that gave Captain Marvel his powers, Katherine admitted the truth. Her marriage had been a mistake. She wanted out.

Carmen sighed as the rapping returned. She hung her head a bit before sliding up to her feet, still leaning on the front door.

She turned around and opened it slowly.

Katherine was on the other side, her hand raised, ready to knock again. She seemed anxious—no, excited. The kind of fluttering you feel when something you'd only fantasized about came to life before your eyes. Carmen hated that she noticed that. She hated that she was in this position, after trying so hard to make it impossible.

"You've got five minutes."

It had all felt predetermined, in a strange way. Locked in. After that first cafecito with Katherine, Carmen just knew it would be something important. But even that gut feeling couldn't prepare her for what was to come, or the journey itself.

The cafecitos and croquetas had evolved quickly into beers in South Miami. Carmen hungered for those conversations, the way Katherine made her feel—made her mind tingle with new ideas and new books to consume. She felt alive in a way she hadn't really considered in her perfunctory, routine day-to-day. Carmen felt herself veering off the path her parents had established for her—the high school boyfriend, the first job, the big wedding, the baby boy. All the things Cuban parents wanted for their daughters. A detour around the fraught developments of life. Unemployment. Heartache. Replaced by security, motherhood, and a Strong Man to keep her safe.

But Katherine awakened a part of her she didn't know existed. A Carmen who didn't have to just do what was expected, but what she wanted. Carmen knew she wanted to be a writer, but it was a hope that had a large asterisk next to it. She could still hear her abuelo muttering to her, just a few days after her tenth birthday, that she should stop telling people she wanted to be a writer. That it wasn't a realistic job for her, or any woman. Carmen remembered the feeling of shame as it spread over her, despite being unsure of why she was experiencing it. It was only through her conversations with Katherine—long discussions about Patricia Highsmith's Ripley novels (and rumors about her comic book work during World War II), the mastery and gender fluidity of Ursula K. Le Guin's *The Left Hand of Darkness*, for starters—that Carmen felt like she could peek outside the window of the house she'd built for herself in her mind. See that there was a path from the front door to something new.

She could still remember that walk to Katherine's beat-up VW Beetle, the car's yellow paint chipped and rusted. The car had been a second-hand gift from her older brother when he left Miami for the University of Michigan. He never came back. An awkward fall during a frat party sent him rolling down a flight of stairs. He broke his neck and died on the way to the hospital. Carmen couldn't remember if Katherine had just shared the story—but she did know emotions were spiking, uncontrollable. They were buzzed, a few rounds further than they usually went at Captain's Tavern off US 1, a divey seafood shack that seemed to have seen better days from the moment it opened.

They were both raw, on edge. Like something was careening toward them at top speed. They somehow also understood that if they dodged, or leapt for the side of the road, there'd be a seismic shift in how things needed to be—like Kang the Conqueror spiraling back in time to prevent the Avengers from being born. The paradox would be catastrophic, unfathomable. This moment had to occur as predestined.

Katherine turned as they reached the car, her blond hair swiveling in the humid Miami night, forming a ring around her flushed face for a moment that seared itself into Carmen's memory.

"That was fun," she said, her eyes at half-mast, her voice huskier than usual, like she'd just awoken from a luxurious nap. "Back to my boring life, huh?"

Carmen didn't respond. Instead she leaned forward to embrace Katherine in the way they usually did—a short, tight hug, her lips grazing Katherine's soft cheek to give her a peck as she pulled back. The sort of kiss that was common in Cuban or Latin culture. Except this time was different, the hug lingering, her hands sliding up Katherine's back, touching for a few seconds too long. As her lips met Katherine's cheek, they moved on a different path—and met Katherine's mouth, which seemed to be waiting.

The kiss was fleeting, but loaded with intent. In the many times she'd relived the moment—the many times she'd felt her lips brush across Katherine's smooth cheek, their dry lips connecting, almost shocking each other with a static zap, Carmen hung on to one inarguable realization. She clung to the knowledge that—at any moment—Katherine could have pulled back, eyes wide, opening the door for them to both laugh it off as a drunken slip. A silly "Whoa, what was *that*?" The kind of moment that would be immediately followed by awkward giggles before being jettisoned into a shared abyss of memory.

When Katherine did pull back, she seemed shaken, as if processing a million different algorithms at once, her brain overloading with potential scenarios and outcomes. She shook her head slightly, a humorless smile on her face as she turned to face Carmen.

"I-I can't, I can't do this," she whispered, her mouth still close to Carmen's, still within reach. "I'm married. . . ."

Then Katherine leaned forward and they kissed again, their mouths connecting and exploring each other. Carmen felt Katherine's hand slide behind her head, pulling her forward. Felt their bodies lean into each other, their hands clutching and pulling. It all happened in a matter of moments, but felt like an endless embrace in retrospect.

The memories flushed through Carmen, a cascading flood of visions and sounds, threatening to overwhelm her as she let Katherine in the door to her tiny New York City apartment. Knowing fully it was a mistake. She could hear her own voice screaming in her head, pleading. *What are you doing? Why? After all she did?* She pushed the voices aside as she inhaled some of Katherine's familiar perfume, her stylish black blouse hanging loosely from her slender frame—stepping out of the hallway's flickering light and into her home. A stranger but also once an intimate, a potent mix of comfort and anxiety that almost drove Carmen to run from her own apartment.

"Thanks," Katherine said, stepping into the cramped space. Carmen watched her as she scanned the room, lingering on the two beds separated only by a flimsy divider. She seemed to nod to herself before turning to face Carmen.

"I've missed you."

"Why are you here?" Carmen asked.

"If you're with someone, I understand," Katherine said, her jaw clenching briefly. "I don't mean to disrupt your life, Carmen. I just—I just wanted to talk to you. I was here, in New York, and I—"

Carmen shook her head. Katherine had only been in her space for a few minutes and she was already exhausted.

"Carmen, please," Katherine said, her arms held stiffly at her sides, as if tied there by some kind of invisible bonds. "I'm here."

"I asked you a question," Carmen said. "Why are you here?"

Katherine cleared her throat.

"Well?" Carmen asked. "I said five minutes. The clock is ticking."

"Oh, for fuck's sake, Carm," Katherine said, incredulous. "What do you want from me? Why am I the villain here? Have you even talked to your father lately?"

"Don't mention him," Carmen said. "I'll ask again—why are you here? How do you know where I live?"

"Come on, Carmen, I'm not a stranger—I asked people we know back home," Katherine said, her tone tighter, more familiar to Carmen. The old attitude bubbling up so easily. "It wasn't hard. Why can't we get past this?"

"I really wish you'd told me you were coming."

"How could I?" Katherine said, exasperation bleeding through her voice. "I don't even know your number."

"You figured out where I work, though," Carmen said. She tried to relish the look of surprise on Katherine's face—no, the look of embarrassment—but couldn't muster the energy. "What do you want?"

Katherine raised her hands in an *I give up, I guess* gesture, followed by a familiar sigh.

"I wanted to see you, okay? That's all I can say. There wasn't some complex, devious plan. I'm here."

A lingering silence followed. Carmen fought the urge to look at her watch. She didn't want this. Didn't want this woman in her apartment. But she'd let her in anyway.

"How are you?" Katherine asked, her voice pleading but not pathetic. A forced politeness masking something else. Through it all, Carmen had only seen that polished veneer crack once—and instead of humility she'd found something else. Anger.

"I'm fine," Carmen said, straining to sound casual. "I like it here."

"I'm glad," Katherine said, folding her hands over themselves. "Can I sit?"

Carmen led her into the main part of the living space and motioned for her to take a seat on the edge of Molly's bed. Katherine self-consciously straightened her skirt as she sat.

"I was here for a conference . . . a writing one. Like the ones we used to imagine going to?" she continued. "I know we haven't talked in so long, but just—you know, being here, thinking about writing, thinking about all the writers we talked about, the books we passed back and forth . . . it just seemed strange to not try to find you. To let you know what happened."

"With Nick."

Carmen let the name hang between them.

"Yes, Nick," Katherine said, looking across the room, not at Carmen. "He's gone. Well, I'm gone. My parents own a place here, downtown on Cornelia Street, so I'm . . . I guess I'm around for a bit. While—oh, damn. This sounds so cliché, Carmen. While I 'figure things out.' There's nothing to figure out, I guess. I'm just confused. Can we really talk? Not just dance around each other?"

"I let you in, so let's talk," Carmen said, moving to her bed, turning to face Katherine as she sat down. "What do you want from me? You left Nick, maybe? Great. I'm happy for you, really. But I don't see what it means for me."

"Nothing," Katherine said, a tinge of anger in her voice. "That's not what this is about. I need to work on myself. I felt so weighed down by everything. By him. By us. By what he wanted or expected of me. I've no idea what it's like to be by myself. To do what I want. I feel . . . frozen."

Carmen fought back the urge to reach out her hand. To slide her fingers through Katherine's. To let her know she was there for her, if she wanted her to be. She reminded herself that there were other times, times when this woman sitting before her—open and vulnerable, emotional and willing—could morph into something else. Something dark and seething.

"You have to go," Katherine said, not a question. "I caught you at a bad time."

"It's fine," Carmen said, her tone flat. It was fine. That's all it could ever be.

"Can we—can we get a coffee or something? Dinner maybe?" Katherine asked, standing up to face Carmen, their bodies inches apart. *Damn this tiny apartment,* Carmen thought.

"Sure, I mean, maybe. Let's see," Carmen said quickly as she stepped toward the door. She waited a moment before wrapping her hand around the knob, the final signal to Katherine that it was time to go.

She nodded as she walked out. "I'd like that," she said. "I could use a friend."

Carmen smiled, or tried to. Katherine seemed to pick up on it, responding with her own strained grin.

"It was nice to see you, Carmen, really," she said, in the hallway now, turning to face her. "I'm not the person I was the last time we spoke."

A silent beat.

"Neither am I," said Carmen.

"I'll call you," Katherine said.

Carmen nodded and closed the door.

As the door clicked shut, Carmen felt herself sliding to the floor, her body crumpling on the ground, a soft sob escaping her mouth.

CRENSHAW WAS HAPPY TO TALK AFTER A FEW HAYMAKERS.

POINTED ME TO AN ABANDONED WAREHOUSE IN THE VOHLAND DISTRICT.

BUT SOMETHING IS OFF.

CAN'T SHAKE THE FEELING THAT I'M BEING WATCHED.

YESSS... SHE'S HERE...

THAT THIS IS WHAT MR. VOID WANTS.

VOIDOIDS.

MR. VOID'S HALF-DEAD HENCHMEN.

BIG ON PUNCHING, BAD ON BRAINS.

GETHER TAKEHERLYNX BADGETHERTAKE HERLYNXBAD

GETHER TAKEHERLYNX BADGETHERTAKE HERLYNXBAD

HI BOYS.

*Excerpt from 1975's **The Legendary Lynx #4, "Into…THE VOID"**—Story: Harvey Stern, Art: Doug Detmer, Letters: Todd Morelli, Editor: Rich Berger, President/CEO: Jeffrey Carlyle. Published by Triumph Comics.*

CHAPTER ELEVEN

She caught a glimpse of them as she turned the corner to Harvey's block on Bleecker Street. Carmen almost kept going, her trajectory taking her right by the pair. She noticed him, even from a distance. It was Harvey. He looked tired, bedraggled. He was wearing the same clothes he'd been wearing when she'd seen him Saturday morning, more than twenty-four hours ago.

He also looked afraid.

Her first instinct was to speed down the street and see what was wrong. But something gave her pause. Yes, he looked afraid—but there was something else happening, too. Harvey was waving his hands frantically, trying to will the person in front of him away.

Carmen was not a lip-reader, but she could figure out what he was saying because he kept repeating it.

"Leave me alone. . . ."

Carmen still couldn't make out the other figure. But whoever it was, he was equally upset, pointing fingers, making sounds that—by the time they reached Carmen—sounded like pained yowling.

She'd come this way to pop in on Harvey. He'd looked shaken when he'd left her in his apartment, and she wanted to know what was going on. Especially if they were going to enter into this creative partnership.

Carmen wanted to help—to rush to his side and see what was going on—but felt paralyzed. Who was this person? What did he want from Harvey? Before she could decide, she saw Harvey backing away from the other figure. Carmen couldn't see past Harvey to get a better look at his sparring partner.

She started walking, her pace picking up with each step. By the time she reached him, a block and change down Bleecker, she felt out of breath. She tapped him gingerly on the shoulder. He spun around.

"Harvey," Carmen said, stepping back. "It's me. Are you okay?"

"What? Oh, hey, hi," Harvey said. "What are you doing here?"

She could see his expression morphing, from one of rage and defiance to something else—something calmer and more familiar to her.

"Who was that?"

"Who?"

"That person, the one you were arguing with," Carmen said, undeterred. "What did they want?"

"Oh, that," Harvey said, an empty laugh following the words. He shrugged. "Just some nutcase, I guess. You know how this city is, right? Bet you didn't see that in Miami, huh?"

His movements were jittery, nervous. Carmen could tell he was trying to play it off.

"It's great to see you, though, seriously," he said, trying to move the conversation away from whatever she'd seen. "I sent Carlyle our scripts. He seemed happy with them. Isn't that great?"

Carmen opened her mouth to say something but thought better of it. Harvey was off-balance. Unreliable. She could smell the liquor on his breath.

"What? Nothing?" Harvey asked. "Is it the credit thing? Is that what's bothering you—"

"Harvey, it's Sunday," Carmen said, squinting her eyes. "You called Carlyle over the weekend?"

"Well, no, I just—it's a long story. I saw him last night. We were playing poker, and I gave him the pages," Harvey said.

Carmen could tell he was vamping, trying to add yarn to an already complicated lie. It was something her mother would do, when Carmen caught her taking nips from a bottle in the middle of the day. She'd try to play it off like Carmen was wrong, then when cornered with the flask or cocktail, she'd turn it around—get defensive. "Y qué te importa, Carmen? Qué tu crees? Yo puedo tomarme un trago de vez en cuando. Eres mi mamá ahora?" The parallels sent a chill through her.

"You're probably still drunk," Carmen said. "You should go home and sleep it off. I wanted to check in on you. You left in such a panic—"

"Panic? No, no," Harvey said, trying to shrug it off. "It was fine. I just had plans. And this—it was just another random whack job. I cut them off in line to get a sandwich, at the deli, you know? People are nuts, Carmen, okay? This city rots your brain."

Carmen gave Harvey a once-over. She knew he hadn't been in a deli. She didn't see a bag. He didn't look like he'd eaten in days.

"I thought you might want to work on the next few issues," Carmen said, patting her bag. "I brought my notes—just some ideas on where we can go after issue six."

"Oh, great, that's great," he said. His eyes locked on her as she pulled out a small reporter's notebook. He almost snatched it out of her hands. "I can't wait to check this out."

Carmen held the notebook, both of their hands on it. Their eyes met.

"You going somewhere?" she asked.

He made a clicking sound with his tongue followed by a forced smile.

"Yeah, look, I have to run—but I'm really happy you came by. Can I keep this?" he said, prying the notebook from her hand. "I'll look it over and blend it together with my stuff. Gonna be a big week for us, you know? We're really doing this. We're making some history."

Before Carmen could respond, she felt Harvey's arms drape around her in an awkward, unexpected hug. She pushed him back gently.

"Are you okay?"

"What? Yeah, I'm fine, fine, okay? Don't worry about me," he said, patting her shoulder briefly. "Let's talk more at the office tomorrow. We can hammer these ideas into the next batch of scripts."

Before Carmen could respond, he was walking down the street, away from his apartment, the notebook sliding into his back pocket haphazardly. She felt a simmering irritation grow into full-on anger. Why had she let him take her notebook?

Carmen took the 6 train up to her apartment, the thrum of the subway helping her regain some sense of calm as she replayed what had just happened. Her eyes danced over the faded, spray-painted walls of the train, over the tired and haggard faces in various stages of consciousness. She couldn't piece together what she'd just seen outside of Harvey's building. But she did know Harvey was in some kind of trouble.

She slept fitfully that night, awakening with a start before dawn from a frantic, haunting dream she could not remember.

CHAPTER TWELVE

The usual Monday morning routines were there—the steaming hot paper cup of coffee shifting from hand to hand, the musty and eerie quiet of the office lobby, the idle chatter on the elevator—but Carmen's head wasn't in the game.

On the packed 6 train, she couldn't focus—her mind kept going back to her meeting with Harvey. She barely heard the blaring car horn and expletives as she crossed the street, just dodging the speeding checkered cab. She was somewhere else, somewhere confusing and hazy.

Carmen figured she'd shake it off once she got into the swing of work, like a ballplayer losing the rust of practice and getting on the field during a game. She'd plow through the stacks of invoices and junk mail and try to power through the day.

Carmen almost stopped in her tracks as she entered the main bullpen area, which was usually library-quiet until around ten thirty most mornings. It still was, but there was a notable difference. Carlyle's office door was closed. Not only that—he was in it.

"Huh," she muttered to herself as she dropped her bag onto her desk.

She waited a beat before she stepped toward his office and rapped on his door. His nose was buried in papers—he was reading something intently. This was not normal behavior. He motioned for her to come in, not looking up.

She stepped in cautiously, placing the still-steaming cup of coffee on the edge of his desk. He didn't seem to notice.

Carmen considered just backing out of the office slowly, but she wasn't built that way. She let her eyes wander over Carlyle's desk. She couldn't make out what he was reading—a stack of printouts, probably a script—but she did see some art. Page roughs—layouts and figures outlining what would happen in an issue, usually.

"Starting early today, boss?"

Carlyle looked up, as if noticing Carmen was in his office for the first time.

"Oh, Carmen, hi," he said. "Are you usually here this early?"

"Sometimes earlier," she said, stepping toward his desk. "Reading something good?"

Carlyle nodded, motioning to the stack of pages on his desk.

"I am. And I'm quite surprised, honestly," he said, stretching his arms out. "I didn't think Stern had it in him."

"Harvey?"

"Yeah, Harvey Stern. You know him. I see you taking breaks together. He works with Berger," Carlyle said. Carmen felt her throat tighten. "I gave him a rush assignment the other day. Told him I needed something by today, this morning. Next thing I know, I've got this story on my desk. Poor boy must've worked all week."

Rush assignment?

Harvey had said something different. Carlyle had no reason to lie. He didn't know Carmen's part in this. So why did Harvey change the details? She tried to keep her voice level.

"Oh, wow, that's something else—and they're good?"

"Yes, quite good, actually," Carlyle said, not looking at Carmen. He missed the wide-eyed expression on her face. "It's a new character. He wants to call it the 'Lethal Lynx,' but that feels too nasty—especially since it's a woman. No one likes a nasty lady. No offense, Carmen."

Carmen didn't respond. Couldn't respond.

The profanities screaming in her skull would've gotten her fired if she'd said them aloud. She felt powerless, watching Carlyle tweak her creation, and she knew all too well the feeling would only grow stronger—and sharper—as time went on.

"What's that artwork?" she blurted out, finally able to speak. The words came out loud, her tone off. She sounded manic. "Those pages?"

"Am I under oath?" Carlyle said, a sneer forming on his face, framing his red, bulbous nose. "You know Doug Detmer? He's drawing the first issue. Maybe more, if I approve. He did some prelim sketches based on what Stern turned in over the weekend. I got so excited I had him start working on it right away."

"It was nice of you to let him pitch," Carmen said, the sound of her own voice distant and muffled.

"Pitch? What on earth are you talking about?" Carlyle said, a baffled look in his eyes. "This was an assignment. That snake Jensen flaked last minute. I had to throw Stern to the wolves. The printer deadline was set; I had some house ad space purchased—I needed a new book, and boy, did Stern deliver. Six scripts over a weekend. Six great scripts."

Six scripts?

She felt her mouth go dry.

The reality of it slammed into her like a wrecking ball. Harvey had lied. There was no casual pitch request. Carlyle wasn't thinking about Harvey's career. No, Carlyle had found himself in a bind and turned to the one person who could fix it without embarrassing Carlyle to his own staff. But why did Harvey approach Carmen? she wondered. She looked over Carlyle's desk and got her answer—the stack of scripts seemed to taunt her. The six scripts that only bore Harvey Stern's name.

"What the hell," Carmen said under her breath.

Carlyle looked up at her.

"Come again?"

"Oh, no—nothing," she said. "I'm just—"

I'm just furious—at myself. For being so dumb. So gullible. Such an easy mark. Blinded by a dream I thought I could touch.

"Well, I'm as surprised as you are, Carmen," Carlyle said. "This story, with Doug on art—that could really sing, I think. I'm glad I asked Stern after Jensen fell apart. It wasn't the obvious choice, mind you. But taking risks—that's what I'm about, you know?"

Carlyle kept prattling on, but Carmen couldn't really hear him, her eyes locked on the comic boards on his desk. She could see the rough pencil layouts more clearly now—and it was definitely the detailed, propulsive style of Doug Detmer. *Doug Detmer is drawing the Lynx,* she thought.

She couldn't take much more of this. She felt elation at the sheer idea Detmer would be drawing the Lynx. But Harvey's betrayal stung—the knife twisting in her side.

Doug Detmer wasn't just an artist. He was an artist's artist. The kind of penciler others imitated and revered. He was the perfect blend of idiosyncratic line work and dynamic, panels-shattering action that felt too good to be true—part Steve Ditko meets Jack Kirby through the filter of Jack Cole. He was also a bit of an urban legend, having made his name in the late forties and fifties working on horror and sci-fi comics for the likes of EC, Continental, Bulwark, and Your Guide publications. When the Kefauver hearings started, and the entire industry was turned upside down, Detmer faded away—refusing to apologize for the work and refusing to put pen to paper on watered-down, generic versions of the stories with which he'd made his bones, shackled by the comic book industry's self-policing "Comics Code Authority." It wasn't a one-way decision, either. Many companies shied away from the vocal and temperamental Detmer. Why pay an aging artist his rates when you could pay a young buck half for less of a hassle? These days, Detmer didn't work much. And when he did, it was for his sole benefactor, Jeffrey Carlyle. And, as far as Carmen was concerned, it was always pure gold.

"Doug Detmer . . . He's . . . he's fantastic," Carmen said, unable to look away from the pages. Even incomplete, she could feel the Lynx coming to life, jumping off the page. She wanted to yank the pages off Carlyle's desk and run into the street, screaming at the top of her lungs: *"This is mine! I made this!"*

But had she? Would anyone ever know?

The realization shook her out of the fantasy.

"Carmen, are you out of your mind? Can you hear me?" Carlyle said. She blinked and caught him glaring at her. "Do you need anything else, or can I go back to more pressing matters?"

Carmen nodded. She needed to leave the office. Needed to think about all of this somewhere safe. But she also couldn't help herself.

"*Lethal Lynx* is much more powerful. It feels new and different, if you ask me," she said, backing out of his office.

"I don't believe I did," Carlyle hissed. "I want something bigger. Broader. Nicer. How about . . . I don't know. The Amazing Lynx?"

"C'mon."

"Right, fine. The Incomparable Lady Lynx?"

"Boring," Carmen said. "And 'Lady' Lynx? Isn't it clear—"

"Legendary," Carlyle said with a glowing smile. "The Legendary Lynx. There! I did it. Now I need a drink. Scurry away, Carmen. We'll talk later. I need to finish reading these other scripts and then you can courier them all to Detmer downtown."

Carmen was in shambles. She wanted to grab Carlyle by the shoulders and scream out the truth—the truth about Harvey, about the Lynx, about herself. She wanted her work to be recognized, not frittered away like some footnote. She wanted to track Harvey down and corner him—give him a final chance to explain away the evidence that pointed to a cruel, calculated lie.

She pivoted out of Carlyle's office and took her seat. Doug Detmer. The Legendary Lynx. Despite it all, this was happening. Her book—well, her book with Harvey, she reminded herself—was happening. It was going to look beautiful, too, she thought. That might have to be enough for now.

But who would know?

She cleared her throat. She didn't want these thoughts to creep in. But they had to. She'd worked on the idea behind Lynx with Harvey—but those six scripts were mostly hers, based on her own work and notes. Sure, they'd brainstormed together and integrated some of Harvey's ideas, but the bulk of the Lynx came from Carmen. The elation over Detmer flickered off, and she was left with confusion and a simmering anger. She'd been duped—if not intentionally, fine, but duped nonetheless. She needed to talk to Harvey, fast. She should've listened to Marion, she realized, even if it just gave her a moment's hesitation before agreeing to Harvey's proposal. His lie. She was as angry at herself as she was at her "friend."

Why had he lied?

"You heading to the coffee cart?"

Carmen looked up. It was Bill Broder, an older, curmudgeonly sales guy who worked for Triumph and Carlyle's other companies. They all shared the same floor space, but she rarely saw Broder outside of all-hands meetings, or when she was forced to take notes during a non-Triumph business conference. He reeked of stale cheese and looked half-asleep most of the time.

"I hadn't thought about it," Carmen said.

"Can you grab me a decaf? Light? Maybe a bagel with cream cheese if they've got any?"

Two dollar bills landed on the desk in front of her. Carmen looked down at the money and then looked at Broder. She felt her face warm up with embarrassment and rage.

"You dropped some money."

"Take it," Broder said, starting to walk away. "Keep the change."

Carmen took the bills and tossed them in the trash by her desk, turning her attention back to the stack of invoices next to her phone. She heard Broder's sharp, surprised intake of breath.

"Hey, what the hell?"

Carmen looked up.

"Is there a problem?" Carmen asked. "Do you really expect me to go fetch you your breakfast, Bill? You're a grown man. You have two dollars. Go get it yourself."

"Well, I just figured if you—"

"You figured wrong. I didn't say I was going, and even if I was, the only person I run errands for is sitting in the office behind me," Carmen said, tilting her head toward Carlyle's glass-encased hideout. "And he signs my paycheck. You . . . well, you can kiss my ass."

She returned her attention to the invoices, but made sure to listen—and savor—the long string of sputtering sounds Broder made as he reached into Carmen's garbage to pull out the money. They were followed by muttered curses as he waddled back to his desk on the far end of the office.

THE CITY IS MY PLAYGROUND.

DAILY TRIUMPH

TRIUMPH CITY LOOKS TO ME. TO BE THEIR VOICE. A HERO ALMOST.

I WANDER THE STREETS AND COLLECT STORIES.

BUT THERE'S ONE THAT I'VE BEEN HEARING MORE THAN OTHERS.

THIS VIGILANTE-- THIS WOMAN-- NAMED THE LYNX. BRAZEN. OUTSPOKEN. DARING.

SHE SAVED THE MAYOR'S DAUGHTER. KID WAS AS GOOD AS DEAD IN VOID'S CLUTCHES.

Friend or Foe?

Masked Woman?

MAYOR'S DAUGHTER RESCUED FROM VOID

WHO'S UNDER THAT MASK? WHAT DOES SHE WANT?

I MAKE THE ROUNDS. POKE EVERY STOOLIE I KNOW.

LET IT BE KNOWN I WANT THE DIRT. FAST.

LYNX? YOU CRAZY, UPTON?

NAH, MAN. I DON'T KNOW S#!+.

HEARD SHE TOOK DOWN MR. VOID.

HE'S GONNA WANT PAYBACK.

YOU MIGHT BE IN TOO DEEP THIS TIME, PALLY.

YEAH, I GOT A LEAD ON HER.

"...JUST MEET ME AT THE DOCKS TONIGHT. CAN'T TALK HERE."

I SEE HIM IN THE DISTANCE. I THINK.

HEY, RUCKA--THAT YOU?

THEN IT ALL GOES BLACK.

NGGHHH!

FWAK!

*Excerpt from 1975's **The Legendary Lynx #5**, "**Dark Truths Revealed**"—Story: Harvey Stern, Art: Doug Detmer, Letters: Todd Morelli, Editor: Rich Berger, President/CEO: Jeffrey Ca[...]
Published by Triumph Comics.*

CHAPTER THIRTEEN

The clock ticked, its minute hand signaling three in the afternoon. Carmen frowned.

Where is he?

She hadn't had the chance to ask Carlyle if Harvey was off. Most of the time, personnel matters went through her. You want time off? Check with Carmen. Need to use your vacation days? Make sure Carmen has it on the calendar. When people called in sick, they didn't ring Carlyle. They called her. It was part of her morning routine—check her messages and update the boss on what kind of staffing situation he'd be dealing with.

But, nothing. Carlyle had ensconced himself in his office for most of the day, only popping his head out briefly to ask for lunch or to scamper to the bathroom. Even the sounds—the boisterous phone calls, and bellowed insults—that usually served as a guide to his moods were muted. When she dared wheel her chair around to catch a glimpse of Carlyle, he was hunched over his desk with a thin cigarette dangling from his mouth, phone cradled on his ear, speaking so softly Carmen had to wonder what the fuck was going on.

But the workday has a way of taking over, and soon Carmen was caught up in other things: putting together a weekly summary on freelancer expenses, ensuring that week's books had arrived at the printer—she served as a backstop to editorial, which had a habit of running hot on titles—and making travel arrangements for Carlyle's annual trip to Italy. In between those tasks, she found herself reading her own work. Or, better said, her own work through the filter of Harvey Stern. Carlyle had asked her to make copies of the first six scripts for *The Legendary Lynx*—to send to Detmer downtown, to route to the book's editor, Rich Berger, and for internal use. She'd run off an extra set of copies for herself before putting a batch in the hands of a courier to run to Detmer, who was surely hard at work bringing Claudia's first handful of adventures to life. As she flipped through the six scripts Harvey had turned in, she realized her collaborator hadn't changed much—the story still remained Carmen's, with some added flourishes that she could trace back to their time together, and some of the ideas he seemed to defend so stubbornly when they brainstormed. The end result was something greater than either of them had, but still mostly Carmen's. She felt her heart sink as she reached the credits page on the sixth script. Her name was nowhere to be found. The rush of sadness was soon replaced by a thrumming anger.

Carmen let her mind drift to Detmer's imaginary studio. Aside from his visit to her desk the week before, she didn't know the man well. She only had a few grainy photos and a brief exchange at a company Christmas party to go on, but she still endeavored to picture the tall, lanky man hunched over a desk, his left hand curled around in that strange way all lefties had, putting pencil to paper—creating the dark, crime-riddled streets of Triumph City, adding leopard-like spots to the Lynx's blue-and-yellow costume as she leapt from rooftop to rooftop. It was all happening—all of the dreams Carmen dared to have.

But it wasn't enough.

She couldn't let the validation of her work—even if it was a secret—cloud her vision. She'd been fucked over. She could treasure compliments and bask in the glow of positive feedback to no end, but there was ink in the water—a black speck spreading quickly, altering everything around it. It was poison. She'd been duped by her friend, who would now stand to accept any credit that came his way and have no reason to tell the truth. Why muddy the waters?

She tried to focus on the positive. The scripts were good. Better than good. Harvey had done a nice job of taking the framework Carmen had provided and managing to blend their ideas together to make something new and alive. He'd found a way to turn their different threads of story and character into—she almost laughed to herself—well, art. The dialogue Carmen had scribbled on the margins of her first drafts, the little notes about details and world-building—like Claudia's orange tabby named Phoebe, or the cross streets of her apartment, Lieber Lane and Kurtzburg Avenue—were just idle thoughts they'd created on top of what was in those initial passes, but Harvey made it work. He'd taken the foundation Carmen had handed him and integrated what they'd brainstormed together. It was more mechanical than creative, but it was work nonetheless. For a moment, it forced Carmen to consider that this whole thing—the subterfuge and deception Carmen had seethed over since she spoke to Carlyle—might be a big misunderstanding. Could Harvey really do this to her? She wasn't sure. And that uncertainty seemed to tighten its hold on her by the second.

Harvey had reworked the scripts with care. Carmen could see his contributions on each page, building on and refining her initial work and the work they did together. Claudia felt like a person to Carmen, not just someone's idea of what a person should be or an amalgam of comic books that came before. Carmen knew that Harvey was not just a hard-core fan. He was a reader of books, too. He had a sense of dramatic structure that wasn't built on just word balloons and panels. It was with that eye that he'd tweaked and tinkered with what Carmen had left in his apartment. The end result was a comic that felt a bit highbrow and aspirational. Lynx basked in the glow of what it meant to be a comic, at least in the script stage—high adventure, stakes, twists, and a character you couldn't forget. Carmen had to remind herself a few times while reading that she'd worked on this. It wasn't just a particularly great script she'd been tasked to mark up. That felt damn good.

She looked up at the clock again. It was close to five. The usual rustlings were happening. Employees covertly heading to the restrooms. Briefcases clicking shut. Bags being zipped. The *click-clack* of typing softening to a hushed tapping. As the workday ended, the work slowed but for a small handful of employees who were either so high up in the food chain that working late was expected, or so low that they had to put in extra hours to impress. Carmen was neither. She clocked in early because that was her nature—to be in first, to scope out the scene, to set the tone. She also didn't mind staying late—looking over page proofs, making notes, reading the stacks of scripts waiting for Carlyle so she'd have something to talk over with him the next day. She knew, instinctively, that the only shot she had of making it here, or in comics, period, was to work harder, longer, and better than any of the men surrounding her. She didn't have the luxury of having gone to college with one of her colleagues. Or of being on the same softball team, or of sharing a drunken memory with her boss. She had to outshine them by a mile, and she was hell-bent on doing it. But she was the exception. Which meant she didn't have much time.

When she got to Triumph editor Rich Berger's desk, opposite Carlyle's much more luxurious space, he was getting up to leave. She looked at her watch: 4:56.

"Oh, uh, Carmen, hey," he said, catching sight of her as he made his way to the door. "I've got to pick up my—"

Carmen smiled.

"Don't apologize," she said. "I'm not the police. You're an adult."

He exhaled.

"Oh, I know, it's just—I know it's a few minutes early," he stammered.

"I just wanted to ask you something before you left."

"Well, yeah, tell Jeffrey I'll have the next *Gray Wolf* script to him tomorrow; it's just that Pellerito's doing some art corrections on the last issue before Rotante can proofread it and I—"

"It's not a Jeffrey question."

He quieted down. Carmen thought if she tried, she could hear a zipper sliding across his lips. He'd said enough already. Smart man.

"It's about Harvey," she said. "Where is he? He didn't call in."

Berger's eyebrows popped up.

"Oh right, yeah, he took today off," Berger said, shrugging, walking past Carmen and turning his face to finish his thought. "He talked to Carlyle. At least that's what he told me. He gave him the day off."

Before she could ask anything else, Berger was halfway to the elevator. He waved absentmindedly at Carlyle as he pushed the DOWN button.

"Huh," Carmen muttered to herself as she walked back to her desk. She took the long way, weaving past the empty accounting desks and through the three or four production and pasteup stations. There she saw it, on the fringe of the editorial bullpen—Harvey's desk. She wondered if he'd snuck in, done some work, and wandered out, outside of the gaze of Rich, Carlyle, and Carmen. But no. There were stacks of routing forms—sheets attached to in-production books that required signatures to be passed along to the next department in line—and proofs. The clincher was the envelope. Fresh mail was usually the first thing you dealt with when you got to work. Harvey Stern hadn't been in today.

As she reached her desk, she caught Carlyle's eye. Except he wasn't looking at her, but past her—distant and pensive. She started to walk toward his office, but was frozen by the sound of her desk phone. It was after five now.

She picked up.

"Triumph Comics, Jeffrey Carlyle's office. How may I help you?"

"Carm, it's me."

Katherine. Her voice sounding relaxed and cheerful.

"Oh," Carmen said. It took her a moment to pull it all back into her mind—that Katherine was here, in New York, that they'd spoken. She'd even promised to see her again. She felt almost dizzy at the rush of imagery and sounds. It had been real, she thought. "Hi, hey."

"I know this is last minute, but I wanted to hold you to what you said to me," Katherine said. "There's this new Italian place, Da Silvano, it just opened up in the West Village, fancy as hell, and—"

"Wait, now? Like tonight?"

"Yes, tonight, silly," she said. Carmen could hear the sounds of the city in the background. She pictured Katherine standing in a phone booth, smiling to herself, her face leaning on her hand like it always did. She tried to pull herself back. To remind herself of what things had been like. But she was failing. "Come meet me. Dinner. My treat. No pressure, of course. But it'd be nice to have that fancy dinner, finally. Not just bars or diners." She paused for a second. "Just a nice restaurant—you and me."

Carmen spoke before she could talk herself out of it. "I'll meet you there," she said. "Six?"

"Deal."

Carmen hung up. She hated herself a little bit. But not enough, she realized. The word rang through her mind as she walked toward the elevator bank, her eyes focused on what was in front of her.

Fuck.

The drive that was supposed to get them to New Orleans had taken forever. The thing about Florida, the thing most people don't realize, is that it's long as hell. Once you drive up the bulk of the state, you still have the Panhandle—the elbow-like piece that juts west, under Georgia and Alabama. It's an awkward, ugly shape—but Carmen, like most Miamians, tended not to think about it. Mostly because the rest of Florida doesn't matter. Miami is the nervous system, the nexus. Nothing else is important. Especially if you're Cuban. Why would you want to go anywhere else?

They'd decided to take the trip on a whim. Katherine's husband, Nick, was out of town on business, and while the kinetic energy from that kiss remained, they'd done little beyond that. Quick embraces, fast, passionate kisses before parting—it all felt very secretive and mysterious to Carmen. The kind of thing that would spoil if they talked about it to anyone, even each other. But Nick being away was a concrete change. It was an exciting, potentially scary opportunity. A chance to act on their impulses and cross a line they hadn't considered. There was an unspoken safety in deadlines, routines, and schedules. The need to get back home to someone else. But with Nick gone, the rules had faded—they didn't have to rush through their affection, or pretend it was something that only happened when they were both drunk. So, of course, instead of spending time together at Katherine's large Coral Gables apartment, they decided to go on a trip.

Katherine had sold it to Nick as work-related. She wanted to research the area for a short story. She'd drive, stop in Pensacola on the way. It'd be fine. Their relationship was strange, she explained—he didn't care, but felt like he *should* care. So while he pushed back she waited him out, and on the night before they were slated to go, she called Carmen excitedly.

"We're a go," she whispered. "Be ready first thing."

"First thing" ended up being closer to noon, and Carmen met her on Thirty-Second Street, a few blocks from her house, her overnight bag stuffed to the gills. She'd told her parents she was going on a writing retreat with some friends. She was a grown woman, she'd argued, once she'd seen the flicker of confusion on their faces. It wasn't so much the going away that bothered them—though it did, their precious daughter leaving the safe confines of Miami to go . . . anywhere overnight—but it was clear to Carmen they had no idea what a writing retreat even was.

It'd felt strange sliding into Katherine's car—different, somehow. They were alone. The privacy felt exciting and alien. Katherine leaned over and placed a quick peck on her mouth, then pulled back—her face flushed and wide open, her eyes on hers, as if to ask, *Was that okay?* It was. It was perfect. Carmen felt the memory carve itself into her mind, the way Katherine's hazel eyes seemed to shine, the way the soft skin of her face glowed with a slight sheen of sweat, the way her blond hair fell around her sharp face.

"You ready?" Katherine had asked, glancing at Carmen briefly as she pulled the car out onto Galloway Road.

She'd nodded yes, but that had been a lie. She wasn't ready. Carmen couldn't even let herself think about what was to come. Surely they'd stay in a hotel, she thought. Would they get separate rooms? No, that didn't make sense. Carmen didn't let her mind wander further, superstition building a wall around the fantasy. As if by thinking about sharing a bed with Katherine, she'd jinx it out of possibility.

They'd barely made it into Palm Beach County before the car started making a low, clanging noise that reminded Carmen of an out-of-tune steel drum. The low *thwack* had started to pick up speed as they reached Delray and hit a fever pitch a few minutes later. Before too long, they'd pulled over at the nearest gas station.

The attendant, a stout older man with an egg-shaped head, seemed half-asleep until he realized his new customers were not only women, but relatively young and in need of help. Carmen had seen this schtick before. Katherine seemed to ignore it. She went into a businesslike mode. Perfunctory. Direct. Eager to finish.

But Carmen had grown up watching her dad work on their beat-up AMC Ambassador—spending hours under the car, or leaning over the engine, basking in the slight shadow the hood provided. She'd heard the sound Katherine's car was making, and it was definitely not good.

"Big problem," the attendant, whose name was Chet, said. "Gonna have to tow it. Not gonna get up to regulation here."

"Regulation?" Katherine said, her brow furrowing. She was holding on to that professional demeanor, but Carmen could already see it cracking, anger sizzling underneath. Their getaway was devolving into a long detour. "What does that even mean?"

Chet continued to chew on whatever bulbous thing was in his mouth. Carmen prayed for gum but knew it was tobacco.

"Means what I said it means, young lady," Chet said, shrugging his shoulders as he draped a rag over one. "You need it in simpler terms? This car's a piece of shit. You're lucky you got this far. You need a proper mechanic. I'm happy to call you a tow—but that ain't free. . . ."

"You can't be serious," Katherine said, a dry laugh skittering out of her mouth. "You're going to charge me to call a tow truck, after you basically said you can do nothing for us? Just give me the towing company's number."

"Well, no, ma'am, I can't do that. Y'see, it's a—what's the term? An endorsement," Chet said, sounding incredulous. "I'm putting you in touch with the best of the best. It's the least I can do for two lovely ladies like—"

"Cut the shit," Carmen said. Chet turned to look at her, his brow furrowed in surprise. "We're not paying you a fee. I can look up a tow truck in the phone book. Either you can be a human being and save me five minutes, or not. Your call, Chet."

Chet stammered for a moment before wheeling around and heading back to the station's main office. Carmen turned to face Katherine with a smile, but instead of gratitude, she was met with something closer to anger.

"What was that?"

"What? What was what?"

"I was handling it," Katherine said. "I didn't need your help."

Carmen could see her pulling back, trying to temper a mood Carmen didn't quite get. She'd never seen Katherine even mildly annoyed before. It unnerved Carmen, and she wasn't sure why.

"I messed up. I should've taken the car in to get checked out before we left," Katherine said. She shook her head, her eyes closing, as if trying to fight off a painful headache. "I'm just, you know, stressed out. This was supposed to be our fun weekend together—"

Our fun weekend together.

The moment left Carmen unsteady. The idea that Katherine, who despite her complicated life had presented herself as calm and capable, could just as easily veer into the opposite left Carmen rattled. But why? Did it bother her to have this idealized woman reveal her flaws? Or was there something else? She filed the thought away for later.

Carmen stepped forward, placing a hand on Katherine's arm. She seemed to fold into her, the embrace warm and comforting.

"Oh, Carm," Katherine said, her breath warm on Carmen's neck. "What are you going to do with me?"

"It's fine," Carmen whispered as she gently pulled Katherine's face toward her own. They shared a brief, fleeting kiss. "Please. It's fine. We'll make the best of it."

Katherine nodded.

Carmen slid her hand into Katherine's for a moment as they walked back toward the car, pulling back hastily as she caught Chet looking them over. She ignored him. Her mind was elsewhere. The pulsing Florida heat unable to erase the chill that seemed to be spreading across Carmen's body.

The skies opened up as Carmen stepped outside of the Triumph Comics offices—the rain coming down strong and coating the grimy, gray streets almost immediately. She raced down Twenty-Third Street toward the subway, dodging soaked commuters and scrambling street vendors, her purse providing little cover from the instant monsoon. She made her way down the subway station steps and took a moment to collect herself before taking the next downtown N train.

She'd lucked out and found a relatively empty car. No odd smells, no blaring noises, no puddles of unknown liquid on the ground. She positioned herself in a corner seat, across from a young couple in the midst of a heated political argument. The boy seemed to be defending Gerald Ford, and his theoretical—and unfriendly—stance when it came to the city's fast-moving financial crisis. The girl seemed bored senseless. Carmen gave her a friendly smirk before looking around the rest of the car. She didn't notice any visible alarm-worthy characters. No strange men talking to themselves. No performers swinging and dancing through the aisle in the hopes of scrounging a few bucks. No passed-out drunks covered in vomit or something else. That was the obstacle course you had to run on the subway—dipping and dodging to get from point A to B, hopefully no worse for wear. Some days were easy. Some were hard—or impossible.

She allowed an exhausted sigh to escape her lips. It'd take a bit to get down to the West Village, so Carmen had a moment to think. And her thoughts floated back to the Lynx, and Harvey, and what was next.

Why hadn't he mentioned he was turning in the scripts to Carlyle? Why hadn't he run his edits by her first? The whole thing seemed rushed and desperate, and it lingered with Carmen in a way that made her more unsettled the longer she thought about it. Harvey had lied.

Even with those reservations, though, she still found herself day-dreaming about what the future held for the character. Carmen jotted down a few notes about Mr. Void, Lynx's main villain. A crime lord with a penchant for controlling shadows and darkness.

She felt energized, putting pen to paper like this. She looked up and scanned the faceless crowd of people sitting around her, trapped in their own bubbles and worries, their minds spinning over whatever they had to deal with. She felt somehow outside of them—on another frequency altogether.

She was writing a comic book.

It was happening—whether she was doing it in secret or not, her words were appearing in those balloons. Harvey had seen to that. He'd been meticulous in weaving in his ideas, but at the end of the day, the scripts were hers.

Harvey. That look on his face lingered with Carmen as the subway doors opened for Fourteenth Street. The mixture of fear and anger as that mysterious figure assailed him. He'd seemed edgy and anxious, as if Carmen had walked in on something personal and intimate. Had the conversation spurred Harvey to finish the scripts he'd turned into Carlyle? The buzz of knowing she had a part in these six stories had clouded her vision, Carmen realized.

The sound of another stop. West Fourth Street.

It took a moment before the street clicked with her, as if she'd willed the train to stop here, at the very place she'd been thinking about. She shoved her notebook into her bag.

Carmen got up and darted out of the closing doors. She looked around the crowded subway platform. Katherine would wait awhile, she thought. This, on the other hand, couldn't. She needed answers.

She needed to talk to Harvey. It couldn't wait until tomorrow morning.

By the time she emerged from the station, the storm had subsided, replaced by a chilly wind and darkening gray sky. Carmen shivered as she walked west, finally turning down Waverly Place toward Christopher Street—and Harvey's building.

She stepped into the vestibule of his building and scanned the names on the building roster, buzzing 6G next to *Stern, H.*

No answer.

She waited a moment and buzzed again. This time longer, the droning sound annoying even her as she lifted her finger.

Nothing.

She jumped slightly as the door to the lobby opened, a man in a rumpled gray suit scampering past her, their eyes not meeting. *Someone's in a hurry,* Carmen thought. She grabbed the lobby door before it shut, and slid into the common area. Harvey's building wasn't memorable—and Carmen's second visit didn't change that opinion. The lobby was empty aside from a collection of boxes near the mail slots and a cockroach skittering toward darkness. It didn't bother Carmen. New York bugs had nothing on Miami roaches. She punched the UP button and took the elevator to the sixth floor, ignoring the occasional lurch and screeching sound.

She stepped off the elevator, the overhead light flickering slightly as she turned right toward Harvey's apartment at the far end of the hall. Despite it being well past the end of the workday, the building felt quiet and abandoned—the sound of a distant radio playing Neil Young's "A Man Needs a Maid" the only thing Carmen could pick up. She knocked on Harvey's door a few times and waited. She knocked again. After a few more minutes she knocked again.

"What the fuck," Carmen muttered. She was about to turn around and head to meet Katherine when she felt her hand wrap around the doorknob and turn, expecting to find the usual resistance.

It was unlocked.

*Excerpt from 1975's **The Legendary Lynx #6**, "Forged by Fire"—Story: Harvey Stern, Art: Doug Detmer, Letters: Todd Morelli, Editor: Rich Berger, President/CEO: Jeffrey Carlyle. Published by Triumph Comics.*

CHAPTER FOURTEEN

The door creaked inward and Carmen felt her entire body tingle, from the fingers on his doorknob to her toes. Something wasn't right, and she wasn't sure she wanted to find out what.

She stepped in, keeping her footfalls light.

"Harvey? Hey, it's me, Carmen," she said, raising her voice to make it carry across the small apartment. If he was here, if he was awake, he'd hear her. "Wanted to check in on you . . . talk about the Lynx. Harvey?"

Still nothing.

The lights in the kitchen and small office area were on—the same stale-beer and old-book smell permeated the apartment. She should turn around, she told herself. She should step back and wait for Harvey to get in touch with her. He wasn't here, that's all. He'd been cooped up inside all day, fighting off exhaustion and a hangover, and he went out. For pizza. For a drink. Anything.

But Carmen was curious. She was always curious. She'd come this far, she rationalized. Why not see what she could find? The apartment seemed undisturbed from the last time she'd seen it—the same cluttered, cramped bachelor pad, loaded with books and records. She noticed the first Velvet Underground record—with the Andy Warhol banana cover—peeking out from a stack near Harvey's desk. The familiar spine of Claire Morgan's *The Price of Salt* jutting from the shelf, where Carmen had pulled it out a few days earlier. All was as she'd left it. So why did she feel a scream forming in the back of her skull? She swallowed hard, fighting off the urge to turn around and leave. To meet Katherine for dinner and ignore the growing anxiety in the pit of her stomach.

She called his name out again as she crossed the tiny living room, still stepping gingerly, like a cat burglar—or their own heroine, tiptoeing through the night, on the hunt for the right clue. But this was different. This was real life, and Carmen was scared shitless.

She saw him lying on the bed before she entered the room.

He was flat on his back, wearing nothing but a pair of dark blue boxers. Carmen felt an immediate wave of shame for walking in on him like this—asleep on his bed after God knows what kind of evening. But that disappeared as her eyes continued to look him over, her steps bringing her into the room.

The bullet hole in his forehead seemed fake at first, like a cruel joke Harvey was playing on Carmen, having somehow known she'd wander into his apartment to see how he was doing. It looked like a thick red dot at the center of his head. But she knew it was real. Would have known even without the short trickle of dark red blood that had crawled down his forehead and pivot left, onto the unmade bed, across his cheek and neck.

She covered her mouth, sure that her scream would flutter up now and echo through this empty, haunted building.

He looked so peaceful, she thought. His eyes closed. Body at rest. She could easily fool herself into blocking out the truth. The gunshot wound. The rivulet of blood. He was dead.

She backed out slowly, or so she thought. She stumbled as she turned around, her footsteps fast and frenetic, desperate for purchase and escape. She felt her heart beating inside her like a riveter in a boiler, like a monster thrashing wildly, desperate to get out.

She made it back to the elevator, her palm slapping at the DOWN button with a manic desperation her brain had yet to register. The doors opened and she hurled herself inside, arms wrapped around herself, trying to pull herself into her own body like some kind of minuscule caterpillar. As the doors closed behind her, she caught a glimpse of one of Harvey's neighbors roughly opening their front door, looking around for something, as if they'd heard a loud crash.

It was only then that she realized she'd been screaming the whole time.

CHAPTER FIFTEEN

he ran.

She could hear the *clack-clack*ing of her work shoes as she raced down the steps from Harvey's apartment.

Harvey.

She felt her lungs desperately pull in as much air as they could as her body transported her down Christopher Street toward the train. Toward anywhere else but where she was right now.

Harvey.

She felt her shoulder slam into something—someone?—as she toppled down the subway steps. She heard the curses and confused words as she hastily dropped her token in the slot, pushing past the line. She had to go. She had to run.

Harvey.

Harvey was dead.

She didn't remember much else. She didn't remember taking the train uptown instead of heading to the restaurant. Or how she got that strange gash on her hand, the dark blood dribbling down her fingers as she reached for the door into her building. Carmen just felt heavy, like a dark, slithering force had wrapped itself around her, pulling tighter with each breath. She didn't remember the transfer—from uptown to the L train, then again to the 6 train uptown—a blur of muscle memory and instinct. By the time she got to her apartment, she was panting, cold sweat coating her skin, her vision blurring slightly.

"What now . . . what now?" she muttered to herself as she crept into her apartment. "Oh God . . . Harvey."

She had to call the police, she thought. But as soon as the idea crystallized in her mind, she knew she couldn't. That fear, the shock she'd felt before was back and spreading all over her, like a patch of thick cobwebs she couldn't yank off.

But she had to.

She felt like she was trapped inside her own body, watching as she backtracked—clumsily stepping outside her door and toward the front exit, her eyes again drawn to the gash on her hand. She felt hypnotized as she stepped out onto the street. She found a phone booth a few blocks west of her apartment, next to a faded bodega, the store's neon sign flickering as she walked into the cramped booth. She looked at her hand as she gripped the booth's handle. It was shaking, the blood caked and smeared on it. She dialed and waited. A female voice—calm, soothing—came on the line and asked Carmen what her emergency was.

"It's . . . There's a body," Carmen said. "Someone is dead."

"Ma'am, where? Is someone hurt right now?"

"He's dead," Carmen said, her voice garbled as she tried to choke back a sob. She needed to get off the phone, she realized. She had no idea if these calls were recorded. But she couldn't *not* call. Couldn't just leave Harvey there to rot. "A young man—he was shot."

Before the operator could say anything else, Carmen rattled off Harvey's address.

"Please, send someone to get him," she said. "Please."

"What's your name, ma'am . . . ?"

Carmen hung up.

She felt her stomach flip inside her as she stepped out of the booth into the New York evening, the air heavy with rain. She let her mind drift back, to walking down Waverly Place just hours before, a street named after a novel, of all things. She'd been on her way to Harvey's apartment. Where his body waited. She could still see the tree-lined street, the old-style streetlamps, the leaf-coated sidewalks. Farther down, where the street would eventually intersect with Fifth Avenue. Carmen knew the area as well as she knew any part of this city, almost as if it were her own neighborhood—but now it was tainted. Haunted. She shook her head, trying to shake off the feeling of despair, or to erase what had just happened. She leaned on the outside wall of the bodega as her vision went black for a second.

She turned around fast, her face resting against the grimy wall of the bodega, the light of a nearby streetlamp and the store's own sign shining down on her as she threw up. She heard the strange sounds she was making—the whimpering sobs that accompanied her sickness—and felt herself start to spin out of control.

She wiped her mouth with her coat sleeve and started back toward the apartment. She needed to be home. She wanted to be home. Not here, not in this dark, dank cluster of concrete towers and shrouded alleys— but home. Miami. Feeling the sun warm her face. Not like this, not like the world was getting smaller, tighter, forcing her to constrict with each breath until she'd just fold into herself completely.

The memory crashed into her vision like a burst of light as she stumbled into the apartment, appearing fully formed and knocking aside everything else. There she was—standing behind her father, late at night, his silhouette visible but unable to make out the details. Another man, slowly getting up, a hand on his jaw where her Papi had punched him. The details started to bubble up, too, like a dream—where everything feels real and fine, and time is fluid. This man had said something to her. She couldn't have been more than twelve. She'd been wearing a new dress. She and Papi had been walking home from the store. Now the bottle of milk and carton of orange juice were on the gray, sun-cracked sidewalk, a pool of soft white spreading slowly, ruining the paper bag. The man had moved off the sidewalk as they approached, courteous, Carmen had thought. She hadn't heard what he'd said—but she hadn't needed to. She'd seen his expression. Even at twelve, she knew to watch out for men. Older men. Mami had warned her. Papi had warned her. *Tienen intenciones, Carmen, entiendes? Cuídate siempre.*

But Papi had heard, and in an instant he'd dropped the bag and swung a hard, polished left into the man's face. He'd fallen fast, a curdled squeal as he dropped. They'd left the groceries, forgotten, on the sidewalk and picked up their pace toward home, Papi looking over his shoulder every few steps to make sure the other man hadn't followed.

"Why did you do that, Papi?" Carmen had asked. "No tienes miedo que llame a la policía?"

Aren't you scared he'll call the cops?

Papi had rubbed her back, in the way he'd been doing since as long as she could remember. Tenderly, but with weight. He was a big, strong man. With presence.

"No te preocupes, mijita. El no llamará a nadie."

Don't worry, daughter. He won't call anyone. She'd tried to push it away, her mind desperate to get back home and wander up the stairs to her room and read an issue of *Betty & Veronica* or the new *Captain America.* Eager to forget. But the moment was burned into her memory. And now she felt transported, back to being that scared girl, back to not believing in the rule of law beyond the power only you could wield, like some kind of grizzled street vigilante.

A choked sob escaped her lips, and she let it go, her body crashing into her tiny bed. She was home. She could crack the shell and be the creature inside. Have feelings and thoughts and ride those waves until she was too exhausted to even think.

Who would kill Harvey?

The answer was, she had no idea. The person he'd been arguing with? An old flame? A rival from a past life? Carmen realized that she didn't really know Harvey Stern that well, beyond their chitchat in the office, or shared laughs between cigarettes. Who was this man who'd stepped into her apartment and changed her life? She wouldn't be able to answer those questions tonight.

Her eyelids closed and soon she was asleep, still in her rain-soaked work clothes, makeup smearing on her pillowcase. She wouldn't hear the phone ringing over and over, call after call, twenty minutes later. She wouldn't feel Molly covering her with a sheet hours later.

CHAPTER SIXTEEN

Carm—Carmen? Wake up, girl. You're going to be late for work."

Carmen felt herself being shaken gently, a hand on her shoulder. She opened her eyes. It was Molly, still in what passed for pajamas for her—a long black T-shirt and not much else. Her makeup was still streaked on her face, the sign that she'd arrived home late from a gig and it hadn't gone particularly well.

"Carmen?"

Carmen nodded, sliding into a sitting position, her palm wiping at her cheek. She gave herself a quick once-over. She was dressed—fully. Her work clothes. What happened? Had she met up with Ka—

Then she remembered.

"Are you okay?" Molly asked. "You were completely zonked when I got home. Like, refusing to wake up. I figured you'd gotten hammered and needed to sleep it off, but . . . I dunno . . ."

Carmen saw it all then, as Molly trailed off. Harvey on his back, the bloody red dot on his forehead. The terror welling up inside her as she approached his bedroom. The panic that consumed her as she ran, screaming, from his apartment.

She swallowed hard before she spoke.

"What time is it?"

"Almost eight thirty," Molly said, her eyes still on Carmen as she got up, her expression loaded with concern. "Before you go—"

Carmen looked back.

"What?"

"This is weird but . . . when I got home the phone was ringing like crazy," Molly said, her eyebrows scrunching over her nose. "They were calling over and over. You know, what you do when you're sure someone's home? Like that."

"Who was it?"

"She said her name was Katherine, and boy, was she pissed," Molly said. "Was going on about you having plans and how she didn't deserve to be treated this way . . . pretty intense—she sounded almost jealous when she heard my voice."

"Fuck," Carmen said as she made for their tiny bathroom. "I'll fill you in later, okay? Thanks for waking me up. Sorry. I need to jet."

"Sure, fine," Molly said as Carmen closed the bathroom door behind her.

Carmen leaned over the sink and looked into the smudged mirror. Her mascara had run and her dark hair was sticking out in various directions, matted and dirty. Her eyes looked heavy and bruised. Her lipstick had faded, but the sharp red was still discernible. If she hadn't experienced the night for herself, Carmen would've thought she'd stumbled home from a one-night stand or an unexpected bender.

"God, I didn't even earn this look," she said to herself as she undressed hastily and ran the shower. Their apartment's hot water was spotty, and she prayed this morning wasn't an off day.

She had completely blanked on her plans with Katherine, but with good reason. Her reaction to being ditched also confirmed to Carmen that despite her claims that she'd changed, Katherine Hall was still Katherine Hall. And that meant she expected to get what she wanted. Especially when she asked nicely.

Carmen stepped out of the shower and wrapped herself in a towel.

She didn't owe Katherine anything. She'd felt pressured and agreed to dinner. So what?

Then she thought of Harvey. Of how serene he'd looked on his bed, as if he'd just shambled into the room and flopped on his flimsy mattress a few minutes before. Had he been taking a midday nap when someone came in and shot him? Was what Carmen saw real? She hoped not.

The answer came fast. Carmen, despite oversleeping, was right on time—which usually meant she'd be the first one in the office. Except again she found Carlyle hunched over his desk. He noticed her walking in and motioned for her to enter. His face looked ashen.

"Another early morning?" Carmen said, trying to keep things light.

"Sit down, Carmen, please," Carlyle said with a dismissive wave. That's when she noticed the weariness. The dark bags under his eyes, the scratchy way the words tumbled out of his mouth, the slight stubble on his face, the wrinkles on his usually pressed shirt. He wasn't put together. Carlyle might be in publishing, but he was all about presentation. He was vain. Not today.

"What—what's going on?"

Carlyle cleared his throat. That's when Carmen realized he wasn't sad, or hurt—he was stressed. Could he be worried about the ramifications of Harvey's death—what it meant to his publishing strategy? She shooed the thought from her mind. She couldn't fathom anyone being that callous. She hoped her instinct had been wrong.

"It's, uh, it's Stern—Harvey. You know, your—" he said, stammering for a moment. "Let me back up. Harvey Stern from editorial. He was found dead, uh, last night. Killed. Murdered. He's dead."

The gasp that Carmen let out was genuine. It was real, she thought, as her hands clenched together. She felt her eyes begin to well up. Whatever distant fantasy she had, whatever strange idea she'd toyed with—one that made what she saw some kind of fever dream, like a sequence from *Doctor Strange* or *Warlock*—was gone. Replaced by a dark, dangerous reality that was heavy, like cement. Harvey Stern was dead.

"Oh, oh my God," Carmen said, covering her mouth with her hands. In the few seconds before she took the seat, she thought she'd have to play some kind of part, act out some kind of grief to sidestep suspicion. But she hadn't expected this. To be gutted by the stark reality of it all.

"What happened? Oh my God."

Carlyle shook his head.

"No clue," he said. She watched as his eyes drifted to a large stack of papers on his desk. "Someone got into his apartment and, well, he was murdered. Killed in bed. Jesus Christ . . ."

He paused. His eyes still on the papers. The scripts, Carmen realized. The scripts for *The Legendary Lynx*. The issues Carmen had written and Harvey had scrambled to rework and turn in. She felt a buzzing in her skull.

"Did you see him?" Carmen asked, her voice sounding distant and cracked. "When he dropped these off?"

Carlyle let out a quick sigh before he started to respond.

"Yes, for a minute, actually," he said. "I'd seen him over the weekend, too, believe it or not. There was an extra seat at this poker game Marv Wolfman and Len Wein were playing at Gerry's place—you know them? They work—"

"I know who they are," Carmen said, her tone short. Normally, hearing war stories about hanging out with comic book royalty piqued her interest. But right now, she was just hungry for more details on what Carlyle did with Harvey a day or two before he was killed. "Who else was there?"

Carlyle raised an eyebrow before continuing.

"The usual crew—like I said," he said, rattling them off—unable to hide the glee he took in recounting these moments, even if it only mattered to comic book insiders like him and Carmen. "We had to call Tony Isabella in mid-game, though, because Harvey just up and left. It was very disruptive. Bizarre."

"Did he seem okay?" Carmen asked.

"Does it sound like he was okay?" Carlyle said. "He just froze when it was his turn—after a few hands. Bolted to his feet and said he had to go. Said he had to talk to someone. He was apologetic, but it basically ruined the game. I doubt they'll want him back. I mean, these guys are a big deal—"

Carlyle seemed to realize he was discussing a recently murdered person and shook his head. Even someone as self-involved as Jeffrey Carlyle had a breaking point.

"Never mind," Carlyle said, standing up. His body seemed to sag despite the motion, as if he'd just run a marathon and hadn't been handed any water. He placed a palm on his desk. "Look, Carmen, this is not good. You know that. He was a nice boy. Meant well. Worked hard. I know you were friends. I'm sorry, all right?"

Carmen nodded.

"Thank you."

He was leaning over his desk now, his head hanging down, shaking back and forth. She'd never seen him like this. Confused and off his game. It was unsettling. He spoke, not meeting her eyes.

"I haven't told the staff, and I probably won't just yet. I'm not sure I have it in me. I might need your help there," he said. "The police are coming by later today. I'll need you to run point—please give them whatever they need. A conference room for interviews, names, addresses, whatever. We want to be helpful here."

"Sure, sure, of course."

A silence hung between them. It felt like hours. In reality, it was probably a few seconds. Carmen let her eyes glance at the stack of scripts.

Why did you turn them in so fast, Harvey? What was the hurry?

Carlyle let out a long, disappointed sigh.

"He was one of ours," he said.

It was the most genuine thing Carmen would ever hear him say.

Whether Carlyle knew or not, the secret was out. People were talking. Carmen knew the minute she took her seat. It was as if everyone turned to look at her at once—their stares questioning and hungry for any bit of information she could share. They were worried. Despite the short time Harvey had been on staff, he'd made friends. He was likable, friendly. And such a fan. He loved comics and his knowledge of the medium was encyclopedic. He could tell you Superman's social security number and the first time Mr. Zero became Mr. Freeze in the Batman comics, and recite the original Green Goblin saga by heart. Or so it seemed. In many ways, his enthusiasm kept the place going. Comics, as exciting as they could be, were work. And a lot of work involved drudgery—late hours, awkward phone calls, invoices, mail labels, deadlines. The stress was high, the pay was low, and the rewards were fleeting. Carmen could see it in the faces of the young staff as they marched in. Saw it as they rolled their eyes when Carlyle shared his latest edict. Work, to them, was just another question mark. Another sign of uncertain times. A city careening toward financial ruin. Weather Underground bombs going off at the State Department. Former government officials convicted of perverting their offices. The sputtering, stop-start conclusion to the inexcusable bloodbath that was the Vietnam War. Each singular event was enough to drive someone to doubt themselves, to doubt the trajectory of the world. To challenge the belief that "it'll all work out." Felt together, it was seismic. It made Carlyle's regular rants about books going over their budgets just one more piece of trash tossed onto the heap. The collapse of the comic book market was background noise to what seemed like the world spinning off its axis.

It didn't help that the market was in a tailspin. To many, comics were a way to bide your time before you got to write something "real"—like TV or a novel, or, wow, even a movie. It wasn't a career unto itself. It was a place where writers honed their craft and left. Left it to the fans, who would write these superhero adventures for free if it brought them closer to the orbit of Stan Lee and his ilk. But today, nothing was selling. Morale was low—and Carmen knew it wasn't just at Triumph. Comic books weren't sticking. There wasn't a path to victory. Would comics fade like the pulp novels that inspired them? Carmen didn't think so. But she wasn't sure. It was, though, the kind of thing she'd talk to

Harvey about—over a shared cigarette or cup of weak black coffee, or standing by the bullpen in those moments between urgent tasks where you could just take a minute and breathe—maybe even think about the world around you and what it all meant.

But now he was gone.

She felt her head drop down into her hands, as if she were seeing herself from above, some kind of astral ghost pondering the human race. The tears didn't come, but she didn't expect them to. She was exhausted. She was conflicted. She felt a heavy stone inside her—but she also felt loss. What would happen to their creation now? Should she burst in and tell Carlyle the truth? That she'd helped Harvey create the character he was about to launch? No. She knew Carlyle well enough. He was taciturn, driven, egocentric, and also prone to grudges. He didn't like to be lied to, much less fooled. It was his biggest weakness—like kryptonite to Superman or spicy food to Spider-Man. This kind of revelation would send him into an apoplectic rage. A petty one. He'd cancel the book within minutes. No, Carmen had to see this through—and that meant keeping the truth to herself until he had no choice but to let her write the book. Assuming anyone read it, of course.

But she'd been lied to, Carmen thought. And she didn't know why.

She stood up with a jerk, grabbing her bag hastily. She needed a cigarette. Some air. She needed to breathe. As she wove around her desk, she could feel Carlyle's eyes on her. She glanced back. Instead of an angry, questioning glare, she was met with sympathetic eyes. He nodded to her before turning back to look at whatever was on his desk.

She was intercepted on her way to the elevator by Rich Berger. He looked stricken and gaunt, the whites of his eyes a light pink. He didn't walk so much as shuffle toward Carmen. She fought back the urge to turn and run in the opposite direction.

"Is it—is it true?"

Carmen didn't respond. What could she say?

"About Harvey?" he asked. "Is it true what people are saying?"

"I don't know what people are saying, Rich," Carmen said, speaking slowly, with care. Trying her best not to seem biting to this man, who seemed so suddenly broken and lost. "But I can't talk about what I think you're asking me about, as much as I want to."

His head drooped in defeat, staring at his plain brown shoes, looking over his stained plaid vest and wrinkled corduroys.

"I told him to be careful. . . ." Berger muttered to himself. Carmen stopped cold.

"What?"

"Oh, well . . . it's nothing, I'm sure—he was such a good kid, you know? Always trying to climb the ladder," Berger said, staring off into the distance, his thick gray mustache coating the grimace his mouth was forming. "I told him over and over again that these things happen at their own pace. That if you do the work, do it well, someone will notice. But he didn't want to wait. He just didn't want to wait. . . ."

Before Carmen could ask another question, Berger had turned around, dragging his feet back toward the editorial bullpen. She saw the other editors and production staffers—Purdin, Conroy, Hahn, Mullin, and Trunick—looking on with a hungry, desperate anticipation that Carmen wanted to immediately forget. She saw them each reacting as they caught Berger's expression. Carmen hadn't confirmed anything, but she hadn't denied it, either.

She took another step toward the elevator when she heard her phone ring. She wheeled around and picked up the receiver before she sat down.

"Where the fuck were you, Carm?"

Katherine.

"I'm at work now," Carmen said flatly. She didn't need this. Didn't want it. Never wanted it.

"We had plans."

"Well, someone died."

"Well, I guess I'm sorry, but . . . you couldn't call me?" Katherine said, her voice a lingering hiss, disdain pinging every other syllable. "You couldn't let me know? Is this some weird thing to get back at me, or—"

Carmen hung up. She hadn't expected to do that, but it felt right.

Katherine came back into her life on her own. She knew the land mines were there but still wanted to saunter across the battlefield. That was on her. Carmen left the phone off the hook and retraced her steps toward the elevator.

Excerpt from 1975's **The Legendary Lynx #6, "Forged by Fire"**—*Story: Harvey Stern, Art: Doug Detmer, Letters: Todd Morelli, Editor: Rich Berger, President/CEO: Jeffrey Carlyle. Published by Triumph Comics.*

CHAPTER SEVENTEEN

They're here."

Carmen felt the tap on her shoulder as she heard Carlyle's words. "They" could only mean one thing—the police. She stood up, straightening out her blouse and long black skirt. She saw them approaching. A stocky older Black woman followed by a tall, twenty-something uniformed officer. The woman seemed to be at ease, smiling and looking around the office with a wonder that Carmen had figured most adults jettisoned at age thirty.

As the two visitors approached, Carlyle placed himself between them and Carmen.

"Detective, this is Carmen Valdez, she'll help you get organized," Carlyle said. "She's my secretary. And a pretty good one, if we're grading on a curve."

"My boss, the comedian," Carmen said dryly. Carlyle sputtered but thought better of it.

The woman raised an eyebrow and extended her hand.

"Detective Mary Hudson," she said. "My escort here is Officer Idelson. He won't do much."

Carmen shook her hand and motioned toward the back of the Triumph offices.

"We've got a conference room set aside for both of you," she said, trying to keep her delivery calm, but feeling a painful churn inside her. *What did they know? What would they ask?* Was she worried they'd connect dots that didn't exist? If she came clean now, about finding Harvey, and they also discovered she'd worked with him on the Lynx—would that make Carmen a suspect? She swallowed hard before continuing. "Just let me know who you'd like to speak to and I can fetch them for you, and if you need any food or coffee."

"That sounds just right, and we thank you for your hospitality," Hudson said, following Carmen down an aisle of desks. She ignored the onlookers. She was used to this part of it. "Busy day for you guys?"

"Oh, well, pretty standard," Carmen said, looking back over her shoulder. "I think everyone is a bit shaken, to be honest."

"Yeah, yeah, I understand that," Hudson said, her smile fading into a pained expression. "Life comes at you fast."

Carmen opened a door and motioned for them to step inside.

"Let me know if you need anything," she said as the two walked into the cluttered, stuffy room.

Hudson immediately started moving boxes and clearing a space on one of the main tables. She zipped around to position a chair facing where Carmen figured the detective would sit.

"Oh, I will, don't you worry," Hudson said, pulling out a tiny notebook from her back pocket. She motioned toward the chair with her chin.

"Do you want me to bring in Jeffrey first? Or anyone else?"

"No, no, we're good," Hudson said.

Carmen didn't respond.

Hudson waited a beat before speaking.

"You gonna take the seat, or do you want an engraved invitation?"

Hudson smiled softly as she looked at Carmen. Carmen couldn't remember the last time she'd used this room for an actual meeting. Carlyle wasn't big on discussions, much less disagreements. He didn't think it worked in publishing. Not if you wanted to have vision. It was bullshit. But as she sat looking at this woman with her mischievous grin, Carmen wished she had at least aired this room out more often, because now she felt stuffy and hot. The redness in her face would soon become a sheen of sweat. Was this what Hudson wanted? To catch her off guard? Well, she had another think coming.

"You're from Miami, right?"

"Yes, born and raised," Carmen said with a dry smile.

"Know a homicide detective down there, Pedro Fernandez," Hudson said, scratching her chin absentmindedly. "Good police. Always thought about retiring down there, me and my daughter. Maybe someday."

Carmen didn't respond. She knew this was typical. Small talk. She waited.

The silence dragged on for a few more moments. Carmen looked up and noticed Hudson was watching her hands.

"Hurt yourself?" the detective asked.

Carmen self-consciously covered the bandage on her left hand, the one that covered the cut she'd somehow gotten rushing out of Harvey's apartment.

After finding him. His body.

She tried to play it off, looking at the bandage with a slight surprise, but she knew she was failing, already making things awkward out of the gate.

"Oh, this, no—it's nothing," Carmen said. "I'm just clumsy. It was stupid."

Hudson nodded. She looked like she wanted to press, but decided against it.

"You know the deceased well?" Hudson asked, looking down at her notebook.

"We worked together," Carmen said. "We'd chat, the way you do with people you're friendly with at work."

"Worked together, right," Hudson said, nodding to herself. Carmen heard Idelson shuffle his feet behind her. "Nothing else? No socializing? No dates? No hanging out?"

"No."

"Gotta ask, you know," Hudson said, noting Carmen's terse response. "Gotta check every box."

"I understand," Carmen said, pulling herself back a bit. "I want to help."

"That's great," Hudson said. "We could use the help. Any detail would be helpful. Like, did you ever—and look, I know you just said no, but I just want to be sure—did you ever, ever hang out with this man outside of work? At a nonwork function? Maybe a drink? Dinner a while back? Concert? Anything?"

Carmen swallowed. She tried to underplay it but she knew Hudson caught it. *Fuck.*

"We—well, no, I mean, we'd have a cigarette at work—"

"Carmen, you seem smart, okay?" Hudson said, leaning forward on the table, palms down. "So please, please, don't try to play me. I'm not talking about smoke breaks or coffee talk. I'm talking about hanging out when you're both not working. Is that clear enough for you?"

Carmen nodded.

"No, we didn't—not outside of work," she said. She hated herself for lying. Hated herself for downplaying her friendship. But what choice did she have here? She was scared, and well beyond the grasp of logic. "We weren't really friends, okay? I mean, I feel bad he's gone—but we were work pals. We'd see each other at the company volleyball games and at bar things after work with work people, but never just us."

Hudson made a brief trilling sound.

"Got it," she said.

Carmen wove her hands together and placed them on her lap. She could feel them starting to tremble.

"Does him coming to your apartment count?"

Carmen felt her entire body spasm, felt her eyes widen.

"What?"

"Spoke to someone who said they spoke to the deceased a few nights before his murder and he told them he was heading to see you," Hudson said, feigning befuddlement. "Must've been a mistake, I guess?"

"That's not possible."

"What isn't, sweetie?" Hudson said, meeting Carmen's eyes for the first time. "That a horny man would brag to a buddy he was going to the pretty girl from work's apartment, or that you'd get caught in a lie? You know which one I believe right now, right?"

Carmen cleared her throat. She could still make this work, she thought. She could get out of this.

"I didn't know he was coming," Carmen said, her words loaded and heavy. "I don't know how he found my address."

"Huh, that's just goofy. This man just showed up, no call? Pretty brave," Hudson said. "Not so romantic these days. What did he want?"

"He wanted to talk," Carmen said, looking at her hands. They felt slick, and she fought the urge to dry them on her skirt. "He wanted to talk about work."

"What about work?" Hudson asked. She was picking up speed now, interested. "What was so important he had to look up your address, show up, and ask you about?"

"He was drunk," Carmen said. "I don't know. It wasn't anything of substance. Just office gossip. Then he . . . well, then—"

Hudson waited, her eyes watching Carmen fidget.

"He made a pass at me."

"Well yeah, I figured as much," Hudson said. "Did he sleep over?"

"What—no, no, not at all," Carmen said, genuine anger in her voice. She was trying to walk the tightrope—to say just enough so she wasn't lying, but also to preserve their story. Their book. For as long as she could. She was failing on all counts. But that wasn't everything. She thought of Harvey for a moment—his drawn and haggard face that day she saw him on the street. The look of desperation and low-grade fear, like someone being held at gunpoint. Carmen realized she was scared now, too. Not just for her book and comic book dreams, but for herself. "I made him leave. That was it."

"That's it," Hudson said. It wasn't phrased as a question. She jotted something down in the notebook and sighed. "It's just . . . so strange, even drunk, for this guy—who from what I could tell, and I get that I'm new to this world, but . . . who was pretty mild-mannered? Is that the right word? Like, a Clark Kent type. So, this quiet, lonely guy gets loaded. Fine. People drink. Then he decides to barge into your place, make a move on you, then politely leaves—but has absolutely nothing to say?"

Carmen shook her head hesitantly.

"No—I mean, yes, that's it," she said. "He was drunk, I said."

"I remember."

"He wanted to talk, to hang out, so I poured him some coffee," Carmen said—walking the tightrope. "But then he tried to . . . he tried to kiss me. I got upset, told him to leave. That was how it ended."

"Then you went to his place?"

"No, what? No," Carmen said, leaning back in her chair, the surprise genuine, even if she knew where Hudson was going. "I didn't."

"Gonna give you one more shot on this one, Carmen," Hudson said. "You seem like a really nice girl. Smart. Very pretty. I'm sure your colleagues say shit to you all the time. Crude shit. Nasty shit. It can get exhausting. I barely remember that because I'm old now, but I know you probably get it all the time. But even pretty girls break, right? Maybe you were drunk, too. Decide, well, why the hell not? I know the guy. He's here. Let's do the dance."

"No, I didn't—"

"Okay, let me slow it down for you, then. You could maybe help me flesh out some of the details of the case, seeing as how you kind of knew the victim," Hudson said, the words delivered so casually that Carmen had to repeat them in her mind to understand what she meant to ask. "Now, the landlord said he heard screaming a while before the vic— Harvey's—body was found. Shortly after that, 911 got a call from a woman saying her friend was dead. Any idea who that might have been, since, you know—it couldn't have been you? Did your friend hang out with a lot of women? Besides you, I mean?"

Carmen started to respond, but Hudson raised a hand to silence her.

"Let me finish," Hudson said, a steel in her voice Carmen hadn't heard before. "I'll quit beating around the bush because I can tell it's making you twitchy, and we don't want that. So, here goes—whoever came into your friend's apartment either had a key, or Mr. Harvey Stern is just about the dumbest guy in New York City, leaving his door unlocked. Pretty goofy, I think. Anyway, so the killer comes in. He knows the place. Knows where this guy sleeps, too. Does a quick recon, finds him dozing, and—"

She locked her eyes on Carmen as she extended her pointer finger like the barrel of a gun.

"Blatt," she said. "Our boy is dead. No question. Killer leaves, the gunshots covered up by the sounds of our fair little town. What'd I miss, Idelson?"

Hudson's colleague remained silent.

Carmen felt a wave of nausea wash over her. She gripped the table. Hudson's eyes looked down at her fingers. The detective knew she was getting somewhere.

"Now, look, you seem like a real nice lady. A real rule-follower and good member of society. So I'm not saying you did that," Hudson said with a relaxed shrug. "But cases are built on evidence, you know? You watch TV, right? It's like that. And if I don't have evidence that anyone else was in that apartment, I have to start looking at the people I'm pretty sure were there. Are you following?"

Carmen nodded, trying to seem detached. To seem like this was okay and normal. But she also felt outside of herself, like a narrator in her own story, looking down on herself—realizing that the detective had Carmen right where she wanted her.

"So help me out here, girl," Hudson said, leaning over the table. "So you sleep with this man, and then feel ashamed. Hell, I would if I looked like you. I mean, Harvey was an okay-looking guy, but you're a ten. We all make mistakes. So, you wake up, take some time to think it over, and realize, shit, let me nip this thing here in the bud. I don't want this boy—this man—to start going crazy on me. It was a mistake, you know? So you head to his place, because look—you're not fooling me. Either you knew where he lived or you could find out easy, all right. You are the boss's secretary. All his secrets are yours. So, yes, you visit this man, you wanna let him down easy and fast—no muss, no fuss. But instead of getting a pleading baby-man, begging you to please give him a shot to be your dream boyfriend, you find a body. And you run out of the apartment screaming, hit your hand real good, too. So hard, you don't even know how you sliced it. Because as tough as you are, you ain't ever seen a body like that, and you ain't ever seen a bullet hole dripping blood like that." She paused. "How'd I do?"

Carmen stood up. She pointed a shaking finger at Hudson. She was falling off the tightrope. The ground was getting closer. She felt dizzy. She felt angry.

"That is not what happened," Carmen said, her voice quivering. That's when she felt the tear streak down her face. That's when she knew she'd lost. But she didn't care. "And I am done talking."

She turned and left, but not before hearing Hudson's parting shot.

"You're done when I say you're done," she said. "And we're a long way from there."

PART II

UNMASKED

CHAPTER EIGHTEEN

The bodega doors made a jangling sound as Carmen walked inside, stepping out of the summer morning. It'd been a confusing summer—more rainy than warm. Molly told Carmen June was a turning point, a peak of humidity and warmth before the moodier months of July and August. Carmen could do without this kind of weather. New York summers were dank—soggy and sticky. So different from the tropical, breezy, permanent summer that she'd become used to back home. The season felt fraught and harried, too—and the news wasn't helping.

Carmen glanced at the tabloid headlines. President Ford had slipped and fallen while stepping off Air Force One in Austria. The city was teetering toward financial ruin, with a lot less money in the bank than what was soon due. It was hard to focus on what was in front of you—made doubly hard in a city like New York, where you had to keep your wits about you to survive. Everyone was on edge, and it didn't feel like things would get better soon, if ever.

Carmen grabbed a basket and dropped a few things in as she walked toward the back of the tiny shop. Bread. Some apples. A six-pack. She didn't eat at home much, but she'd been raised to have a stocked fridge, so the push-pull continued into her adult years, even up in New York, living on her own. Plus, she knew Molly didn't eat—so she felt some motherly concern for her wayward roommate.

She caught sight of the two girls crouched near the newsstand as she made her way to the register. They seemed to be about ten or a bit older, but Carmen was always terrible about kids' ages. What caught her eye, though, wasn't the kids, but what they were holding. The girl on the left—smaller, long red hair, bright green eyes—was looking at her friend with angry defiance, her hand clutching a comic book.

"Wonder Woman is boring, okay? You know that," she said, spittle coating the words. "She's just not realistic, Winnie."

Winnie shook her head, looking more like a disappointed parent than a preteen.

"And what? The Lynx is cooler? She has, like, not even three issues out, Martha," Winnie said. "We don't even know if it's gonna stay good."

"She's fast, she's strong, she's smart—she's like Batman or Daredevil but, I dunno, better—she feels like a real person," Martha said, pushing the comic into Winnie's hand. "Check this out. For real. She fights this guy—Mr. Void—who is, I dunno, like a criminal boss. And she figures out what he's up to in her real identity and then fights him as a hero— it's pretty intense."

As if on cue, both girls turned to look at Carmen, who was standing a few feet away, enraptured. It took her a second to realize she'd been caught. She mostly didn't care.

"Oh, sorry, I was just—I work at that company," Carmen said, pointing at the issue of *The Legendary Lynx* Winnie had in her hands. It was the third issue, also drawn by Doug Detmer. The artist's cinematic style was on full display: The cover featured an up-close shot of the Lynx, pinned to a wall by a mysterious hand, the heroine clawing to loosen the villain's dark grip. "We make those comics."

The girls seemed unimpressed and concerned, as if Carmen was going to mention to the bodega owner that they were reading without paying. She backed off.

"I'm just glad you're enjoying them," Carmen said, placing a hand over her heart absentmindedly. "It means a lot."

Carmen walked outside, propelled by embarrassment and her own desire to be alone and truly savor what she'd seen and heard. Half a block from the store, Carmen realized she'd left her basket on the floor near the spinner rack of comics. She shook her head and kept walking down East Seventy-Second Street. The mixed emotions—seeing the girls reading a comic she'd written, forgetting why she'd gone inside in the first place—were enough to propel her west, past even the Dakota building and to the West Side Highway. She'd choose that over sheepishly walking back into the store.

She blinked at the sun. She had a little more time before she'd have to really deal with the arrival of New York weather—snow, slush, and all the things Miami girls just saw on the television. Harvey had been murdered three months ago, and little had changed. Detective Mary Hudson was still on the case, ostensibly, but her visits to the Triumph offices had become infrequent and brief. Carmen could tell she was flailing. But she hadn't stopped probing Carmen, though she was much more subtle about it now. Hudson was smart. A plodder. The kind of person who would push every button in every combination to figure out what each one does. Eventually, she cracks the code. That's what worried Carmen. Hudson would eventually find out. It wasn't so much the truth that mattered. Carmen hadn't done anything but go over to Harvey's apartment and run out. But the lie was now bigger than the truth. The fact that she was hiding something was more problematic than what she might have done. What was it they said about Nixon? It wasn't so much the crime, but the cover-up.

Carmen wondered how much those two young girls knew about the morbid narrative surrounding their favorite comic. How the writer— well, cowriter—behind *The Legendary Lynx* was dead. She wondered how

Harvey would react to the book's sudden success. After one issue, the series had leapfrogged even *Avatar* to become Triumph's bestselling book. Earning rave reviews in the few comic book trades and a buzz that shocked Carmen, it'd revived what was left of Doug Detmer's career as well—pulling him out of the depths of obscurity and back on the map. He was no longer a name only pros mentioned to each other. At fifty-two, he was reborn. Though the book wasn't selling enough for Marvel or DC to take notice, it was on its way to becoming the company's flagship. Detmer's art was a big reason for that. Carmen had even overheard Carlyle grousing about trying to keep Detmer working on the series. But she wasn't sure if there was another outfit in town that could put up with his peculiar brand of surly artistry.

Carmen was happy for Harvey. For their idea. But she also felt an emptiness. Like a limb was missing from her body. She was watching her own story unfurl, but she couldn't engage with it. Or talk about it. Claudia Calla—the Lynx—was her creation as much as it was Harvey's, and no one knew it. Carmen knew she could march into Carlyle's office, toss her notebook's worth of ideas at him, and come clean. But to what end? Getting fired and still being unable to write a story featuring the character she created?

She wasn't alone in this, she knew. She'd heard every horror story in the book. She saw it, too. How Jack Kirby had helped cocreate dozens of Marvel's top characters, only to see Stan Lee take the lion's share of the credit. And still, the company owned them all, no question. You did the work, sold your idea, and then it was out of your hands. Maybe someday that'd be different. But Carmen wasn't sure. In the short-term, she was watching her precious creation live out her life from a distance, like a mother snooping on the child she left at a friend's doorstep. Even worse? The clock was ticking. And she was no closer to finding out the truth—the reason why Harvey had rushed those stories to Carlyle.

She reached her apartment building and made her way toward the building's dimly lit stairwell. She felt the steps creaking under her feet. She needed to think.

Harvey had reworked the six scripts Carmen wrote for the Lynx, integrating ideas they'd discussed and adding a few things he'd seemed to favor. He'd revised them at an almost inhuman speed. But that stack of work was finite. The third issue of *The Legendary Lynx* was out now, and the fourth was halfway drawn. In a few months, there'd be a seventh issue—written by someone else. But who would Carlyle choose? Was there anything Carmen could do to make him realize he should give her a shot?

As she reached her floor, she heard a flurry of steps fading down the hallway. She tried to follow the sound but only saw a tall figure turning the corner and taking the stairs on the opposite end of the hall down. Carmen felt a static tingling spread over her skin.

It'd been a woman. Carmen was certain of that. But it wasn't Molly. Whoever it was hadn't been expecting Carmen to come up this way. She walked to her door and unlocked it. She waited a moment, her hand on the knob, half expecting the person to come back up and reveal herself. She felt the knob turning on its own and stepped back. She watched as the door opened inward, revealing Molly in a bathrobe, a pink toothbrush in her mouth.

"You coming inside or what?"

Carmen stepped in.

"Thought you were gonna grab some milk."

"I left them—the groceries," Carmen said, sitting down on her bed. "Long story. Hey, did you notice anyone out in the hall?"

"I mean, you were just out there," Molly said walking toward the bathroom. "Did . . . you?"

"I think so," Carmen said, looking up at her roommate. "But they ran when I got there."

"Maybe it was your creepy ex," Molly said.

She was joking, of course, but it stuck with Carmen for a second. She hadn't heard from Katherine since she'd hung up on her months ago. Carmen had just figured she'd gone back to Miami, back to Nick. But could Katherine still be here?

She didn't feel guilt over the missed dinner. She'd just found Harvey, her friend, dead in his own bedroom. She had no desire to talk it over with Katherine. For a long time, Katherine was the last person she ever wanted to see or think about. Her reaction to the missed date just cemented that.

So why was Carmen thinking about it at all?

She heard the bathroom door close and the shower start. Carmen plopped back onto her bed and closed her eyes and let her mind take her somewhere else. Another time.

She could smell the carne asada almost before the Versailles waiter appeared. She watched as he slid the plate in front of her. The restaurant had been open for a few years, tops, but had already become a nexus point for Miami's exile community. An extension of a life left behind. The food, the music, the fellowship—it felt like home. Even to Carmen, who'd left the island as a young girl, more American than Cuban. It'd been Katherine's idea. "I want to experience your world—see you speak your language, eat your food, everything."

Carmen hated it when she said shit like that.

But everything else about that night felt special. Like they'd graduated to something of substance, not just sneaking kisses or making discreet visits to Katherine's apartment when Nick was out of town or watching football with his friends. They'd been doing this dance for months, Carmen realized, and never been out to dinner. They'd had drinks. Cafecitos. Quick lunches. But never a date.

It wasn't like they could be open about it, of course. Miami was not that kind of town. Cubans were not that kind of culture. For Carmen, it'd been a gradual realization, one that predated Katherine.

In quiet moments, when she'd be sitting in her bedroom, her parents asleep, the only light coming from the Miami moonlight outside, she'd ask herself: *Am I in love?* The answer had to be yes. You didn't ask yourself if you weren't.

The early part of the night felt almost magical—like they'd crossed some imaginary threshold together and become more than whatever they had been to each other.

That was as good as the night was going to get, Carmen remembered.

Katherine had seemed on edge from the moment Carmen stepped into her car. Mostly silent on the way to the restaurant. The one or two times Carmen asked if anything was wrong, she was met by a shrug or a terse "Nothing, don't worry—let's try to have fun tonight."

Carmen wasn't stupid. There were complexities in even the most mainstream relationships, much less those that involved a third person. A spouse. It was the cloud that hung over them. The barrier that prevented them from any kind of momentum or reality. To go beyond dark bars and faraway hotel rooms to something more genuine.

By the time they got to the restaurant and ordered, Katherine seemed to calm down, trying to smile when appropriate and ask Carmen about her day. But it felt perfunctory and automated, like she wanted nothing more than for this to be over—despite how much she knew it meant to Carmen, and how much Carmen thought it'd meant to her.

"You're very quiet," Carmen said, popping a piece of tostada into her mouth, savoring the buttery flavor. "Almost feels like I'm eating alone."

Katherine smiled. A humorless, distant smile. The kind of smile you'd give to someone at the DMV or when you're offended but just need to get through it. It stung. Who was this person? Carmen thought. This woman who didn't even seem to want to be here? She felt her own temper begin to flare.

"It's Nick, isn't it?" Carmen asked.

Katherine's eyebrows crept up for a moment, before she seemed to force herself back to her serene, uninterested facade.

"Yes," she said.

"Do you want to talk about it?" Carmen said, reaching a hand out and placing it on her arm. "I'm here. It's okay if you're upset. You don't have to pretend to be having—"

"No, I don't want to talk about it," she said, each word hitting Carmen like a jab to the shoulder. "Please don't mention him."

Carmen felt it bubble over then. Months of secrets, denials, missed calls, late arrivals, winding drives to drop her off blocks from home.

She'd had it. Carmen wasn't deluded. She knew what this was. But her heart thought it was something else. And at a certain point, in a battle between what you think and what you feel, something has to break.

"So we just pretend he doesn't exist?" Carmen said, pulling her hand back. "Like we're just two friends having dinner after work before we go back to our husbands? I want to be with you, okay? I'm willing to wait, I know this is hard for—"

"You don't know," Katherine said, her voice hushed, her eyes darting around. That humorless, thin smile still on her face—as if breaking it would shunt her back to reality. "You don't know what I'm dealing with. What I have to do. How I have to be."

"Well, then fucking tell me," Carmen said, her voice rising.

An older woman sitting at a table behind them spun her head around briefly, her mouth forming a small O. Carmen glared back, willing the nosy woman to turn around. Is this what Marvel Girl felt like? she wondered. Moving objects with her mind?

Katherine tilted her head, as if trying to see Carmen from a slightly different angle.

"I think I have to go," she said, her lips pursing in a strange, unsettling way. Was she seething with anger? About to cry?

She started to get up, placing her napkin daintily next to her untouched plate of food.

"Wait, no, why? Please, why are you doing this?" Carmen said, ashamed of what she was saying, but desperate to cling to some remnant of hope. Some shred of possibility that this night—which was going to mean so much—could be redeemed. "Katherine, come on, sit down."

She felt Katherine's hand wrap around her arm. The fingers tightening on her wrist. Before she could react, before the surprise could kick in, she felt Katherine's fingernails dig into the soft flesh near her palm. She let out a slight squeal—like a captured animal. *Just surprise,* she thought. But no. She was in pain. Katherine was hurting her.

"I'm leaving," Katherine said. "Don't call me. Don't come to my house."

"Let go of my—"

"There's another person involved in this," she hissed, her thin, superficial smile long gone now, replaced by bared teeth. "And you need to leave that be. I'm married, okay? Why can't you accept that?"

"You're hurting—"

Before Carmen could finish, Katherine had let go of her arm, pushing it back, like some unnecessary rag, a nuisance. She looked around, disoriented, before finding the exit and walking toward it briskly. Carmen looked at her arm. The marks that would become bruises. The dark red lines where Katherine's nails had dug into her skin. They'd bleed soon, she thought. They'd scab over after that.

Carmen welcomed the pain. She wrapped her own hand around her wounded wrist and felt the pulse of her own veins, beating through the pain the woman she loved had caused, keeping her alive.

But she couldn't find refuge in the hurt. No. Not with the same words pounding inside her, slamming outward, propelling toward the lining of her skull. Over and over and over.

What the fuck have I gotten into?

"Earth to Carmen, are you there?"

Carmen blinked her eyes to see Molly standing before her, fully dressed, a blue towel wrapped around her dark hair, backlit by the morning sun. Carmen allowed herself a moment to admire her roommate. Her tan skin and sharp features. Her large dark eyes. Carmen felt strange. Disoriented and lost. Why had she allowed herself to fall into that well of memory? To relive those times with Katherine?

She felt relief wash over her, at least for a moment. Katherine was gone. The temptation to reunite had been derailed by Harvey's death, and that was for the best. She had enough on her mind, on her plate.

"Hey, yeah, I'm fine, sorry," Carmen said, standing up. She was inches away from Molly, who was giving her a confused, expectant stare. "I've got—I've got a lot on my mind."

"Seems like it," Molly said, taking a few paces back. "You still hung up on your friend? That cop still hassling you? You know you don't have to talk to them anymore. Not unless they have something new to say, right? Seems like they're just chasing their own tails."

"You're right," Carmen said absentmindedly. She looked at her watch. She needed to get to work. The day had already started poorly—no groceries, no relief. But her mind kept going back to the bodega. To those two girls.

They were arguing about comics, which was a victory in and of itself—two girls debating the merits of two heroes in adventures created mainly to entertain boys their age. But one of the heroes was *hers*. A character she created. Sure, with Harvey. And Doug Detmer certainly brought some of his stark, minimalist line work to it—neither could be discounted. But neither could Carmen. She had a piece of the story. And it was resonating.

Except she didn't. No one knew she'd done a thing when it came to the Lynx. Harvey had taken credit for her work when he turned those scripts in. Hadn't even consulted her. No one would ever know. Soon, within days, Carlyle would be forced to make a call—to find the next writer to pen the adventures of Carmen's baby. He might have made it already.

Carmen looked around her small, crowded apartment. Saw the vestiges of her Miami life intermingled with the new one she was building here. She hadn't moved to New York City to be a spectator to her own career. A footnote. A means to an end.

She heard Molly gasp as a pot clattered to the kitchen floor. The sound pulling her back to the moment. To the problem. She snatched her purse, gave Molly a half-hearted wave, and sped out the door.

Carmen could be patient, but she wasn't passive. That wasn't going to change now. Still, the question remained: What could she do? Was there a way to save this character, this creation that felt like an extension of her very being?

Carmen Valdez was about to find out.

CHAPTER NINETEEN

A **publishing office tends to move** in a cycle, like the moon—it picks up speed as it heads toward a cluster of deadlines, then plateaus as those deadlines are met. The valley of quiet usually tends to last a day or two longer than it should, sparking another flurry of activity that gradually revs up until the whole cycle begins anew. Carmen had gotten used to the Triumph office's particular rhythms, and as she walked in, Carlyle's coffee in hand, she had to fight the urge to lift a finger in the air to gauge just which part of the office was blowing the most hot air.

She knew it was bad when the production grunts were in early, poring over art corrections with glue, Rapidograph pens, and brushes at the ready. She heard Trunick's hushed, pleading voice as he bargained for minutes, desperate to make sure the new issue of *Freedom Alliance* made its release date. She saw Mullin's figure dart across the back of the office, X-Acto knife in hand, trying to correct a piece of art that could derail an entire sequence in the new issue of *The Dusk*. Carmen loved the bustle. She loved how things seemed to be spiraling into chaos only to jell at the last minute and produce art. It reminded her of working overnight shifts at her college paper. Not overnight shifts by design, but beer-and-coffee-fueled benders to get the paper done and in the hands of her fellow students by their Wednesday morning deadline. It was the same thrill, Carmen realized, except they weren't writing stories about Vietnam War protests or corrupt student government elections—they were putting together four-color adventure stories about urban vigilantes, or teams of alien warriors, or godlike men pretending to be mortal.

She stepped into Carlyle's empty office and placed his coffee next to a stack of papers on his desk, making sure to leave enough room in anticipation of her boss's usual clumsiness. She heard a throat-clearing sound and spun around.

He looked like shit. Again. Another set of dark bags under his eyes, his tie barely knotted, a blue stain on the collar of his white shirt. He even seemed unsteady on his feet, as if he'd just gone twelve rounds with the Hulk and survived.

"Rough night, boss?" she asked.

Carlyle looked at her, his eyes flickering to life; his dazed, reflexive frown suddenly shifting into a bright, manic smile.

"Not at all, actually," Carlyle said, stepping around her and tossing his blazer onto a chair. He slid into his own seat and spun it to face Carmen. "In fact, I think I may have solved our Lynx problem, Carmen."

"Lynx problem?"

"Don't play coy, it doesn't suit you," he said with a low harrumph. "You know as well as anyone we need to find someone to write this book—if this continues for a few more months, it could be the one book that keeps the company afloat. Everyone loves *Avatar*, raves about it. But I don't think anyone's buying it. Yet people can't get enough of this damn Lynx character. They can't stop talking about the Lynx. She might not be pulling Marvel or DC numbers—but she's a damn hit!"

Carmen smiled. She could feel her face flush, but she didn't care.

Carlyle grabbed a pencil and tapped it on his desk, eyes on Carmen.

"Well? Don't you want to know how I did it?"

"Did what?"

"Solved the problem. Are you following me, Carmen? I found a writer," Carlyle said, his grin now conspiratorial. "And it's genius."

"Maynard?" Carmen asked meekly. If it had to be someone else, Carmen would at least understand their top, best writer getting the gig. It'd still sting, though. Of that she was sure. "Do you think he can handle two books a month? I mean, Wolfman at Marvel does six."

"No, not Maynard—that bad Jim Morrison impersonator would ruin this book, no way," Carlyle said, waving his arms derisively in Carmen's direction. "Please, be serious. No, this is even better. It's not a big name, but he's a true professional—someone I know we can rely on. He'll keep the train on the tracks and we can see just how far this idea will go."

Carmen felt her heart begin to sink.

"Who is it, then?"

"Jensen, Mark Jensen," Carlyle said, pride slathered on every word. He leaned back, hands cupped behind his head. "You know him, right? I don't think he's ever come into the office, but we've used him before. He also did a few things for DC. A truly great plotter—I mean, one of the best. With style, too. I think he can really elevate the series—take it past this, I dunno, whatever cultish, lefty propaganda Stern was trying to sneak in—you must've seen it, too, right? Just bring the character back to its roots. I have to thank Harvey, actually."

"Harvey?"

"Yes, he left me a note on the back of the last page. It was brief, almost illegible, but it said, 'Pass on to Mark Jensen if series continues.' Can you believe that, Carmen? It's fate. The poor boy wanted this veteran, this talent, to carry the torch. Imagine the press about this? A great big *Times* piece on this company and how we're redefining—"

Carmen didn't hear anymore. Her brain was spinning out of control. She couldn't believe what she was hearing. She could feel the character being pulled further away from her. First Harvey had taken it upon himself to rework Carmen's six scripts, with not even a thought to what Carmen might want, or a chance for her to make changes. She wondered if his death had somehow softened her anger toward him. No, the embers were still hot, and thinking about Jensen pulled her back to that original resentment. Harvey had used her. Had picked her brain and taken the bulk of her work and added a coat of cliché paint to it. Then he'd taken complete credit for it.

Look, just be careful with Harvey, okay?

Marion's warning flooded her mind. What had she meant? What could Carmen do now, with zero control over this idea that felt so much like it was a part of her?

She knew the Lynx wasn't hers. Carmen understood that there was a chance, even in a best-case scenario, that they'd lose control. She'd braced herself for that, as best she could, but now she felt their creation being sent into the arms of something else, something perverse, something wrong.

She'd never even met Jensen—he was one of the few freelancers willing to wait until a check appeared in the mail, she guessed. But she'd read his work. He was certainly fast—but he was never, ever good. He didn't have the chance, some might argue, always getting the rush work and desperation calls, but never the chance to really shine on a book. But Carmen knew that was bullshit. There was a saying, one that Carmen had heard early on in her days at Triumph—you were lucky if a freelancer was two of three things: fast, nice, and good. Jensen was just quick. His writing was subpar on a good day, and no one in the bullpen had any idea why he kept getting work. Aside from the "fast" part. So to think that Harvey, whom Carmen knew had called on Jensen to bail his ass out of the editorial fire on a few occasions, would note how much he wanted Jensen to take over the Lynx was baffling. Almost as baffling was Carlyle strutting around like a rooster in a henhouse. Where was the win here?

"You're joking, right?"

Carlyle's gleeful look morphed into a petulant glare.

"Is there a problem?"

"You know Jensen's work as well as anyone—it's shit," Carmen said. She could feel her temperature rising, could sense the words careening out of her mouth faster, angrier than they normally would. "He's our glass case. Shatter in case of emergency. This is hardly an emergency! I can think of a handful of writers who'd be great with Lynx, right off the top of my head." She gave it a beat. "Hell, *I'd* be great at this."

"That's quite enough," he said. "I'm not fond of your tone, Carmen. Plus, we've already talked about this. Anyway, it's decided, all right? We're done here."

Carmen stiffened. Despite Carlyle's perpetually dismissive attitude and cranky demeanor, she'd always felt like they had some kind of bond—a mutual respect. He could be flip, but there were lines he wouldn't cross. He wouldn't overtly disrespect her, or demean her. He'd done that now, shrugging her off like some kind of nag.

She heard him muttering as she turned around, but the words were lost as his door slammed behind her.

The clacking of her shoes on the office's linoleum floor echoed the pulsing in her head. The droning scream that told her she had to do something to fix this.

Something was very wrong, and Carmen knew the only way to figure out what it was involved retracing the last steps Harvey Stern ever took.

"Who got you, Harvey?" she whispered to herself, as she approached the office's far wall. Looming over her was a giant poster, a blue-and-black-clad vigilante staring down at Carmen, leopard-like spots flickering over her boots and sleeves, her masked eyes and grim smirk immediately letting you know this hero was someone not to be messed with. Tough. Streetwise. Independent.

Carmen knew she couldn't save her friend. She knew she should hate him for betraying her like this. But Harvey Stern was dead. If she could salvage something of theirs, something they made together, she would. Even if she couldn't find it in herself to forgive him yet.

She had to untangle what was going on, fast.

The Legendary Lynx depended on it.

CHAPTER TWENTY

She caught **Rich Berger** as he was beginning to unpack a soggy-looking sandwich and a bottle of Coca-Cola for lunch. He seemed annoyed to hear her gentle knock, but it faded once he realized it was Carmen. Despite their book club friendship, Carmen's presence could still intimidate. The perks of being the boss's henchwoman, she thought.

"Hey there, Carmen," he said, hands on the sandwich as he reluctantly looked up.

"This won't take long," Carmen said, closing the door behind her.

Berger's mouth scrunched together in confusion. This was a comic book company. There weren't many closed-door meetings. Not unless someone was getting fired or there was money trouble. Both happened from time to time, but most of the day's work was accomplished by editors screaming to staff outside their offices. Closing doors would hamper that.

"Everything okay?" Berger asked, letting his sandwich drop onto his desk with an odd *schlop* sound.

"I think so," Carmen said, trying to figure out just why she'd walked into Harvey's boss's office without a plan.

The conversation with Carlyle had left her in a daze. She felt completely rattled by the thought that someone like Mark Jensen would be writing Claudia Calla's adventures. It was anathema to her. Not only was Jensen a joke, he was a salacious, thickheaded, and misogynistic joke. His scripts were littered with crude double-talk and cumbersome innuendo. An editor's nightmare, one that was only remedied by the sheer speed with which he cranked his shit out.

"I just wanted to check in on you," she said softly, trying to show genuine concern. "I know it's been a few months since, well, since . . . Harvey."

Berger nodded slowly, still not truly understanding the reason for Carmen's visit, but apparently appreciative for the human connection.

"Well, I appreciate that, I do," Berger said, looking down at his desk. "He was a good kid. I just wish it seemed like the police knew more, you know? It's been months and nothing. I know you had some bad chats with them, but to me, that detective Hudson seemed to be pretty capable. So it's just frustrating that they can't seem to move the needle on it."

Carmen nodded. Berger's intel wasn't anything new to her, but it was fresher—and confirmed what she'd thought. Hudson had hit a wall. Despite routinely pestering Carmen for more details, she was coming up empty. Whoever killed Harvey had done a careful job covering their tracks, she thought.

Carmen hesitated, unsure if she should say anything.

Then a vision of a disheveled Harvey entered her mind—walking into Carlyle's office with a stack of scripts under his arm. Scripts she'd written, loaded with her ideas but credited solely to him.

She was sure now.

"I wanted to ask if you'd talked to Carlyle about the Lynx book," Carmen said.

She had to tread carefully here. As far as Berger knew, despite their casual book club, Carmen was in his office as Carlyle's envoy. If she spoke out of turn, Berger's internal alarm would go off. He'd been with Triumph for a while, and knew the landscape better than most.

"Not today, no," Berger said, a tinge of confusion—or was it worry?— in his voice. "I know he wanted to finalize who was taking over, so I sent over a few suggestions. I hope he'll take them into account. But you know Jeffrey—he wants it to be his call, too."

Carmen nodded.

"Who'd you pick, if you don't mind me asking?" Her voice was hushed, secretive. Berger responded with a knowing smile.

"Fishing for gossip, eh?" he said. Carmen almost cursed under her breath. Berger was no rookie. "You'd know better than me. Did he pick someone? I'd like to know. I'm the one stuck cleaning up whatever they deliver."

"Fair trade," Carmen said with a smirk. "You first."

Berger shrugged.

"Fine. Well, it's our top book, and with Harvey, uh . . . well, gone, it makes sense to put our top writer on it. So I figured Maynard would get a shot. I threw out a few other names, too—Hart, Post, Cosby, Rozan, Rosenberg, hell, even Allen Ulmer, the guy behind Micro-Face—y'know, guys we use who might elevate things if given a shot. I can't see how he wouldn't pick one of those, but it's always a crapshoot with him. I know he hates Maynard's scripts, but the fans love *Avatar*. It's like an obsession."

Berger was half right. The fans who did read *Avatar* loved it. But not that many people were reading it. Not that many people were reading Triumph's comics, period. That had come into focus now, with the Lynx's book sales topping anything Triumph had ever done—and still tracking miles behind anything Marvel and DC were putting out, with dwindling returns from the newsstand. Now *Avatar* was a solid number-two for them, but one that didn't feel as essential. *How quickly we forget*, Carmen thought.

"This goes in the vault," Carmen said, her look stoic and without emotion. "Okay? If I hear this gets back to me, I will not hesitate to make your life a living hell."

It wasn't an idle threat, either. Carmen, despite "just" being Carlyle's secretary, had access to many tools that could reflect poorly on any of the employees. Late invoices. Miscommunications with the printers. De-layed shipping to the distributor. All things Carmen would never do, but Berger didn't need to know that.

He gave her an incredulous frown, but she could tell he understood. He had to.

"Well, look, of course, I'm not an office gossip," Berger said, pushing his thick glasses up the bridge of his nose. "I appreciate the information. Though, now I'm worried it's not any of the very qualified people I sug-gested to Jeffrey. I mean—"

"It's Jensen. Mark Jensen."

Berger's jaw hung open. She could see the filling in one of his molars. He didn't make a sound for a few moments.

"Rich, are you—"

"You're kidding, right? This is some kind of bullshit prank the pro-duction staff put you up to? Because that is not fucking funny."

Carmen lifted a hand. Berger's voice was rising and she didn't need an incident. She needed information.

"I wish I was," she said softly. "I just wanted to warn you. I also wanted to ask if—I dunno, you'd suggested him?"

"No, why in the hell would I do that? Jensen's a waste," Berger said, shaking his head. "His writing is puerile. He's more trouble than he's worth. You get one of his scripts, you spend as much time fixing his work as the time you'd lose from giving it to an actual writer. I don't get why Carlyle keeps going back to that infested well, it's insane."

"Wait, what?" Carmen asked. Her plan was out the window. She hadn't expected this.

"You know better than me," Berger said, looking over his glasses at her. "Jensen gets more work than many more capable writers. He's the cleaner. Our utility man. It's not because any of us like him. But for whatever reason, your boss keeps him fed."

Carmen waited a beat. Berger was right, of course. But it connected dots Carmen didn't know existed. She got the invoices from the assistant editors. And yes, Jensen got a decent amount of work—but Carmen assumed all creative decisions sprung from Carlyle and Berger. She also understood that Carlyle was in charge—and often made demands. But she just figured Jensen got work because he was fast, quality notwithstanding. But the way Berger seemed to tell it, Carlyle was *forcing* people to use the freelancer.

Carmen doubled down.

"Do you think Harvey wanted Jensen to take over?"

Berger scoffed.

"What, like a last, dying wish? That's ludicrous. Harvey couldn't stand the guy's work—he railed on Jensen, every time Carlyle hired him to do a fill-in. He almost got into it with Carlyle himself over it," Berger said, pushing his sandwich away absentmindedly. "He hated the guy, and he'd never even seen him. No one has, really. He can't even be bothered to come pick up his checks. I can still hear Harvey prattling on about it. 'It's not worth it, Rich. The stories would be better if you just let me write them.' I used to think it was just Harvey's own aspirations, but then he handed me a script Jensen had sent in, and my eyes almost rotted in their sockets. Sexist garbage. And, look, we make comic books. I get it's not high art. Hell, who knows if we'll even be around five years from now—but there's a minimum level of quality that we—well, at least I—strive for. Mark Jensen ain't it."

Carmen stood up.

"Vault, okay? Act surprised when you get the news."

Berger nodded.

"Believe me, I'm erasing it from my mind," he said, picking up his sandwich and examining it. "I actually kind of resent you telling me."

Carmen shrugged.

"The truth hurts," she said as she stepped out of his office, leaving the door open behind her.

As she made her way back toward her desk from Berger's office, she caught sight of Harvey's own work space, across from Trunick, a production assistant. He was out to lunch. Carmen glanced over Harvey's old desk, which had been left mostly untouched. Carlyle, ever eager to scrimp and save, hadn't replaced Harvey yet—so there'd been no need to clean out his desk. Since the case was still open, Carmen imagined Hudson wanted to revisit their searches as needed.

Carmen hovered over it for a few moments.

She couldn't be here long, she realized. At least not now, when everyone was in the office. But she let her eyes skim over Harvey's belongings for a few moments longer. Then she saw it—scribbled in red marker on the edge of a make-ready, a preliminary, prepublication proof for an issue of *Gray Wolf,* the protagonist's lupine face screaming in anger on a crowded splash page. The issue had already come out. Another sign that Harvey had been gone for a while.

Under the art were two words, written in Harvey's clunky, blocky handwriting: *VISIT DD.*

She made her way back to her desk, the message floating through her mind.

As she sat down, a plan began to formulate. "DD" was, of course, Doug Detmer—the artist on the Lynx. But did Harvey know that? He was dead before Detmer even got the scripts. Had Carlyle told Harvey who the artist was going to be? Or was there another reason for Harvey to meet with Doug Detmer? Carmen glanced back at Carlyle's office. He was on the phone, leaning back in his chair and motioning toward the large windows that overlooked Twenty-Third Street. Standard afternoon routine.

She flipped through the freelance contracts in the file cabinet next to her desk and found the address. She stood up and made a gesture at Carlyle—something that seemed to say *I'll be right back.* He waved her off, too embroiled in his own call to care. She had been counting on that. Carmen grabbed her bag and left.

Detmer's studio was on the Lower East Side, on Ludlow and Rivington, above a bar named Iggy's. The area was relatively quiet by New York City standards—a tight-knit immigrant community, in contrast to the Bowery's Skid Row aesthetic just around the corner. A group of four children watched as Carmen scanned the addresses, their eyes wide and cautious. They stood by a decrepit-looking building with a fading HOTEL

ON RIVINGTON sign flickering in the late-afternoon light. The foot traffic was sparse. Carmen noticed a few people perusing the few stores, but nothing close to a crowd. Carmen rarely ventured this far south, for obvious reasons. But this felt important. It felt like a last gasp, too.

Doug Detmer was a tainted legend. The kind of talent you'd hear mixed things about from the same person. Messy drunk. An artist's artist. Difficult. Genius. Problematic. Trailblazer.

Everyone who'd dealt with him had a war story, and those tales became their own currency. Legend was he'd studied under greats like Bernard Krigstein, Graham Ingels, and Jack Cole, destroying relationships with each one. Dave Cockrum, a rising star artist known mostly for his *Legion of Super-Heroes* work at DC Comics, had briefly apprenticed with Detmer, only to bail after a few short months.

Carmen buzzed the door, pushing the button that featured a hastily scribbled *Detmer Studios* next to it. She waited a moment, and was about to buzz again when a crackle of static broke through. The voice on the other end was hoarse and sedate.

"Yeah?"

"Uh, hey, Mr. Detmer?"

"Who's asking?"

"It's Carmen Valdez, from Triumph Comics," she said. "Carlyle sent me to check on you."

A pause. She heard a wet, hacking cough.

The door buzzed, and Carmen walked in. She noticed the crudely posted OUT OF ORDER sign on the elevator and took the stairs up, the dark, dank steps strewn with trash and dirt. Carmen tried to focus on her destination, ignoring the scurrying sounds of what might be bugs or rats or something else. She reached the sixth floor and turned the doorknob. It was unlocked.

She wasn't sure what she'd expected, but it wasn't this. The space was large—art tables and chairs spread out. It felt almost as big as the Triumph offices, except completely empty. Bottles collected by an overflowing garbage can. A brown, dusty couch near the far wall. That's where she caught the only glimpse of life—a tall, gangly figure spread out on it, arms over his face. This was the great Doug Detmer, she thought.

Detmer was the kind of artist other artists raved about. He was that good. His line resembled the work of a master like Alex Toth—a cleanness and curve that felt natural to the eye. His layouts were dynamic and lively, his attention to detail mesmerizing, and doubly impressive considering his aversion to excessive cross-hatching or needless noodling.

Carmen took a tentative step forward. Detmer rustled. How messed up do you have to be to buzz someone in, then completely pass out a moment later? Carmen wondered. She'd dealt with drunks before. Her parents, mainly. It was why she was mindful of her own intake. She didn't need to be a doctor to realize the drive to be a drunk was at least partially genetic. She didn't need to get dragged down into that well.

Despite the universal love for Detmer's quirky, unforgettable style, and despite the fact that his skills as a draftsman and stylist had only nominally eroded over the last twenty years, time had finally caught up with Doug Detmer. His work with Charlton, Warren, Quality, and Bulwark had dried up—leaving Triumph as the only place willing to put up with his shit. Carmen wondered if even that would've continued, if *The Legendary Lynx* hadn't become a relative hit.

Detmer moved with more purpose now, rising to a sitting position, a hand sliding over his balding head. He looked gaunt and unruly, even from this distance. Carmen walked toward him, the sound of her feet on the hardwood floor confirming what his whiskey-addled brain couldn't register minutes before. There was someone else in the studio.

"Mr. Detmer?" Carmen asked, raising a hand in a slow wave. "It's me—Carmen? From Triumph?"

Detmer stood up. She could make out his long, thin face now, as he zombie-shuffled toward her—wearing an ink-stained white polo shirt and wrinkled gray jeans. He didn't have shoes on, and his hands seemed to shake slightly as he put on a pair of flimsy glasses.

She looked past him for a moment, noticed the small cooler by the sofa, and the toothbrush and cup placed carefully by the windowsill.

This wasn't just where Detmer ran his studio. It was where he lived. And from what she could tell, it was a solo operation.

"Carlyle sent you here?" Detmer croaked. He was a few feet away now, swaying slightly. He looked twenty years older than the fifty or so Carmen knew he was.

"Yes, he wanted to make sure—"

"Don't bullshit me, sweetie, I wasn't born yesterday."

Carmen froze.

"He wanted to check on the next issue," she said, pressing. His expression didn't change.

He let out a raspy, humorless laugh.

"Issue's done. I sent it a few days ago. You should have it in hand."

Carmen let out a long sigh.

"Fine, you got me," she said. "I'm not here because Carlyle sent me. I need to talk to you. About Harvey Stern."

A low "huh" was Detmer's only response before he turned around, motioning for Carmen to follow. She did. He led her into the only room in the space, and—from what she could tell—the only area that was cleaned regularly.

Unlike the rest of the barren studio, the office was immaculate—original art and awards framed on the walls, animation cels and pictures surrounding them. It was a shrine to Doug Detmer's career, she realized. Carmen caught a page from his chilling story in EC's *The Haunt of Fear*. A picture of Detmer and EC Comics founder Bill Gaines, smiling innocently, mere months before the comic book empire they'd all built together would begin to crumble. There was a framed gag comic from his *Playboy* days. A few pages from an *Avengers Annual* that Detmer had filled in on. Some animation turnarounds for a failed cartoon she couldn't recognize. It was all here, like a tomb, waiting for the pharaoh to die.

"This is amazing," Carmen said, leaning in to inspect an original *Lynx* page of art. She loved this page, had loved it from the moment she'd first seen it come in. A shot of the heroine leaping through an apartment window, in search of reporter Simon Upton. Instead, she finds a bloody message from her foe, Mr. Void, scrawled on a mirror. She was in awe at Detmer's mindful use of shadow, and the way the color subtly played on the mood of the page. She felt her eyes watering as they scanned the art. Felt herself reminded yet again that there was a piece of her on this page. A piece she needed to get back.

"That was a good one," Detmer said, collapsing into his desk chair. "That script . . . was something else. Something special. It was the only reason I took the gig. I'm just about ready to retire, I guess. Or be retired. But when Carlyle called with this, well, I had to say yes. Didn't read like Stern, though."

Carmen turned her head around to face him.

"What do you mean?"

"I've read Stern's past work. It was . . . fine," Detmer said, his face moving slightly to meet Carmen's inquisitive gaze. "But that's it. You can tell pretty fast what someone's range is. He was never going to be more than a decent writer. Nice guy who worked real hard. Every time I'd see him, he'd go on and on about wanting to work together. Wanted to come see my studio, 'talk shop,' he said. It was nice, but there was an air of desperation to it. Because people liked him and wanted to help, not because he was some kind of rising star. But this *Lynx* script . . . it felt, eh, I dunno. Almost like . . ."

Before Detmer could finish, he was seized by a loud, hacking cough. When it ended, he seemed dazed—his train of thought derailed.

"You okay?" Carmen asked.

He wiped his mouth with the back of his wrist.

"Fine, I'm fine," he said. "So tell me the real reason you're here. I don't have all day."

"You didn't seem to be doing much when I got here."

"I have my schedule. It works for me," Detmer said, standing up. He moved closer to Carmen. It wasn't threatening, but she felt herself on edge in the small office space. "So, tell me—why are you here? I know the Harvey kid got murdered. But like I said, he wasn't writing those scripts anyway. At least not the good parts. Any idea who was?"

"Oh, I don't know, I mean . . ." she faltered. She didn't know this man at all, but the temptation—to come clean to someone, even if it was this talented wretch of a man—was impossible to resist. "I think he did it himself."

Detmer shook his head.

"So he conned Carlyle, eh? That slick asshole was never as smart as he thought he was," Detmer said. "I'd love to shake the hand of the person that did help Stern, because—that?" He pointed at the framed *Lynx* page. "Now that's something special. That's how you write for an artist like me."

Detmer started to walk past her. Carmen would never be able to recall what drove her, or why she did it, but she would never regret it, even after the tragedies that would follow.

Her right hand jutted out. Detmer met her eyes, a slight smile on his face.

He took her hand. His skin felt cold and scaly. Carmen fought the urge to pull back.

"Knew it," he said.

"I helped him . . . we did it together," she said, her body shaking. "You're the only person who knows."

Detmer nodded, the empathy on his worn face genuine—a wounded soldier appraising another one who had fallen on the field.

"Well, fix that. Get Carlyle on the phone," he said. "You need to step in. I imagine they're running out of scripts, right?"

Carmen opened her mouth to respond, then hesitated. As alcohol-addled as Detmer seemed to be, he still picked up on it.

"Wait, he has someone already?" Detmer asked. "That sneaky fuck. Who did he go with? Maynard? Or someone out of the box, like Isabella?"

Carmen tried to speak, but the words wouldn't come. She shook her head.

"Who then?"

"Jensen—Mark Jensen," she said softly. Detmer's expression quickly shifted from genuine curiosity to something almost feral.

"Jensen? That's absurd," he said, pushing past Carmen toward the studio. "Jensen?"

"Yes, do you know him?" Carmen asked. "Have you met him?"

"Met him?" Detmer spat, a maniacal grin on his face. "Have you? Has anyone?"

Carmen tried to respond, but Detmer was out the door, picking up speed with each step.

She followed. He was pacing around the space. Arms waving around as he tried to process her news. Before she could react, Detmer had grabbed a stack of pencils and rulers from his art table and tossed them across the room, the tools clattering to the ground. Then he grabbed the table and flipped it over, watching as ink and pages crashed together, spreading out around the fallen table like blood after a shooting. He kicked it, muttering curses and "Jensen, fucking Jensen" over and over.

He froze, remembering he wasn't alone. Carmen watched as he whirled around, his expression tight and awkward.

"You should go," he said, each word sounding strained. "I need to think. Figure out what to do next about . . . everything. Okay?"

Carmen nodded and backed away cautiously.

She thought about reaching out, placing a hand on his shoulder, anything—but the man was gone. In a whirlwind of anger and hate she couldn't understand. As the tantrum escalated, she moved toward the exit, closing the door to the studio behind her as quietly as she could manage.

As she made her way down the steps, she thought she should feel something else. Concern. Anxiety. Fear. But instead, she realized she was feeling elation and relief. She'd finally shared the truth with someone. A man she barely knew, yes, and a man who was clearly unstable, but a colleague. Someone knew. Someone would know, no matter what happened.

She let herself enjoy the moment as she rode the train uptown. She let herself enjoy it as she walked the handful of blocks from the 6 train station to her building. She continued to enjoy it as she opened her front door, despite the brief, jarring feeling that she was being watched.

CHAPTER TWENTY-ONE

Carmen had walked through the vast Commodore Hotel a few times during her brief tenure as a New Yorker, but never like this. The Commodore felt very "old New York" to Carmen, even if she hadn't been in the city long enough to truly understand what that meant. She wasn't sure if it was the rusted, stuffy-looking statue of the hotel's namesake, Commodore Cornelius Vanderbilt, or the giant fading awning that draped over the Commodore's entrance. Whatever it was, it carried some weight—like a piece of a larger puzzle, nestled right next to the nexus that was Grand Central Terminal. But the hotel had seen better days, with rumors swirling that the aging building was bleeding money and would soon be shut down.

Now, the expansive lobby—which often seemed airy and spacious—felt cramped and crowded, with tables and boxes and wandering people taking up the bulk of the space. A part of her didn't want to go past the front door. She wasn't big on crowds. She'd brave one if it was worth it—a great concert or dance club. But she'd never seen anything like this. These people weren't here for a rock show or political rally. They were here for comic books.

"Your industry's dead, huh?" Molly said, tugging on Carmen's arm to get her deeper into the crowd.

"I never said that," Carmen replied. She felt her hand weave into Molly's as her roommate led her through the throngs of people.

Carmen pulled back to grab a program book—Marvel Comics' sleek, shiny space hero, the Silver Surfer, on the cover, drawn by the character's creator, Jack Kirby.

"Who's that?" Molly asked.

"The Silver Surfer," Carmen said, unable to hide the disdain in her voice. "C'mon, Molls."

"Girl, you know I don't read your mainstream tights-and-fights shit," Molly said with a dismissive wave. "I came because you needed a pal to ride with. Here I am. Your pal."

Carmen jabbed her shoulder. Molly feigned pain before laughing.

Harvey had told Carmen about the Comic Art Conventions—how the most legendary of the New York cons had been run by a local teacher, Phil Seuling, and how it'd grown each year. It was a place for fans to congregate, to meet fellow fans selling comics, to interact with the people behind the books they loved. In their short time indoors, Carmen had already spotted a few—longtime Marvel editor and writer Len Wein, flanked by his Swamp Thing artist, Berni Wrightson. Young DC assistant editor Paul Levitz, who'd made his name in fan circles and even wrote some of the copy for the program books that were distributed at the show. Prolific Marvel writer Roy Thomas. And the "King" himself—Jack Kirby. She'd known Kirby would be here—he was slated to be on a panel with Walter Gibson, creator of pulp hero the Shadow. They were both guests of honor. But catching a glimpse of the living legend made it feel all the more real.

Carmen looked at her watch. The panel was a few hours away. She had time to wander. If she could find a path. The area was a sea of tables where dealers looked to move copies of older comics. It was creating an entirely new market, Carmen mused. When she was a kid, you got the comics as they came out, and that was it. There was no opportunity to search for back issues. Maybe you'd luck into a friend or playmate who had some older ones you could trade for, but, like anything else on the newsstand, the life span of an issue was finite. If you missed it, your loss. But Carmen was there to people-watch, too, and she'd already gotten a glimpse of a few comic book stars—like cosmically tinged *Warlock* writer/artist Jim Starlin.

She stopped at a small table at the space's far corner, manned by two kids who couldn't be older than sixteen. Their table was loaded with boxes, meticulously labeled. Carmen started flipping through one casually— spotting a number of comics she'd either left behind in Miami, or would have murdered someone to get a copy of. Galactus's first appearance in *The Fantastic Four*. The first issue of the epic Stan Lee / Steve Ditko "Master Planner Saga" from *Amazing Spider-Man*. The first appearance of the Justice League of America in *The Brave and the Bold*. Kid Flash's debut in the pages of *The Flash*. How did these kids know where to find these? she wondered.

"Need any help?" one boy asked.

"Oh, no, I'm just browsing," Carmen said, but then stopped herself. She was a professional, she thought. She stuck out her hand. "I'm Carmen. I work at Triumph."

The two kids seemed genuinely impressed, and Carmen tried to keep a straight face, even as she felt Molly's knee jab at the back of her leg playfully.

"Wow, nice to meet you, ma'am," the older boy said, his floppy brown hair whipping back as he stretched to shake hands. "I'm Greg. This is my pal Joey. We live on Long Island, but we come down to these shows whenever Phil gives us a table."

"Nice to meet you," Carmen said.

"Well, uh, what do you do at Triumph?" Joey asked, his pointed face sporting a curious and hungry look. "You know Jeffrey Carlyle?"

"Of course. I'm . . . one of his writers," Carmen said.

"Huh, that's amazing," Greg said, a trickle of doubt in his voice. "Which books? Can I ask? I mean, I pick up all the Triumph books and I don't remember any lady writers."

Carmen frowned. She'd pushed too far. Now it stung.

She pulled back her hand and nodded.

"It was nice to meet you," she said.

The boys seemed confused but were too polite to say anything. They waved brightly as Carmen walked on, Molly trailing behind.

"What was that about?"

"I dunno, it felt like the right thing to say."

Molly's look went from curious to distracted, her face looking past Carmen.

"Hey, is that your creep boss, I think, standing over there?" Molly said, pointing across the space. "Talking to some wino-looking guy?"

Carmen turned to follow Molly's arm. She was right. Carlyle was in a corner across the room, looking almost buoyant, a tidy rum and Coke in one hand, his other raised up, as if he were conducting the New York Philharmonic. Looking up at him was another man—it took Carmen a moment to register who it was, because the last time she'd seen him, she'd tried very hard to not meet his red-eyed stare.

Stephenson. Carlyle's drinking buddy.

Before she could keep moving, Carlyle seemed to sense her stare. He turned to face her, his joyous expression suddenly serious and awkward. He motioned for her to come over to them. Stephenson's smile melted into a humorless smirk. Carmen nodded.

"I gotta hit practice," Molly said, watching Carmen begin to move toward the men. "You okay?"

"Yeah, fine," Carmen said in a faux-sunny voice. "I'll catch you later."

She didn't really want to talk to Jeffrey Carlyle or his stooge Stephenson. As much as this convention was work-related, it felt like her own personal adventure, and she didn't enjoy blending her two worlds together. But maybe she needed to.

By the time she reached Carlyle and Stephenson, the two men were back to their convivial conversation. She caught a snippet of Carlyle's story before they turned to face her.

". . . then the girl tells me, 'No, sir, this isn't just comics people—it's for adult stars, too,'" Carlyle said, struggling to hold his laughter in. "And I ask, 'Well, miss, do you mean actors that aren't children?' And—Dan, seriously, I tell you, she looks at me like I was growing a third eye. Then this woman says, 'No, sir—I mean porn stars. This party is a porn and comics party.'"

Stephenson started to laugh, a hiccupy, rhythmic laugh that made Carmen think of a bloated woodpecker, his entire body shivering with glee at Carlyle's tale.

Her boss raised a hand to Carmen, as if to say *One minute, please,* before continuing.

"It was completely wild, Dan, just insane. Then I look over my shoulder and there's Gerry Conway, and he's looking at me like the world is upside down," Carlyle said, chuckling with every other word. "I tell you—"

"Hey, boss," Carmen said, tired of standing in silence. "How are you?"

"Ah, Carmen, hello there. You know Dan Stephenson, right?" Carlyle said, motioning to his friend, who seemed to crouch back slightly. "He's edited comics all over the place. We go back quite a while."

"Yes, I know Mr. Stephenson," Carmen said coolly. "In fact, we spoke not long ago."

Stephenson averted Carmen's glare, but Carlyle noticed it immediately. Over the short time they'd worked together, they'd picked up on each other's habits and moods. He could tell she was pissed.

"Is that right?" Carlyle asked, giving Stephenson a sideways glance. "What about?"

Carmen knew she could have stopped there. Could've just pumped the brakes and made her day a little easier. But she wasn't built that way.

"Mr. Stephenson came by the office looking for you, boss," she said, one eyebrow raised slightly. "He seemed—well, a lot like now—more than tipsy. But definitely angrier than today. You were out, but he didn't seem to accept that."

Stephenson straightened up his shoulders and finally turned to face Carmen, his face contorting into a painful grimace Carmen would never forget.

"Now that's not fair, young lady," he said, his voice sounding hollow and husky. "We had a disagreement, that's all, I—"

"We didn't have a disagreement. My boss wasn't there, and you wouldn't leave. So I threatened to call the—"

Carlyle waved his arms, a referee breaking up two boxers refusing to let each other go.

"That's enough, all right? Enough," he said, trying to keep his voice light and playful but clearly frustrated. "Carmen, what brings you here? Looking for a new job?"

Carmen had to strain to stop herself from rolling her eyes.

"Just enjoying this whacky industry of ours," she said. "While it lasts."

"That's for sure," Stephenson spat. "Comics are dying. The stuff these people produce now—just overwritten garbage. You can't make a pulp into literature, you know? Just be who you are, accept your place. Right?"

Carmen felt her skin crawl as she looked at this disheveled lump of a man.

"Have a nice day," she said before walking away. She didn't try to decipher the words the two men muttered to each other as she walked off.

She wandered down the main aisle, tables and colorful displays on either side, but it all blurred together for Carmen. Whatever rush of inspiration she was hoping to find here—among comic book fans, readers, writers, artists—she had missed. She still felt outside. Someone who loved the medium, who wanted to join the chorus of talented people creating it, but still couldn't get a foot in the door. As much as she treasured the Lynx, the character she and Harvey had labored over, she had no claim to her. Aside from Detmer, no one knew the truth. Carmen also didn't know how anyone ever could. Would anyone believe her? Would her word stand up to Carlyle's? To the industry as it worked now?

She felt someone brush past her, shoulders bumping into each other. Carmen turned to look.

"Oh, hey," the woman said. She looked familiar, her long red hair framing a naturally expressive face. "How are you?"

It took Carmen a moment, but she recognized her. Marion Price. Harvey's old friend. From the volleyball game.

The relief she felt was unexpected but welcome. The sight of a friendly face, someone she'd at least spoken to before, softened the hard edges that she'd felt forming after the awkward exchange with Stephenson. It anchored her.

"Oh, hi, hey," Carmen said, trying to form a smile. "Good to see you."

"It's Marion," she said, patting Carmen's arm gently. "Carmen, right? Harvey's friend?"

Carmen nodded. The mention of Harvey sent a shock through her, making her feel momentarily off-balance.

"Hey, are you all right?" Marion asked. "I know Harvey was your friend, too, right?"

"Yeah . . ." Carmen trailed off, letting her eyes skim over the crowd of fans, pros, and everything in between. She felt so outside of this, despite everything. Would she ever feel like she belonged? Like she could talk about her work?

She felt someone tugging at her arm and turned to see Marion pulling her along.

"Hey, wait—"

"No, you're coming with me," Marion said, her expression playful. "You need to get out of here. I need a drink. Think we can find something to do that gives us both what we want?"

Carmen let herself be pulled away by Marion, out of the Commodore Hotel—and out of this fanciful, four-color world she so desperately wanted to be closer to, but still felt miles away from. The thick New York air crashed into her as they stepped outside, Marion smiling slyly as they walked down the street. She felt an electric charge between them as their eyes met—like the bolt of lightning that turned Billy Batson into Captain Marvel. Carmen looked back through the closing hotel entrance doors and thought for a moment about what she might miss, leaving like this—the names and faces she'd connect. But those worries seemed to fade the farther she wandered from the crumbling hotel.

CHAPTER TWENTY-TWO

They didn't walk far.

Marion made a beeline across the street, to a chipped, faded BAR sign that simultaneously screamed "dive" and "perfect" to Carmen.

They entered the dimly lit, nameless watering hole and almost immediately felt the gush of cool air that signaled an empty bar at midday. The hustle of Grand Central was gone, muted by the dark, secluded bubble they'd entered. The bartender nodded as they took two stools at one of the many empty square tables past the main bar. Carmen wasn't sure, but it'd sounded like she and Marion both sighed upon reaching the grimy seats and counter. They'd both wanted out of the convention, even if they hadn't realized it.

"Long day?" Carmen asked, trying to make some small talk. She realized she barely knew this woman—their only link was Harvey, and it was a tenuous one.

"Oh, it was fine," Marion said, rifling through her small purse. "I did my duty and manned the Warren table with Louise for an hour. Then

Jim set us free. Told me to 'network.' So I did for five minutes, but then I found you."

She looked up and gave Carmen a soft smile.

"You showed up at the right time."

"That's what they say," Carmen said, still trying to keep it light. Before she felt the need to say anything else, Marion was walking toward the bar.

"You a whiskey girl, or no?" she asked.

"A beer is fine," Carmen said.

Marion scoffed.

"C'mon, my treat—there are no smelly boys around. We don't have to pretend to be one of them here," she said, her arm motioning toward the empty bar that housed them. "It's just us badass bitches."

Carmen laughed, the sound rich with relief. Marion was right. This wasn't a continuation of the convention, or of their day jobs. She didn't know this woman, no—but she and Carmen had more in common than she did with most of the people at the Commodore, and that was worth something.

"Johnnie Walker Red on the rocks, if they have it."

Marion shook her head.

"I can't allow that," she said, reaching the bar, her back leaning against the long, chipped wood paneling. "Black Label or we're done here."

Carmen nodded, smiling.

"You're the boss."

Carmen watched as Marion ordered the drinks—the ease with which she carried herself; airy, light, no stress. Carmen felt a tickle of jealousy. She prided herself on being cool and aloof, keeping people at arm's length when it was required. But that was also a defense mechanism. A skill learned over years of compartmentalizing everything going on outside. If she didn't show what she was feeling, she didn't have to think about it. Even better—no one would ask.

Marion returned and slid Carmen's drink over to her. She took a short sip, feeling the liquid warm her mouth and throat. It felt good. She needed this, needed some kind of release from everything she'd been feeling and pondering the last few months. The Lynx, Harvey, her job, Katherine, her papi—if it wasn't one thing, it was the other, but it was always *something*. It was nice, if for just a moment, to sip a stiff drink with an attractive woman across from her. She felt like she was outside of herself.

"Isn't that better?"

Marion's question shook Carmen loose for a second, bringing her back to the bar.

"What?"

"The Black Label," Marion said, giving Carmen a quizzical glance.

"Oh, yeah, yes—much better," Carmen said, taking another sip. "Fuller, I guess. Is that the right word?"

"Oh, I dunno, I'm not a whiskey snob. Literature, comics, music, that's where I raise my nose," Marion said, looking down into her own glass. "But drinks? I'll have whatever you put in front of me. If I'm buying, though, I get the strong stuff. Comic book salaries don't go very far in New York."

"You're not from here, right?"

"No, I was born in San Fran," Marion said. "I moved out here a few years ago to work at Bulwark. I can't say I regret it, but it's certainly different."

"What do you mean?"

Marion leaned back in her chair, as if trying to get a better look at Carmen.

"I'm not a mainstream comics person, I guess. I think that makes me sound like a snob but I really don't give a shit," she said, smiling. "I made my bones putting together 'zines and writing and drawing comics about real stuff, like getting your period and dating, and the real world, you know? Kind of a poor woman's version of Trina Robbins, I guess? She's someone I really admire. But I'd write and draw real things—stuff that happens to real people, that I wake up and think about. Not male prepubescent fantasies—guys in tight underwear punching each other because they don't understand. I never liked those kinds of books. I still don't. At least at Warren we don't touch the cape stuff as much."

Carmen shrugged. She'd heard this before. Not in exactly the way Marion was saying it, but from others—people who looked down at comics, especially superhero ones. People who thought they rotted your brain or wasted your time. But for Carmen, it was the opposite. She'd learned to read English with Archie Andrews and Betty and Veronica, had come to appreciate the literary aspirations of Stan Lee's operatic Silver Surfer as a preteen, and marveled at the pseudoscience of the Flash's cosmic treadmill in high school. Comics were in her blood, and she didn't want it any other way.

"Did I offend you?" Marion asked.

"No, that's your take," Carmen said, running a finger over the edge of her glass. "I just don't share it. I mean, to me, it's about how you use the medium—"

"The 'medium'? Well, look at you," Marion said with a gruff laugh. "It's comics, girl. People crank these out like pizzas. You think anyone is trying to produce high art? The ones who are do it to bide their time before the real thing comes along."

Carmen bristled.

"It's not all crap, is my point. Look at Avatar, or what Harvey was doing with the Lynx . . ."

The mention of Harvey froze them both. After initially discussing him at the convention, they seemed to avoid mentioning him for fear of jinxing the potential of their own budding friendship. But now the lid was off.

"What was he doing with the Lynx?" Marion asked, her eyes probing, an expectant look on her face.

Carmen took a long pull of her drink. Her buzz was spreading, her entire head tingling in a way she rarely allowed herself.

"You warned me before . . . before he, uh, died," Carmen said. "At that volleyball game. What did you mean?"

Marion looked away for a moment, then turned to meet Carmen's gaze.

"I guess I did. Look, I like you," she said, reaching over and placing a hand on Carmen's arm. It felt warm. Familiar. "So I won't bullshit you. But I also don't have to tell you all my secrets, either."

Marion straightened up, and for a second Carmen thought she was going to stand up and walk out, but instead Marion stuck a hand in her purse and pulled out a pack of Parliaments. She offered the pack to Carmen, who took one.

Marion lit her cigarette and handed it to Carmen. She held the burning cigarette to her own. The pause in conversation had helped. Carmen felt more at ease. The cigarette helped, too.

"It's just not Harvey," Marion said, exhaling a cloud of smoke toward Carmen. "You know?"

Carmen didn't move or respond. The truth was, she didn't know. What she meant, or what she was getting at.

Marion motioned to the bartender for another round. He nodded and moved to the back of the bar. In what felt like an instant, their empty glasses were replaced. Carmen's head felt fuzzy. She could hold her liquor, but that was usually a handful of beers or some wine drunk over a long stretch. She wasn't a marathon bar drinker. Marion seemed like a cat on a blanket—comfortable, sleepy, and hungry.

"You're single, right? Don't have a steady guy?" Marion asked, narrowing her eyes as she looked at Carmen, as if she were trying to see through her. "Must be tough working at Triumph."

"Probably as tough as it is for you," Carmen said hastily—more bite in her words than she'd wanted, but unable to stop herself. "Right?"

She nodded.

"Most of the boys at Warren know to leave me alone," she said with a sly smile. "I bite."

Carmen waited a beat before speaking.

"I'm not sure what you're asking me," she said. The jukebox was playing something irritating—McCartney's "Band on the Run," the *neener-neener* guitar riff momentarily distracting her.

"I'm not asking you anything, baby," Marion said. "I'm just saying it must be tough for you. An attractive, smart, independent woman forced to work with a bunch of horny men who don't think they should have to struggle for anything they want. Isn't that Jeffrey Carlyle in a nutshell?"

"I know how to navigate it," Carmen said, nodding to herself. "You call them out on it early, then they learn their lesson. They learn to leave you alone."

"Right, but then you're the 'frigid bitch' or the 'conceited slut,'" Marion said. "Or worse. You become a pariah just because you don't want to hang out with your coworkers, or date them. It's a drag. I regret moving out here at least once a day. Usually after being stuck in an elevator with some dipshit from work."

"Why did you move out here?"

"I was doing a lot of cool stuff out West—this collective I was a part of, we were putting together these great, intense comics," Marion said before finishing off her drink and wincing slightly. "But I wasn't making any money. I was living with this guy and it was—I dunno, it was time to go. I was drinking too much, smoking too much weed, just numbing out. And that's not me. I like to be busy. To be creative. I'd met Harvey a few years back when I was visiting the city, and he called me—breathless, in that way he gets—well, got. So excited and enthusiastic. Said Bulwark needed an editor. I'd be his boss. Imagine hiring your own boss. How trippy is that? I never thought I'd be making comics people would actually read, much less drool over like they do with Vampirella. But I wanted to do something else."

Carmen knew the Harvey who Marion was describing too well. Her mind flashed back to the drunk man showing up at her door, his eyes wild with the ideas that would become part of the Lynx. Was that just who he was, or something he put on to get what he wanted?

"What was it like? Working at Bulwark?"

"It was a mess, a complete disaster," Marion said. She ordered another round.

Their third? Fourth? Carmen had lost count. The music had changed.

A few people had wandered in. She wasn't sure of the time. Her tongue felt thick and heavy. She wanted to get up and go to the bathroom, but the idea seemed so exhausting.

"The guy who ran the place was a complete mess," Marion said. "Used all of his savings to start his own publishing company. Before that, he'd worked as an editor at a bunch of places, and before then, he'd run a packaging company—like forever ago, when companies would farm out work to places like the Eisner studio. They'd get paid and have to produce X amount of pages and then they'd deliver them to National or Timely, and they'd print them. It was the way things worked, until the publishers just cut out the middle man. After he bounced around as an editor, people got burnt on his tastes. So he was left in the lurch. He had all these freelancers and knew how to make comics, but no one was buying his shit anymore and no one wanted to deal with him. So he decides to package, print, and sell it himself. Except no one taught him how to run a company—or do the things he didn't know firsthand. So, I get there, expecting to be a Band-Aid on a scrape—instead, I'm trying to salvage a submarine with a leaky bucket and a few napkins."

She stubbed out her cigarette on the table. Carmen caught a glimpse of the bartender shaking his head in frustration before Marion continued.

"It was bizarre. I mean, the editors were doing all the writing—not because we were good, but because we needed the money," she said. "We'd create these names, these pen names, and then we'd write under those names, but cash the checks for ourselves. Harvey knew it, too. He schooled me on it before I started. It seemed shaky, but I also needed some money. Moving from California to New York was expensive, even if you just swing over with a knapsack and a few bucks. A few days in, I knew the place was going under. So it became a springboard to finding another job and keeping my rent paid."

Something about what Marion said made Carmen's sloth-like synapses fire. Her eyelids fluttered.

"What did Harvey do?" Carmen asked. She wanted to know more, to ask a more thoughtful question, but the words wouldn't come. This caveman-speak was as good as it'd get. She needed some water. She needed to go home.

"Harvey?" Marion asked. "He was in on it like everyone else. He was trying to get his own career going. He knew the ship was sinking, so we were all turning in scripts like maniacs."

Carmen felt her vision widen, felt herself see the pieces floating in front of her—like a giant map of the world, the continents hovering around freely, but inching closer to forming something else. A bigger picture.

"Carmen?"

She looked up. Marion seemed concerned. Her hand on Carmen's arm again. Tighter now.

"You there, kiddo?"

"Yeah, sorry, brain drifting, I guess."

"You need another drink."

"No, no, I don't," Carmen said. She felt dizzy. She needed to go. But she also had a question. What was it? "I have—"

"Where do you live? I'll get you home. You're drunk."

"No, wait, what happened?"

"With what?"

"Bulwark," Carmen said, the word sounding thick and stunted, as if she were speaking with gobs of gauze in her mouth. "What happened?"

"It went under, before any of these scripts—these ideas—were printed," Marion said, as if everyone on the planet knew the answer. "No one bothered to tell us. One day the doors were locked."

"What about Harvey?"

Marion raised an eyebrow.

"Harvey, Harvey, Harvey," she said. "I get it. You miss him, too. But he was long gone by then. He'd been fired a few weeks before. I could never get a straight answer out of him."

Carmen didn't respond. She placed a foot on the floor, trying to center herself. To stop the bar from spinning. How many rounds had they had?

"Enough of that—what about you?" Marion said, ignoring Carmen's disorientation. Or was she drunk, too? "It was clear he was pining for you."

"Who?" Carmen asked, able to focus her mind on Marion for a second before shifting back, trying to retain her balance. "Harvey?"

"Yes, though he was so focused on his career—or making a career in comics—I'm surprised he ever had time for someone else," Marion said, looking down at her lap. "He was always looking for a way up, you know? To climb that ladder, get that shot. I didn't have the heart to tell him there was no shot. Comics are a dead end."

Carmen watched as Marion's expression changed, from the jovial, free-spirited woman knocking back whiskeys to something else, something haunted and sad. Almost as if she were changing shape before her eyes.

"I have to go," Carmen said, lurching out of her seat. She shoved her hand into her purse and slapped a few bills on the table before turning toward the exit. Marion grabbed her arm. Carmen leaned into her, their faces close.

"Don't leave," she said. "We just got here."

Carmen could smell the whiskey on her breath, blending with her sharp perfume. She saw the tired look in her eyes—a look of defeat. Of a lot of nights like this, nights that started with such potential only to end up alone in a shitty bar.

Marion leaned in. Carmen turned her face in time, feeling Marion's lips slide across her cheek.

"I have to go," Carmen said again, stepping back, feeling the cobwebs fade away—at least for the moment. "See you around."

She didn't look back. She didn't hear the brief plea for her to stay, for just one more round.

The evening air was brisk and sharp, chipping at Carmen as she stepped out of the bar. She half expected Marion to come outside. To plead with her to stay. To make her stay. It made Carmen pick up her pace, the buildings and people whizzing by her, blurs she could only navigate on instinct, the whiskey churning inside her.

She had wanted to kiss her. She knew that much. Had wanted to feel her mouth on hers and think back to a time when that was easy and normal. Or easier than now. To Katherine and dark booths in Miami bars, hands clenched under tables and long, lingering kisses when they thought no one was looking—only to realize everyone was. Even to the string of cheap, barren airport hotel rooms that marked the last, chaotic gasp of whatever they'd had together.

Carmen shook the memories away as she stumbled down the 6 train station steps, her hand sliding along the grimy wall for balance. She felt an energy charging through her—a desire she'd pushed down and ignored because it'd only brought her pain and anguish in Miami. Anger. The energy felt good. Powerful. Like she was sifting through piles of sand and finally getting to something solid—to herself. But this feeling came with a price.

Old memories that stung as much today as when they'd just occurred.

"You don't know what it's like, all right?" Katherine had said, sitting in her beat-up car, her eyes red and wet from another argument, her hands clutching the steering wheel. "I can't just do what I want, okay? I can't just meet you for dinner, or hang out with you whenever you want, okay? I have obligations. I have a family."

A family.

Carmen remembered hating herself in that moment. Hating the way her stomach twisted, her body finally realizing something her brain had concluded weeks before.

It hadn't just been that Katherine was married. Carmen knew that. It wasn't just that Nick was around and existed in a space Carmen couldn't occupy. That was normal, as far as these things went—these *affairs.* These illicit encounters. No. There was something else. Someone else. A child. She had a child.

The roar of the subway seemed to shake Carmen awake, her feet moving on autopilot as she tried to navigate the station, her mind paralyzed by memories long buried.

Carmen felt her shoulder brush up against a tall man, heard him mutter something low and offensive as she stumbled into the subway car. Heard the familiar *ding* as the doors closed behind her. Carmen flopped into the seat, tried not to get too comfortable, tried to stay awake. She had to get home.

Her head made contact with the seat as she leaned back. The low *thump* sound felt familiar, and triggered something else. Another memory. Another piece of her Carmen wanted obliterated forever. But this time, the sound persisted—and she was gone again.

Thump.

Thump.

Thump.

The slapping sound, the pounding sound of Katherine's fist on the dashboard, over and over. The car shuddering with every second of contact. The look on her face—pure rage, tears of anger and hate, makeup that had been smeared by kisses now adding a clown-like gloss to her manic expression.

"You have a kid?"

The question had come out, and it should've come out sooner—but now Carmen felt bad, ashamed for having asked it, for having disrupted what had been a perfectly nice night between them. A pleasant night after so many awkward and stilted ones, still an improvement over that aborted dinner at Versailles. They'd been building back to something, Carmen had felt, but that was gone. It was gone. All that remained was Katherine's fist, slamming into the dash. *Thump-thump-thump.*

"You bitch, you fucking bitch," she'd said, as much to Carmen as to herself. "How could you ask me that? How could you make me choose?"

It'd all seemed to click together that night. The night Carmen had to walk home from the bar, unable to hail a cab. The night she had to step out of Katherine's car because she refused to listen to anything Carmen said. The strange pills in Katherine's purse when Carmen would rifle through it for a cigarette. How she'd always be two drinks ahead no matter how quickly Carmen knocked them back. The terse phone calls that'd happen once or twice every time they were out—from restaurant or bar pay phones.

"I'm on my way. . . . Yes, I understand what this is like for you. . . . No, no. You know I don't want it to go there. . . . Don't do that. Don't do that. Do not put him on the phone. . . . Please, Nick, come on. It is not like that. I have to work."

Thump-thump-thump.

"Why?" Katherine had wailed, her eyes closed, her forehead on the steering wheel now. Her knuckles red and limp on her lap. "Why can't you just let it be? Isn't this enough? Isn't it enough that you do whatever you want? See whoever you want?"

The intimation—that it was not Katherine who was cheating on her spouse, but Carmen being unfaithful to Katherine—would've made any rational person laugh cynically. But for Carmen, in that twisted, obsessive state she found herself in, walking down Bird Road from Coral Gables to Westchester, it crushed her. It was proof that the chasm between them had been much larger than she could even imagine. Possibly too large for her to ever traverse.

That's what had broken her. She remembered leaning over, the bile and vomit rushing out of her mouth on the side of the road. The hot liquid slapping the concrete and splattering around her feet.

She hadn't been drunk. But she was sick. She was torn. This was not the person she thought she should be, Carmen had realized. *But we drift away from those ideals as time goes on,* she'd thought. *And the more we drift, the more we rationalize. The more we rationalize, the less of ourselves remains.*

Her vision came back into focus. She wasn't dizzily wandering Miami. She was in New York—and she was very drunk. She rubbed her eyes with the palms of her hands and tried to propel herself forward. Away from the past. It'd worked so well before. Why not now?

Carmen felt for her keys and heard them drop at her feet, clattering on the floor of the vestibule of her New York apartment. She'd made it. She always made it, she thought. She could take care of herself. No matter what anyone said. No matter whom she upset. She was a survivor. She didn't need help.

She slid the key into the lock and felt back to a time her hand had been in the same position, outside of her home in Miami, tears streaming down her face, her feet blistered and sore, her entire body shaking with a potent mix of rage, shame, and love.

She had known her mother was on the other side. She'd known she'd tell her what happened. What had been happening. And she'd also known nothing would ever be the same. Like the last page of a cliff-hanger—the Red Skull, Captain America's Nazi war criminal arch-foe, wielding the nigh-omnipotent Cosmic Cube and switching places with the patriotic hero. How could our hero win, trapped in the body of his worst enemy?

Carmen saw the figure the second she stepped into her apartment and it just seemed too perfect. Like the past and the present had schemed to concoct an event so powerful, so intoxicating, even Carmen could not resist. The figure turned to face Carmen as she approached. Sheepish. Hesitant. Beautiful and alive, like Carmen had willed her into being here in New York, away from Miami and away from everything that had come before.

Katherine noticed Carmen step toward her, and that smile appeared on her face—replacing the fear and anxiety that had seemed etched into her being.

"I left him, Carm," she whispered, each word growing quieter as Carmen approached, as Carmen wrapped her arms around her.

Carmen kissed her then, and it felt as if nothing had changed, as if the idealized version of them—this pair they'd both fantasized about and tried to will into existence—had returned. It felt natural and good and comforting, pushing away the hot stench of the city and Carmen's own fears and regrets. All that remained was this woman, this woman she'd hated and feared and at times loved, who was waiting for her like a gift from the gods, a woman of wonder sent down to scuffle in Man's World.

Carmen leaned her head back and gave Katherine a closer look, her fingers gently running down the sides of her face, as if trying to confirm she was real. That this was happening. Then she kissed her again.

"I left him," Katherine said.

CHAPTER TWENTY-THREE

Carlyle's bellow—low and hoarse—sliced through his closed office door.

"Carmen? Carmen? Get in here, please."

Each syllable seemed to mirror the pounding in Carmen's skull, the dirty, lingering hangover still sticking to her like bubblegum on the bottom of her shoe—even a few hours into the workday. She wasn't used to this. She was used to being in control. To having a few drinks, getting home, chugging water, and getting to bed early. Pacing herself. She was definitely not accustomed to getting shit-faced, stumbling home, then stumbling further—into bed with the last woman she'd loved. A mistake, for sure. How bad was still to be determined.

Carmen groaned as she got to her feet and moved toward Carlyle's office.

He was standing in his doorway, his face reddening more by the second, his left hand clutching the doorknob.

This was bad. He couldn't even wait for her to get inside.

"Everything okay, boss?" Carmen managed as she stepped into his office, Carlyle's door clicking shut behind them.

He didn't respond until he got behind his desk, hands clenched into fists.

"He quit."

Carmen started to open her mouth to respond, but Carlyle beat her to it.

"That egomaniacal washout Detmer, he quit. Out of the blue. He gave no reason. No explanation. He just came by, it must have been first thing this morning, before I got in and dropped off his last issue," Carlyle said, motioning toward a stack of fresh Detmer Lynx pages. Carmen fought the urge to let her eyes linger over them—she would appreciate his draftsmanship another time. "He had the gall to affix a note, too—'I QUIT.' That's it. Nothing else, no 'Thanks for the opportunity,' nothing. That's what I get, you see? That's what I get for propping up that sloppy drunk, that lush, for years. Keeping him alive when no one would touch him."

"I'm sorry, I—"

Carlyle acted as if Carmen wasn't even in the room. He had to rant. He had to vent this anger or it'd consume him.

"After all I've done for him," he said, shaking his head. "No one would touch him. He was toxic. He came to me hat in hand, begging for work. Now he's too good for Triumph? How soon people forget."

"Maybe we should pause the series," Carmen said, her voice picking up speed. The hangover had given her some kind of drunken bravery she didn't normally have, like a new twist on her existing powers. Maybe she could flip this to her advantage, she thought. "Maybe it's moving too fast? Bringing in Jensen, now a new artist—it's too much."

Carlyle waved a hand in her direction.

"Carmen, do you think I survived this long by sitting around panicked and desperate? Haven't you learned anything? You don't just pause a series—that's not an option," Carlyle said, turning his seat to look up at Carmen. "I made the call thirty-five minutes ago."

Carmen felt her stomach lurch.

"The call?"

"Yes, to Steve Tinsler," Carlyle said, leaning back in his seat, resting his head on his hands. "He knows Jensen. They did some war books at DC. Before that, I think he did a few issues of *Teen Titans* and some of the Quality characters. He's good and fast."

"He's definitely fast," Carmen said, not biting her tongue.

"What would you suggest, my dear?" Carlyle said. He seemed genuinely curious. As if he'd just won a big bet and was intrigued by what might happen if he rolled the dice again.

"Jensen's a hack. Tinsler's a hack. You've gone from a book that has personality—charm, even—and turned it into something you can get anywhere, boss. *The Lynx* is special. It has a voice. People read it because it's different, quirky, strange. Detmer's art is miles above Tinsler. Detmer's an artist who other artists drool over. If he had his shit together, people would say his name in the same breath as Toth or Cole or Wood, or hell, even Kirby," Carmen said. She could feel her skin growing hot, the last vestiges of the hangover sweating themselves away as she spoke. "Harvey's story was important, too. It wasn't just a punch-'em-up. We cared about Claudia Calla. We cared about her struggles and her reason for putting on the costume. It was a love letter to characters like Spider-Man, Daredevil, Batman—but different. It feels present, like, I dunno, what might really happen. To hand that book—our best book—to Jensen and Tinsler? It just feels so . . . I don't know, it just feels cheap."

Carlyle smiled. A humorless, annoyed smile. Carmen knew she'd overstepped. She just wasn't sure where. Her pounding headache and clammy palms made figuring that out impossible. But somewhere along the road, she'd veered off, and that's where she'd lost Carlyle, who was looking for a polite challenge, not a complete insult to his being.

"Let me tell you something, Carmen, and I'm going to be as honest with you as you just were with me," Carlyle said. He was standing up now, taking a few steps toward her. "Comics are cheap. They're disposable and fleeting. Comics are about primal entertainment. They are for the masses. They're for the kids that buy their candy at the pharmacy and want something to read on their way to the playground. Can they be high art? No. They just can't. They're beneath that. The intellectual charge you get from reading the greats is a feeling no stapled stack of crude drawings can ever, ever match. But can we try? Certainly. So, I think you're also underestimating what we, what Triumph, can do here. We're granting Jensen and Tinsler a grand opportunity to reach the masses. A chance to drive our best car. A chance to—with some guidance, with some help from me, from us—to elevate comics to something else. I like to think I'm not risk-averse. I let Maynard do his thing on *Avatar*.

"I gave Stern a shot here, on the Lynx. I hired you, with no experience, to be my right hand. I savor those opportunities—to cater to the people but still hit the right notes and appeal to another audience, too. But things aren't always that wide open.

"We're in a bind here, Carmen. Harvey is dead. Doug Detmer quit. All I can do is, by sheer will, impose some sort of style and quality on what's left of this book. But it needs to be done. We can't miss a deadline. I need someone to create the template. Otherwise, we'll just be sitting around this office, wondering for weeks who might be just perfect to take over.

"And by then, my dear? The world will have passed us by. Comics—hit comics—are ephemeral. Comics as a whole might be, too. You don't think I see it? You don't think I'm preparing for the day our distributor shuts down, or Marvel or DC get into a bidding war over paper and we're left in the lurch? I am ready to pivot to the next thing. The real thing. By then, who'll care about who was the right person for *The Legendary Lynx*?

"I agree with you, in theory. We should strive to tell better stories. Reach to make sure the people reading these books have their vegetables along with dessert. But not at any cost. It's comics, for chrissakes. The Lynx is a headache now. More problematic than energizing. I need bodies. I need people to do the work so we can patch it up while the train is on the tracks. Otherwise, what's the point? Otherwise, we might all be begging Jim Warren or Carmine Infantino or Chip Goodman or even Len Wein for a job in a few months. And you know what? They'll say no. And that'll be that."

Carmen took a few steps back.

"Get Tinsler on the phone for me. I want to lock down his rate and get him Jensen's first script," Carlyle said. The heat and rage was gone, replaced by a steely resolve. He was back to business. This was how they worked. They flared up at each other and came to some impasse. Except this time, Carlyle wasn't giving any ground. Carmen *had* shamed him, she thought.

"How's the script?" she asked.

Carmen understood her role. She wasn't an editor. Maybe someday, if Carlyle's grand design was enacted, but not now. But still—he'd never passed a script along to editorial, much less to a freelancer, without running it by her. He was more upset than she'd first thought.

"Get Tinsler on the phone," Carlyle said, returning to his seat.

He didn't look up as Carmen walked out of his office.

She sat down at her desk, the hangover haze fading. She felt shaken. No longer dizzy with the remnants of her drunken night, of her time with Katherine, or anything else. Carmen let her memory dance around the blurred details of the night before. Both of them half walking, half falling into her apartment, locked in each other. Leading her toward the bed. The lights being flicked off. The sudden jolt of awareness, hours later, that Molly would be home soon. Rushed dressing and repositioning of things they'd knocked over. Hurried kisses goodbye and empty promises to talk later. Had this been another time, in Miami—she'd be replaying these moments over and over, desperate to catch any missed detail, analyzing each frame of mental film for signs and meaning. But now? She just felt empty, a worn-out husk at her desk with no real idea of what to do next except sit and watch the mess she'd just made.

Steve Tinsler's art was almost raunchy and definitely crude—like a teenage boy's dirty drawings, the ones his parents would find under his bed. There was no craft to it. No nuance. The subtleties and texture that Detmer had infused into the series would harden and shatter within a page or two under Tinsler and Jensen's watch. The Lynx was as good as dead.

Jensen and Tinsler were quite the pair, she thought, as she looked through her files to track down the artist's number. They were both hacks who'd outlived their value with most companies, but still managed to find work at Triumph. A disheartening trend if there ever was one, Carmen thought.

She started to dial Tinsler's number and stopped herself. She noticed her hand was shaking. She felt her eyes begin to water. Carmen looked around, but no one was looking back. The bustle of the office continued apace; whatever distraction Carlyle's closed-door tirade caused had since faded. Everyone was in their own routine—Mullin sped across the office, a stack of script pages in his hand. Trunick leaned back in his chair, on the phone with a freelancer. Carmen saw Hahn near the back, scouring the old bound volumes to find a story to reprint and fill a gap of pages. No one knew what Carmen knew, or what she was thinking. No one would know if she just sat back and let Tinsler and Jensen pick up where Harvey and Detmer—and she—had left off.

She hung up the phone and started dialing again. A different number this time.

Doug Detmer's line rang and rang. No one picked up. It took her a second to notice the figure approaching her desk. The same figure she'd threatened with police action the last time he'd entered the Triumph offices.

Dan Stephenson smiled, his furry eyebrows obscuring his eyes. At least he seemed sober, she thought as she hung up the phone.

"Mr. Stephenson," Carmen said, looking up at him. "Can I help you? Mr. Carlyle's in a meeting."

"Oh, I know," Stephenson said, still smiling. "I thought he'd updated you."

"Updated me?"

"Oh, yes, about my new role," Stephenson said. Still with that stupid, knowing smile. "Maybe you should check with him?"

Had this been a normal day, she would've sent Stephenson to hell. She didn't have the luxury for games most of the time. Today, though, she felt off-balance. Her hangover didn't pair well with the conversation she'd had with Carlyle. Nothing felt secure.

She heard his door swing open.

"Dan, great, great, you made it," Carlyle said, looking at his watch. He turned to Carmen. "You know Stephenson, right, Carmen?"

"I do," Carmen said. "We talked about this yesterd—"

"Right, okay, well, he's joining our team," Carlyle said. "We're short-handed with Harvey eh, well, gone—so Stephenson will be working with Berger on his books. He's been all over and needed a break. Never say I don't have a heart. Help him get settled."

Carmen's mouth opened. She couldn't control it. Was this really happening? She flashed back to a day before—to seeing Carlyle and Stephenson huddled at the Comic Art event. Had they been plotting this?

"Joining the—"

"I leave you in her capable hands," Carlyle said, swiveling around and heading back into his office.

Carmen turned to Stephenson.

"Welcome to Triumph," Carmen said, the monotone clear. "I'll take you over to Rich."

"You don't seem happy."

"You don't know how I seem," Carmen said as she stood up to face Stephenson. "Follow me."

Stephenson did just that.

As they reached Harvey's old desk, Carmen could feel the staff's eyes on her and Stephenson. The disruption had shushed the floor, the only sound coming from Rich Berger's office as he yelled into his phone. Carmen could already guess what he was going on about. Not only had Carlyle force-fed him Mark Jensen as the new writer on *The Legendary Lynx*, but Tinsler and now Stephenson. None were ideas Carlyle had sought Berger's counsel on.

She grabbed a small box and started putting Harvey's few remaining belongings away. Hudson had let Carlyle know the police were done going over his work space, so Carmen felt comfortable storing what was left. It was mostly out-of-date page proofs, scrawled notes to himself about deadlines and whom to call, and a collection of office supplies that would put a storage closet to shame. But as she cleared most of the stuff off his desk, she noticed something else—something that had been buried and not easily visible.

The notebook was unremarkable, but something had caught Carmen's eye. Perhaps it was its size—small, dark blue, worn out, and bent. It had been used. And used regularly. It'd also been tucked away, buried under papers, as if Harvey wanted to be the only one who could reach it. Or was she just projecting?

She snatched the notebook and tossed it into the box.

"Feel free to grab some supplies from the closet down the hall to the right," Carmen said, not bothering to point, or to even look at Stephenson. "I'm sure Rich Berger, your supervisor, will be in touch shortly."

Stephenson scoffed.

"Berger? No, no," he said. "I'm flying solo here. I only report to Jeffrey."

"Is that right?" Carmen said, turning her gaze toward him.

"Yes, that was part of the deal," Stephenson said, taking Harvey's seat and doing his best to get comfortable. "Is that a problem?"

"Oh, not for me," Carmen said, turning around and walking the box back to her desk. She heard Stephenson say something but ignored it. She was done with him.

Before she could get to her desk, she was intercepted by Berger, who looked bedraggled and on edge.

"What in the world is going on?" he hissed, trying to keep his voice down, just a few feet from Carlyle's open office door. "What is he doing here?"

"Stephenson?" Carmen said, feigning ignorance. "Why, he's our newest editor. But he only reports to the boss."

Berger shook his head, then started rubbing his temples. Carmen worried the man might explode right in front of her.

"I don't understand what this guy has on him," Berger said.

"Hmm?" Carmen asked.

"I just—what kind of qualifications does he have? To be worth the hire? It's not like we're flush," Berger said, looking at Carlyle's office.

"Last time I spoke to him, we weren't even filling Harvey's slot. To save. To get by 'hard times.' Now we're hiring a has-been editor? His last publisher folded."

"Bulwark?" Carmen asked.

"Right, it was an utter disaster," Berger said. He seemed distracted now. "I gotta talk to Jeffrey. I'll see you later. Swing by, I have another book for you."

Before Carmen could say anything else, Berger had disappeared into Carlyle's office, the door slamming behind him.

She placed the box on her desk and pulled out the small notebook. She slid it into her purse and made a mental note to skim it when she was alone.

"You coming by later?"

Carmen turned around. It was Trunick, one of the younger editors.

"Coming by?"

"Yeah, we're all hitting up Tommy's," Trunick said. "Think the staff needs to blow off some steam. Been a long week."

"Been a long year."

Trunick laughed.

"What time?" Carmen asked. The idea of heading back to her apartment—to answer Molly's probing questions or, worse, to find Katherine popping by—did not appeal to her.

"Right after five," Trunick said. "Think most of production's going."

"Even the new guy?"

Trunick shrugged. He was the epitome of a nice guy, all Midwestern charm and innocence. She'd expect no less from him.

"See you there."

Tommy Makem's was a dive on Park near the Marvel Comics offices. To anyone else, Tommy's would appear to be your run-of-the-mill Irish pub—the muted green-and-brown décor, the smell of Guinness and fried foods, and an obscure Dubliners track on in the background. But it meant a lot more to Carmen and others trying to climb the precarious comic

book industry ladder. It was a meeting point, not just for the freelancers and editors swapping stories and angling for work at Marvel, but for
everyone else—people from DC, Warren, and what was left of Atlas/
Seaboard, the company started by Marvel founder Martin Goodman and
his apparently less-talented son, Chip, who was shown the door when the
title of publisher was passed on to Stan Lee.

Carmen liked the vibe well enough, but, even more, she liked the idea
of being part of something bigger—and when she was at Tommy's she
felt like she was a writer toiling away in the same mines as the rest of
them. She liked the idea that maybe, just maybe, she was part of something vibrant and creative. An art form.

At the moment, it was far from full. She scanned the sparsely popu-
lated bar and caught a few familiar faces beyond the huddle of Triumph
employees sitting near her. Artist Bob Brown sharing a laugh with his
Daredevil creative partner, writer Marv Wolfman. She thought she saw
writer and Marvel editor Archie Goodwin sliding money across the bar,
but couldn't be sure.

"No booze tonight, Valdez?" the dark-haired production assistant,
Mullin, asked as he returned to the small table, a tall glass of dark beer
in hand.

"Taking it easy," Carmen said, sipping her water.

She was sitting at a high-top table, surrounded by the younger tier of
the production department. Dreamers—like her—who saw working at
Triumph as a foot in the door to the medium they loved. She wondered
how jaded they'd become over their time at the company. Trunick was to
her left and Hahn, slightly older and somewhat shy, to her right. This trio,
along with Harvey, had made up the company's future, she thought. The
staffers who, if given the chance, might've been able to steer Triumph away
from the impending industry crash.

"Hey, what's your take on the new guy, Stephenson?" Trunick asked
before polishing off his beer. "He seems, I dunno—how do I say it?"

"Like an asshole?" Carmen said.

The table laughed, drawing attention from some of the surrounding

seats. Stephenson was sitting off to the side, with Berger the closest colleague to him, but not necessarily sitting *with* him. Just a few hours in
and he'd already managed to make himself a pariah.

"You got that right," Hahn said under his breath. "I can't believe
that's the new Harvey."

"There is no 'new Harvey,'" Carmen said, surprising herself with the
bite of her reply. Hahn seemed taken aback.

"Sorry, I just—I'm still dealing with the whole thing," Carmen said.
The trio nodded. They were all dealing with it, too—in their own ways.

"I'm just bummed about the *Lynx,* you know? That book was so
damn good," Mullin said. "I've been hearing some crazy shit about who's
taking over."

The young editors turned to Carmen. It was no secret that the best
way to any good intel was through the boss's secretary. But Carmen wasn't
a novice. She wasn't going to feed the gossip mill if she could help it.

"C'mon, boys, you know I can't talk about that," she said, wiping
some condensation from her glass. "I'm a vault."

"Yeah, I know, but—that book was so good," Mullin said. "So good,"
he repeated, drawing out the word in an almost comedic way. "I didn't
know Harvey had that in him."

"It's something, all right."

Carmen and her tablemates turned to see Stephenson, dragging his
own chair a few inches toward them. She felt her face flush red. Had he
heard them before?

"What is?" Hahn asked, his low, whispery voice almost lost in the
hazy noise of the bar.

"The *Lynx,*" Stephenson said, dabbing some seltzer on a medium-sized
ketchup stain on his dress shirt. "I mean, I can see why you're impressed. It's
not like anything Triumph's done. But, let's not act like Mr. Stern forged
anything, well, new."

Carmen bristled. She started to respond, but then caught a glimpse
of Stephenson, his eyes wide and hungry, as if he wanted this moment
exactly. A debate. A chance to show his fangs.

Trunick beat her to it.

"What's your point?" Trunick asked. "What didn't you like about it?"

Stephenson squirmed a bit in his seat before lifting his chin toward Trunick, his eyes distant from drink and grease. He did not look well, Carmen thought. The glaze on his splotchy skin looked unhealthy and slimy.

"My point, young man, is that the Lynx is cute, but not compelling," Stephenson said. "She's not going to save this company or save comics. She's too quiet. Fans don't want complexity—they want action, they want suspense, they want color, sex appeal. Not gravitas or deep thinking."

He cleared his throat.

"Now, don't get me wrong—Harvey was a fine person, a fine writer, and of course, pairing him with Doug Detmer was a stroke of genius," Stephenson said, talking faster now, sounding almost out of breath. "But it didn't add up. I'd just finish each issue and ask myself, 'Who cares?' They just lacked the pizzazz of good storytelling."

Carmen couldn't bite her tongue any longer.

"Is that so?" she said. "Like what? She didn't have cool powers? She didn't look sexy enough? Her tits were too small? You just weren't turned on enough as you flipped through the pages?"

Stephenson seemed surprised by the attack. He'd underestimated her.

"Ah, you're a reader, *Ms.* Valdez," he said, a toothy grin appearing on his face.

"You're the one who slithered toward us," she said, immediately regretting her words. She was angry. She hated getting angry. She wanted to be calculating Bruce Banner, not his green-skinned alter ego. But it was too late now. "We were having a perfectly fine—"

"Isn't this a work soiree? A chance for me to meet my colleagues? Instead, I'm feeling alienated and disliked, on my first day, no less," Stephenson said, a faux pout in his voice. "Just for sharing my opinion on Stern's mediocre—well, let me rephrase that—unoriginal stories."

"Unoriginal?" Carmen asked.

Trunick had left the table for another beer and Mullin had wandered toward the bathroom, leaving Hahn as the only witness to the increasingly testy exchange.

"You heard me," Stephenson said, standing up shakily. "Stern was a nice boy, but not exactly a thinker. Or a new voice. I've read those stories before."

He clasped the edge of Carmen's table, leaning in slowly. She could smell his stale cologne, the fried food he'd been shoveling into his maw blending with cheap whiskey and grungy, dank body odor. She didn't hide her disgust.

"I'll be going now, it's past my bedtime," he said, his smile turning into a lascivious sneer. "It'd be nice to have someone warm to tuck me in, though."

She only realized her heel had slammed into Stephenson's shoe when he groaned in surprise and anguish, his body bending forward as his hand still clutched the table. She heard Hahn's sharp intake of breath.

"You little b—"

Carmen didn't wait to hear more, shoving past Stephenson, her purse slung over her shoulder. She heard Hahn blurt out, "Holy shit!" as she darted by, the handful of coworkers still at the bar watching her leave.

She stepped outside, her fists clenched. She could feel her fingernails burying themselves in her palms. She looked down at her hands, red marks slicing down her pale skin.

CHAPTER TWENTY-FOUR

She waited until she was a block down East Fifty-Seventh Street before she opened her purse and pulled out Harvey's tiny notebook.

Every page had something on it—a scribbled note, a half-complete grocery list (*Milk, beer, cold cuts, deodorant*), some vague reminders (*Talk to JC about the project* or *Check in with $$*), or a directive Carmen figured only Harvey would understand (*Borrow the good stuff only!!!*). But it wasn't what Harvey wrote that spurred Carmen to action—it was what actually fell out while she was flipping through the notebook's pages.

Under normal circumstances, Carmen would have missed it—but everything relating to Harvey now was loaded with meaning, fraught with potential. So the ticket stub was more than just a slip of paper. She turned it over to see stacked, blocky letters, the venue—CBGB—printed above the handful of band names. Television and Patti Smith. Carmen remembered this show. Well, she remembered missing it. Harvey had invited her, and Carmen had begged off, only to later hear Molly raving about this woman—this "musical poet"—who made a lasting impression on the landscape that night, as part of a longer, chaotic residency. It'd also been the last night Richard Hell played with Television before quitting. March 23. CBGB had only been open a few years, from what Molly had told Carmen, but it had quickly become the spot for bands to play in the East Village. Once the Mercer Arts Center had closed in '73, bands had nowhere to go if they were playing new songs. Enter Hilly Kristal's bar. Had Harvey been there? A week before he was murdered? Could the venue provide some kind of clue to what happened to him, almost three months later?

She doubted it, but it was the only lead she had. She turned left on Lexington Avenue, the wrinkled ticket stub still folded in her hand. She found a pay phone a block down. She dialed the number fast.

"Hey," she asked, out of breath. "You have plans tonight?"

Carmen felt Molly gripping her hand as they walked toward the entrance of CBGB, the off-white awning with its crooked red letters beckoning to them. She could feel the bass pulsing out from the tiny stage even before they handed the doorman their admission. Molly smiled knowingly at the shaggy, scraggly college student manning the door. A moment later, they were in another world. A world of grime and sweat. Of faded, beige walls and cheap drinks paired with menacing stares and a kinetic, untapped energy. Carmen felt like they'd cut through a thick cloud of smoke; the smell of cigarettes, spilled beer, and dirt blended together to form something intoxicating and exciting. Something new. The throng of bodies, people moving in different directions, shouting, laughing, kissing, arguing, seemed to be its own massive organism, unlike anything Carmen had ever seen. Carmen felt like an invasive virus, trying to weave her way farther into an unknown black void.

Carmen thought she heard the lead singer of the band—Talking Heads, according to the flyer—singing in French, but she was sure she'd been mistaken. They were opening for a band Carmen did know, the Ramones, a dour-looking Queens quartet that blasted through their three-chord tunes with an abandon and enthusiasm she'd never experienced before. But watching this trio now, she felt like she was on another planet. The lead singer was tall, gangly, and awkward, shifting jerkily, his wrist pivoting over the strings on his guitar. His complete opposite sat behind the drums, a jocular, almost gleeful expression on his face as he kept a constant, driving beat that supported the song but didn't overpower it. No, the engine was standing in front of him in a tiny, pristine package. The woman's dirty blond hair was in a boyish cut, but there was no doubting the band had a lady bass player—and she could carry the bottom as well as anyone Carmen had ever heard.

"She's good, right?" Molly whispered to Carmen, her breath hot next to Carmen's ear.

Carmen turned to face her roommate.

"Yeah, they're weird—but it's cool," she said, looking back at the band, their view obscured by the rowdy crowd revving up for the Ramones.

"I feel less alone now," Molly said. "It's tough to play here—to play in front of dudes, next to dudes. Just trying to hold your own when everyone, from the people watching you play and sing to the guys in your own damn band, just want to rip you apart, you know?"

Carmen did know, sort of. She didn't want to know.

"Magna Carta played here?"

Carmen, of course, had seen them plenty of times in various living rooms, dive bars, and basement "showcases," but never at CBGB.

"No, but we're trying," Molly said, scanning the cramped, sweat-and-beer-soaked room, the throb of the music keeping everything in the club vibrating at its own frequency. "You said your friend was here before he got shot?"

Molly's words sent a jolt through Carmen. The blunt delivery—"He got shot"—was jarring, a reminder that she wasn't just here to pick up some gossip about her friend, but to actually try to piece together what ended his life. But why? she wondered. Because she cared for Harvey? She did, somewhat. He was a good person. Helpful. Kind. But was she doing this because she wanted to figure out how to clue Carlyle in on the truth about the Lynx? Did she think that answer was somewhere in the wrinkles of what happened to Harvey? She wasn't sure. She might never be sure.

"Carm, did you forget why you're here?"

Carmen turned to Molly and gave her a distant smile.

"No, sorry—I just got lost for a second," she said. "But yeah, he came here—he saw Patti Smith."

"Right—in March," Molly said, nodding to herself as she stared at the band onstage. She was looking at them in a different way. In a way Carmen couldn't. Catching guitar chord changes, drum rhythms, and musical synergy. She was scoping out her competition. Trying to figure out what they had that Magna Carta didn't yet.

"That was one of her first gigs, too," Molly said. "She was amazing."

Carmen watched Molly, her face expressing every droplet of emotion— the excitement in her eyes, the slight smile as she described Smith's debut. She had to fight back an urge to hug this weird, quirky woman.

Molly raised a hand quickly—pointing toward the bar.

"See that guy? With the beard?"

"Yeah," Carmen said, following Molly's gaze. "Scruffy looking?"

"That doesn't narrow it down, Carm, but yeah—curly hair?" Molly said. "That's Hilly. He's the owner and manager. If anyone here knows anything, it's him."

Molly grabbed Carmen's hand and led her through the crowd, her fingers interlacing with Carmen's as they wove between the dancing and gesticulating throngs of people. Elbows, shoulders, and knees jabbing and bumping into them as they tried to navigate their way past.

Carmen felt coated in grime, but didn't mind—the music the band was making, jerky, rhythmic, and cerebral, seemed to propel her and everyone in the small bar into each other. It was a release, and she'd desperately needed something like this—a chance to cut loose and just feel what was happening around her. By the time they got to the bar on the other side of the venue, she was swaying to the music, not an ounce of alcohol in her system.

"Hilly, hey, it's me, Molly," Molly said, waving down the older man.

He noticed her and began a slow approach. Molly leaned back to talk-prep Carmen. "Let me talk to him, okay? He knows me."

"Sure," Carmen said.

"Molls, how are you?" the man named Hilly said, his voice low and gruff. Carmen could smell the faint scent of beer on his breath. "Who's your friend?"

"This is Carmen," Molly said, pointing a thumb over her shoulder at her roommate. "Had a few questions for you, if you got a minute?"

"Look, Molly, I like you—I like your band, too," he said, lifting his hands slightly, as if trying to soften the inevitable blow. "But I'm booked solid—the bands, Television, Blondie, Talking Heads, they're all fucking fantastic. I can't push them aside, or push the Ramones—"

"No, no, no, it's not about Magna Carta," Molly said. Carmen noted a slight tinge of embarrassment on her friend's face. "It's not that, okay? I just need to ask you about a gig from a while back—you remember Patti Smith's gig on March twenty-third?"

"My friend, Harvey, was here that night," Carmen said, interjecting. She could feel Molly's eyes boring into her neck as she leaned over Molly to get Hilly's attention. "I dunno if anything, well, anything else notable happened that night? That you might remember?"

"You asking if I saw your friend?"

"No, but I mean, if you had, that'd be helpful. I'm trying to piece together what he was doing during those days."

"What? Is he dead?" Hilly said, a humorless laugh spilling out of his mouth. "What kind of question is this?"

"He is dead, Hilly," Molly said, straightening up. They were basically yelling at each other, trying to be heard over the music. "Carmen's got her cute little detective hat on. The police don't know what the fuck happened, and this guy was a friend."

"Shit, I'm sorry," Hilly said sheepishly. "I was—I dunno. I was mainly watching the stage, like everyone else in the club, honestly. We were mesmerized."

"Did anything else happen? Anything strange?" Carmen asked. She could hear the desperation in her voice and it shamed her. Why did she think she'd find anything here? she thought.

Hilly scratched at his chin.

"Your friend, what'd he look like? Young?"

"Tall, skinny, dark hair, glasses," Carmen said. Hilly was right next to her now; she was basically yelling in his ear. It felt intimate and strange at the same time. "Kind of a quiet kid?"

"Hrm, well, he wasn't quiet that night, if it's the guy I'm thinking of," Hilly said.

"What happened?" Molly asked.

"It was a loud night, as you can imagine, and a late one—everyone was on a high, celebrating Patti's big show. But those are usually safe nights, because everyone's just celebrating. Just riding the high, I guess," Hilly said. "But as we're cleaning up, these two guys—one young, lookin' like your friend, how you describe him, the other one older, harder to figure out—start screaming at each other. I couldn't hear about what, but the younger guy—he seemed frantic, kept telling the other guy to leave him alone, to stop hounding him."

Carmen felt her mouth drop open.

"What else did they say?" Carmen asked, grabbing Hilly's arm. He pulled away gently. "What else were they talking about?"

"I had some of the guys escort them out, one at a time, you know? So the scene doesn't spill into the street and I get fined? Anyway, the older guy goes easy, starts walking out, but the kid—man, that kid could scream. You should've heard him."

Before Carmen could ask, Hilly kept going.

"He just kept sayin', 'Leave me alone, leave me alone,' and 'I don't owe you anything—it was mine! It was always mine,'" Hilly said, clearing his throat before continuing. "Before he was done, he was screaming nonsense, you know? Just brutal shit."

"Like what?" Carmen asked.

Hilly paused and took in a long breath, as if he were finding any way to delay what he had to say.

"Well, he was screaming," he said. "Just screeching, you know? Stuff like, 'You'll have to kill me for it, okay? You'll have to kill me.'"

CHAPTER TWENTY-FIVE

Hilly's big arm swung outward, his finger pointing at a shadowy figure near the entrance.

"That guy can help," he said, motioning with his chin. "He was with your friend that night."

Carmen wheeled around. The shadowy figure looked clearer now: a lanky man with dark, close-cropped hair, in a baggy sweater and a pair of large, thick shades. He seemed to notice Hilly's sudden attention.

"Hey," Carmen said, hopping off her barstool and stepping toward the man. "Hey, wait a sec . . ."

The man didn't wait.

He bolted.

"Carmen, hold on," Molly said, but Carmen ignored her. She could hear Hilly saying something but that was as far as it got. The next thing Carmen knew, she was darting out of CBGB, the man's sneakers slapping loudly on the wet concrete of the Bowery. Carmen gave chase, but she knew it was a lost cause—the man was quick, as if he was used to chases like this. As he turned left on East First Street, he looked over his shoulder briefly and caught sight of Carmen in pursuit.

"Get the fuck off my back, lady," he yelled before turning his attention toward the alley in front of him.

Carmen picked up speed. She was no slouch. She didn't exercise much, but she was in shape—the benefit of a fast metabolism and years of cross-country in high school. Still, she hesitated for a moment as she approached the alley. By then, it was too late.

She felt her arm being yanked into the dark stretch, then the cold, hard wall of the rain-soaked building as her back slammed into it. Another jolt of cold now, except this time it was at her throat—a small, sharp blade centimeters from her neck. The lanky man's hot breath pelted her face, his wide, wild eyes almost embedding themselves into her mind. She tried to speak—could feel her mouth opening—but no sound came out.

"What the fuck do you want?" he spat. "Who the fuck are you? Chasing me around like this?"

He pulled back slightly with his knife hand, and Carmen let out a brief whimper. She took another moment to compose herself before she could speak. Even then, her voice was a stuttering, hoarse croak.

"My—my friend, you, uh, you knew him," she said, reaching for the words but unable to find them at the right speed. She felt like a giant clock was ticking above her, and there wasn't much time left. "Harvey, Harvey Stern—"

The man's expression changed slowly, from panicked anger to confusion to genuine surprise. As it did, Carmen found herself wondering how she'd resolve this situation under different circumstances. If, say, she wasn't Carmen Valdez, overeager interloper, but her own creation, Claudia Calla, the Legendary Lynx? Carmen pictured herself sending a knee hurtling up into the man's midsection, followed by a volley of punches and perhaps a roundhouse kick, each one sending the thug farther back into the alley, until his body slammed into an array of half-empty garbage cans, his head bashing into one with a loud, satisfying *thunk*.

"Harvey?" he asked, pulling Carmen back to reality. "Harvey?"

He repeated the name again, almost to himself, before pulling the knife back.

"What, you his girlfriend? Is he okay?"

His concern seemed genuine. As he stepped away, Carmen felt her equilibrium return. She pivoted a few steps to the left, their eyes still locked on each other.

"He's a friend," she said. "Well, he was."

"Was?"

"He's dead. Shot in the head a couple months ago. That night you saw him at CB's—that was a week before he was killed."

"Shit," the man said, looking down at his hands. "The fuck? Harvey? That kid wouldn't hurt a fly."

"How do you know him?" Carmen asked, tilting her head to make eye contact with this strange, violent man who was now apparently experiencing the five stages of grief at hyperspeed. "Who are you?"

"Me? I'm nobody," the guy said, shrugging, as if he hadn't just had a knife to Carmen's throat a second ago. "I mean, I just know Harvey from the clubs and stuff. From around."

Carmen stepped toward him. He seemed shaken by her approach. They both were.

"Harvey was murdered," she said, feeling the cold steel in her own voice as she spoke. "The cops have no idea what happened to him. You saw him not long before that happened. Don't you think they'll want to talk to you?"

Carmen knew the threat was risky. This man could easily overpower her, maybe press down on her throat with the knife he'd been wielding just moments ago. But she'd come this far, she thought. She'd run through the night, chasing after this mystery man. She wasn't going to let this clue slip past.

"I'm nobody, all right? I sell Harvey some shit—nothing big; weed, pills, a little horse, but not much," he said. "I can get in real trouble, so I don't need you sniffing around me, or bringing my name to the cops—"

"The cops don't believe me anyway," Carmen lied, desperate to form some kind of bond with this man who might know something about what became of Harvey Stern. "I'm working on . . . on this, on my own. I'm trying to figure out what happened to him. Who his enemies were."

Carmen reached out her hand to the man. He shook it quickly, his palm slick with sweat.

"I'm Carmen."

"I'm Andy," he said, sliding his hands into his pockets, as if he wanted to bury them there.

"Nice to meet you," Carmen said, straightening out her blouse. "And I'm sure you're a nice guy, but you also did have a knife on me—so, can we talk somewhere . . . with better lighting?"

"Sure," Andy said, looking around, as if expecting the shadows to come alive and attack him. "But you're buying."

They settled for dollar pizza a few blocks up, a rustic place named Stromboli's on Saint Mark's Place, past the mission. It was the kind of pizza counter that felt ever-present in New York—the series of warm pies, some missing slices, the distant employee watching as customers mulled over a piece of pie. It was too late for a proper restaurant, and Carmen didn't feel safe enough getting drinks with "Andy." They stood by the counter in the half-empty corner spot, as people in varying degrees of inebriation stumbled in and ordered food—usually to stumble back out, steaming slices shoved in their liquor-laced mouths. The place smelled of tomato sauce and burnt bread, with a dash of pine oil.

"Okay, you got some food—now talk to me," Carmen said as she put her massive cheese slice down on its oil-soaked paper plate. "You were Harvey's dealer?"

"I mean, yeah, if that's how you want to look at it. I like to think we were friends, too."

"Did you ever hang out when you weren't giving him drugs for money?"

"Uh, well, no, but—"

"Okay, so you were his dealer, that's fine," Carmen said. She was feeling more uneasy as the night progressed, realizing she'd left her only friend behind at CBGB and unsure of just where Andy's info would lead her. "But tell me about that night—at the bar. Do you remember anything?"

"I don't, not really well, I guess. It was so whatever, you know? Harvey wanted to cop, so he called me. We had a code—he was so, like, cloak-and-dagger about something so basic, like—this is what I do, man. I sell drugs," Andy said, shaking his head, as if Harvey were right there, talking to him. "It's not Philip Marlowe shit. But he'd call and say, 'Hey dude, I need a few apples and maybe a banana bunch if you have any.' Apples were coke, bananas were heroin. He didn't do many bananas, honestly. Harvey was kind of stiff, a stick-in-the-mud, I guess. So I figured he was really stressing lately to be asking for the hard stuff."

The idea of Harvey shooting or snorting heroin seemed alien to Carmen. Even at his worst, he seemed so buttoned-up and frozen. But people probably thought that about her, she mused. You never know what someone's stewing over on their own time.

"What was he like when you saw him that night?"

Andy took a bite of his slice, which was almost done. He chewed slowly, savoring the food. Carmen wondered how well the guy ate. He was skinny, sure, but it didn't seem by design. It was thinness born of hunger and cutting the corners of life. She scanned his arm, the skin near his veins pocked with needle marks in various stages of healing. The dealer was dipping into his own supply.

"He seemed edgy, I guess, talking fast, looking around a lot," Andy said with a shrug. "But once we made the exchange he calmed down. Wanted to hang out, talk music—I mean, Patti Smith was playing, too, so we were almost hypnotized by that. It was fucking amazing. That voice. Her vibe. She just took over the room. So we're standing there, mouths on the floor at this woman and her band, when I see Harvey get bumped. I figure it's just some idiot not watching where the fuck they're going, but Harvey seems to know him."

Carmen inched closer.

"What did he look like?"

Andy looked down at the counter, a frown on his worn, scarred face.

"He was old, that's all I remember—not ancient, but definitely not the type that comes to CB's, you know? Like a dad," Andy said. "But I couldn't get a good look at him. Next thing I know, Harvey's turned around and is all up in this guy's face, shoving, yelling, asking the guy to leave him the fuck alone. I thought he'd spilled a drink on him at first, but then it seemed like, I dunno—"

"What?"

"Like they knew each other . . . like they hated each other."

She decided to walk home, despite it being late. Despite the idea of wandering New York City from the Bowery to the Upper East Side. She hoped Molly hadn't made the same choice. But she needed time to think. To digest the rest of what Andy had said.

Harvey was dead. There was nothing Carmen could do about that. Even if she did walk into Hudson's office tomorrow, admit to her what she'd seen—they'd be no closer to figuring out who killed her friend. So what was she trying to do now? Solve the murder herself? Or was there another, more selfish reason? Was she scared that whoever gunned Harvey down might look to Carmen next? Carmen had to admit that was part of it. In no time, Jensen and Tinsler would turn in their first issue of *The Legendary Lynx* and her character would be gone, transformed into something else—something corporate and boring. One of many, instead of one of a kind. The idea made Carmen sick.

But she also knew that Carlyle would fire her on the spot if he learned the truth—that she'd written the Lynx with Harvey in secret. Or if he thought that Carmen was trying to weasel her way into an assignment in the wake of Harvey's death. Without any real evidence, she'd have no standing in Carlyle's eyes, and that was all that counted at Triumph.

Carlyle hated many things, but being made a fool of was the worst. She'd have lied to him and tricked him, and that would not be tolerated. She'd have no recourse then, either. There was no proof Carmen had created anything, even if Carlyle knew it to be true.

No. Carmen needed evidence. Not only of what happened to Harvey, but what happened between them. Her own notes wouldn't be enough. The scripts Harvey turned in were useless—they were the ruse. They only featured his name. The original ones she'd written and brought to Harvey's apartment were probably gone, too. Or were they? she wondered. If she wanted to have any kind of shot, she needed to show Carlyle that the Lynx was as much hers as Harvey's, and it'd be in his best interest to let her keep writing it.

It wasn't unheard of. Carmen knew Triumph was an outlier when it came to carving out creative opportunities for women. Linda Fite had written *The Cat* for Marvel. Ramona Fradon had been drawing at DC for over a decade, cocreating the mixed-element hero Metamorpho. Louise Jones worked at Warren. Those were just a few. But Carmen was stuck. She couldn't quit her job. She had nowhere to go. Definitely not Miami. She had to thread a needle somehow.

These thoughts crowded her mind as she took each step toward her apartment, the dark, angular corners of the city seeming to bend inward, as if pointing at her, questioning her.

If Andy's story was to be believed—and Carmen had little reason to doubt him, trade aside—someone had been harassing Harvey. This dovetailed with what she'd seen with her own eyes, hours before he was killed. But why?

She felt her feet beginning to ache. She sighed and took a seat at a nearby bench, the long branches of Central Park looming over her. The brisk September chill seemed to wrap around Carmen, the warmth of the walk eliminated by an early fall. She rubbed her eyes and took a deep breath.

"What do I want?"

She almost jumped at her own words, her voice booming through the New York night, a message from her own brain to her ears.

She didn't know the answer. Not clearly. But she knew part of it. Her words echoed something else, though. A dark, clouded memory she'd tried to bury with new experiences and friends, and a cobbled-together life in another city, far from the only place she'd ever called home.

"Is this what you want, mijita?"

She could see her father, sitting on the edge of their large, uncomfortable couch. The tacky neon fabric muted in the living room's pale light. It was late at night. Carmen had just gotten home. Katherine's pounding still echoing in her mind. Her face was wet with tears. Her feet blistered from walking. Her hands shaking.

She knew she shouldn't have said anything. Least of all to Mami. A woman Carmen would never understand. They had nothing in common. Her mother embraced her role—housewife, cook, keeper of the home, and fervent caretaker. Quiet, religious, respectful—at least when sober. She was loved by many. Except Carmen. Well, she loved her mother—she knew, somewhat, that she was a product of another time. But she didn't *understand* her. Carmen loved books. She loved speaking her mind. She loved doing as she pleased. She was responsible, of course. She was cautious. But she wasn't secondary to anyone else. Certainly not to a man.

The divide had created friction. Carmen's desire to carve out her own place—at the expense of what her mother saw as not only tradition, but akin to law—alienated her from Clara Valdez to the point where the two barely spoke. Carmen bided her time, saved her money. At some point, she knew, she'd be able to move. Afford her own place. In wilder, more freewheeling moments, she even dreamed of sharing a space with Katherine—equally liberated from her husband (and son!). But Carmen was also too much of a realist to believe those dreams would come true for very long.

Her body ached, her heels throbbing from the long walk. She was tired. Too tired to be reliving this now, alone on a desolate New York street, a few feet away from the swirling patch of green that was Central Park.

But why? The question seemed to rear its head again.

Why had she decided to confide in her mother in that moment? Had she just been that weak? That powerless? Her mother—this person she'd vilified and ignored for years—still retained great power. Her familiar mannerisms. Her smell. Her affection. Her entire self—it screamed warmth and safety to Carmen. It'd made sense in the heat of that moment to not only tell her why she'd walked all the way from Coral Gables to their home, alone in the middle of the night, but who she was. Who she'd known herself to be for so long.

She let out a quick, empty laugh, remembering her optimism in the wake of the conversation. Her belief that her mother not only understood what she was saying—that Carmen was in love with a woman her mother had never met, that it was who she *was*—but accepted it and loved her for it.

Maybe she did, deep inside—maybe the love, such a deep-seated and basic emotion, couldn't be disrupted by anything. But Carmen wanted to be loved not in spite of who she was—but because of it.

"Is this what you want, mijita?"

Of course she'd told Papi. Despite how Carmen had begged, cried, pleaded. Her mother had agreed, nodded with great care as she ran a hand over her head, let Carmen sob into her shoulder, Mami's familiar *Agua de Violetas* perfume filling her with love and comfort. It would be okay, she'd thought. It could be okay. For the first time she could remember in a long time, Carmen had felt safe and whole and like herself. Empty, but alive— the conversation cathartic and painful, but also rejuvenating.

Papi.

Over time, even after today, Carmen would slowly learn one ever-present and stinging truth about life. That it wasn't a series of epic widescreen moments—seismic battles like the Avengers' Kree-Skrull War, or the various crises on Earth-1 and Earth-2. No, life was a series of hasty skirmishes—little things that chipped at you, that nudged and poked and prodded. Little insults. Little offenses. Little suspicions. Rarely would people stand up and walk out of your life, like some defeated villain being dragged to some unnamed superprison. There was no Ultimate Nullifier–style weapon you could use to defeat that which plagued you. Even the big moments—the culminations of major, essential stories you'd crafted in your own mind—didn't resolve through climactic battles over the George Washington Bridge, nor did the ground shake, as if struck by Thor's mystical hammer, Mjølnir. Big thoughts would spin out of your mouth only to disintegrate into particles of dust—the meaning of your message watered down by polite society, their power drained by atmosphere.

So when her papi, her ally, her friend—her hero, a man who'd introduced her to a pantheon of fictional superbeings—confronted her that night, she knew immediately what had happened. Could already visualize her mother taking him aside to tell him the truth about his querida Carmencita. She didn't do it with glee, Carmen was sure. Her mother wasn't vindictive. Nor was she stupid. But she was weak. A sloppy drunk. Subservient and dutiful. And even though her papi was a good man, an honest man, he was still a man of his time. Religious and stern. Honest, humble, but also didactic. And that man could not overcome himself—no matter how much he loved his daughter.

Carmen felt the tears now, her hands wet as they covered her face. She wanted it to be rain, she thought. She wanted to feel something external overpowering her, making her feel these things. But it wasn't coming from outside. It was in her. No matter how hard she tried to bury it, to ignore these moments—they lived and festered inside her. They made her what she was now, and how she was.

She remembered her hand wrapping around the small piece of luggage. She remembered the Miami morning dusk peeking through her plastic red blinds as she walked down the stairs of her house, her footfalls light. The sound of the door sliding shut as she walked toward the cab. There was no note. There was no speech given with hands on hips. Just a space that had grown much wider in a short amount of time. An aching sadness that would need to be numbed and avoided until the scab formed and the bleeding stopped.

The barrage of memories paralyzed Carmen. It wasn't just tears now, but racking, spasmic sobs as she sat alone on this grimy bench in Midtown. She felt the stares as a handful of people walked by—out on the town. She didn't care. She'd tempted fate for too long. She should've just ignored the memory. Shoved it back down and wrapped her fingers around its neck. Instead, she'd opened the door a crack—allowing herself to slip back into that world, to remember what it'd felt like to not feel completely, utterly alone. To not live every moment unmoored from any past or home.

Like an alien stranded in a world she could not escape.

*Excerpt from 1975's **The Legendary Lynx #7**, "Lynx Reborn!"—Story: Mark Jensen, Art: Steve Tinsler, Letters: Todd Morelli, Editor: Rich Berger, President/CEO: Jeffrey Carlyle. Published by Triumph Comics.*

CHAPTER TWENTY-SIX

Can you believe this shit?"

Carmen looked up to see Trunick from production, a sharp frown on his clean-shaven face.

He tossed something onto Carmen's desk. It took her a moment to realize what it was—a makeready of *The Legendary Lynx* #8. The book would hit stands in a few weeks, the second installment in the Mark Jensen and Steve Tinsler era. To the complete surprise of everyone, the first issue had not only maintained the sales numbers of the original Stern/Detmer issues, but improved on them. Significantly.

"What now?" Carmen asked, looking around.

"Read it," Trunick said. "It's . . . it's an abomination."

"I can't," Carmen said, hoping that her tone implied she was busy, and not the truth—that she just couldn't bring herself to crack the book open. She'd studiously avoided the comic at every stage, from script to pencils to inks to colors and letters. She was not going to break that streak now.

Trunick leaned over her desk and opened the issue he'd tossed on it. He pointed to an interior page—featuring a very buxom, purple-swimsuit-clad woman with long raven hair. The suit was skimpy, to say the least, and her posture left little to the imagination. A few steps behind was a younger, more nubile woman with blond, slightly shorter hair. Her suit was orange, and she had a dark spot over her nose and lines crisscrossing her cheeks, signifying whiskers. She knew she shouldn't, but Carmen couldn't help herself. She read the dialogue.

"Jump on my back, Kitty, this might be our only chance!" the character purporting to be Lynx exclaimed as she leaned forward, motioning for the younger sidekick to basically mount her. "We'll crash through that window and put a wrap on the Red Rascal's dastardly plan!"

"With pleasure, Lynxie!" Kitty rejoiced as she hopped aboard with a knowing wink.

Carmen flipped to the next page, her stomach twisting.

It was a full-page splash, featuring the Lynx, her sidekick Kitty riding on her back, arms seductively wrapped around Lynx's small waist, her face placed squarely next to the hero's ample bosom. Shards of glass sliced through the heroes' already minuscule "costumes" to leave even less to the imagination, their faces forming powerful grimaces that could either be read as extreme focus or . . . ecstasy.

Carmen closed the issue hastily and slid it over to Trunick. She'd seen enough.

"Please, take this," she said, not meeting his gaze. The only sign that he'd left were his light footfalls on the linoleum floor toward the editorial bullpen.

Carmen felt her hands clenching together. She reached for the phone. Before she could dial the number, she heard Carlyle's door opening.

"I think we might have a real hit on our hands, Carmen," Carlyle declared, waving a stack of what she assumed were sales reports. "Jensen and Tinsler are making something special, I can feel it. I trust my gut. I know when a book is going to be a home run. It's how I got this far."

He was gone before she could reply. She was thankful for that, unsure what she might say to his victory dance.

She grabbed the phone receiver and dialed.

He picked up on the third ring.

"It's Carmen."

It was silent on the other line except for the sound of low, inconsistent breathing. She continued.

"Can we work on this?" she said. "Can we do this our way?"

"I thought you'd never ask," Doug Detmer said. He cleared his throat. "Meet me at my studio. Tonight."

Carmen hung up. For the first time in months, she felt empowered.

For too long, she'd been on the defensive. She'd tried to adapt to the circumstances that seemed to change around her. Reacting to what the world had laid at her feet. Harvey's death. Katherine's sudden reappearance. The loss of the Lynx.

That's not me, Carmen thought as she stood up, pulling her purse strap over her shoulder. *Not anymore.*

She remembered sitting at the foot of her bed, a red pencil scribbling on a blank sheet of paper—the first few strokes of something. A possibility. She could see the stack of comics on her childhood nightstand—endless universes and characters, heroes and villains and sidekicks and lovers. So many possibilities. A chorus of colors and ideas that never seemed to end. That always seemed to inspire and engage her. When Carmen Valdez opened a comic book, a good one—whether she was six or twelve or thirty, the feeling never waned—she was enveloped by a sense of wonder and enchantment that not only promised something new and exciting, but also beckoned to her. That seemed to welcome her. It called to her. To be more than a bystander. More than a reader. To be a part of something. To create for herself, to join the litany of letters bursting from every page.

It was a feeling she'd lost, she realized, when Harvey died. A sense of hope and possibility that had been short-circuited when her first and only shot faltered. But she was tired of feeling hopeless. That wasn't who she was. If her dream wasn't beckoning to her, she would chase it. She felt a determination pulse through her, like a being endowed with the Power Cosmic. Or Jack Kirby and Stan Lee's regal and silent creation, the Inhuman Black Bolt, who could shatter worlds with but a whisper.

It was not a feeling she would give up easily.

PART III

TRUE BELIEVER

CHAPTER TWENTY-SEVEN

Just pretend it never happened."

Detmer's voice was haggard, each word crawling out of his cigar-chomping mouth. Carmen watched as the artist leaned over his drawing table, his left hand swiftly bringing to life a dynamic, lively sketch of the Lynx. She was swinging through the city, her face determined. Her original costume restored, her figure looking more fit than foxy. This was the Lynx they knew. The real Lynx, Carmen thought.

Detmer, on the other hand, had changed in the months since Carmen had last visited. His already thin frame seemed but a wisp now, his skin pockmarked and stretched, dark bags under his eyes, with a faint scent of one skipped shower too many. The studio was still empty—no sign of any new artists moving in to share the burden or keep things going. Bottles of beer had been replaced with bottles of liquor. Ashtrays overflowing. A thickness to the air Carmen didn't want to place. Her mind flickered back to the envelopes she'd spotted stacked near the door—more PAST DUE notices than she'd ever seen in her life.

She knew that after his abrupt exit from the Legendary Lynx series, Detmer had been unable to find new work. Even with the buzz surrounding the series's success, it wasn't enough to get him steady employment. Sure, some offers came in—inks on an issue of *Defenders,* a fill-in on *Sub-Mariner,* a short story in *House of Mystery*. But nothing he could live off of. Nothing sustainable. He'd burned the final bridge, it seemed. Though the man was apparently unfazed by this development, it was clear to Carmen that comics—inasmuch as you could describe the fading industry in singular terms—had passed Doug Detmer by. Despite decades of work ranging in quality from superlative to solid, Detmer was now an artifact. A name that might come up at a convention or in conversation between two hardcore fans. A "Whatever happened to?" query that might go unanswered more often than not. He was a recluse—by default, not design.

"Just pretend what didn't happen?" she asked, bringing the conversation back to Detmer's earlier comment. "What did you mean by that?"

"I mean, we just pick up where *we* left off," Detmer said, not looking up from his table, adding a few motion lines to the pinup before tossing it onto a nearby pile of pages. "We do a whole issue—script, art. As much as we can do. Then the second Jensen and Tinsler fall apart, we swoop in with it ready. Carlyle will have no choice. He'll need the issue to keep the gravy train rolling, so he runs with it. Then it hits and people will go wild."

Carmen paced around Detmer's desk, fingers rubbing her temples.

"But what if they don't?" she asked. "What if they keep going? I mean, the book is selling well. Carlyle seems over the moon. They might not give this up."

"They will, trust me," Detmer said, grabbing a new sheet of paper and starting to doodle. "Those hacks can't keep it going. They have two ideas that they rub together, over and over again, and eventually they burn out. Just be ready. Get a story going. Reference what they've done—but negate it. Tear it apart. Make it the bad dream we all know it is."

Carmen smiled. She liked this. Having an ally. A coconspirator. She'd missed it, in the wake of Harvey's death. Detmer's plan was sound, too.

"What if it is a bad dream? Like you said?" she asked.

"Too easy," Detmer said, starting the preliminary lines that would eventually make a person. It was a villainous pose—a tall figure with a hand outstretched. "Too trite. You can't have her just wake up and it's all gone. Even to hacks like Jensen and Tinsler, it'd be a slap in the face."

"What if it's a dream caused by a villain? Someone who has an ax to grind with Claudia?"

"Now that's something," Detmer said, nodding. "Some kind of mental trick."

"Mindbender."

"What?"

"That's her name—that's the villain."

Detmer smiled as he erased some of the lines around the figure— deftly turning what he'd envisioned as a man into a woman. He started to play with details. A black cloak, white; pupil-less eyes; a pale, angular face.

"Mindbender . . . I like that," he said, more to himself than to Carmen. "I like that a lot."

Carmen picked up her pace, walking along the office's long center aisle. It was a crisp November afternoon. Thanksgiving was right around the corner. Carmen avoided thinking about where she'd spend it. She was avoiding a lot of things, she realized. A lot of people, too.

"She's a crime lord, a psychiatrist, maybe? Someone professional and skilled who takes a dark turn," Carmen said. She could see Detmer continuing to sketch out of the corner of her eye. "She wants to step in to fill the, ahem, void left by Mr. Void's defeat."

"Why, though?" Detmer asked.

"Why what?"

"What is the question," Detmer said. "What made her go from a professional career, maybe a family, to being a psychopath? Someone who suits up and uses their knowledge for ill gain? And don't tell me her parents are shot outside of a theater."

They shared a brief laugh.

"I mean, why can't it just be greed?"

She saw Detmer raise an eyebrow. It wasn't critical. He was intrigued.

"She wants to make money?" he asked.

"Maybe she's tired of always having to answer to anyone, to have to be a cog in the machine," Carmen said, walking up to Detmer's art table. "But instead of choosing the path of good—like Claudia—she decides she can use her knowledge of medicine and the human mind to cash in. She snaps. Maybe she gets fired or sees the underbelly of her industry, or something makes her doubt herself to the core. Then she goes the other way, and the Lynx just happens to be blocking her path."

"I hope you have a good memory."

"Why?" Carmen asked.

"Because this is good," Detmer said.

He lifted up the piece of paper he'd been doodling on. There she was. Mindbender. Standing tall, her look ethereal and menacing. A mix of the evil queen from Disney's *Sleeping Beauty* and a street-brawler—dark, sinewy lines surrounded her. Her eyes seemed to stare right into you.

"How did you . . . just do that?"

Detmer chuckled.

"It's what I do," he said.

Carmen thought she heard a slight catch in his throat on the last word.

Carmen didn't respond, so Detmer spoke, as if trying to push the conversation away.

"Think we've got enough for you to get started," he said, sliding a stack of sketches into a drawer near his large drawing table. "Think you can get me a plot to start sketching out this week?"

"Sure, I'll bring it by tomorrow," Carmen said.

"Great," he said, slapping his drawing table gently. "Then I'll put the visuals together and we'll have a book. With your damn name on it this time."

Carmen felt her eyes well up. She hadn't expected that. She hadn't expected this moment. This life.

She imagined opening the book Detmer had yet to draw. Her fingers sliding across the flimsy cover paper. The loud reds and greens and blues of the image—the Lynx hunched over, hands on her skull, as floating versions of her closest friends and enemies hovered around her, taunting her. *What lurks inside the Lynx??* the cover text would read, two large, italicized question marks capping off the query. *How could you not open the book?* she thought. She imagined a dynamic, panels-shattering image of the Lynx kicking off the issue. Drawn by Detmer—in his crisp but quirky style, no line or shadow wasted, a perfect balance of light and dark—a fluidity of action that was mesmerizing and deceptively simple. A master at work. And he was drawing something Carmen wrote.

She smiled at him. She knew she was crying. That her face was wet with tears. But she didn't care. This was going to happen, and the rest didn't matter right now.

Detmer nodded. An odd silence followed before he spoke again.

"What do you think happened?" Detmer asked. "To your friend? To the Stern kid?"

Carmen's brow furrowed.

"He was shot."

"I know that," Detmer said, trying to rein in his incredulous tone. "But what else? Why? I knew Stern a bit. He was harmless, mostly. A nice kid who wanted to make a name for himself. Why would someone kill him in cold blood?"

Carmen shrugged.

"I'm not sure," she said. "I've tried to figure it out. To talk to people he knew. I feel like there's something else—something about him just beyond my reach. I know he upset someone, and that's what I'm trying to figure out. But I keep drawing blanks. It still feels so extreme. For someone to do that to someone like Harvey. But then I also feel like I didn't know him all that well to begin with. That there was—"

Detmer raised a hand. Carmen stopped talking and watched as the lanky man stood up and walked across the large office space to a set of file cabinets. They looked rusted and broken, and had probably not been used in years. A loud screeching sound confirmed it as Detmer opened the bottom drawer. He seemed to find what he was looking for quickly, then shut the drawer and returned to his seat. He handed Carmen a small piece of paper with a number scribbled on it.

"Give that number a call," Detmer said. "Friend of mine. Woman by the name of Marion Price. Works at Warren now. Know her?"

Carmen nodded.

"A bit, we met at a volleyball—"

"She knows everyone—Marvel, Charlton, DC, you name it," Detmer continued. "Smart. Personable. Great editor. She's too good for our world, honestly. She gave me work when I needed it, but not because she felt bad. Because she knew I could deliver. She might know some of the skeletons in your friend's closet."

Carmen took the paper and slid it into her purse. She saw Marion's face for a moment, warning her about Harvey several months back. Here she was again.

"There's always more to people than what we know," Detmer said, his voice hoarse. He reached into a drawer and pulled out a faded, chipped silver flask. He took a quick swig before continuing. "Secrets. Vices. Darkness. Tap that vein—that takes you to their heart. And the truth."

Detmer looked at Carmen, his eyes dark and hollow. She didn't know what to say. She started to make her way toward the studio door.

"Don't look so worried, okay? The industry's done anyway," Detmer said, changing gears. "I can see your face. I'll find work. Maybe I'll be a janitor, but I'll find some work."

Carmen ignored Detmer's lie. She'd seen this happen to many men in her life before. Her father included. The long fade-out instead of the burst of flame. Her tolerance for it was gone, she realized, even if she did feel some fleeting sympathy for this once-great talent.

"What?" Detmer asked, meeting Carmen's expectant gaze.

She shrugged sheepishly. She couldn't believe she was going to do this.

"What is it?"

"Nothing, it's just—this is silly," Carmen said, her nose scrunching up for a second. "But would it be crazy if I asked you to take a photo . . . with me? I just want to—I guess, remember this?"

Detmer couldn't hide the smile sneaking onto his face. He got up fast, his movements swift and mechanical. He stepped toward a nearby desk and pulled open a large drawer. He found what he was looking for immediately: a large, bulky camera that couldn't have been less than a decade old. He set it up in front of them—balanced on Detmer's own desk rather precariously. He walked over to Carmen and draped an arm over her shoulder. His skin felt clammy and hot at the same time. She tried not to think about it as the bulb flashed, blinding her momentarily. She hoped she was smiling. He didn't bother to take another shot.

"I'll send you the print when it's ready," he said, not meeting her eyes as she started to move toward the door.

"I'll bring by the plot tomorrow," she said, opening the door and looking back. But Detmer was working. His pencil feverishly pistoning up and down the page.

He must have heard her, she thought.

He didn't look up as she left.

CHAPTER TWENTY-EIGHT

Carmen's smile faded as her feet hit the sidewalk outside Detmer's decrepit studio.

She'd let the fantasy overtake her, she thought, but the reality was in control now. The reality that her character was in someone else's hands. That Jeffrey Carlyle, no matter what flashes of kindness he exhibited to her, would never let her write a comic book.

She stopped in the middle of the sidewalk, her hands buried in her secondhand coat's pockets. She heard the watered-down tinkling of James Taylor's saccharine cover of a Marvin Gaye classic sputtering out of a passing car. A burly man cursed under his breath as he sidestepped her, his feet stomping over the day's *Daily News*. The headline read ABE JOINS TALKS ON MUSIC STRIKE. She shook her head. She couldn't process the news now. Her head was elsewhere. Despite the fall chill, she still felt a buzzing energy that warmed her over. She was resolved.

No, she thought. *I won't just cave.*

She'd come too far for that.

The train ride to Harvey's apartment was uneventful, at least on the outside. But in Carmen's head, she found herself leaping from Triumph City rooftops—her eyes trained on a figure below. She felt the cool wind slap against her face as she swung between buildings. The sting of her knuckles after knocking back a gang of thugs. This story was hers, Carmen realized. The Lynx was hers. More than it'd been Harvey's or Carlyle's or Triumph's.

She buzzed the apartment building's super as she entered the vestibule. This journey had probably been a waste of time, Carmen realized. It'd been close to eight months since Harvey'd been murdered. This was New York City. You were lucky if a place stayed empty for a week.

The main door swung open and an older man with a wisp of white hair on his sunburnt head stepped into the entryway. He looked more concerned than annoyed.

"You buzz me?" the man asked, an Irish lilt to his voice.

"Yes, my name is—Claudia," Carmen lied, hoping the man didn't notice her hesitation. "I'm a relative of Harvey Stern. He died in his—"

The older man let out a low shushing sound, a finger over his lips.

"Enough of that, missy, I know what you're talking about, all right. No need to alarm anyone," he said. He motioned for Carmen to follow him. "You says you were his cousin or something?"

"Yes, that's right," Carmen said, not correcting the man. "Who are you?"

"Name's Jimmy Dubin," the man said, extending a hand. Carmen shook it. "Building superintendent. Been here for thirty-odd years. Never had anyone die on me before. Least not from that, you know? Sorry if he was close kin, but honestly, I was just about to toss that one pile we had left."

Carmen felt her heart sink.

"His apartment's been occupied?"

"Occupied? Sheesh, there was a line around the block it seemed like, the day he died," Jimmy said, laughing to himself as they walked toward the elevator. "People are desperate for deals. Rude awakening they got, I tell you."

He punched the DOWN button and motioned for Carmen to follow. She hesitated.

"Oh, yeah, well, look—some of his stuff is still here," Jimmy said. "I'm figurin' you want to go through that, no? Cops have already been over it more times than I can remember. So you came at the right time. Was gonna leave it on the curb Wednesday mornin'."

Carmen stepped into the elevator.

"Did you know him well?"

"Your cousin?" he asked. Carmen winced slightly. "Yeah, good kid, good kid. Friendly. Kept to himself. Never made much noise. Never had lots of people over. The night he died—well, there was a woman in there. Heard the screams all through the building, I tell you."

"Do you think the police will find who did this?"

Jimmy shook his head.

"No, naw. Case has drawn on too long," he said as the elevator chimed, signaling they'd reached the basement. "Killing comes easier to some, I guess."

She followed him out. He turned right, down a low hallway that led to a wider open space crowded by laundry machines and garbage cans. The dank room smelled of sweat and garbage. Jimmy pointed to the left, toward a far corner. Carmen saw a familiar piece of furniture. Harvey's desk.

"He hadda bunch of stuff in there," Jimmy said. "Cops didn't take much, just rifled through it."

Carmen tried to give him a genuine smile. She felt bad taking advantage of this kind man.

"Thank you so much," she said. "Can I have some time alone with his things?"

Jimmy took a moment to respond, processing her question before waving her off kindly.

"Oh, yeah, sure," he said. He pointed toward the other side of the basement. "Just let me know when you're done so's I can lock up and get on with it."

"Thank you, Jimmy."

"Oh, think nothing of it," he said as he walked away, leaving Carmen alone with the desk. "Only thing I had to move—there were some half-burnt pages in his trash bin next to his desk. I stuffed those pages in the top drawer. Just a handful of them."

Carmen froze. She felt her fingertips begin to tingle, then her hand. Like she'd been sleeping in the wrong position for hours.

"No problem," she said, her tone robotic and flat. She waited for Jimmy to step away before moving toward the desk.

The piece of furniture itself wasn't memorable. Faux dark wood, chipped in places. It felt flimsy and disposable. The front seemed to wobble a bit, too. It was small. A few drawers on each side and a twisted lamp atop it. If Carmen had seen it on the side of the road, she wouldn't have blinked. But what lurked inside?

She considered searching it from top to bottom, but then thought better of it. She grabbed the top drawer and yanked it open.

The pages were there, as Jimmy had promised. She touched them gingerly. A stack of about five typed sheets, the bottom third browned or blackened by flame, partially unreadable. But Carmen didn't need to see the entire page to know what they contained. It was hard to make out most of it, the damage sporadic and tough to piece together.

From what she could tell, they were notes—a bit scattershot and stream-of-consciousness, but threads that she assumed Harvey had wanted to tie into a bigger idea later. They were dated a few years back. Carmen knew that Harvey had worked as an editor at Bulwark before he left—or was fired. This seemed like a comic pitch he'd been working on at the time. But Carmen couldn't tell much else from the decaying documents.

She knew Harvey had always wanted to write, so why did this bother her? Maybe he had a few ideas in his back pocket, Carmen thought. That couldn't be the worst thing, right? She'd integrated some of her own thoughts and concepts into the first six Lynx scripts—ideas she'd been scribbling and taking down since she was a kid. So why did this bother her, then?

Why did she feel lied to?

She stuffed the pages into her purse without thinking. She wanted to look at them more closely. It was impossible to piece together what they meant here, in some dingy basement, with Jimmy hovering nearby. But they meant something. She knew that. He'd wanted to burn them for a reason.

Was it enough to get him killed? And if someone killed Harvey for this idea—what did it mean if someone found out she'd cocreated the Lynx, too? Could someone out to get Harvey also want to hurt her?

She looked at her hands. They were shaking. She gripped the desk to stabilize herself. After a few seconds, she kept rummaging.

The desk, aside from the burnt pages Jimmy had left in there, was unremarkable. Paper clips, a stapler, and a checkbook. She flipped through the checkbook, unable to make out Harvey's carbon-copied scribble. It seemed inconsequential, though. Rent, bills, the usual. She could have stopped there, Carmen thought, still gripped by the irrational fear that there was something—or someone—eager to destroy Harvey and anyone he'd worked with. But she didn't. She opened the desk's main drawer and looked in again.

She noticed something else. Something familiar. She reached into the drawer, her arm straining slightly as her fingertips grazed the pages of a familiar notebook. Carmen yanked it out and saw her own writing notebook, the one Harvey had gingerly swiped from her the last time she'd seen him alive. She went through each page of the notebook. It was all as she'd left it, aside from certain pages being folded at the corners. The ones that focused on Claudia and her dual life as the Lynx. The character traits that eventually made it into the book she'd written with Harvey's help. She flipped to the next page absentmindedly and stopped cold.

The handwriting was different, not hers or Harvey's. Large blocky letters replaced Carmen's tight cursive or Harvey's illegible scribble. It was not a note to himself. It was a message someone wanted Harvey to see. A message the cops had missed. Maybe Harvey had, too.

IF YOU THINK YOU CAN FUCK WITH ME ON THIS
YOU ARE IN FOR A WORLD OF HURT
DO NOT EVEN THINK OF SHARING THIS W/ ANYONE
YOU KNOW WHAT YOU TOOK AND IT IS TOO LATE TO FIX IT
PAY ME WHAT YOU KNOW I DESERVE OR LET US TALK
NO TIME FOR BULLSHIT—CALL ME ASAP

　　　　　　　　　　　　　　　　　　—YOUR PAL

Carmen had to will her mouth to close as she heard Jimmy's footsteps in the background. She dropped the notebook in her purse and turned around hastily. The older man was wiping his hands with a stained cloth. He nodded at her as she got to her feet from the crouch she'd been in.

"Find anything you could use?"

Carmen swallowed.

"Nothing, really," she lied. "But it was nice . . . nice to be around him one last time."

Jimmy nodded in an effort to show some empathy, but Carmen could tell he just wanted her to go. She was disrupting his day. She needed to leave, too. Needed some air. Anything else.

"Thanks . . . thank you," she said, waving half-heartedly at the unsuspecting man she'd tricked. She felt bad. She knew it was wrong. But she also knew she had to figure this out, and he'd gotten her a step closer to that. "I'll see myself out."

"Have a good one," Jimmy said as Carmen reached the elevator. The doors closed slowly.

She let out a long breath as it climbed up to the lobby. She closed her eyes, her fingers at her temples. *What in the world was going on?*

She opened her eyes at the ding of the elevator doors. She gasped as she saw the person waiting on the other side.

"Well, huh," Detective Hudson said. "Funny seeing you here."

CHAPTER TWENTY~NINE

You gonna tell me what the heck you're doing here, Ms. Valdez?"

"Detective Hudson," Carmen said. "What are—"

Hudson motioned for Carmen to step off the elevator. She did. She forced herself not to clutch her purse.

"I got a call from the building super," Hudson said, motioning her head toward the other side of the lobby. "Telling me Harvey Stern's cousin was here to go through his belongings. 'How nice,' I thought. Then I remembered Mr. Stern has no cousins. Not much family at all, honestly. So I figured I'd swing on by his place and see who this mystery relative was."

"I can explain," Carmen said.

"You will explain," Hudson said with a quick nod. "At the precinct."

Carmen felt a cold shock knife through her. A sense of endless free fall she wasn't sure she could end. Her life unraveling, out of reach.

"Please, no, I haven't done anything wrong."

"Yeah? Then why are you here?" Hudson asked, genuine curiosity in her voice. "Just passing through?"

Carmen felt her mind racing, fingertips frantically flipping through the pages of her memory for something—anything—that could salvage this.

"I wanted to help," Carmen said. "Help find out who did this to Harvey."

Hudson's features softened, but not by much. She was a cop, after all. Not a school nurse. But Carmen did notice the change, and it gave her a sliver of hope.

"You know what would help?" Hudson asked. "You being straight with me for once."

Carmen let out a hesitant laugh.

"Something funny?" Hudson asked, confused.

"I just—I'm not feeling great. I want to help, that's why I'm here—I wanted to see if there was something you missed," Carmen said, looking at Hudson, keeping eye contact. "I just . . . It's bothering me. What happened to Harvey. It affects me, too."

Hudson let out a short hissing sound. Carmen couldn't tell if it was good or bad. The detective took a step toward the door.

"C'mon, let's talk outside. I'll spare you the trip to the interview room," she said. "But you're not getting away without talking to me."

Carmen followed her out onto Christopher Street. The November chill felt good on her skin, balancing out the sheen of sweat that had formed. The air signaling a liberty she craved. She still hadn't figured out what she was going to tell Hudson, but she knew she had to tell her something. Like she needed Detmer, she also needed Hudson, she realized. She needed allies. She needed help. Especially if whoever was after Harvey might be after her, too.

Hudson leaned against a streetlight and lit a cigarette. She motioned her pack toward Carmen, who gratefully snatched one of the Parliaments. Hudson shared her fire and they both took hungry drags. The sky was gray and cloudy. Felt like a cold rain was coming. Carmen almost craved it. A cleansing.

"Start from the beginning, because I know your ass has been lying to me since the jump," Hudson said. "So, if you want to pull yourself out of this, you need to come clean. Then I can see if you can be saved. And if you have anything that might help me work this deadbeat case."

So Carmen did.

The words came slow at first, but after a few moments, Carmen couldn't stop. She did as Hudson instructed. Started at the beginning. With Harvey—their friendship, their routines. Then his visit to her apartment. His proposal—to work together. How they created the Lynx that night. She detailed seeing the man arguing with Harvey near where they now stood. The air of uncertainty and fear that surrounded them both as Carmen came upon the scene. She talked about coming to visit him, worried after he'd missed work. His body, placid and lifeless on his bed. Her scream. She told her about the drug dealer at CBGB. She shared the lies she'd told Hudson out of fear. Of being implicated in some kind of crime. Fear of Carlyle discovering her secret collaboration. Just fear. Of the police. Of everything.

When she finished, she let out a long, deflated sigh. The kind of sound you make at the end of a brutal day, when all you need to do is brush your teeth and collapse into bed. A sigh of defeat and resignation, but one of clarity and relief. She'd told *someone* everything. Even Detmer couldn't see the full picture. Carmen felt lighter. Though she wasn't sure it'd help her avoid Hudson's wrath.

She scanned the older detective. Her dark, deep features. Smoke dancing in front of her face as she watched Carmen's story wind down, expressionless and stony. She wasn't giving anything away, and Carmen hungered for any little bit—any small clue pointing to how this stoic woman might react. She needed a sign that she would be okay. That she'd not only live, but have a shot at something more. Carmen realized in that moment how tired she was. Of everything. Of the weight of this lie. Of the weight of the Lynx. Katherine. Her father. This new life that she'd created that still felt empty—without history, but freeing and liberating in a way she'd never experienced before. She was alive, able to do as she pleased with whomever she wanted. But she was also numb. Alienated from her heart and her history and her home in a way she couldn't easily fix. A woman without a past desperate to create a future for herself.

"You stirred up some serious shit, huh?" Hudson asked, her face still not giving anything away. "Well, I'm glad, at least you were honest. I could tell. Been doing this for a while and that, my friend, is the first time you've talked to me and talked to me straight. So, gold star for you. Welcome to basic citizenship."

Carmen didn't respond. Didn't know how to respond.

"That was you then, that called?" Hudson asked. "About his body?"

Carmen nodded yes.

Hudson nodded to herself.

"Figured as much. So, that checks that," she said. "Now, I'm guessing you don't have a lead on Harvey's drug buddy?"

"I just know his name is Andy."

"Great, should help us find him. New York is a small town," Hudson said. It wasn't a snarky comment, Carmen realized. Hudson had a way of rattling off asides, almost as if she were trying to keep herself entertained. "Look—I need to process this stuff. See if it opens any new avenues for me. I said I'd spare you a trip to the station, and I'll stick to my word. But you have to give me yours."

Carmen started to open her mouth to speak, but felt her entire body start to shake. Hudson seemed to notice and spoke, as if to spare Carmen.

"All right, all right," Hudson said. "Don't leave town. Don't do anything stupid. And if something comes up—and you will know what I mean by that, because you're as smart as you are pretty—you call me. If I'm not there, you leave me a message and I will get back to you within the hour. There's something funny going on here and I don't like it. Whatever it is, you're in the middle of it."

"Yes, yes, of course," Carmen said eagerly. "I'll keep you posted—"

Hudson shook her head.

"No, no, girl, you don't understand," she said. "You need to stop whatever the fuck you're doing, like, yesterday. You're not a cop. You're not helping anyone by snooping around and getting your fingers dirty, messing with evidence or whatever else you touch or mess around with, you hear me? Let it be. If a cat crosses your path and you think it might have something to do with that dead friend of yours, call me. If you roll out of bed and remember something you think you want to check on? Call me. You get it? You do not act. You do not interview anyone. You. Do. Nothing."

"I got it."

"Good, then I think we're done here," Hudson said, lighting a new cigarette with the still-lit butt of her first one.

Carmen thanked her and started to turn away toward Waverly, feeling a strange, nervous elation. Like a kid who'd managed to avoid punishment despite a few Cs on their report card.

"One more thing, though," Hudson said, her delivery slow and thoughtful. She'd planned this, Carmen thought. But it was too late to prepare. Too late to brace for what was coming.

"Yes?"

"You know a lady named Katherine Hall?"

Carmen took a second too long to answer. Could feel Hudson's stare scouring every inch of her for a clue.

"She's a friend," Carmen said, choosing her words, letting the sounds hang between them. "From back home."

"A friend?" Hudson said, nodding to herself. She pulled out a small notebook and flipped a few pages. "From Miami, right? How well did you two know each other?"

"Just friends," Carmen said. "School friends."

"Seen her lately?"

Carmen swallowed hard.

"A few times, yes," she said. "She came up here a while back. She was having some personal problems."

"Yeah? That's too bad. What kind? Bad hair day?"

"She was leaving her husband," Carmen said, her voice sounding stilted and formal.

She knew honesty was the best path with Hudson, but that was bumping up against her own life. Her own problems. She wasn't sure how much she needed to reveal about Katherine. She wasn't sure why Hudson even knew her name. Alarm bells blared in her head. Something was wrong. Very wrong.

"Oh, wow, that's rough," Hudson said, flipping to the next page in her notebook. "Looks to me like she's here because of a new job, though. I mean, she might still have left her husband, but I dunno. What's his name? Nick? Nick Hall?"

Carmen's throat went dry. She nodded.

"Right, well, Nick Hall's name is on the lease of her new place," Hudson said. "Which, again, could just be some part of their divorce. I dunno much about that."

"His name is on the lease?" Carmen asked. She hated herself for the incredulous tone in her voice. But she couldn't stop it. Couldn't stop the anger from surfacing.

Hudson seemed to smile without smiling.

"Seems like a weird setup, but who knows what happens between man and wife," Hudson said. She gave Carmen a quizzical look. "You okay?"

"I'm fine," Carmen said. She was not fine. She knew that.

"It's funny, because, this woman—this Katherine Hall," Hudson said, flipping a few more pages. "She was spotted right around here, on the night of your friend's murder. And a few nights before, when he came home late. Seemed like she really liked this neighborhood, I guess. Maybe looking for her own place, huh? For when she really leaves her husband?"

Carmen froze.

"Or maybe something else, who knows?" Hudson continued. "Was enough for your friend Harvey to complain about this Miami friend to some people he knew. Saying some woman was trailing him. Strange, right?"

Katherine following Harvey? How could that be?

Isn't it enough that you do whatever you want? See whoever you want?

Had Katherine been trailing her? Did she come to the same mistaken conclusion Hudson did? That Harvey and Carmen were more than friends?

"Why are you asking me about her?" Carmen blurted out. "Is she a suspect?"

Hudson hesitated, as if waiting for Carmen to say more.

"We don't have any real suspects, if I'm being honest," Hudson said, a wan smile on her face. "You looked good for a split second. But you also don't strike me as the type. This friend of yours—well, from what I can tell, she has no connection to Harvey Stern aside from you. That's a whole 'nother thread for you to mull over."

Hudson cleared her throat before continuing.

"I like to think I'm good at this, been at it for a while," she said, not looking at Carmen. "But no matter how good you are, you eventually get a nut you can't crack—because the perp is actually fucking smart. You play the game long enough, you learn that most criminals are dumb as shit. And most murders? They're the spouse. Or the business partner. Someone the victim screwed over. Usually, that person did it in a fit of rage—which leads to dumb mistakes. But sometimes you get something else. Someone who knows what they're doing. They know to wear gloves. They stake out the scene. They learn their vic's routines. They hunt. They time it just right. Listen, I've taken down a bunch of bad people. I've left a few in the cold case file, too. It's part of the game. Big picture, you get more than you miss. But I'd really, really like to get this one."

Carmen took a step back.

"I need to go," she said. "Is that okay? Can I go?"

"Sure, kid, of course, we're done, remember?" Hudson said. "You feel all right? I know talking to the police is never easy. But you seem worse than when I found you. Is it about your friend?"

Carmen shook her head.

"I'll be talking to her soon," Hudson said, her eyebrows popping up. "Should be interesting. See what you all might have in common. Probably nothing. But you know, have to chase down every lead, I guess."

Carmen wanted to bolt down the street and never come back.

Katherine.

Carmen hadn't seen her in months. They'd barely interacted, but somehow remained in touch. The dance was painfully familiar to Carmen. Katherine would go off the grid. Ignore calls, visits, messages, then suddenly reappear as if nothing happened and all was fine, eager to pick up where they'd left off. But this time was different for Carmen, too. She didn't have the energy or desire to track Katherine down. Her heart didn't ache at the thought of never seeing her again. But Katherine was still cloaked in a romantic nostalgia Carmen couldn't quite shake. She wanted to be next to Katherine. Wanted to kiss her and hold her and breathe her in. It was an exciting detour she'd let herself wander down—a fantasy she could play in her mind's eye when she needed it. But now Hudson had injected a jagged edge of malice into the whole affair. Both predictable and painful.

What's his name? Nick? Nick Hall?

He was here. In New York. They'd followed her to New York, Carmen thought.

But no, it wasn't that. It was probably worse—simpler, cleaner. Katherine and Nick had just moved to New York, the way millions do each year. It was just a happy coincidence that Carmen was here, too. A chance for Katherine to entertain herself once more, to have an easily accessible off-ramp for when things got too real at home. The story of leaving him—of being here on her own, attending a conference—was just that. A fanciful tale she'd probably made up as she took the train to Carmen's apartment. And Carmen had fallen for it. Again.

Hudson waved as Carmen stepped away. She raised a half-hearted hand in response before turning around, the wind slapping her face. It felt sharp and angry, like the world was shaking itself out, a spinning dervish of frustration taking out its rage on anyone. Carmen just happened to be in the storm's path. The sounds of the city were overwhelmed by the fast clacking of her shoes on the sidewalk as she speed-walked to the train station.

The pelting of the wind continued, unceasing. She couldn't bear it any longer, and closed her eyes in response, feeling the warm tears trickling down her cheeks.

CHAPTER THIRTY

Carlyle's door slammed with a low *thrum* that reverberated throughout the small Triumph Comics office. Even Carmen, who'd become accustomed to Carlyle's petty tantrums and pouty displays of authority, shuddered as her boss stomped toward her desk. Something was wrong. Very wrong.

"You okay, boss?"

"Jensen's done," Carlyle said, the words drawn out and pained. "Two issues and he's done. We need someone else. Fast."

"What happened?"

Carlyle raised a hand; he didn't have the energy to deal with it. But Carmen had to know. Damn everything else, she thought.

"It's just . . ." He sighed. "It's just terrible, and late, and, well, you were right, okay? The scripts are impossible to salvage. If Detmer hadn't left, at least we could've reached for mediocrity. But Tinsler . . . It's just a disaster and I need to fix it. I could swallow it because the sales are strong, but they're also running weeks behind. We might have to slot in a reprint if things keep spiraling. Get Berger—tell him to come to my office with his best ideas in five minutes. I need a moment."

She watched as he made a beeline for the men's room. She turned her seat to the phone and dialed. But she wasn't calling Rich Berger.

Doug Detmer didn't pick up. Carmen hung up and looked around the office.

She got up, unsure of what to do with herself. This felt like an opportunity—but she felt frozen and adrift. She knew Detmer was drawing the plot she'd dropped off, but it was nowhere near ready. What if Carlyle found someone else today? No, she couldn't let that happen.

She walked around her desk and headed for the bullpen. She was moving toward Berger's office when she caught sight of two of the production staff, Trunick and Mullin, chatting in hushed tones by the bullpen.

"What's the good word?" Carmen asked, a conspiratorial smile on her face.

"You know better than us," Mullin said, a playful grin on his youthful face. "Is it true?"

"Is what true?" Carmen asked coyly. "You know I can't reveal everything I know."

"Jensen, is he done?" Trunick asked. "Please be true. That guy was a complete hack. Every line of script was a piece of pure dog shit."

Carmen cackled. She needed a laugh.

"I can neither confirm nor deny," Carmen said, a wicked grin on her face. She caught sight of Berger wandering toward his office. "But I'll know more in a bit."

She stepped away from the gossip circle and followed Berger, rapping her knuckles lightly on his open door. The older editor looked up, his bushy eyebrows raised expectantly. Carmen could already tell he was having a day.

"Got some news for you, RB," Carmen said.

Berger sighed and pointed to a chair across from his desk.

"That kind of day already?" she asked.

"You work here, Carmen, you know the drill," Berger said, rubbing a hand over his forehead absentmindedly. "My artists are late. My writers are late. We don't pay them enough to threaten them and we don't have people to replace them if we have to fire them. I love comics. Have I mentioned that?"

"Well, then I hate to add to your malaise, but I do have some news."

Berger stifled a groan.

"What now?"

"Boss wants Jensen off the book, immediately."

Berger leaned back in his chair, letting his eyes scan the ceiling briefly.

"I don't know if I should be happy or scream," he said.

"How bad was it?"

"Which part? The scripts were shit—but I can make a shit script workable," Berger said. "But they were also late, so then I have to rewrite a script last-minute to make it go from idiotic to just nonsensical. Pair that with an artist who doesn't really understand basic principles like perspective, proportions, or narrative, and we're in quite the pickle, my dear."

"So what's your backup plan?"

Berger gave Carmen a quizzical look. She was stepping outside of her usual role—a courier of information. An intermediary relaying questions or desires from her boss to his staff. She rarely got into the logistics of things. But this time she needed to know. Berger was sharp, she knew that. It was a calculated risk.

"Who's asking?"

"I am," she said.

Their eyes met for a few seconds.

"Hmm, well, if someone was interested in applying for the job— the job of writing this book—I'd need to know relatively soon," Berger said, riffling through some pages on his desk. "I'm assuming our fearless leader wants some options yesterday?"

"Right."

"Right, right, so ... well, I don't have any options. Maynard can't handle another book and this isn't really his wheelhouse. He's more of an acid-trip kind of writer," Berger said with a dry laugh. "Little is running behind on *The Dusk* and I don't think Gallagher can do much more than what we're asking of them on *The Black Ghost*. Aubrey Hamilton is barely caught up on *The Fantastic Flame*. We're maxed out. The usual second-stringers are busy, too. And with the rates we pay, I'd be lucky if the janitor were interested."

Carmen nodded.

"Now, here's my question—why are you asking me that?" Berger asked. "And don't say you're just curious, please."

Carmen paused. She wasn't sure she could trust Berger. She didn't know him all that well. He was the closest thing she had to a friend in the office, sure—they swapped comics and talked craft, but that felt more like an intellectual exercise than actually hanging out. Carmen was absorbing knowledge from a veteran. They weren't really meeting on equal footing. As nice and friendly as he was, he was still an older man—a mild-mannered one, sure. All that aside, Carmen knew one thing: She needed an ally. Rich Berger was her best bet.

"I might know someone," she said.

Berger let out a grumble.

"I'm not stupid," he said flatly. "I know you and Harvey were friends before he, well, died. I'm sure you talked about his idea, right? You knew he was working on this book for Carlyle?"

Carmen gave Berger a placid smile. She needed to think.

"Harvey was my friend, yes. I knew he was working on this," Carmen said, playing it close to the vest.

"He didn't write this whole thing. I see flourishes of him, but the bulk of it isn't his," Berger said, tapping his desk. "I know that. I think Carlyle has some idea, too. It didn't read like his past work. It felt greater-than. Better. I was blown away when I read those first few scripts. I was tempted to take him aside and ask who he'd cribbed them from."

Carmen nodded.

"I wonder what he would've said."

They were in a theoretical realm now, dancing between the raindrops. Carmen knew she had to tread lightly.

"I think he would have lied," Berger said, leaning forward. "But I also think the truth is clear. At least to me. Someone helped him come up with this story. Someone good. Someone who, maybe, felt like they couldn't get the gig themselves. Ring a bell?"

"Maybe."

"Good," Berger said, standing up. "I have to visit our overlord, I guess. But, if by chance, you discover who Harvey's secret collaborator was— tell them they should throw their hat in the ring. We can be creative about some things. Names are just words on paper."

Carmen nodded at Berger as he stepped out of his door. He stopped a half step before leaving.

"Oh, one thing—so you know, Stephenson's out today. He called in this morning," Berger said. "Probably hungover. People can't seem to keep their shit together these days."

"Sure thing, and . . ." she said, watching as Berger waited. "And thank you, Rich."

Berger responded with a brief, awkward nod before leaving his office.

Carmen sat in the chair for another moment, looking at the muted floral pattern of her skirt, the floating colors dancing next to each other. There was a path now, she thought. Something.

She reached into her pocket and pulled out a small scrap of paper. She saw the smudged name and number. Marion Price.

If she was going to do this, she needed to figure out what kind of risks that'd involve. She needed to find out what had happened to Harvey so she could avoid the same fate.

She stood up and left Berger's office, the sounds of the bullpen drowning out the drumming in her skull.

CHAPTER THIRTY-ONE

Carmen leaned back against the bus stop terminal, her eyes on the building's front doors. She'd tried to find another way to handle this, but struck out, and she was running short on time.

She saw the figure step out, looking frustrated but focused. Carmen walked to intercept her.

It took Marion Price a second to recognize Carmen, but her reaction remained calm, almost content.

"I was starting to wonder about you."

Carmen laughed.

"What do you mean?"

"I can't believe it was Doug Detmer that got you to call me," Marion said as she slid her arm through Carmen's.

Carmen started to respond, but Marion raised a finger, almost touching Carmen's open mouth before she interrupted.

"I know somewhere nice you can take me."

They walked down the block and ended up at an Italian restaurant, Giordano, which Marion claimed was affordable and decent, on Thirty-Ninth Street off Ninth Avenue, near the mouth of the Lincoln Tunnel. It was popular with the theater crowd, Marion said as they entered the restaurant. The lighting was low, the dark wood paneling giving the crowded space a shadowy, ethereal feel. The waiter sat them in the back, at a small two-seater in the corner, Marion's back to the far wall. She ordered a martini as the menus arrived. Carmen scanned the offerings and soon realized Marion's perception of "affordable" was different from hers. But she'd have to make it work.

The urgency she'd felt after talking to Hudson only seemed to increase with every passing hour. Everything was moving, and not in concert—Katherine, Detmer, Carlyle, Berger, Harvey—every piece felt important and alive, but Carmen wasn't sure which one she needed to tackle. She only knew she had to figure out what had happened to Harvey so she could take ownership of her work, so she could solve the murder of her friend, and so she could avoid the same fate. But in what order? She felt a pang of guilt. Was she desperate to figure out just why Harvey was killed so she could absolve herself? Was she more concerned with her comic book career than her dead friend?

Two things could exist at the same time. Two feelings could share the same space, she told herself. And right now, she needed to find out from Marion Price just what Harvey had been into at Bulwark, and what it might have meant for him at Triumph.

She looked up from her menu and met Marion's sharp green eyes. They seemed to smile at her.

"It's Italian food, not another planet, Carmen," Marion said, patting her hand gently. "Should be easy to find something you like, right? Or do you not eat meat? I'm a veggie, too, we can find—"

"No, no, it's fine," Carmen said nervously. "Look, I'm sorry about last time. I was drunk. I needed some air."

"Oh, it's okay, totally," Marion said, her smile losing some of its fire. "I had fun. I like you. It was a good chance to blow off steam. There aren't many of us around, you know? Women in comics, I guess. At least not at places like Warren or Triumph."

Carmen tried to smile. Marion took a sip from her drink, then pressed on.

"So what made you track me down? Finally realize you need a friend?"

"Something like that," Carmen said. "I need some help. I'm trying to—"

Her brain stalled. She knew herself what she was doing, but she wasn't sure how to explain it to others—especially someone like Marion, who was sharp, and could easily read between the lines of whatever Carmen tried to say.

Marion raised an eyebrow.

"To what, girl?" she said. "You seem so nervous. Is everything okay?"

"I'm trying to figure out something about Bulwark," Carmen said, pushing her chips to the center of the table. "I think it might have had something to do with Harvey's death."

Marion seemed to fade back into her seat, her smile gone, her eyes suddenly dull.

"Oh."

"Am I crazy?" Carmen asked. "I could be wrong. This is just me thinking out loud. But I know you worked there, and—"

"You're not crazy, but that doesn't mean what you're doing is smart," Marion said. "Bulwark is old news. It doesn't exist. Whoever owned the place ran off with everyone's salaries and ideas. It was theft, pure and simple. I'm not sure what any of that has to do with Harvey, though."

Carmen watched Marion as she took a hurried final sip of her drink. Her relaxed and almost eager demeanor had been replaced by an edginess that was new. Her defenses were up. Carmen had struck a nerve. Now she had to decide how to play it.

"Harvey worked there," Carmen said slowly. "And now Harvey's dead. It could be nothing, you're right—but I'm trying to figure out if there's anything here."

"Isn't that what the cops are for?"

"Have they solved it yet?" Carmen snapped.

Marion tilted her head slightly. Carmen wasn't sure if that meant she was impressed or annoyed.

They ordered. Carmen stuck to a salad and appetizer. Marion went for the stuffed shells and a bottle of Cabernet to share. Carmen tried to calculate how much this would cost, and if it would put her next rent check in peril.

"Did you talk to anyone before me?" Marion asked as the waiter left their table. She took a long, slow sip of her wine. *Another few bucks shredded,* Carmen thought.

"A few people," Carmen said. "One of them suggested I speak to you."

"Ah," Marion said, a sleepy smile on her face. Her stark, beautiful features seemed suddenly more human, more wounded. "And here I thought you just wanted to spend some time with me. Silly me."

"I'm sorry, I mean, I do, but—"

Marion lifted a hand.

"Please, don't try to fix it, it's fine. I'm a big girl," she said. "It's nice to see you. It's nice to be here in an okay restaurant after a long day. I wasn't expecting it, so it's a treat, I guess."

A treat. Carmen felt herself let her guard down. Let her eyes linger over Marion. Her red hair. Her emerald-green eyes. The way the black dress she wore seemed to become a second skin. Marion Price was beautiful, in the way that made people stop and look—even people not prone to doing things like that. It was a relaxed beauty, too, not overmannered or too thought-out, Carmen mused. Would it be so bad to just enjoy this moment? To just slide Harvey, the Lynx, Triumph, Bulwark, Doug Detmer, and all the other bullshit polluting her brain to the side for the night, and enjoy the company she'd stumbled into?

Carmen reached for her own glass of wine and took a brief sip. She felt the tingle on her lips and noticed Marion watching her intently, a slight smile on her lips.

"It's hard to talk shop when you want to have fun, huh?"

"Yes," Carmen said. "It is."

Marion's hand slid across the table, resting over Carmen's. She didn't look around. She didn't act like what they were doing was in any way out of the ordinary. Perhaps it wasn't, for her.

"Why are you really here, Carmen?"

"I told you," Carmen said, her words crashing into each other, clumsy and drunk even though she'd had hardly anything to drink. "Bulwark. I want to learn—"

"No, I mean, really," Marion said, her voice sounding lower, slower than Carmen remembered it, as if she was trying to spell it out for Carmen and having little success. "When you heard my name, did you feel even the slightest jolt? A little shock of excitement? I really hope so."

Carmen turned her hand palm up and wrapped her fingers around Marion's, their fingers hot at the touch.

"Yes, yes, but I—I really need to talk to you about this," Carmen said, pulling away, straightening out the napkin she'd laid out on her lap. "Please."

Marion nodded, that smile still on her face—a viper waiting in the shadows.

"I'm not really sure what else I can tell you that you don't know," Marion said. Their food arrived, the steam rising from Marion's dish, giving her face an ethereal, otherworldly gleam. She nodded a thank-you to the waiter before turning back to Carmen. "It was a bad place to work. Harvey and I did our best to survive. We all made some bad choices there."

"Bad choices?"

"We talked about this. Harvey was a climber—he wanted to be the next Stan Lee or Robert Kanigher," Marion said. It was clear she wanted to speed through this, to get to something, anything else. "He saw Bulwark as a stepping-stone. I saw it as a job, to pay my rent and maybe make a little money doing the things I did for free in California. But it wasn't anything like Warren, or what I'm guessing Triumph is like. Looking back on it, I guess it was one big, long con. Just a grift. They wanted us to really push the talent, to get as much as we could out of them. The contracts were atrocious, even by today's standards. The page rates were a joke. It was a way to keep some aging hacks working, and the books never seemed to come out."

"How did Harvey fit in?" Carmen asked.

"He was the golden boy at first," Marion said, poking her food. "He rose fast. He was writing a lot. He was a good employee. People liked him—I mean, you know Harvey, he's—he was—a lovable kid. Bright, nice, a bit of a charming nebbish. A taller, more attractive John Cazale. If anyone there was a lifer, it was Harvey."

Carmen put down her fork.

"Then what happened? I mean, Harvey rarely talked about his time there when he got to Triumph," Carmen said. "Did he quit?"

Marion shook her head and swallowed a bite of pasta.

"No, no, he was fired," Marion said, nodding to herself. "But I can't tell you why, beyond what he told me. When it comes to the actual truth, I have no idea. He was there one day, gone the next—and a few days later, there was a break-in. Next thing I know, we can't even get into the office. Then I'm out of a job."

"Didn't anyone notice the comics were never coming out?"

"Of course. We're not all dense, you know?" Marion said. "But there was an excuse every time. Printer problems. Release date changes. Cash flow. Some better than others. The whole operation ran for maybe a year and change, so it's not a long runway. Stuff would get greenlit, the editors would be tasked with making the books, then next thing we knew, we had another job to do. You did as you were told. I wanted to pay my bills and have some fun money; plus I was young and living in New York. At a certain point you stop caring."

"Except for Harvey."

Marion looked up and Carmen noticed the pained expression on her face.

"Harvey never saw it as just a job," Marion said. "It was his life. He hated it toward the end. Hated the 'scam,' as he called it."

"Scam?"

Marion looked around the restaurant. She pulled out a cigarette and lit it quickly, offering one. Carmen waved it off.

"Yes, it felt like some grand, Watergate-style conspiracy," she said, looking past Carmen, as if reliving the story in her mind's eye. "Bulwark was a fraud; it was some kind of ethical breach to have people create characters for this company and see no money, or ever have their stories printed. He was more invested than I was. He was actually writing a lot for the company at that point, at least a script a week. I didn't really care. I'd edit his work from time to time. It was fine. He knew the tropes and he wrote like the people he read. But it didn't make me feel great hope for the medium, okay? So when he'd go on these tirades—these heated bitching sessions when we'd go out for a drink and I'd just want to soak in a martini—it was fucking exhausting. But I think back to it now and wonder just how much he knew, or how right he was."

Carmen straightened up.

"He thought Bulwark was stocking up on characters? Why?"

Marion shrugged.

"I don't know, like I said, I didn't particularly care and I tried to move on with my life when it seemed like he was just set on ranting," she said. "The idea that these characters—these comic books—will have any lasting value beyond the moment they're printed is insane. But Harvey thought the company was stealing ideas, having staff create characters that they'd then use for something else down the line, as if that was ever a thing."

"I mean, there's been a Batman show and other stuff, so it's not completely out of the realm—" Carmen said.

Marion laughed. It was a melodic sound, but also heavy with defeat. A lived-in laugh that made Carmen sad instead of cheerful.

"C'mon, Carmen—what? Do you think there's going to be an Avatar television show? The characters Bulwark had were so derivative and forgettable," she said, digging into her food. "I mean, maybe, but I don't know. It feels like a strange business model."

Marion ordered another bottle of wine. Dinner pressed on. They shifted away from Bulwark to other things. The weather. Marion's life in

California. Bands they'd seen recently. Favorite bars. It felt light, natural, breezy. It was pleasant. Not fraught and perpetually perilous, like her time with Katherine. It felt natural. Carmen didn't want to move past it. But she had to.

As the waiter delivered the bill, Carmen leaned over and looked at Marion.

"I have one more question," she said.

Marion rolled her eyes playfully.

"Go ahead, detective."

"Why do you think Harvey got fired? Just speculate. I'm curious."

Marion's playful demeanor disappeared.

"Harvey was a good guy," she said. "But even good guys cut corners. They feel like they deserve a certain slice of the cake. It's an attitude you or I can't really take. We have to work our asses off just to be treated close to the same. But Harvey had this feeling that if he was going to be scammed by Bulwark, he was going to make a name for himself. He was going to write as much as he could and really create a body of work. It was admirable."

"How is that bad?"

"Well, that's not bad," Marion said, lighting another cigarette and taking a long drag. "But I'd heard rumblings that he was doing some things that weren't kosher. Asking talent to pitch ideas, rejecting them, then refashioning the ideas for his own purposes. I'd only heard this, never experienced it. He worked under me, so anything he did as an actual editor had to be run by me. But that didn't mean he couldn't come to a writer or artist under the guise of his job and ask for ideas, then twist them and turn them into something else, something for himself."

Carmen placed her hands on the table, palms down, as if trying to stop herself from falling. She felt dizzy. Her body was heavy. Marion seemed to blur in the distance. Had she said what Carmen thought she'd heard?

"Are you all right?" Marion asked, reaching for Carmen in a show of concern, not intimacy. "Carmen?"

She was not all right. She was not all right.

"Harvey did that, didn't he? He's done this before," Carmen said. "Please just be honest with me."

Marion gripped Carmen's hand.

"Of course he did it," she said, her tone labored, as if talking to a confused child. "He did it all the time. But he did it one time too many, I think. And the last time he did it at Bulwark—well, he really hurt someone else."

Carmen pulled her coat around her body as she stepped out into the fall evening, Marion a few steps behind. She heard her say something but didn't comprehend it. Her mind was in a tailspin.

Harvey had manipulated others. Other writers. Poked and prodded for ideas. Taken ideas. Made them his own.

Did he do that to me?

Carmen was sure he had. The thought felt like a cold knife to her midsection.

"Thanks for dinner," Marion said, stepping in front of Carmen, her striking red hair and lightly freckled skin contrasting against the dark, dreary evening. She was smiling, her hands encircling Carmen's wrists.

"Of course," Carmen said, forcing a smile. "It was nice."

"If you like police interrogations, I guess," Marion said, moving into Carmen, their bodies warm against each other. "But yeah, it was fun."

Carmen leaned into her. The kiss was brief, their lips barely touching, but it felt nice. Comforting. She could feel Marion's smile grazing over her own mouth, the warmth of her wine-tinted breath caressing her face.

"I'm terrible at playing hard to get," she whispered.

Carmen let out a short laugh.

"That's okay."

"I hope so," she said as she slipped something into Carmen's coat pocket. A torn piece of paper.

"But I promised myself I'd be better, even if I like you," Marion said, taking a step back. "So call me again, okay? Don't play head games. You're sharp. I'm smart, too. We can keep talking."

Carmen stepped toward Marion, their hands intertwined.

"I'd like that," she said. "Maybe we can talk about something else, too."

"That'd be more fun, I think," Marion said, an eyebrow raised. Did she have more to say? Carmen wondered.

Marion stepped toward Carmen and gave her another kiss, longer, more intentional, each motion lingering over the last. After a while, she pulled away.

"I'll see you, okay?" she said, her voice husky. Neither of them wanted to leave, Carmen knew.

"Yeah," she said.

Carmen watched as Marion stepped into the crowd toward Ninth Avenue, her red hair blending in with the bright lights and blaring sounds of their chaotic city, like a fading, wayward beacon.

CHAPTER THIRTY-TWO

Now this is a damn comic book!"

The words accompanied a stack of pages landing on Carmen's desk—full line art, about a comic's worth. She noticed a typed-out script paper-clipped to the boards. She pulled up the script and looked at the art. The familiar, stark line work of Doug Detmer was unmistakable. The character, too. It was the Lynx—not the Lynx that had been appearing in the Jensen-penned issues of the series, but the one from before. Except . . . this wasn't from those early issues.

"What—" Carmen started to say, before Carlyle shushed her.

"You won't believe it. I didn't believe it myself," her boss said, hovering over her shoulder as they both looked at the pages. As Carmen flipped from one page to the next, it started to take shape. This was a new story. Drawn by Detmer. It was *her* story drawn by Detmer. He'd finished it. She knew that was coming. She hadn't expected him to turn it in.

Her skin felt cold and electric. She reached back to the script, her fingers scrambling for the top page.

"I know what you're wondering, Carmen, you sharp-eyed vixen, you,"

Carlyle said in a voice that felt more disturbing than playful. "'Who wrote this book, boss?' Well, I'll tell you—I have no idea, no clue, at all. Detmer dropped this off late last night. Showed up at my apartment, unannounced. Like some kind of phantom. Said he knew the writer, but he had to keep it under wraps 'until they wanted to reveal themselves.' Can you believe that? So utterly dramatic. Anyway, this is good—great, even. Get this to Morelli for lettering immediately. We've got another issue! That traitorous lush saved us all without even knowing it."

Carlyle didn't wait for a response. Carmen slumped into her chair. Whatever had just happened had happened too fast. She needed to process it. But wouldn't have the chance. She looked up to notice another figure: Dan Stephenson. He was flipping through the script Carlyle had left, a disdainful look on his dour face.

"This doesn't feel right. Jensen was just getting warmed up, it seemed," Stephenson said, shaking his head. "How can he believe someone like Detmer? He drinks more whiskey than water. He's a has-been."

"You should talk," Carmen said, snatching the script back. She didn't need this now. She just wanted one goddamn minute to bask in a victory, and this sad sack had to come by and sludge around her desk like a wayward maggot. "Don't you have work to do?"

Stephenson shrugged and walked back toward the bullpen, muttering something to himself. *Good riddance,* Carmen thought.

"Holy shit," Carmen whispered as she looked over the stack of art pages.

They were beautiful. Detmer's already cinematic and chiaroscuro style seemed even more lively and playful in this story. Without even reading a word of the script, she could see what Detmer was doing, could feel and understand the story Carmen wanted him to tell. She watched as Claudia Calla awoke, wires and machines hooked up to her brain. Flipped a page as the heroine realized she'd been trapped and manipulated by the Mindbender. Cheered as the heroine donned her familiar costume and hit the grimy streets of Triumph City, hungry for revenge. It was perfect, Carmen thought. It erased what came before deftly, and set the stage for what was to come. It was happening. She was writing this comic. Her dream was in her grasp, almost there.

"Ms. Valdez."

Carmen looked up at the voice, thinking it would be Stephenson again, eager to get the last word in, desperate to be relevant despite all signs pointing to the contrary. But it wasn't Stephenson. No, it was much worse.

"Detective Hudson?"

"That's me," she said. She looked grim, the slight humor and understanding she'd showed Carmen the last time they met gone. In fact, she didn't seem interested in Carmen at all. "Your boss taking visitors?"

Carmen nodded jerkily before she got up. She motioned through the glass wall surrounding Carlyle's office to him, noting that Hudson was there. He got up from his seat hastily and stepped out.

"Detective, good to see you," he said, his tone forced. "I hope you've got some good news about the case."

Hudson shook her head.

"I have no news about the case, Mr. Carlyle, which is never good news," Hudson said. She didn't seem to mind Carmen standing on the fringe of their exchange. "But I have come to let you know that we think we have a similar case. A similar attack."

"What?" Carlyle asked, confused. "I don't follow."

Hudson lowered her voice.

"We think whoever killed your staffer, Mr. Stern, has acted again," she said, looking around to make sure others didn't overhear. "I wanted to check in with you to see if you know the victim. She's in a coma at the moment. The doctors aren't sure she'll pull through."

"Well, who is it? I don't know if I know them unless—"

Hudson raised a finger to her mouth.

"Please shut the fuck up," she whispered.

"Sorry, sorry, I apologize," he stammered.

"She never worked here," Hudson said.

She.

"But I know it's a small industry, everyone knows everyone else, so I wanted to touch base with you," Hudson said, rummaging through her handbag. She pulled out a small photo. It was black and white, but Carmen recognized her immediately. "Do you know this woman?"

Marion.

"No, no, I mean, she looks familiar, but—"

"That's—that's Marion Price," Carmen said.

Hudson and Carlyle turned to her. He seemed surprised. The detective did not.

"You know her?" Hudson asked.

"Not well, but she worked at Warren," Carmen said. She tried to keep herself together. Tried to keep her face from reddening, her eyes from tearing, but she felt the edges fraying. She wanted to run. To hide. To scream. What was going on? "I met her a few times—we hung out after the convention in September. . . . She was very . . ."

Then the tears came. Long, ugly sobs that Carmen hadn't expected. Tears that probably weren't just for Marion but for everything. Harvey. The Lynx. Detmer. Miami. She couldn't stop. Soon, she was shaking. She felt a large arm wrap around her. Smelled Carlyle's cheap aftershave as he whispered it would be all right. A pat on her shoulder as Hudson asked if she needed to sit down.

No. She needed to run. She needed to run as far away as she could.

It took a few minutes for Carmen to settle. For the tears to dry off and the shaking to stop. Hudson was there, crouched down next to Carmen's chair. Carlyle had left, allegedly to get some water, but Carmen knew the old man couldn't handle seeing people cry. Much less a woman. It unnerved him. It was fine.

I'm terrible at playing hard to get.

The last moments of the night before, their last moments together, thrummed in her mind—had anyone seen them? she wondered. Had anyone seen what happened?

"You okay?" Hudson asked, a hand still on Carmen's shoulder.

"Yes." Carmen sniffed. "Yes, I'm fine. I'm sorry, it's just a lot—there aren't that many women in this industry and Marion is, well, I don't know—a friend, I guess."

Hudson nodded. She didn't say anything. Carmen knew the detective was probably trying to figure out just how close Carmen and Marion had been. But perhaps those questions could wait. Carmen knew she needed some time to ponder just how to answer them.

"What happened?" Carmen asked, surprised by her own shaky query.

"Seems like someone snuck into her apartment—attacked her in bed. Whoever was doing it woke her and she fought back. Stuff was all over. Looked like a twelve-round brawl in there," Hudson said, eyeing Carmen warily. "We didn't find a weapon, but my guess is the assailant didn't expect to find his vic awake. Probably wanted to come in, get a shot off, and leave. Same as your other friend, Harvey. She's lucky to be alive. Lucky she was able to fight off a stranger like that. Or maybe she knew the attacker . . . ?"

The question lingered in the space between them. Carmen felt herself get light-headed. Hudson had intimated there was more between Carmen and Harvey. Was she doing the same here? She'd be closer to the truth this time, at least.

"Heard from your Miami friend?" Hudson asked, shaking Carmen from her mental detour. "Mrs. Hall?"

Carmen shook her head no. It was the truth. She hadn't spoken to Katherine in months. Had no idea where they even stood. She'd felt a slight pang of guilt as she took the subway uptown the night before, in the wake of her kiss with Marion, but shook it off with disdain. If Katherine cared, if she'd ever cared, she wouldn't pull this disappearing act whenever things didn't go her way. For all Carmen knew, she was back in Miami, making dinner for her husband and son as if nothing had ever happened.

"We're not in touch anymore, not really," Carmen said. "I don't even know if she's in New York, honestly."

"I believe you," Hudson said. "But she is still in New York. And I'm still trying to get ahold of her. Lady never seems to be around when I swing by her place. I did have a nice chat with her husband, though. Seems like an easygoing fellow."

Nick is here.

"Oh?"

"Yeah, good dude, loves sports—big Dolphins fan, seems pretty down to earth," Hudson said, standing up and wiping an invisible speck of dust from her coat. "Seemed surprised when I asked about marital trouble, but don't worry—I didn't linger on that too much. According to him, they'd both been itching to get out of Miami for a while. Though, of course, they keep a residence down there. Family and all."

Carmen stared at Hudson, letting the words filter into her brain. She'd figured as much, if she was being honest with herself. Katherine and Nick would never split up. The romance of it—the idea of running away with Carmen, or some other Carmen-esque woman, of course ran wild in Katherine's mind, but she was too old-fashioned. Too set in the idea of a marriage, a house, a child. Those were the things that defined a "life" to her. The rest were just detours you took to keep things interesting. How had she been so foolish? How had she ever thought Katherine would leave him?

"That's nice," Carmen said, giving Hudson a wan smile. She didn't have the energy to fake it. Hudson responded in kind. And her words jolted Carmen.

"She's not worth it, you know?"

Carmen hesitated, but Hudson's eyes stayed on her.

"Stay around, okay?" Hudson said as she turned to walk toward the elevator. "Something tells me we'll need to talk again before too long."

Carmen watched as the stout detective left the floor. She waited a minute or two before Carlyle buzzed out of his office and made a beeline for Berger. She wrote out a few pending invoices, too. She knew what she was going to do, she knew she had to do it fast, but she was scared. The pieces seemed to be inching closer to each other, but she was worried about the image they'd form. Worried the picture would resemble a woman she thought she'd loved. A woman she'd almost loved again. Still did love somehow, she corrected herself.

Katherine Hall was a jealous, irrational woman, Carmen thought. A woman that had been following Harvey Stern in the days leading up to his murder. A woman not averse to trailing Carmen. Had she spotted her with Marion? Had she seen them together?

How had she been so blind? Carmen wondered. Could it be true? She picked up the phone and dialed her apartment. Molly answered on the second ring.

"It's me," Carmen said. "I need to warn you about something."

"Carm, I'm so glad you called," Molly said. She sounded out of breath. Anxious. Carmen wasn't used to this version of her cool and collected roommate. It set off alarm bells in her mind.

"What's wrong? Is everything okay?"

"Yeah, well, no—not really," Molly said. She was whispering, as if trying to keep what she said from someone else. But who was there? "I think you need to come home. Now."

"Molly, what's going on?"

"Come home, Carmen," Molly said. "Please."

*Excerpt from 1975's **The Legendary Lynx #9, "The Awakening"**—Story: "TBA, Dear Reader! Stay Tuned!" Art: Doug Detmer, Letters: Todd Morelli, Editor: Rich Berger, President/CEO: Jeffrey Ca[...]
Published by Triumph Comics.*

CHAPTER THIRTY-THREE

What are you doing here?"

Carmen's question seemed to drape over her one-room apartment as she stood across from Katherine Hall. Molly looked shaken, angry, vulnerable. That, in turn, worried Carmen even more. What could this woman have done or said to unsettle her steely friend?

"I'm leaving," Katherine said.

Her expression was blank, empty. Carmen knew this version of Katherine well. The version that'd appear out of the smoke, make an edict, and disappear back into the fog—like some kind of emotional phantasm, unreal and uncaring.

Not again, Carmen thought.

"So what?" Carmen said. She took a step toward Katherine, her hands balling into fists. "You're really coming here to tell me that you're leaving? Where've you been? I haven't spoken to you in months. Why should I even care?"

She could feel Molly squirming behind her, pacing around, worried.

What did she think? That Carmen was going to take a swing at this woman? The thought almost thrilled her.

"I just wanted you to know," Katherine said, still retaining that hazy, vacant stare, that robotic tone that only meant one thing to Carmen—that Katherine had cycled through every option, had considered every alternative, and she'd reached the end. There was no benefit to this for her anymore, even if her body had figured that out long before her mind did. "I'm going back home. I'm going to work on my marriage. I need to do this . . . for myself. For my family."

Carmen spat out a laugh. "Oh, fuck you," she said, shaking her head, a rage-filled smile on her face. "You don't get to swoop in here and act like you're driving the car, okay? You're not fooling anyone. You don't think I knew Nick was here? With your son? That you'd just transplanted the same shit, the same secrets we dealt with in Miami to New York? You lied to me then and you've been lying to me now."

Katherine's expression remained blank, though Carmen did enjoy the brief flicker of surprise that passed over it as Carmen confronted her with the truth. It'd probably be the only victory Carmen would clock today, so it would have to be enough.

"This is just not going to work, Carmen. I can't do this."

"Do what?" Carmen asked, shrugging. "Do what? Please, explain it to me. I haven't seen you in months. You came to me. You came to New York. Or was it just a convenient little escapade? Your husband gets a new gig, so you decide to find some new hobbies while your nanny watched the—oh, wait, this woman you used to fuck on the side is here."

Carmen was barely pausing for breath. It was as if the attack on Marion had cracked her wide open, and now all her carefully built defenses were gone.

"Why not take up that hobby again?" she said. "It's like crochet or playing guitar. Just something to pass the time while Nick is away, or your kid is asleep. A good way to avoid being bored. Or facing the real problem. You're the problem, all right? You're the person that isn't working,

Katherine. To think I ever cared for you. To think I ever wept for you. It makes me hate myself. But most of all, it makes me sad for you. But you can't be my problem anymore. I'm done."

Carmen's final barrage landed hard, cracking Katherine's steely expression. Her dark eyes watered. Carmen heard Molly's sharp intake of breath.

"Why were you following me? Following Harvey?" Carmen asked, the rage in her voice tempered, the words cold and calculated. She needed answers. "The police want to talk to you. You know that, right?"

Katherine looked away. Not toward Molly. Not toward anyone. Just away for a moment, as if desperate for a second to think.

"I made a mistake," Katherine said. Carmen had to strain to hear her. "I—I wanted to see you. I wanted to be . . . I don't know. I felt unhinged there—just desperate to be near you."

"So you followed me around? Scared my friends?" Carmen spat. "What am I supposed to believe now? What have you done?"

"No, look, it was nothing," she said. "It's a big nothing, Carm, you have to believe me—"

Before Katherine could finish, Carmen stepped to the side, her arm outstretched toward the front door.

"Get the fuck out of my apartment."

Katherine did. Their eyes didn't meet. Carmen didn't watch her leave. The sound of the door slamming shut the only confirmation she was gone.

"Holy shit," Molly said, stepping toward Carmen. She wrapped her arms around her roommate, pulling her in tightly. Carmen could feel Molly's mouth near her ear. "Are you okay?"

"Yeah, I think so," Carmen said, disengaging from the hug and starting to walk around their small studio. She was a pacer. She liked movement. She needed to think. There was too much going on. Too much happening at once and she wasn't sure if she'd done the right thing. But fuck, it felt good.

"I just didn't know what to do," Molly said, sitting on the edge of her bed. "She came in here, ranting and raving, saying she needed to talk to you and she wasn't going to leave until you came by. She was scary, Carm. Eyes wild. I was worried, I didn't know what she'd do."

Carmen crouched down, her hands on Molly's.

"I'm sorry you had to experience that," Carmen said. She felt different. Awake. Alert. The adrenaline coursing through her. Was this what it felt like to swing through the streets? To punch a street thug? To slip into a black-and-blue costume, a mask over her eyes? It was thrilling and haunting, all at once. "I'm sorry."

"Hey, it's fine," Molly said. "I just, man, I just had no idea you had so much baggage to deal with back home. When I met you I was, like, 'Damn, this girl probably just sits at home and reads all day.'"

They shared a laugh.

"What's her deal?" Molly asked, after a few minutes of silence.

"We had something once," Carmen said, almost as much to herself as to Molly. "But that ended a long time ago."

"I get that, but . . . why is she here, then?"

Carmen looked at her roommate. Her friend, she thought.

"I don't know," she said. She'd never felt more honest about herself. "I guess we like to hold on to things too long. Try to keep them close."

"She's a creepy bitch," Molly said, standing up and walking toward the kitchen. "I think we might want to change our locks. How do we know she's not gonna wait outside to corner you when you head to work or whatever else? She went ice-cold with you, then lost it."

Carmen thought back to her conversation with Hudson. Her revelation that Katherine had been following Harvey. Carmen's own paranoid thought about Marion—*Marion*—and how Katherine had been almost devoid of emotion just a few minutes before. Could Katherine have been so possessed by jealousy that she took extreme measures? Twice? If so, why was she leaving New York?

"She's not well," Carmen said. "But she's not a killer."

"Not a killer?" Molly said, her expression confused and a bit worried. "What are you talking about?"

"Sorry, talking to myself," Carmen said. "I'm just trying to piece together what happened to Harvey. The detective investigating his murder said Katherine was following him before he died."

"Did you ever think she was just following someone that was *with* Harvey? Like, a hot little Cuban girl named Carmen?" Molly said, jabbing Carmen's arm gently. "Right? Weren't you hanging with him a lot before he died?"

Molly was right. It seemed too easy an explanation. But there it was.

"But then what about Marion?"

"Who the fuck is Marion?" Molly asked, bewildered. "Carmen, I'm like ten issues behind you here—what's going on?"

"Marion is a friend of mine—well, someone I know. She works at another comic book company. And we . . . hung out last night," Carmen said, not sure why she was being evasive now, but it came naturally. "I was wondering if maybe Katherine saw us, and jumped to conclusions."

"And attacked someone?" Molly asked. "I mean, I guess anything's possible. But if she wants you back—it didn't seem like she was working toward that right now."

"You're right," Carmen said. "Stupid. I'm not cut out for this. I should leave it alone."

"Leave Harvey alone? Not if he was your friend," Molly said, wrapping an arm around Carmen's shoulder. "You're doing what any real friend would do. But maybe this idea that your ex has gone all Norman Bates is probably a little off."

Carmen ran her hand through her dark hair. She felt out of sorts. Shaky. The confrontation with Katherine, the revelation that Marion had been beaten—it was pushing her over an edge she hadn't realized existed. And now, she felt adrift. What had happened to Harvey? Could Marion's attack have just been a coincidence? She refused to believe that. She didn't think Hudson thought that was the case, either. And that meant someone was murdering people very close to Carmen—hours after she'd seen them. She felt her mouth go dry at the thought.

"Bulwark," Carmen said, her voice a hushed whisper.

"What?" Molly asked as she pulled a beer out of their aging fridge. "Who's Bulwark?"

"It's where Harvey worked before Triumph," Carmen said. She was on the floor now, rummaging through a small box—flipping through a stack of comics. "I think it's here. I don't even know why I brought it with me."

Carmen crouched down. She could feel Molly walk over to her. Carmen tossed back errant issues of comics like *The Avengers, Daredevil, Justice League of America, The X-Men, Avatar, The Dusk,* and *Blue Beetle.* She was digging for something else. Something she hoped was real.

"Here it is," Carmen said, one comic in particular in her hands. "I thought I'd imagined it."

She showed it to Molly, victorious, even if to just herself.

"Tyrant . . . Tyranticles?" Molly asked, her eyes squinting as she looked at the tattered comic book in Carmen's outstretched hands. "Are those, like, bug people?"

"They were an insect warrior race, I guess," Carmen said, flipping through the book. She stopped at the third or fourth page, a finger pointing near the bottom. "Here it is. Holy shit."

Molly stepped around to look over Carmen's shoulder.

"What? This art is gross," she said. Then her eyes landed on Carmen's finger—and the text hovering above it. "Oh."

In the credit box, under BULWARK COMICS PROUDLY PRESENTS, were a handful of names. But three in particular stood out to Carmen. One was dead. Another close to it.

MARK JENSEN, WRITER.

HARVEY STERN, ASSISTANT EDITOR.

MARION PRICE, EDITOR.

CHAPTER THIRTY-FOUR

She buzzed the bell again. Still nothing.

The skies had opened up as Carmen exited the subway and made her way down Ludlow toward Detmer's studio. She was soaked, her coat sopping wet after just a few blocks. She stood in the doorway of Detmer's building, the sound of the buzzer providing a strange comfort. She'd been doing this for at least ten minutes, she thought. Where was he?

"Yeah?"

The voice cut through the static and sounded muffled, as if spoken underwater or through a sheet. But it was Detmer.

"Doug, it's me—Carmen," she said. "Can you let me up? We need to talk."

He buzzed her in.

As she made her way up to his studio, she knew immediately that something was wrong.

The neat piles of mail were gone, replaced by envelopes strewn over the floor, bottles collected in corners, and a stale, fetid smell that could only be attributed to body odor, liquor, and vomit. All of that crystallized in her mind before she saw him. There was still some sliver of doubt in her mind that he wasn't all right, that perhaps she'd just come at the wrong time—not given him any time to prepare for a guest, or to get his shit together enough to look human.

What she found was a ghost of a man—pallid, bony, slow-moving, and distant. His skin seemed jaundiced. The dark bags under his eyes were so large that they seemed to just blend into the rest of his face. His shirt was wrinkled, splotches of red and orange and brown near the collar and sleeves. His movements were slow and unsteady, like someone who'd just woken up. But this didn't look pleasant. This wasn't a buzz. This was the end, she thought.

She gasped when she caught a good look at him, as he stuffed a stack of art pages she couldn't make out into a large envelope.

He seemed to recognize what his appearance had done to her, his usually stoic expression cloaked in a sadness that immediately burned itself into Carmen's memory. He was ashamed, but he could do nothing about it. She'd seen this before. She'd known people so desperate for a drink, so desperate to ride out their life numbed and detached from the reality of the world, they'd willingly sacrifice everything—their appearance, their health, their friends, their passions. Doug Detmer was a dead man walking, Carmen knew. It seemed that Doug Detmer knew it, too.

"Didn't know you were coming," he said, the laggard words not calming Carmen in the least. "Would've tidied up a bit . . ."

Detmer finished packing the envelope and tossed it onto his art table. He wobbled toward Carmen. That's when she noticed he had a bottle of wine in his hand. Twist-off. The cheap shit. It was almost empty. Red wine residue stained his mouth, like some kind of morbid lipstick.

"Are you okay?" She didn't know what else to ask.

"Fine, fine, just tired," he said, flopping down into a stray chair. "What's the emergency?"

The studio space felt more like a storage area, a place where people dumped furniture that once meant something—drawing tables, office chairs, file cabinets, art folders. Things that once had use. Things that once were special. Now they were just stuff—overflow, detritus. Like Doug Detmer, the world had passed this space by—and all that was left was the ticking clock and a bottle of dollar red wine.

There was so much she needed to ask him. Her mind flashed back to the first time she'd been here and they'd talked about the Lynx. How enraged he'd become at the mere mention of Mark Jensen. He'd quit the book soon after. But now Carmen knew the name had more meaning to him—and to her. He was a link to both Harvey and Marion, and a link to Bulwark.

Molly, always-wise Molly, had been clear: Call Hudson. She can take it from here. But take what? A coincidence at best? Comics was a small, fading industry. Everyone had worked with everyone else at any given point. So what if the hack that wrote the Lynx also wrote something else for Harvey and Marion?

"Someone else has been hurt, almost killed," Carmen said, stepping farther into the studio, but keeping her distance from Detmer, who seemed to be melting into the uncomfortable chair he'd collapsed into. "Marion Price. The editor at Warren you connected me to."

Carmen thought back to that night. The kiss. She let her imagination guide her through what happened next, and she felt herself shudder.

Detmer nodded dismissively.

"Right, right. I heard. Sad. Like I told you, I liked her a lot. Very smart. Very polished. Hope she pulls through," he said, the last few syllables slurring into nothingness. It was as if every part of his body, every muscle, didn't have the energy to keep going. "But what does it have to do with me?"

Carmen opened her purse and pulled out the issue of *Tyranticles*. She handed the book, now wet from the rain, to Detmer, who took it gingerly. He looked at her like she'd handed him a strange fruit, as opposed to a comic book.

"What's this? Huh. So Bulwark actually did produce some comics, I guess," he said, carefully opening the pages, trying to avoid ripping or damaging the wet pages. "So what?"

"Look at the credits."

Detmer stopped on the opening splash page. His reaction told Carmen nothing. Just a slight, slow nod. A movement that could have easily been a muscle spasm or delirium tremens. She felt a sadness pour over her as she watched his shaking hand let the comic drop to his lap, as if he was too tired to hold it up.

"What about them?"

"Harvey Stern. Marion Price. Mark Jensen," Carmen said. "Coincidence?"

Detmer's glossy eyes didn't change. Awareness didn't kick in. Was he so far gone? Carmen wondered.

"Harvey is dead and Marion could be," she continued. "Jensen took over for Harvey. Doesn't that feel like something? Some kind of link?"

Detmer shook his head.

"Doug, don't bullshit me here. You flipped over a table when I told you Jensen was taking over for me and Harvey. You quit the book in a rage," Carmen said. "Why? What is it about Jensen that set you off?"

Detmer sighed, as if Carmen had just asked him to do a sprint or lift a weight instead of just talk.

"Mark Jensen is a fraud, the worst kind of person, a nothing," Detmer said, his voice suddenly clearer and focused. "He was a scam artist. He stole more than he created. The absolute worst of our industry. A craven opportunist."

"You worked with him?"

"If you did work at Bulwark, you worked with Mark," Detmer said. "He was their main writer. He handled everything that wasn't farmed out to the staff."

Carmen tried to breathe. She was missing something here; she could feel its shape in front of her—like a shadow dancing on the edge of her vision. But what?

"I still don't get it," Carmen said. "How can you hate him? This is more than a professional dislike. I deal with our freelancers all the time. They range from nice to annoying to assholes. But I don't hate any of them. What did Jensen do to you? Have you ever even met him? Is he even real?"

Carmen had muttered the last sentence as more of a joke than anything else, but Detmer's eyes seemed to glimmer.

"Do you really want to know?"

"Of course I do," Carmen said.

Detmer shivered slightly, but there were no open windows, and the temperature inside the stuffy studio had to be close to eighty.

"Track down the money, follow it," he said, his body seeming to fold into itself more, like he wanted to curl up into his shell and disappear. "Whoever owned Bulwark, whoever signed the checks—they shuttered the place for a reason. I wish I had the answers. The guy who ran Bulwark behind the scenes . . . they've got them all."

Carmen tried to respond, to prod Detmer for more, but the artist waved her off. She thought she heard his body creak as he got to his wobbly feet, swaying as he shuffle-stepped toward the studio's bathroom.

"Let me know what you dig up," he croaked, before closing the door behind him.

Carmen thought about staying, thought about seeing how she could help. Instead, she turned around and left.

She caught Berger reading *The Legendary Lynx* #9—Carmen's latest, still-anonymous story that featured Detmer's finest work to date. He was leaning back in his chair, feet on his desk, truly savoring the experience. She couldn't help smiling as she stepped into his office, a stack of memos in her hand. She dropped them at the edge of the older man's desk. She started to turn around when she heard him speak.

"Nice work."

"Excuse me?" she said, spinning around.

Berger tapped the comic.

"This. Nice work," he repeated.

Carmen nodded, tried to play it cool.

"Detmer did a great job," she said. "It's my favorite issue so far."

Berger tossed the comic onto his desk and brought his feet back to the ground. His friendly smile was now a sharp smirk.

"Your secret's safe with me, Valdez," he said. "I'm just grateful to have a small hand in making a few readable comics."

Carmen tried to stay cool, but she couldn't hide the smile on her face. Berger noticed and nodded before turning to the stack of pages she'd dropped on his desk.

She made her way back to her desk, her head still buzzing. From Berger's compliment, but also from her encounter with Detmer the night before. What were the pages he'd been hastily stuffing in an envelope? More importantly, what did he mean by "follow the money"? Who would know about something like that?

As she reached her desk, she saw Carlyle speed out of his door, a flustered look on his face.

"Not coming back today," he muttered. "Have to deal with something at home."

"Sure thing, boss," she said. "Everything okay?"

"Don't worry about it," he said, turning around briefly. "Can you give Maynard a ring? Tell him we need to get lunch. His number's in my Rolodex on my desk."

"Consider it done."

He started to pivot back, but slowed himself—his expression softened.

"You doing okay?"

"Sure, why?" Carmen asked.

"Just—well, just checking, Valdez," he said. "I know you're tough. We all are. But almost losing two friends so fast can't be good for anyone. I don't want to get all mushy on you, but if you need anything, let me know. Otherwise, get back to work."

Carmen nodded.

"Thanks, boss," she said. "Glad to know that heart of yours can work when shocked into action."

He ignored her and headed for the elevator bank.

She stepped into his office and took his seat. His desk was huge, regal—befitting the head of a major publishing company. A bit ostentatious for the head of a third-rate comic book publisher. She started flipping through the stuffed Rolodex on the far right of his desk, looking for Len Maynard's home number.

Track down the money, follow it.

Detmer's words hovered above her as her fingertips flicked through Carlyle's contacts. Jeffrey Carlyle wasn't a comic book lifer, but he was a social climber. He knew who to talk to and who to chase. He had made fast friends in every corner of the industry. From talent to editors to production staff to the fan press. Could this Rolodex hold the key to the info Detmer dangled in front of her? She flipped more slowly. Past Len Maynard. She almost skipped over Stuart Alford, too. But something called to her about the entry, scrawled on a card in hasty blue ink—*Stuart Alford—the Comics Journalist.*

Carmen had never heard the name before. Or the news outlet. She'd read her share of comic book fanzines, but had never heard of this one. But she knew very well that there was a fervent base of readers who just wanted to write about the comics they read and loved, who treated it more like a passion than a disposable, passing hobby. People like her. She jotted down Stuart's number—along with Maynard's—and stepped back to her desk.

She rang Maynard and left a message, following Carlyle's instructions. Then she dialed Alford.

"Hello," a voice said. It was low and laconic. Relaxed but not disconnected.

"Hi, is this Stuart Alford?" Carmen said, trying to lower her own register without alerting anyone in the office. "I've heard good things about your work."

"Oh, that's nice," he said. "Can you cut the voice? It's weirding me out."

"Sure," Carmen said, reverting to normal. "I need some help with something. I hear you're good at digging things up."

"I'm not sure what that means," he said, with a slight tinge of humor. He sounded intrigued. "But I do write about things, yes."

"Can we meet? I have some questions."

"No, we can't meet—at least not until I know what you want to discuss," Alford said. "And until I have some kind of idea about who the hell you are."

"I need to know some things about Bulwark."

The line went quiet for a moment. Carmen thought she'd lost him.

A throat-clearing sound.

"You sure?"

"What do you mean?"

"I mean, are you sure you want to stick your nose into this?" Alford asked.

"Yes," she said, her eyes darting around the office, making sure no one was eavesdropping on the conversation. "Please. It's important."

"All right, well, you don't sound threatening—but stranger things have happened," he said. "You know Umbertos in Little Italy? The spot where they shot 'Crazy Joe' Gallo?"

"Yes."

"Let's meet there, I've always wanted to go there," Alford said. "Eight o'clock."

"All right, but—"

It was too late. Alford had already hung up. Carmen put the receiver down and waited a moment before collecting her purse and making a beeline for the bullpen area. As she made her way across the office, she felt a growing sense of inevitability. Carmen wondered just how long she'd be able to avoid the same fate that had consumed Harvey and Marion.

CHAPTER THIRTY-FIVE

Carmen crossed **Mulberry Street,** the flickering pink neon sign that read UMBERTOS CLAM HOUSE beckoning her. It was a few minutes before eight. She liked to be early. Especially when it felt as cloak-and-dagger as this.

She'd cornered Trunick at his desk before leaving the office. She knew the younger staffer was more tapped into the fan press and people "covering" the industry, as it were. She feigned ignorance, noting that the name had come up while doing something for Carlyle. Trunick seemed to buy it.

"Alford? Wow, yeah, he's a big deal," Trunick said, eyes opening wide in that sweet, Midwestern way he had. "I mean, in terms of comic fans. He has this newsletter, *The Comics Journalist.* Kind of like *Comic Reader,* but a little more defiant, I guess. He mails it from his apartment. Just, like, really scathing but lovable takes on everything—reviews, his life. I get it each month. Sometimes it's late, but it's always good. Even his missives are well-written. The design is atrocious but it's not about the look. You read it for his words. He's like some sort of comic book Lester Bangs, minus the acid weirdness."

Carmen thought that was enough intel, but Trunick had pressed on.

"He gets to the root of why he—and I guess, we—love comics. The magic of it. But he's also not afraid to call people out, to point out the shitty things," Trunick said, not looking at Carmen, as if he were trying to propel himself into a better, fairer world. "He's great. I love his writing. Why did you want to know about him again?"

Carmen rehashed her excuse, which seemed to mollify Trunick. Before he could ask anything else, she was gone.

She stepped into Umbertos and took in the atmosphere. A few years back, mafia pariah "Crazy Joe" Gallo had been gunned down inside of the restaurant, one of the bloodiest scenes of mob violence in a long line of bloody scenes.

A tall, stocky man in the back raised a hand. He was bald, a salt-and-pepper beard lightly covering his face. His clothes seemed well-worn and comfortable. He smiled easily, but it wasn't without some tension. Carmen guessed he didn't get out all that much.

She reached the table and rested a hand on the chair across from him. "Stuart?"

"Yes," he said calmly. "Nice to meet you."

She took a seat and scanned the plastic menu that was resting on the table.

"I have to say, I was intrigued by your call," Alford said. "Mainly because not many people have my direct line. So that made me wonder who the hell you might be."

Carmen reached out a hand. He took it.

"Claire Morgan. I'm a freelance writer," Carmen said. The lie came naturally, and she couldn't deny the thrill she felt as the words left her mouth. "Like I said on the phone, I'm interested in digging into Bulwark."

Alford scoffed.

"Claire Morgan?" he said with a chuckle. "You'll have to do better than that."

"What?" Carmen said, doing her best to seem slightly offended. She couldn't back out now.

Alford leaned forward, resting his face on both hands, like a toddler looking at a butterfly.

"You're not being fair," he said, still smiling. "If you want me to be honest with you, I need you to be honest with me, okay? And I'm a reporter. I dig things up. I also read. A lot. Claire Morgan was Patricia Highsmith's pseudonym—so, points for being literary and obscure, Ms. Carmen Valdez, executive assistant to Jeffrey Carlyle of Triumph Comics. That explains how you got my number. It doesn't explain the more important question: Why?"

Carmen met Alford's eyes. The waiter arrived to take their drink orders, providing her with a brief respite. They each ordered waters. She hadn't expected Alford to be so direct. His demeanor was deceptive. He was sharp and he was on the offensive. She'd underrated him. That was her mistake.

"I'm not calling on behalf of Triumph, or Carlyle," Carmen said, ignoring her metaphorical unmasking. "I don't want to get in trouble, either, but I need some information. I've heard you're very good at your job, so I thought I'd try you."

"Flattery will get you everywhere," Alford said with a smirk. "Well, at least further than where we are now."

Carmen sighed.

"I'll just be straight with you, because I'm not really sure where else to go here," she said. "My friend Harvey Stern was murdered. Recently, another friend, Marion Price, was almost killed, too. They both worked at Bulwark. I'm not a detective, but I think whatever happened to them has something to do with that company. There doesn't seem to be a lot out there about them, so I wanted to dig a bit deeper. I just need to learn more about the company to confirm my suspicions. I could be totally off base."

"You're not," Alford said, before taking a long, hasty gulp of water. "And I think we should take this conversation elsewhere, now that I know what you want and why."

Carmen started to get up, but Alford waved her back into her seat.

"I meant eventually, my dear Claire," Alford said with a playful smile. "I'm still gonna eat some clams."

Dinner itself was uneventful, though Carmen had trouble focusing on her food. The small talk was just that—fleeting and tiny. As they left the restaurant, Carmen paid the bill, the second hefty dinner she'd have to figure out how to finance in almost as many days. She followed Alford out the door.

"I live near Spring," Alford said, walking toward Broadway. "I share a loft space with some friends. It's technically a performance space, but we make it work. I couldn't find any other place to store my files."

"Are we safe to talk now?" Carmen asked, trying to keep pace with Alford as he sped along the sidewalk, belying his size. "Now that my dinner-buying abilities have been vetted?"

"Yes, thank you, that was nice," Alford said, not meeting Carmen's stare. "I just don't like getting into the nitty-gritty somewhere I'm not comfortable. I also wanted to make sure you weren't some kind of, I dunno, double agent."

"Double agent? This is comic books, not le Carré."

"Exactly," Alford said as they turned right on Lafayette.

Alford's apartment was close to what he'd described—more of a space than a home, with few walls or demarcation, littered with boxes, file cabinets, and one gray, unhealthy-looking couch occupied by two black cats.

Carmen made a beeline for the felines. Both seemed receptive to her pets.

"That's Ditko," Alford said, motioning to the cat currently rubbing his face on Carmen's hand. "The other one's Gaines, for Bill Gaines."

Carmen smiled.

"Cute."

She could feel Alford moving around behind her, shifting boxes and stepping between areas of the spacious loft. She couldn't hear anyone else around and felt a brief, passing tinge of fear.

"So, Bulwark," Alford said, a finger tapping his chin as he stared at a set of file cabinets. "I think this will do for you. It's . . . a lot. But I can't think of anything not in here. I'm not really sure what you're looking for, so that could help."

"I'm not sure what I'm looking for, either," Carmen said, moving to look at the two large cabinets. "I just need a sense for the place—an idea of who was behind it."

Alford nodded, still staring at the rusty cabinets.

"Well, that information is quite something," he said, a tinge of worry in his voice.

Carmen stepped toward the first file cabinet, a loud, painful screech announcing the first drawer opening. She'd come to be pretty fast at skimming files, a skill picked up working for Carlyle and at previous odd jobs back home. The files were organized, but a bit scattershot—employee records, comic book scripts and plots, invoices, internal memos. The kind of stuff you wouldn't find dumpster diving, she realized.

Carmen turned around to look at Alford, who'd ensconced himself on the couch, one black cat on each side.

"How did you get all this stuff?"

"I know some things," Alford said ominously. "Things I can't say until the right people die and I can finish this book."

"Book?" Carmen asked. He'd sidestepped her question, which was already a red flag.

She turned her attention back to the cabinet, moving slowly to the next drawer. She'd pulled some pay stubs—one for Marion, one for Harvey. Nothing unremarkable about either. It just confirmed what she already knew—that they'd worked for the company, on staff and as free-lance writers. But it didn't explain her big question—who was signing the checks? The stubs just said BULWARK/RAMPART COMIC PUBLICATIONS. Which meant nothing to Carmen. It meant nothing to anyone, really, unless you knew who Bulwark even was. But Rampart? That was new.

After about half an hour, her eyes started to tire. The memos blurred together—requests for sick days, vacation time, copier rules, and general edicts were making her dizzy. She did stuff like this all day for Carlyle, and reading the Bulwark version just made her realize how mundane office life could be, even if you were working in the exciting world of comic books. Then she found it.

The clipping was short—a few inches, from the business section. It was dated March 15, 1968—a few years, as far as Carmen could tell, before Bulwark would even attempt to publish a comic book.

COMIC BOOK EXEC LOOKS TO EXPAND WITH INVESTMENT IN START-UP

The story was brief, but it was enough to knock Carmen back.

Silver Claw Publishing owner and Triumph Comics publisher Jeffrey Carlyle was announced as part of a small investment group backing the launch of Rampart Comic Publications, a boutique newspaper strip, comic book, and literary novel publisher looking to debut in late 1970. Rampart will be overseen by Daniel Stephenson Jr., a veteran of the entertainment publishing industry with a focus on comic books. Stephenson, the husband of Carlyle's late sister, said in a press release he hopes the two companies will complement each other in the struggling comic book market. . . .

Carmen felt her hands begin to shake. She dropped the clipping back into the file cabinet, her hands still on the furniture to balance herself.

Dan Stephenson owned Bulwark—Carmen had known that much. But he was Carlyle's brother-in-law?

"You all right over there?" Alford said, getting up from the couch. The cats scattered. "What'd you find?"

"Stephenson," she said. "He owned Bulwark."

"Well, yes," Alford said. "He owned it because they let him."

Carmen shook her head.

"What do you mean?"

"Dan Stephenson is one of the many comic book mysteries that will never be solved," Alford said, a humorless smile on his wide face. "One of these guys that just keeps getting work—keeps getting hired. I get why Carlyle chipped in. He's his brother-in-law, for God's sake. But it was bound to fail. No one wanted a company run by Stephenson. Which is a big part of why it was such a secret."

"Why did he want it, though?" Carmen asked. She reached back into the file cabinet for the clipping. She pulled it up to her face and read it again, as if hoping the text had changed in the interim. No such luck. "I don't understand."

"You're still not getting it, are you?"

Alford stepped around Carmen and reached for the bottom drawer of the other cabinet. It opened with more ease, a sign that it was being used more often, she thought. Alford pulled out a thick manila envelope and opened it carefully. Inside was a stack of pages separated by large clips. He flipped through them and handed her one from the middle of the pile.

Before she got to the middle of the page, Carmen knew what it was.

BEWARE! THE FERAL CLAWS OF . . . PANTHENA!

Famed archeologist Caterina Clauson uncovers an ancient artifact on a journey to the wilds of Africa—a golden, cat-shaped scarab that seems to beckon to her with a wailing cry.

On her return home to Rampart City, Clauson discovers she is unable to dream, haunted by visions of wild animals and a lifetime of centuries past. She awakens in a cold sweat and notices the scarab by her bedside. Bringing it close to her chest, she learns she has been imbued with powerful, catlike abilities—including the power to leap from any height, sharp and deadly claws, and stunning vision that borders on a sixth sense! Driven to defeat the villains who might threaten the innocent, Clauson dons the striped yellow-and-blue costume of PANTHENA, protector of the night!

Carmen stopped reading. She flipped back to the top of the page. There was no cover page. No sign of who the author of the pitch was.

But Carmen knew something wasn't right. What were the odds that someone at Bulwark would think of a cat-themed superhero? Not impossible, she guessed. Marvel had the Cat. DC had Catwoman and the Cheetah. But it didn't fit. Some of the elements of the story seemed almost . . . familiar.

"Figure it out yet?" Alford said, shaking Carmen from her train of thought.

"What?" she asked.

"Why Stephenson did this? Why he started Bulwark?" Alford said, his eyes widening. Carmen felt that slight tinge of fear again. "He put all his money into it. Every last cent. I know because I followed it. He spent a small fortune on launching the company, even with the investors. This was his last shot at relevance. He'd burned every other bridge he had. He thought he had it all figured out."

"I don't—I don't follow."

"It was a character mill, basically," Alford said with a gruff laugh. "A way for Stephenson to create a universe of characters he could own all for himself. That pitch you hold was one of them. 'Panthena.' What a dumb name. What a silly idea, right? But Stephenson thought he'd struck gold. But he made one mistake."

Carmen watched as Alford paced around his loft, cracking his knuckles and stepping around her, forming a wide circle.

"The robbery," Carmen said. "The break-in at the Bulwark offices."

Alford pointed a finger at Carmen.

"You've done your research," he said.

"I spoke to Marion a few times—before," Carmen said. "Was that Stephenson? Did he break into his own company?"

"Ding. Almost, but not quite. You're a smart one, Carmen," Alford said. "You're close. See, Stephenson wasn't organized. But he was meticulous about one thing. His characters. These ideas and concepts that would make him rich. He was convinced they'd set him up. So he started storing these pitches, these ideas. He published maybe a handful of books, but in the meantime, he had his staff cranking out these ideas for him, then tucking them away."

"But then someone took them," Carmen said, reaching the conclusion Alford was guiding her toward. "Before he could lock them up. Copyright them for himself, for Bulwark."

Alford nodded.

"The bad thing that happens when you invest all your money into something is, well, you run out of money," Alford said, shaking his head in judgment. "Stephenson couldn't run the company. He needed investors. Carlyle only got him so far. So he went into hock with a loan shark. Then he started bouncing paychecks. Moving cash around. But he was hopeful—he had this one idea . . ."

Alford tapped the Panthena pitch Carmen was still clutching.

"This one pitch for a character that was sure to sell."

Carmen stepped back, still holding on to the pitch. She felt the loft getting smaller. Alford seemed to loom over her. She took in a quick breath. She wasn't sure what it all meant, but she knew it wasn't good.

"Someone took it," Carmen said. "Someone took . . . this?"

Alford nodded, a conniving smile on his face.

"Where . . . where did you get these files?" she asked cautiously.

"Stephenson lost everything. Shuttered the company. Sold it to Carlyle for pennies on the dollar. But there was nothing to sell—just equipment, paper . . . stuff, not ideas. Not magic," Alford said, a slight hiss glossing over his words. "From what I heard, Stephenson never let Carlyle forget it. Kept begging for work, all the while trying to figure out what happened to his secret treasure trove."

Alford took another step toward Carmen.

"How—Stuart, how did you get these files?" she stammered, though she thought she knew the answer now. "Who gave these to you?"

"I have my sources," Stuart said, his voice softening. He rubbed his chin. "The black market is a fun place. Comic fans are crazy. We're crazy. We'll buy and sell anything. This was just in some storage space in Long

Island. The guy I bought it from said he was storing it for a friend, but they'd never come to get it, so he wanted to unload it. He had no idea what he had—no idea the history these files contained. He just thought it was a bunch of pay stubs and office-closing memos. But you—you figured it out fast. You see what I've got here, right?"

Carmen nodded, still a bit shaken, still processing.

"Yes," she said, looking back down at the Panthena pitch. What *was* this? "I think I do."

"Take it," Alford said, shrugging, suddenly casual. "I want you to have that. It's yours."

Carmen wanted to be polite. To argue. But she also wanted the pitch. She needed it in a way she couldn't fully describe or comprehend.

"Thank you, thanks," she said, almost hugging the pages to herself. "I think I need to go . . . it's getting late."

Alford walked her to the door. He leaned against the doorway as she stepped out.

"Let me know what you dig up, all right?" he said, that smile still on his face. "I'm invested in this story. I know there's an end to this thread. We can find it together."

"I will," Carmen said, stuffing the pitch into her purse, folding the pages gently. "I'll call you if I learn more."

"Good night, Carmen," Alford said as he closed the door slowly. "I hope you find what you're looking for."

The click of the door closing, followed by the sound of Alford's locks sliding into place, echoed down the tiny hallway. Carmen stepped into the elevator and pushed the button for the lobby. She let her body lean back into the elevator car. Felt herself sag. She was so tired. Everything seemed to be happening so fast.

Dan Stephenson had run Bulwark. Dan Stephenson was Carlyle's brother-in-law. Someone at Bulwark had worked on a pitch that seemed to echo what Carmen and Harvey would do with the Lynx. Had it been Harvey? The stories were different enough, but it still nagged at Carmen. There was no cover page. Nothing that linked it to Bulwark beyond being in a file cabinet with other files. Something was missing, Carmen thought. Had someone robbed Bulwark only to leave the prize in a warehouse somewhere for Alford to find? It made no sense.

The cold air shocked her momentarily as she stepped out onto Broadway. It was late, she realized. She didn't like being downtown at this hour alone. She started to make her way back toward the train. She took out the pitch again gently. This time she tried to read the text carefully. That's when she saw it—something scribbled on the top page, in light pencil. Something she hadn't noticed at first glance.

Looks good—JC

Carmen felt her memory unfurl, felt herself transported to the basement of Harvey's apartment, a charred document stuffed into his empty desk. The only real sign of creative work. Had that been an earlier, less final version of the pitch Carmen held in her hands? What was Harvey doing with it?

"What have you done, Harvey?" she asked herself, still flipping through the pages as she crossed Grand Street.

"Look out!" she heard someone scream, but it was too late for Carmen.

She didn't hear the footsteps behind her, or the whooshing sound of something being lifted and slammed down. But she did feel it.

She was outside herself—and seemed to feel and watch her body crumble, a pulsing pain in her neck, then in her head, then in her entire body, in seconds. Maybe less.

She looked up. Saw someone hovering over her—a dark, muted shape, looking around, desperate and scared, but also . . . angry? Panic hit her then. Carmen thought to ask something, but she felt sluggish, dazed. She wanted to rest. To sleep for a long time.

Then everything went black.

*Excerpt from 1975's **The Legendary Lynx** #10, "Once More, Into the Void"*—Story: "Still a Secret, Dear Reader!" Art: Doug Detmer, Letters: Todd Morelli, Editor: Rich Berger, President/CEO: Jeffrey Ce
Published by Triumph Comics

CHAPTER THIRTY-SIX

Flickering light. Sounds—beeping, hushed voices, clattering. Then pain. Aching, dull pain, impossible to pinpoint.

"She's coming to," someone said.

"Get the doctor."

"He's on the way."

"Hey, you there? Carmen? Carm?"

She felt her eyes open. The blurry shapes coalesced into something familiar. A bed. Faces around her. A hospital. She tried to speak, but her throat felt cracked and dry.

"Just relax, okay?"

Molly.

Carmen felt herself start to nod, but the pain froze her. She closed her eyes again, felt the tears forming around them, trickling down her face. She tried again. She would keep trying.

This time she could see more clearly. Molly. Detective Hudson. Where was she?

"You had us going there for a minute, girl," Hudson said. Carmen could see her now. The shape of her dark face. Her kind eyes. Felt her hand gently on her own. "Doc is coming to fix you up some more. But in a little bit . . . we're gonna talk."

Carmen thought better of nodding, or moving at all. She closed her eyes and let herself drift away.

Carmen watched as the door to her hospital room swung open. It was Molly, Detective Hudson a few paces behind. Her roommate smiled.

"You up for some food?" Molly asked, a conspiratorial look in her eyes. "Got you something they don't serve here at St. Vincent's."

Molly lifted a box of pizza up over her head like a prize, walking it around the small hospital room as if she were presenting a championship belt at a prize fight.

"Nothing, I mean nothing, can top a fifty-cent slice," Molly said. She dropped a piece on a plate, the cheese and sauce already creating a crater of oil on the flimsy paper. Carmen shook her head no. She wasn't ready for that.

Molly shrugged and steered the slice into her own mouth as she sat down at the foot of the bed.

Carmen smiled. She'd lost much sense of time. But from what Molly had told her, she'd been there for a few days. She'd awoken a few hours after her arrival, but had been in and out until this morning. Carmen couldn't shake the headache that seemed to be a permanent fixture in her brain. But aside from the concussion, she'd dodged any permanent damage.

"You got lucky, girl," Hudson had told her. The detective hadn't waited to let Carmen know what happened. As Carmen had left Alford's apartment, she'd been hit in the back of the head—by something hard. A bat or a club. Had it not been for a worried bystander, whoever had struck her would have kept going. The screams of the concerned citizen saved Carmen's life.

"How's the patient today?" Hudson asked, taking a seat next to Carmen's bed. "Up for a few questions?"

Carmen sighed. She'd known this moment would come. Hudson was persistent. She'd given Carmen a few days to recover. A few days to mull over just what had happened. But she wouldn't give her much more time.

"I'm . . . I'm not ready, Detective, I'm sorry," Carmen said, leaning back, wincing. "Can we talk tomorrow?"

Hudson shook her head.

"No, we can't talk tomorrow," she said. The tenderness in her voice wasn't totally gone, but it was clear to Carmen that Hudson was done waiting. "You've been laid up a few days, I get it. Seems like you can speak fine, though. So let's talk."

Carmen licked her dry lips and nodded in agreement.

"So, let's start from the beginning," Hudson said methodically. "Why were you there? Downtown, that time of night? By yourself?"

Carmen was tired. Too tired to try to sidestep the detective with any Claire Morgan–esque antics. She just told it straight. How she'd found Alford's number. Their awkward dinner at Umbertos. The conversations back at his apartment. She didn't mention the Bulwark files, thinking that it might end up coming back to bite Alford.

Hudson nodded along, not interrupting, soaking Carmen's story in. When Carmen stopped to take a sip of water, she finally spoke.

"That it?"

"I think so," Carmen said.

"Well, all right. Here's the truth," Hudson said, leaning forward in her chair, her eyes on Carmen. "Whoever did your friend in—and whoever probably hurt your other friend, Marion—they're gunning for you. You got real lucky there was a Good Samaritan around that time of night. You're lucky you're a pretty girl, too. If it'd been a dude passed out in the street, I'm sure he'd have kept walking."

Carmen didn't respond. She let her eyes close briefly. She felt the pull of medicated sleep.

"You fading on me, Valdez?"

"I'm tired."

"Walk me through what you remember before you got hit. What happened right before?" Hudson asked. "Maybe we can learn something that'll help catch this son of a bitch. Can you do that for me?"

Carmen nodded. She thought back to those steps. What had she been doing? Leaving Alford's apartment. The elevator. Rummaging through her purse.

The pages. The pitch.

She grabbed Hudson's arm.

"The papers," she said. "Where are the papers?"

"The papers?" Hudson asked. "What?"

"Did they find the papers with me? Any pages?" Carmen asked, trying to backtrack, kicking herself for saying too much. "Anything?"

"Just your purse," Hudson said, looking at Carmen warily. "Seemed like everything was there. Nothing stolen. What papers are you talking about?"

Carmen shook her head.

"It's nothing, nothing," she said. She groaned slightly as she leaned back down in bed. "Sorry. I'm just not up for much else today."

Hudson rested her hands on the railing around Carmen's bed. The look on her face said much more than she could say with words.

You're bullshitting me.

"I've got a lot more questions," Hudson said. "And you should know by now that I like to get them answered. I'm patient. I can wait until tomorrow. But I can't wait forever."

She patted Carmen on the shoulder and turned toward the side table next to her bed. She pulled out a business card and shook it gently.

"My card. Gonna write my home number on the back. Hardly anyone has that number. Prized knowledge. Pick up on every ring when I'm home," she said as she jotted the number down on the card, not looking up at Carmen. "I know your type. You're a good person. That's nice. But you're nosy and you have a weird sense of justice. I get that, too. Still, I'm sanctioned to feel that way. You're not."

She straightened up and tapped the card with a finger.

"And if my gut is right, you're going to do something stupid again. Soon, even," Hudson said. "I want you to promise to call me before you do. You understand?"

"I do," Carmen said, her voice barely louder than a whisper.

Hudson turned around and headed for the door. She gave Molly a quick nod before turning to look at Carmen.

"I'll be back tomorrow. Then the next day," she said. "You were out there, that late at night, for a reason. I want to know more than why. I want the details. What you learned. I warned you about getting your nose up in this shit, and it seems like you weren't listening to me. Best get your story straight."

Carmen could only nod in response. Hudson left without another word.

"That was intense," Molly said, standing up and walking over to Carmen's bedside. "Wonder how many friends she has?"

"She's not bad," Carmen said, wincing as she tried to sit up. "She means well. And she's right."

"Right about what?" Molly asked. "What the hell happened, Carm?"

"I don't really know, to be honest," Carmen said, cursing under her breath as she swiveled her legs over the side of the bed. "I thought I was close to figuring it out. To finding out what happened to Harvey and why, but I don't think I am. And I lost something that would've been a big help. I was sloppy. I should have kept my eyes and ears open, and instead I was walking around like a teenager reading a dirty novel."

"Where the hell are you going?" Molly asked.

"I need to get up, move my legs," Carmen said, standing up for the first time in what felt like years. She was wobbly, her head light. The hospital's bright, all-encompassing lights didn't help. But she felt better than she expected. "I don't want to be here forever. Have to get home, get back to work."

"You're insane, but that reminds me," Molly said.

She turned and walked to a nearby chair. She pulled out a long package from under her purse.

"Forgot to tell you, this came for you yesterday, a messenger dropped it off," Molly said, sliding the large box onto Carmen's bed. "Lucky they came by while I was home. My hours aren't exactly normal."

"Huh," Carmen said. She looked the box over. The return address set off alarm bells. DETMER. She felt her fingers tearing into the box, opening it up roughly.

It took a moment, but Carmen recognized the contents. They were pages, a stack of original art. Detmer's art. The top piece was a cover—to *The Legendary Lynx* #11. It featured their heroine being lifted into the air by her archnemesis, Mr. Void, his evil on full display. There were rough lettering notes on the bottom right of the cover—*Final Confrontation!*

Carmen smiled.

"What is this?" Molly said, looking over Carmen's shoulder, her hand on Carmen's arm.

"It's our comic," Carmen said, moving to the first page of the story. It was a full splash page of the Lynx crashing through a warehouse skylight, glass sprinkling through the sky, a group of the Voidoids, Mr. Void's goons, staring up in surprise. She felt a lump in her throat. Could feel her face reddening with pride. The tears came soon after, when she read the tiny credit box Detmer had scrawled on the bottom of the page.

Story by Carmen Valdez / Art by Doug Detmer.

"That's you," Molly said, leaning her head on Carmen's shoulder. "Wow. This is great."

Carmen nodded, unable to form words. This was their story. With her name on it.

No one could take this away from her.

She almost missed the tiny slip of paper that was at the bottom of the box. Molly snatched it, her eyes narrowing as she read the handwriting on the yellow scrap. She handed it to Carmen without a word, a look of confusion on her face.

Carmen recognized the handwriting immediately. Detmer. These were the pages he'd been stuffing into the envelope when Carmen arrived at the studio.

Don't let them keep you in the shadows anymore.

This has nothing to do with you.

Thank you for your friendship. Don't forget me.—DD

Her eyes hovered over the last words for an extra moment. Trying to process what they meant, trying to understand if they could mean anything but what she understood. Then, she panicked.

"No . . . Oh God, no . . . Oh my God," Carmen said, dropping the paper. The rest of the pages fell onto the bed, some of the art boards sliding onto the ground as Carmen struggled into her clothes. "Jesus . . . No . . . Fuck."

"What happened?" Molly said. "Who is this person? Carmen—where are you going?"

But Carmen was gone, the only sign of her exit the handful of Doug Detmer art pages floating down onto the grimy Saint Vincent's Hospital floor.

CHAPTER THIRTY-SEVEN

The funeral was a light affair. Ten, maybe twelve people in attendance.

Doug Detmer had died by a self-inflicted gunshot wound six days prior.

Carmen's hand shook as she signed the guest book. The funeral home was quiet and somber, as one would expect such places to be. Carmen, in her limited funeral experience, was used to the Catholic Cuban way—a viewing, a burial, a gathering. Detmer was Catholic, too, she learned—at least technically. But there would be no open casket here. She stepped into the room, saw the coffin that would usher him into the hereafter in the middle of the space. She recognized some of the guests. Jeffrey Carlyle. Rich Berger. Dan Stephenson. Some of the younger production staff at Triumph—Hahn, Mullin, and Trunick. She kept to the back. Nodding slightly as Carlyle turned and gave her a brief wave before returning his gaze to the giant wreath of flowers positioned in front of the casket. She slid her hands into her coat pocket. She felt the slip of paper weave through her fingers. She'd last worn this coat at dinner with Marion, she realized.

Carmen knew she was too late the moment she forced her way into Detmer's building. When she saw his feet poking out from behind his drawing table, a pool of blood forming on the opposite end.

She wasn't sure if she'd screamed then. She couldn't remember. She'd just known her friend was gone. Her only ally in all this. The only person who truly knew what went on. Who truly understood.

Yet in the flurry of times they'd worked together, Carmen never took a moment to get to know the man beyond the surface. Beyond the clear drinking problem. The surly demeanor. The knight-errant trying to preserve some kind of rule of law in an industry that was spiraling into something else, something darker. Who was Doug Detmer? What demons found a way to crawl inside of him? His name should've been listed along with so many other greats, like Ditko, Toth, Eisner . . . but instead, she feared, he'd be a footnote. A name someone would bring up to impress his colleagues, a sign of deep insider knowledge, nothing more. A trivia answer in a game that not many people seemed interested in playing for very long.

She turned to see Carlyle sidling up next to her, placing a hand on her shoulder.

"Carmen, so good to see you," he said. "I know this is hard. For Triumph. For me. For everyone."

She smiled at the platitudes. She knew the same questions she had for him could be asked of her.

Why were you there?

Carmen thought back to six days earlier. She'd been in Detmer's studio for just a few minutes when she heard footsteps. She turned and saw Carlyle, a look of shock on his face as he glimpsed Carmen, a look of pained understanding as he recognized Detmer's body on the ground.

"We have to carry on, you know," Carlyle said, leaning his head toward Carmen so the other funeral attendees couldn't overhear. "Detmer was troubled. Always had issues. I liked the man, a truly great artist, but he was not well. Hadn't been for almost twenty years. We'll figure out what to do next."

Carmen shook her head in disgust. She saw Carlyle's shocked reaction. She didn't care.

"He was a person, boss," she said, looking up at Carlyle, her face streaked with angry tears. "He worked for you. You knew him, what? Twenty, thirty years? Least you could do is not talk shit about him at his own damn funeral."

Carlyle opened his mouth, but thought better of it. He nodded.

Carmen looked toward the front of the small group. Felt the thin piece of paper in her coat pocket. A talisman of sorts, she thought.

Stephenson stood in front, hands clasped, head bowed. He turned to look at Carmen, their eyes meeting. She stared back. After a moment, he looked away.

"He was my friend," she said, choking back her words. "He was a good man."

Carlyle nodded.

"Why were you there?" she asked. "Why did you come to his studio?"

"Let me get you a cab," Carlyle said after a bit longer.

She brushed him off. Could feel him lingering behind her as she hailed a taxi and stepped inside. The tears started to come then, as she saw Carlyle fading into the cityscape. She buried her face in her hands.

By the time she got to her apartment, the tears had dried—a steely resolve in their place.

She reached under her bed to find the box that contained Doug Detmer's final issue of *The Legendary Lynx*. She flipped to the last page, turning it around slowly. She saw the scribbled words there, again. The words that would haunt her for years to come.

Bulwark → Triumph
$$$$

She put the pages back into the box gently. She got up and went back to her coat, draped on her rumpled bed. She pulled out the small scrap of paper. She'd almost forgotten it. How Marion had slid it into her coat pocket as she kissed her goodbye. Hours before she was attacked. She looked at it again now, for what felt like the thousandth time since her friend had been assaulted. The message was a question. The final two words—the name—underlined three times.

Who is <u>Mark Jensen</u>??

She let the note drop back onto her coat.

She whispered a prayer.

Then she lay down in bed, pulled her knees up to her face, and cried again.

CHAPTER THIRTY-EIGHT

She saw Alford's shadow before she caught sight of the burly man as he approached the front door of his apartment, a bag of take-out Chinese in one hand. It was late. Close to ten. Carmen felt tired. It'd been a few days since Detmer's funeral and a week and change since she'd left the hospital, but she still didn't feel right. She wasn't sure she'd ever feel right. But there was work to be done.

She heard Alford's key slide into the door. She took a step. He spun around, eyes wide in surprise.

"We need to talk, Stuart," Carmen said, her black coat enveloping her like a flowing cape. "You have something that belongs to a friend of mine."

Alford's expression went from surprise to understanding. He wasn't shocked to see her. It had only been a matter of time, Carmen realized.

"What do you want?" he asked. "I didn't help you so you'd keep coming back."

"But you knew I would be back, right?" Carmen asked. "If I was smart."

"I wasn't sure you were," he spat. "But here we are."

He opened his door and held it open for her. Carmen hesitated for a second, the bump on the back of her head seeming to pulse with pain at the thought of turning her back to a strange man, but she walked in anyway.

"I need to see those Bulwark records again," Carmen said, walking toward the two file cabinets she'd skimmed before. "I need to look through them myself."

"Why? Why should I?" Alford sputtered. He seemed jittery, defensive, standing between Carmen and the files. "You can't just come in here—"

Carmen raised a finger to silence him.

"I can do whatever I want right now, Stuart," she said, a dark smile on her face. "Because something tells me you won't want to explain how you got all these files in your apartment. I checked you out, you see? You're not just some enterprising comics reporter—you've worked in comics, too. In fact, you interned at Bulwark. Seems like a much clearer line to you and these files—these *stolen* files—than you led me to believe before. I think Detective Hudson would love to hear about it. You know cops, right? They love to speculate about motive."

Alford swallowed hard. His face flushed red with anger.

"You can't just—" he said before stopping himself, a low whine to his voice. "Fine. Just, well, just be quick about it. I don't have all night."

"Expecting someone?" Carmen asked as she walked to the second file cabinet. "I don't need this, okay? I know what happened. I just need confirmation. You're just helping me check my own work, okay? Just sit back and I'll be out of your hair in a few. If not, it gets more complicated."

Carmen knew what she wanted to look at. Had been glancing at it when Alford had dangled his magical stack of pitches. Had pulled her away. As she flipped through the folders, she spoke to Alford. "Who gave you the files? Was it Doug?"

Alford started to pace, taking a moment before responding.

"I can't say, I just—"

"He's dead," Carmen said. "You knew that, right? He blew his brains out two weeks ago. It doesn't matter anymore. But I have to figure this out. For Harvey. For Marion Price. For Doug. Can you help me?"

Alford looked down at his feet, his head shaking.

"Yeah, it was Doug," he said. "Doug thought Bulwark was gonna be his last shot. Stephenson and Carlyle promised him the world. They'd make him art director. Let him nurture new talent. Guide the look of the line. It felt like a dream gig. But Doug was a mess. He couldn't do it. And pretty soon, he realized what a scam Bulwark was. Doug saw it before anyone else. Started talking, complaining—about how Stephenson was ripping people off, abusing his staff, bilking talent. It was sloppy. But no one should have been surprised, okay? Doug Detmer was never a team player. By the end—he knew he was quitting. But he knew—"

"That's when he told you about these files? He knew how much it'd hurt Stephenson?"

Alford nodded.

"And you took them and started your enterprising journalism career," Carmen said, disdain dripping from each word. "But you're not telling me everything, either."

Alford only stared at Carmen.

"That's okay," Carmen said, pulling out a thick folder. She reached for one page in particular. "I got what I came for."

She stood up, the small stack of papers safely tucked in her purse. This time, she thought, she'd save the close reading for when she got home.

She sidestepped Alford and walked out of the loft space without another word.

CHAPTER THIRTY-NINE

Carlyle flicked on the lights and seemed to jump a few centimeters.

It was barely eight in the morning. He hadn't expected to find Carmen there, sitting at her desk in the dark—a large box in front of her.

"What the hell is going on here?" Carlyle asked, trying to shake off his discomfort. "I almost jumped out of my own skin."

"Wanted to deliver something," Carmen said, standing up and stepping around her desk. She motioned to the box. "Couldn't wait."

Carlyle grumbled as he walked over. He looked in the large, thin box. Carmen caught the slight flicker of recognition and the pivot to ignorance.

"What is this?" he asked, flipping through the pages. "You're sitting here in the dark because someone mailed in some artwork? Are you feeling ill?"

"These are Doug Detmer pages. You know that, though," Carmen said, half sitting on the desk. She placed a hand on the top page—her pointer finger hovering over the credits. "It's for a new issue of *The Legendary Lynx*. It was the last thing he did before he died."

Carlyle scoffed and took a half step back.

"What in God's name for?" he asked. "We didn't even have a script for that issue. Did he write it himself?"

"No, boss," Carmen said, waiting a moment. She felt the weight of what she was going to say. Felt it rising off her shoulders as she spoke the words. "I did. I wrote it."

Carlyle shook his head, his confusion almost plausible. But Carmen was past that. As she'd told Alford—she knew the answers. She was just seeking confirmation now. And she knew Carlyle had never been as dumb as he'd pretended to be.

"What are you talking about?" Carlyle said. "Did you go around me to get Detmer to draw one of your—one of those—what? Spec scripts? Vanity projects?"

"Boss, I respect you. But c'mon. You know me well enough to know I wouldn't do that," Carmen said. "So, please, don't try to twist what I'm saying."

Carlyle scoffed. He tried to move around Carmen, to head into his office, but she stepped in front of him. "What are you doing?" he asked.

"I know the truth," Carmen said, looking up at a man she'd once considered a mentor. Perhaps even a friend, flaws aside. "I know what happened with Bulwark. I know that you bought the company from Stephenson for pennies, to help your brother-in-law pay off his own dangerous debts. Not only that, you kept people like Stephenson—and other guys who were fading fast, Detmer, Mark Jensen—you kept them working here at Triumph. Busy enough to make a living. Why, boss? That's the thing I don't get. What did they have on you?"

"You know nothing," Carlyle said. His voice was low, hushed and angry. It unnerved her. "And you should watch how you toss accusations around, dear."

Carmen reached into her purse and pulled out a stack of pages. They looked like itemized records. Banking transactions. Lots of them.

"How do you explain these?" Carmen said, dropping one of the pages onto the desk. "Payments from you to Stephenson, regular, big sums."

She dropped another page onto the stack.

"Then another large sum—right before Bulwark closed down for good," Carmen continued. "Enough to pick up some cheap equipment, maybe a few file cabinets' worth of characters and ideas?"

Carmen looked up at Carlyle. His face was reddening, his mouth twisted into a painful grimace.

"It doesn't end there," Carmen said, adding another page. "These are invoices you've signed here at Triumph—to Mark Jensen—for work we never published. Now, I can't tell you how to spend your money. This is your company. But it makes you wonder why a successful publisher like you might pay a hack like Jensen thousands of dollars to do . . . nothing?"

Carlyle picked up one of the pages and scanned it. Then let it drop back onto the desk.

"You're doubling down pretty hard," he said, ever the poker player. "I could just fire you right now."

"Yeah, you could," Carmen said with a brief nod. "And you probably will, and there's nothing I can do about it. Except take these pages to Detective Hudson. I'm sure it might make for interesting reading."

"What in the hell does this have to do with anything?" Carlyle said, his voice rising. She'd hit a nerve. "How I spend my money is none of her business."

Carmen stood up. She grabbed the stack of papers and straightened them on the desk before putting them back in her purse.

"Maybe, maybe not," she said. "Doesn't hurt to ask, I guess."

Carlyle raised a hand.

"Fine, fine. Look, Carmen, you're a good person at heart, okay? This isn't you. I know your dream is to write. So, just tell me what you want, we can figure something out," he said. "Let's be sensible about this. We don't need any more trouble these days."

Carmen put a hand on Carlyle's arm. He felt tense, ready to strike.

"No, *Jeffrey*, no. I don't want to blackmail my way into this," she said. "I want to earn my place in comics. My own way. But I will ask that you run this story—Doug's last story. For him. And you'll use my name. I wrote it. And I helped Harvey write those scripts he turned in, too. But

I won't make you keep me on. Or force you to give me work. That's kind of what got you into this mess, huh?"

Carlyle seemed to sag a bit. Was it relief . . . or defeat?

"There is one more thing I want to know," Carmen said. "One more bit of information."

CHAPTER FORTY

The *ding* of the elevator alerted her.

Carmen watched as the figure stepped out and looked around the dark office.

It was late in the evening. The office was empty aside from Carmen, who—once again—was waiting in the dark.

The figure stepped into the office, arms trying to find a light switch on the wall and having little luck.

"Jeffrey?" the figure asked, taking another hesitant step into the Triumph offices. "You called—I'm here. What's going on? Why can't we just meet at McGee's? Can't even see my own hand in front of me."

Carmen turned the lights on, illuminating the figure that stood across the office from her. Dan Stephenson. He tried to blink away the sudden brightness. Once his eyes grew accustomed to the light, he settled his gaze on Carmen, seated calmly at her desk.

"What is this?" Stephenson said, his eyes narrowing as he approached. "Carlyle called to tell me he had a check for me. You got it?"

Carmen didn't respond immediately.

Stephenson looked even more disheveled than usual, the beard more scraggly, the clothes wrinkled and stained.

"Hm, wasn't expecting you, Dan," Carmen said, feigning concern. Stephenson came a few steps closer. "I do have a check. . . ."

She pulled out a blank envelope.

"But it's not addressed to you," she continued.

"Who's it for, then?" Stephenson asked. "What is going on here? Carlyle never sends people to pay me, it's between me and him. Who's the check for?"

Carmen placed the envelope back on her desk and looked up at Stephenson, no longer hiding her humorless grin.

"It's a check for Mark Jensen," she said. "Do you know him?"

Stephenson stopped in his tracks, about a foot from Carmen's desk. His face formed a sly smile.

"Ah, so you figured it out—my own little pseudonym. Goodie for you. Now what?" Stephenson said. "You're going to complain to your boss that his own damn brother-in-law's been double-dipping? Gimme a break, you nosy little bitch. You think he didn't know?"

Carmen didn't let the insult rattle her. She persisted.

"I'm more curious about what you knew," she said, lifting up a stack of charred papers. The notes she'd found in Harvey's desk. "About Harvey Stern. And about the Lynx."

CHAPTER FORTY-ONE

The fuck are you talking about?" Stephenson barked.

"I'm talking about you, Dan," Carmen said, a thin smile on her face. "About your ability to just keep hanging around. Surviving. Like some kind of disgusting barnacle. Somehow, toward the end of your career, when pretty much everyone wrote you off, you found enough money to start your own company. Then when that went under, you land a cushy editorial gig here at Triumph while making money for hacking out scripts under another name. Now, I get that Carlyle's your brother-in-law—but it had to be more than that, huh? Family has a ceiling, too, right?"

Carmen leaned forward, her elbows on the desk.

"So I did a little digging. It took a minute—I had to compare what I had to public filings, then I had to talk to people. Then I had to cross-reference it all," Carmen said, ticking off topics with her fingers. "But from what I could tell, Carlyle bought you out of Bulwark, left you a nice retirement package, and paid off Doug Detmer, too. Seems like a really generous brother-in-law."

She noticed Stephenson's shoulders relax a bit. He scratched at his unkempt beard.

"Do you want a prize?" Stephenson said. "Jeffrey was in business with the wrong people. His desperate quest for legitimacy—to somehow achieve fame as some kind of literary wunderkind—blinded him. Forced him into bad deals. Bad debts. How do you think he was able to buy Triumph out from under his father? He had to make some promises to some shady guys. Promises I knew about. Promises that could ruin a guy like him. His sister told me, when she was alive. She didn't realize that info would save my life years later, when I couldn't get work from anyone. When I needed to become someone else just to pay my rent. Detmer knew it, too. Yeah, that sure came in handy then."

Carmen didn't respond. Stephenson seemed wound up. Her gamble was right. He kept talking.

"Detmer . . . he was no angel. He knew where Carlyle's skeletons were," Stephenson said. He seemed desperate, out of breath, as if he were trying to convince Carmen of something only he understood. "So we did it. We survived. We had no choice. Comics had left us behind. No one would hire us, so we had to carve out our own path. Doug could still draw, too. So it was easy to give him an assignment here and there. But I couldn't live off that. I needed something else, I realized. I deserved something else. I needed a paycheck. I wanted that."

"What else did you want?" Carmen asked. She pulled out the charred pages of the Panthena pitch—the one that resembled so much of what Harvey had brought to the table when they'd created the Lynx. "Revenge?"

Stephenson scanned the paper.

"What about Harvey?"

"Stern? That little shit?" Stephenson said, looking up from the burned pitch. "This idea—this paper—is mine. I can't even begin to figure out how you got your slimy little hands on it, or what you're trying to pull here."

He took a few steps toward her, his palms on the edge of her desk as he leaned forward.

"It's mine," Stephenson continued, leaning into Carmen's personal space, his rank breath clouding the air between them. "And I want it returned to me."

Carmen leaned back, moving her chair away from her desk and Stephenson.

"You created a character for him, when he was an editor at Bulwark," Carmen said. "Right?"

"Wrong," Stephenson said, his grin widening. "Mark Jensen did. That little twerp had no idea we were one and the same. But then the Bulwark offices are robbed. Suddenly Stern feels like the company's doing some dirty dealing, so he quits—it took me a while to piece it together. That this uppity shit had stolen from his own employer. I'd lost focus. My company was going under, and even with Carlyle keeping me afloat, I'd lost everything. I was distracted. By the time I pieced it all together, Stern was gone."

Stephenson stood straighter now, looming over Carmen.

"But then Stern ends up here, at Triumph," Stephenson said, his eyes glazing over, as if he were transporting himself somewhere else. "Then I see he's taken my idea, my work, and turned it into this Lynx bimbo character. . . ."

Stephenson reached into his coat. He pulled out the revolver as if he were taking out a comb. There was a silencer affixed to the weapon. Stephenson had come prepared.

"I fought in Korea, my dear," he said, shaking the gun hastily. "I don't take shit from anyone—not Carlyle, not from a punk like Harvey, not from a skinny, ugly dyke like you."

Carmen stood up. Felt her hands twitching at the insult. Saw as Stephenson shakily lifted the gun barrel to match her movement. He was off-balance, she noticed. He had expected fear. Timidity. Instead, he got something else.

"Yeah?" Carmen said, her vision locked on Stephenson's own bloodshot eyes. "I don't take shit from anyone, either. Not anymore."

CHAPTER FORTY-TWO

Stephenson took a hasty step forward, the barrel now pointed at Carmen's chest.

She felt a streak of sweat slide down her back. Stephenson seemed calm, but Carmen had rattled him enough to pull a gun. She had to keep him distracted.

"But why kill him, then?" she asked. "Why not just tell Carlyle that Harvey had stolen your idea?"

Stephenson shook his head jerkily.

"Because the damage was done, you idiot," he spat. "Stern fucked me. Once I heard Jeffrey had him working on the book, it was over. I couldn't put the genie back in the bottle. Stern tried to fuck me, and I don't like that. He tried to fuck Jensen. At least that bitch Price was smart enough to keep her mouth shut. She knew how to leave well enough alone . . . but then I see her with you, and I knew. I just knew she'd broken . . . knew she'd spilled what little she had. I hope it was worth it."

Stephenson rubbed his eyes roughly, as if trying to keep himself focused. His eyes looked electric.

"You see, Stern knew that idea was gold, but he got mad when he realized Bulwark would own it, lock, stock, and barrel. So he stole it and saved it for a rainy day, not realizing I'd find out. He didn't even know I was Jensen, not until I got into his apartment and explained it to that whimpering fool. Oh, he cried, begging for his life—said he just wanted his own break. . . ."

Carmen remembered those moments with Harvey—brainstorming the bits and pieces that would blend together to form the Lynx, now forever screened through a new, darker lens.

Maybe we give her cat powers? he'd asked.

Harvey had been smart enough to piggyback on Carmen's ideas—to take the things that would make the Lynx different enough from the Panthena pitch, but retain the elements he knew would make it a hit. Carmen thought back to how prepared he was. How generous he'd seemed. How willing he was to brainstorm on some things, but how definitive he'd been on others. Why had he looped her into his fraud? she wondered. Was there something more sinister? Or had Harvey just wanted a colleague to validate his own feelings about what he was doing? A good deed—giving Carmen a shot at her dream—erasing a bad one?

Stephenson's words crashed into Carmen's brief remembrance.

"Oh, wait, now I get it. It was you," Stephenson said, the gun raised higher, pointed at Carmen's head. "You were what he was talking about. The ghostwriter. He cried over you. Said you helped him. Even in the end, he didn't give up your name. I was surprised by that—Stern showing a slight bit of backbone. . . ."

Stephenson seemed to be reveling in the memory of Harvey's final moments, like some strange high. He snapped back to the present and his stare chilled Carmen all over.

"Stern was a thief," Stephenson said. "A hack—a nothing. All he had were those notes Jensen—well, I—wrote. He knew he needed something else. Someone else. But why pair with a real writer? Someone he'd have to credit? When he had you lying around, desperate for any foot in the door? Even an invisible one?"

Carmen felt her hands begin to shake, Stephenson's words shooting through her.

"You were the perfect tool for him," Stephenson said. "The partner he could use and ignore as he saw fit. Once the comic was printed, once his name was on the book—no one would know or care about Carmen Valdez."

The final piece clicked into place, as if falling from the skies. Carmen saw the full picture, and it broke her heart.

Stephenson had murdered Harvey to get revenge, then used his relationship with Carlyle to not only reclaim his character, but to take over from the man who'd stolen it from him. Then, in a panic, he'd attacked Marion Price—desperate to keep himself in the shadows and retain his hold on the character. But Stephenson had miscalculated one thing.

The Lynx wasn't Harvey's character to lose.

Her hands stopped shaking. She felt the resolve spread through her like a smooth, pleasant sedative. She'd been in the shadows too long. For so many different things. She'd hoped and pined for someone to hand her a shot, an opportunity. Had been patient and dutiful. No more.

The Lynx was hers.

"It's not yours," Carmen hissed as she moved toward him, surprising Stephenson. She took another step around her desk. She ignored the gun. "The idea Harvey took from you, from Bulwark, was nothing—a few lines, cliché crap, like most of the stuff you've cranked out for years. But Lynx is mine. She's been inside me since I can remember. I won't let you hurt her anymore."

Stephenson smiled.

"Oh my, the little kitty has a bite," he said, only a foot away from Carmen. "Do you think anyone will care . . . or remember you when you die? I can read the headlines now, if there are any: 'Former comic book secretary found shot at her desk.' A blip on the radar. A footnote. A forgotten piece of comic book history. A nothing."

Carmen moved. She took two quick steps toward Stephenson, grabbing his gun arm and pushing it up. He fought back, but he was older, slower, and the surprise gave her an advantage, leaving the older man momentarily off-balance.

"Maybe Stern was right to pick you," Stephenson said, pushing back, slowly regaining control of the weapon. "But no matter. It ends here."

Carmen panicked. She pushed Stephenson backward and away, hoping to knock him off his feet. Instead, he just stumbled, his arms flailing as he struggled for balance.

Then a noise, a muted, shunting sound.

The gun.

Carmen fell to the ground. Before her brain could register it, her hands were at her midsection. They felt wet and hot. She didn't look down. She couldn't look down.

She closed her eyes. She heard Stephenson stepping somewhere—toward her? Labored breathing. Then a louder noise. Footsteps. A familiar voice.

"Freeze! Put the gun down. You're surrounded."

Carmen's eyes fluttered open, hazy and tired. She was so tired. Stephenson was on his knees now, a few feet from Carmen. She heard his gun rattle to the floor.

"No, no, what is this?"

Carmen felt her body splayed on the grimy Triumph Comics floor, the linoleum cool and calming as she struggled to breathe.

"No good hero . . ." she said, her voice a whisper only she could hear. "Goes into battle . . . without backup . . ."

CHAPTER FORTY-THREE

Two Months Later

t was late. Well after one in the morning. Carmen felt dizzy and light-headed, her body caked in dried sweat.

She'd never felt better.

She still felt a pinch of soreness when she walked too fast, or stretched too far. Bending over to pick things up sometimes stung, too. But tonight—it didn't matter. She smiled at Molly as they walked crosstown from the Upper West Side, away from the Beacon Theatre. They felt euphoric and other-dimensional.

"That was amazing, Carm," Molly said, leaning her head on Carmen's shoulder, her face sleek and glowing. "I mean, I knew Johnny and Celia were amazing, but damn. Together? That was something else."

Carmen just smiled. Celia Cruz was a legend musically to all, but especially to Cubans like her. La Guarachera de Cuba had been singing since the fifties, and would probably go on for another handful of decades doing her thing. "Quimbara" was an anthem. To hear her sing it with another legend, Johnny Pacheco, was something Carmen had never thought possible.

"I still can't believe you got tickets," Carmen said.

Molly shrugged.

"Sometimes people do me favors, you know? One of the benefits of playing gigs all over the city," Molly said with a soft smile.

She slid her hand into Carmen's and they walked a few more blocks in silence.

The cold air felt good on their skin, cooling them off from the heat and rush of a good show.

Carmen knew she should be grateful. To have survived. That Dan Stephenson was in jail, awaiting trial for the murder of Harvey Stern and the brutal attack on Marion Price. He'd killed Harvey out of anger—at Harvey's theft of his idea, an idea that ended up forming only a slice of the Lynx. Then he'd assaulted Marion out of fear—worried she knew something and was talking. He hadn't expected her to be awake, much less to put up such a fight. Marion was better now, Carmen knew. She'd visited her a few times in the hospital when Carmen was finally out herself. She'd moved back to California. She was done with comics, she'd told Carmen, but she promised to keep in touch. Carmen hadn't heard from her. *That's how these things go,* she thought. You get close to a light and then it flickers and fades.

Stephenson facing a judge brought her some relief. But it also left a pain inside her. A sadness she couldn't shake. She'd trusted Harvey. Thought his intentions had been real. Maybe they had been. Maybe the truth resided somewhere between what Stephenson had said—that Harvey was a hack desperate to use someone to create his ticket to fame, or that he genuinely wanted to help his friend achieve her dream. Both things could exist at once, Carmen thought.

"You're thinking too hard, girl," Molly said, elbowing her gently. She stopped short, realizing she was hitting too close to where Carmen had been shot. "Oh, Carm, shit—I'm sorry."

"It's fine," Carmen said, trying to smile. "I'm good."

They fell back into a comfortable silence as they crossed Madison Avenue. Carmen let her eyes close for a moment. She could hear Celia singing one of Carmen's favorites—"Vieja Luna"—her lush, melodious voice sounding wistful and pleading at once, begging to escape with the aging moon when the night dies. "En el momento en que la noche muere."

The plaintive music seemed to live in Carmen's head, pulsing through her as they kept walking, kept moving. Celia's sad, somber ode to an old moon, and her own fears for tomorrow, stuck with Carmen.

"You heard anything from your job?" Molly asked, her question dangling between them cautiously. She knew Carmen didn't want to talk about this. But, like a good friend, she was asking her the tough questions anyway.

"No, but I haven't checked," Carmen said.

It was the truth. Carlyle had been unexpectedly kind to Carmen while she was hospitalized and now, paying her as if she were working and treading carefully around their conversations. Carmen knew it came from a place of fear, and she was fine with that. Carlyle had known more than he let on—he'd known Jensen was a fraud, funded Stephenson and Detmer and Bulwark, pouring money into a sham operation and then trying to cover it up to avoid anyone finding out just where his own money came from. But that was an investigation for someone else. She wasn't interested in bringing Jeffrey Carlyle down. Honestly, she thought, she wasn't sure what she was interested in at the moment. But she knew one thing—Jeffrey Carlyle would find a way to survive—to thrive, even. He'd find a corner to cut or a deal to swing. Triumph Comics would live on.

"You're gonna quit, huh?"

Carmen nodded.

"Yeah," Carmen said. "I think I'm done."

Carmen's words seemed to turn into smoke and spread out before them—meaning so much and saying so little.

While she'd been laid up in the hospital, *The Legendary Lynx* had continued. Rich Berger had resigned from Triumph and gone freelance, picking up where Carmen had left off and taking the series in a solid, if unspectacular, direction. The art was solid, if still in the shadow of Doug Detmer, in the hands of a newcomer named Henry Zdarsky. It wasn't that the comics were bad—they just lacked the spark that she and Harvey and Detmer had brought to the series. Carmen felt fine thinking that. She'd earned that much, she thought.

Carlyle had kept her posted on what was going on, seemingly afraid of whatever stink Carmen would raise upon her release. But nothing happened. Carmen would nod politely, give a suggestion or two on story or the art, and Carlyle would be on his way. Eventually, he stopped visiting. Her paycheck would arrive every other week by messenger. First to her hospital room—sponsored by Triumph Comics—then to her apartment. She didn't question it.

Celia's voice flowed through her mind again. The forlorn, escapist plea to an aging sky. It reminded Carmen of the humid, sunny Miami air. Of sitting in her air-conditioned room, dropping a stack of new comic books on her bed—flipping through the pages, her eyes wide with anticipation. She felt her mami's hands sliding over her face before bed. Felt her father's chapped lips kissing her forehead as he left for work in the morning, the dusk barely illuminating the world outside their window.

She turned to Molly.

They were almost home, halfway down the block. She grabbed her roommate's hands and started a simple salsa shuffle, her steps moving instinctively to the music in her head.

Molly played along, sliding her hand around Carmen's waist as they moved, their smiles mirroring each other. Carmen twirled Molly around, letting her drop back, her arm holding her up. As the imaginary song drew to a close, Molly stood up, her face close to Carmen's.

"It's nice to see you happy," she said.

"I am happy," Carmen said, a genuine smile now.

Carmen turned her head. She noticed the bank of pay phones near the corner bodega.

She looked at Molly.

"Can I meet you at home?" she asked. "I need to talk to someone."

Molly nodded.

"Be careful, okay?" she said as she walked toward their apartment, turning back to look at Carmen. "I'll see you in a bit."

Carmen waved at her and made her way to the pay phone. She asked the operator to make a long-distance call.

The phone rang three times. Four. Carmen thought about hanging up—but then she heard his voice. Her heart seemed to fill—not with anger or fear, but with love.

"Oigo?" he said, sounding confused. Carmen realized how late it was. She didn't care.

"Papi?"

"Carmen? Carmencita?" he said, confusion and elation blending together in his words. "Cómo estás, mijita? Estás bien? Necesitas algo?"

"Hi, Papi," Carmen said, the tears forming in her eyes as she leaned into the phone booth and addressed her father. She placed her face in the corner of her arm, fighting back the tears that were coming too fast. "Sí, sí, Papi, estoy bien. Ya estoy bien. . . ."

Excerpt from 1976's **The Legendary Lynx #11**, *"Revelations"*—Story: Carmen Valdez, Art: Doug Detmer, Letters: Todd Morelli, Editor: Rich Berger, President/CEO: Jeffrey Carlyle.
Published by Triumph Comics.

EPILOGUE

October 10, 2018

She was pouring herself a cup of coffee when she heard the car pull into the driveway.

Their house was a few blocks off Route 6, the main thruway that cut through Cape Cod, on Stoney Hill Road. She walked toward the large bay window at the front of the house and saw a woman who was probably no older than thirty step out of a black rental car.

She gave the living room a once-over before walking toward the door to greet her guest. She loved this house. It was quaint, small, and comfortable. The kind of place where you lived—as opposed to the barrage of summer homes that littered most of this end of the Cape. Her house was in constant use, she thought. It was alive.

She opened the door and waved at the visitor, who'd parked behind her own faded blue Subaru. She noticed a flicker of recognition on the woman's face as she walked toward the door, past her well-kept garden.

She reached out her hand as the visitor walked up the porch. They shook gently. The guest had warm, kind eyes.

"You must be Laura," she said, giving her an easy smile.

Laura seemed to be trying to absorb every detail of the moment. As if she'd been waiting for it for quite some time.

"Yes, Laura Gustines," she said. "Nice to meet you, Mrs. Valdez."

"Please, call me Carmen," Carmen said, following with a quick laugh. "I may be old, but I'll never be that old."

Carmen led her visitor into the house, which was meticulously clean and organized—stylish, even, the décor giving off a vibe that was both standard Cape Cod but also thoughtful and measured. Carmen saw Laura smiling as she caught a glimpse of a framed piece of comic book art down the house's main hallway, which led to Carmen's office.

Carmen caught her expression and nodded.

"That's a Detmer," she said, motioning her chin toward the piece. "There are a few more in the office. Can I get you a glass of water? It's a long drive from the big city."

The "big city" was, of course, New York. Carmen didn't do interviews often, and when she did, she wanted them to count—or at least be conducted by someone she respected or trusted. Ideally both. She knew Laura Gustines was the main graphic novel reviewer at the *New York Times*, which both awed and surprised her. To think, there was someone whose sole job was to write about comics for the paper Carmen used to pilfer from the Triumph offices to stay up-to-date with the world.

Carmen had gently grilled Laura before she decided to agree to the interview. She knew Laura lived in Astoria, in a small two-bedroom with a friend. Was originally from Charlotte. Grew up reading comics, had a nice CV. But Carmen had been reviewed in the *Times* before. What made her consider the interview was that Laura was working on something more. Something Carmen felt was long overdue.

"No, I'm fine, thanks," Laura said, following Carmen into the living room. "I stopped for lunch on the way and I'm still wondering how I stayed awake."

"Oh?" Carmen asked, feigning interest. "Where'd you go?"

Laura's face reddened.

"Well, 'lunch' is being generous," she said with a laugh. "I stopped for ice cream and a bathroom break."

Carmen smiled.

"Ah, Sweet Escape," she said. "We go there from time to time. It's a treat, that's for sure. But that's not why you're here, is it? To talk about Cape Cod ice cream?"

Laura shrugged, as if to say, *Well, yeah.*

From what Carmen had learned, Laura Gustines was here for a few reasons. On paper, she was in the final stages of reporting for her nonfiction book, *Secret Identity*, which she described as "a look at women who'd shaped the comic book industry, with a special focus on those whom history might have forgotten or ignored." That had piqued Carmen's interest. Not because it hadn't been done before, but because it hadn't been done when Carmen was ready.

Laura had been effusive in her initial email to Carmen, calling her one of the book's holy grails, the interview Laura knew she needed before she could properly sell this book to a publisher. Carmen was flattered, of course. She'd made a name for herself over the years. She also frequently got emails and texts with links to long, winding internet message board threads intimating knowledge about what had happened before. At Triumph. But she wasn't looking to have her ego stroked. She liked the idea of helping another woman, one close in age to her when she had first set out on her own writing journey.

It felt like the right thing to do. It was also a chance to do much more.

In many ways, Carmen had left Triumph behind. Months after her encounter with Stephenson, on a whim, she'd moved to San Francisco, getting in touch with an old friend of Marion Price's and starting to get work as a freelance writer and, eventually, a cartoonist. Her illustrated memoir, *The Things That Saved Me*, was an unsung classic of the graphic novel medium, a look at coming of age in Miami during the early days of the Cuban exodus to Florida. It painted a picture of a young girl raised by conservative, hardworking parents, straining to adapt to a culture and country that felt completely alien to her—and how her own passion for comics, especially superheroes, kept her going. *Things* was Carmen's first and only published work in comics, aside from the sole issue of *The Legendary Lynx* that bore her name.

After the acclaim that followed the release of *Things,* Carmen had pivoted, carving out a healthy and vibrant career penning a series of noir-tinged science fiction novels set in the not-so-distant future, a blend of Ray Bradbury and Ursula K. Le Guin. Some had been optioned for film and were critical darlings if not international bestsellers. They paid for the house, her used car, and her groceries. More importantly, Carmen loved the books— and they let her play with the tropes and ideas she'd obsessed over as a child.

Carmen could tell Laura was smart. Not just fact-checking smart, but detective smart. She asked the right questions and seemed to feel there was something missing.

Why did you only do that one issue? she'd asked Carmen over email, a question she sidestepped gingerly.

But Laura persisted. It was clear to Carmen that the reporter was putting the pieces together. To something.

There's something missing here. I'd love to hear your story. And to help tell it in this book.

That's what had sold Carmen, finally, as she teetered between ignoring the polite reporter's last email and diving in.

"Follow me," Carmen said, her words snapping Laura to attention.

Laura followed Carmen down the house's main hallway, turning left before the bathroom. They were in Carmen's office now—expansive shelves cluttered with novels, art books, and photos, the walls loaded with framed artwork and sketches.

Carmen watched as Laura's face lit up, slowly soaking in everything. The book spines, the art on the walls, the décor. Carmen was a writer. She knew what it took—how you recorded all you could and wove it into something new, something special. Carmen allowed herself a moment to admire everything, too, and to think about what had come before. From the wreckage of Triumph she'd carved out a place for herself—as a writer and artist, but most importantly, as a person.

They sat across from each other, Carmen facing the door, both seated in front of the medium-sized desk and drawing table that took up most of the space in the office. Carmen relaxed a bit as she sat, the comfort of her working space casting a spell on her. She caught a glimpse of herself in a mirror hanging near the door. She retained the same pale skin, dark eyes, and knowing smile—except now her face was framed by her straight, shoulder-length gray hair, tucked away in a hasty ponytail. She felt at peace, too, something she didn't know was possible before. There was a clanging sound. Laura flinched. Carmen smiled softly.

"That's my wife," Carmen said. "Probably dropping a pan in the kitchen. She likes to cook, but isn't particularly good at it. I don't have the heart to tell her, though."

They laughed. Carmen watched as Laura looked over the framed artwork hanging just above Carmen's seat. An interior page from *The Legendary Lynx* #11, the one issue Carmen was credited as having written—the vigilante heroine overcoming her archnemesis, Mr. Void. The other, a cover proof of *Things,* signed by Carmen. Finally, a photo—of a younger Carmen, raven-haired, slender, and mesmerizing, standing next to an older, gaunt-looking man, in what appeared to be a studio or office space.

"That's Doug," Carmen said, following Laura's eyes. "Doug Detmer. I have a lot of his art around. I really wanted that photo taken. For some reason, it all felt so fleeting. I needed evidence."

Carmen watched the young reporter's face. She was clearly eager, but also professional—waiting for her chance. Carmen had just given it to her.

"He was a great artist," Laura said.

Carmen smiled, but said nothing.

"Now, I know you probably expected me to want to talk about your graphic novel, and your other work—your novels, which I love," Laura said. "But that's not really it."

Carmen tilted her head slightly, as if to say, *Well?*

"I want to talk about Triumph," Laura said. "I know this ground has been covered by many writers—probably more capable than me—"

"Don't sell yourself short," Carmen said, raising a hand slightly. "Just go on."

"Well, I guess I've been keeping you in suspense."

"Good writers can do that," she said. Laura responded with a polite smile.

"My book is about women in comics, generally—notable creators and editors and people who worked in the medium," Laura said. Carmen could tell she'd practiced the pitch; it sounded smooth and precise. "But my main focus, the real reason I'm writing this is here—in this room. You see, I grew up reading the Lynx—I mean, it wasn't coming out. My brother had them in his room and I was just so, I dunno, relieved to find a hero who was a woman, who wasn't a damsel in distress, and who also seemed to have a real reason for being, you know? It was eye-opening. It felt like this lost gem, and as a kid I just loved the stories—but as an adult, as a jaded adult, if I'm being honest, I returned to them. And I just had some questions that I thought you might be able to answer."

"Sure, I can try," Carmen said, leaning back, bracing herself.

"Okay, well, here goes—the book, I mean, when people talk about that comic—it's the first chunk of issues anyone cares about," Laura said excitedly. "The opening half dozen and the ones penned by the mystery writer and then your issue. I don't think people mind the later stuff, but—"

"Rich was a nice guy, great editor," Carmen interjected. "But yes, his issues felt . . . perfunctory. They were solid, but not memorable. Triumph was dying by then."

"Right, right," Laura said. "So, I've done a lot of research. Especially on the people involved. Harvey Stern—who I know was your friend—was killed before any of his issues came out. It's not a major part of comic book lore, which I found weird—but I think a big reason was that the man who was charged in his murder, and in the vicious attack on another comic book editor around that time, Marion Price, well, he died in prison—Dan Stephenson. He died before he could go to trial. So the murders seemed to fade away in history. It didn't help that Triumph was such a small company, and while the Lynx was a hit for them—it was easily overlooked. It was relative, you know?"

Carmen raised an eyebrow.

"Anyway, Harvey Stern had a body of work—nothing huge, but he'd written a stack of issues for this other small company, Bulwark. I dug those up and . . ." Laura hesitated. "And, I read those and thought, well, I guess it just didn't fit."

Carmen remained silent. Laura moved forward in her seat.

"His stuff was . . . well, it was fine, is what I mean," Laura said, grasping for the right words. "But when you compare it to his work on the Lynx, it's night and day. And then it goes off the rails, with, uh—"

"Jensen," Carmen said, almost spitting out the name.

"Right, Jensen—his work with Tinsler, well, that was just hack-y and bad," Laura said. "So, then this mystery writer—who, even up till his death a few years back, Carlyle refused to name—comes in, and you feel almost like we're back. But it's actually, for my money, even better than the first batch of issues. More confident, clearer. More—ugh, I hate this word, but more literary. More lived-in and comfortable with itself. And your fill-in, Detmer's last issue before he—well, you know."

"He killed himself," Carmen said. "You can say that."

Laura nodded.

"You seem very smart, and I appreciate you coming here—it's a great test of wills, you know? Living here—it makes the people who do show up that much more worthwhile," she said, each word sliding out with ease. "And I know you must be nervous, though you shouldn't be. I'm a person, like you. I'm not famous. I have a phone bill and a cat I take to the vet. So, at the risk of sounding rude—what can I help you with? I don't read comics now. Not many. I wrote a few, I plan to write a few more. But they're my own, outside of the thrum of the industry, outside of the trends and the buzz. So, I guess my question is, what do you want from me?"

Laura cleared her throat and waited a beat before speaking.

"I'll cut to it," she said, speaking slowly but not passively. She had probably practiced this speech, too, Carmen thought. "I've done my research. I've spoken to people who worked at Triumph at the time. I've read everything the company produced and just—well, immersed myself in all of it."

Laura paused for a second, and seemed to stare off into the distance before looking at Carmen again.

"Well, I guess, I—I just want to know if you knew anything about what happened," Laura said. "I know you were friends with Harvey, at least based on the handful of people I spoke to."

"Who was it?" Carmen asked. "Mullin? Trunick? Hahn?"

"All three," Laura said, trying not to smile and failing.

"Nice, I hope they're doing well," Carmen said. "I miss them."

"They're doing well, I think," Laura said. "Trunick writes about movies now, has a few books out. Mullin works in advertising. Hahn is a novelist, too."

Carmen's eyes seemed to brighten.

"That's wonderful," Carmen said. "But you're still avoiding your question."

Laura let out a nervous laugh.

"You're right. Well, huh. I promised myself I wouldn't crack, but here I am."

Carmen reached over and placed a hand on Laura's.

"It's okay, you can ask me whatever you want," Carmen said, giving this reporter she'd just met as soothing a smile as she could muster. "I'm all yours."

Laura smiled at the unexpected kindness, gave Carmen a quick nod, and continued.

"Well, I think the record is wrong," she said. "I don't think Harvey Stern created the Lynx and just handed it to Jeffrey Carlyle at Triumph. The story of some kind of last-minute miracle might be true—the comic crackles with the energy of something that came together fast. It's loaded with legends like that. But the truth always comes out. How Bill Finger helped with Batman, for example. How he basically created him but Bob Kane got all the credit. Comics are full of stories like that.

So, my point is—I don't think Harvey Stern wrote *The Legendary Lynx*. Not alone, at least."

Carmen started to respond, but Laura politely raised a finger.

"I think you did," Laura said, almost phrased as a question—but clear enough. "I think you created her, and poured yourself into her, and for some reason decided to let it fade away. You chose to let this part of your story be anonymous. You didn't take credit for your wonderful, historic work. And I want to know why."

Carmen straightened up in her seat and looked at Laura, any semblance of a polite smile gone—replaced by a drive and focus that had been simmering just under the surface before.

"The Lynx," Carmen said, choosing her words carefully, "was complicated. I love her. In the way you love someone you gave your heart to, but who didn't return the favor. She was important to me. She still is. But I've had to keep her at arm's length. Because it hurt too much."

Laura didn't speak. Seemed hypnotized by what Carmen was saying—was about to say.

"You see, it's hard—because for years and years, all I heard about is how great her story was, how many fans became writers and artists because of what they read," Carmen continued. "And, wow, how nice it must have been to be able to add a little riff at the end of this seminal, overlooked story. This brief coda to a character most had forgotten."

Carmen watched Laura. The reporter didn't reach for her pen. For her tape recorder. For anything. She wanted to experience this in real time, for herself. Carmen could appreciate that.

"I thought I could get past it," she said. "I moved to California. I did my own thing. Made my own name for myself. Got married. Moved back east. But life isn't like that. We can't just bury things. They crawl back. They reach up and poke at you. You have to make peace with what you did and what others did to you."

"You didn't answer my question," Laura said. Carmen felt herself bristle. She caught the reporter's expression but could sense no remorse at the brusque, cutting statement. She was a reporter, Carmen realized. A real one. They weren't afraid of asking the tough ones. But Laura was right. Carmen had evaded the question. She was tired of dodging it, too, she realized.

Carmen leaned back, waiting a beat that seemed to drag on for decades. Then she turned to face Laura, her face serene and honest, as if she were just talking about the weather—not digging into a hidden history of comics most fans, critics, and readers didn't know existed.

"Finally. I didn't think it'd happen, honestly. But yes, you're right, Laura—the Lynx is mine," Carmen Valdez said, her voice echoing through the office, the words almost melodic—as if she'd memorized them in private, in front of the mirror, but was speaking them to someone else for the first time. "I created her. It's time people knew that. I've been waiting for someone, anyone to figure it out."

Laura let out a brief, excited gasp. Carmen pressed on.

"And I want to tell my story."

ACKNOWLEDGMENTS

Secret Identity is a book I've had percolating in my mind for years. It was the novel I always wanted to write but also one I wasn't sure I was ready to write. It blends so many things I love—comic books, noir, New York, Miami, flawed characters, and more—that I needed to be sure I was doing it justice. At the end of the day, that decision rests with you, the reader.

I was lucky to have a number of sensitivity and beta readers who share some aspect of Carmen's background and were able to nudge and guide me during the writing journey. Their insights were (unsurprisingly) invaluable and meaningful, and I'm so humbled by their generosity. Thank you to Kelly J. Ford, Kristen Lepionka, Amanda de Bartolomeo, and Andrea Vigil. Additionally, Carmen Maria Machado's genre-bending memoir *In the Dream House* and Alison Bechdel's two graphic novel autobiographies proved particularly helpful—and were just flat-out amazing to read. Trina Robbins's essential works, specifically *A Century of Women Cartoonists*, *The Great Women Cartoonists*, *The Great Women Superheroes*, and her memoir, *Last Girl Standing*, were a massive resource to me as well. Alexander Chee's excellent essay, "How to Unlearn Everything" originally published in *Vulture*, and Nisi Shawl and Cynthia

Ward's essential *Writing the Other: A Practical Approach* helped me numerous times. I also spoke to a number of comic book industry friends—women who worked in comics and publishing during or around the time described in the novel. Their recollections, anecdotes, and memories of comics and New York at the time were huge helps in making the world Carmen, Harvey, and others inhabit feel real. Thank you to Linda Fite, Louise Simonson, Karen Berger, Isabel Stein, and Laurie Sutton, legendary, trailblazing women who blessed me with their time and stories.

The world of comic books and publishing was vastly different from the one I now inhabit today as a writer, editor, and executive of graphic novels. Before comic shops sprung up to create a specialty market and long before traditional bookstores and digital outlets made selling comics standard, the industry had one narrow funnel to reach an audience: newsstands. During the midseventies, the industry was spinning out, and few saw what it might become. Surely no one was thinking we'd be lining up to see a movie or streaming TV shows based on then B-list characters like Ant-Man, Peacemaker, or the Eternals. Well, maybe just Dan Stephenson. I relied on a number of well-researched comic book histories and fictional stories to give me a better sense of what things were like in 1975 in comics and in New York City, while understanding what came before and after. Each one is worth your time. They include Megan Margulies's fantastic memoir about her memories of her grandfather Joe Simon, *My Captain America: A Granddaughter's Memoir of a Legendary Comic Book Artist; James Warren: Empire of Monsters,* Bill Schelly's fantastic biography of the Warren founder; Nathalia Holt's history of unsung women animators during the early days of Disney, *The Queens of Animation;* Ed Brubaker and Sean Phillips's fictional Criminal graphic novel set in the comic book industry, *Bad Weekend;* Grant Morrison's trippy, heartfelt, and personal love letter to superhero comics, *Supergods;* Jill Lepore's incisive and meticulous look at the origins of Wonder Woman, *The Secret History of Wonder Woman;* Marc Tyler Nobleman and Ty Templeton's heart-wrenching look at the sad tale of Batman cocreator Bill Finger, *Bill the Boy Wonder;* David Hajdu's tour de force look at the horror comics boom and bust of the 1950s, *The Ten-*

Cent Plague; J. Michael Straczynski's entertainment memoir, *Becoming Superman;* Glen Weldon's fantastic history of Batman's place in pop culture, *The Caped Crusade;* Art Spiegelman and Chip Kidd's look at the tragic life and enduring legacy of artist Jack Cole, *Jack Cole and Plastic Man;* Hillary Chute's indispensable guide to comics, *Why Comics?;* Douglas Wolk's thoughtful and welcoming analysis of the medium, *Reading Comics;* Austin Grossman's enjoyable superhero deconstruction novel, *Soon I Will Be Invincible;* Alex Grand and Jim Thompson's exhaustive and informative *Comic Book Historians* podcast; TwoMorrows' insightful and entertaining Bronze Age publication, *Back Issue* magazine; Abraham Riesman's powerhouse biography of Stan Lee, *True Believer;* and last, but certainly not least, Sean Howe's compelling and comprehensive Marvel history, *Marvel Comics: The Untold Story.* In terms of setting, I also found myself relying heavily on Will Hermes's snapshot of New York in the 1970s, *Love Goes to Buildings on Fire;* Judith Rossner's potboiler of a mystery, *Looking for Mr. Goodbar;* and Don DeLillo's satiric masterpiece *Great Jones Street.*

While research is, of course, invaluable, I gained much from direct conversations and interviews with people who were there. I am beyond lucky to have many friends who've been in comics for a long time, and doubly lucky to have been able to lean on them for their time and remembrances of the era—or their knowledge of comics history as a whole. I'm eternally indebted to a who's who of comic book legends, including Paul Levitz, Stuart Moore, Gerry Conway, Robert Greenberger, Brian Cronin, Paul Kupperberg, Kurt Busiek, Scott Edelman, Alex Simmons, Michael Gonzales, and the aforementioned Fite, Simonson, Berger, Sutton, Howe, and Riesman, who were exceedingly generous with insights and guidance. They all made this story stronger and better.

One of the best things to happen to me over the last year—a twelve-month span full of so much anxiety, stress, and chaos for all of us—was forming a writers' group with three super-talented writers who also happen to be truly good people. Their support, feedback, humor, and friendship have been invaluable. I don't think you'd have this book in your hands if not for Kellye Garrett, Amina Akhtar, and Elizabeth Little. I also suggest you pick up their novels—but if you're a smart reader, you already have. They're simply the best, and I'm a better writer by association.

In addition to my writers' group and my sensitivity readers, I was also quite lucky to have some of the best beta readers and volunteer copy editors ever—people who were willing to sacrifice their own time to read my work and make suggestions that helped elevate and improve *Secret Identity*. Thank you, Elizabeth Keenan, Phoebe Flowers, Rob Hart, Emily Giglierano, Chantel Acevedo, Erica Wright, Isabel Stein, Michael A. Gonzales, Ellen Clair Lamb, and the inevitable person I thoughtlessly forgot—I blame my schedule, young children, and lack of sleep. I'd also like to thank the many author friends who, whether they know it or not, helped me bring this book to life—through a kind word, bit of advice, or just by being around. Special thanks need to go to organizations like Sisters in Crime, Mystery Writers of America, and my beloved Crime Writers of Color. We need to lift each other up, speak out for what's important, and celebrate our victories, and these groups help do that. I'd also like to thank my many friends in the world of comics—my colleagues at Oni Press, the many writers and artists I've had the pleasure to work with and call friends, and the many professional contacts and colleagues I've made over my two decades of work in the medium.

Secret Identity was particularly unique in that it featured comic book sequences woven into the prose narrative, and I certainly could not have created those pages alone. Artist Sandy Jarrell, a talented and (in my opinion) underrated draftsman, was my top choice to bring the Lynx to life. He did not disappoint, going above and beyond what I could have ever imagined. His art perfectly encapsulated the tone and style of the time, and his attention to detail and flexibility made him the ideal creative partner. I've known Sandy for a long time, probably longer than either of us would care to admit, and I'm so proud we've finally been able to collaborate directly. Taylor Esposito, one of the best letterers in the comic book business, was able to evoke the style of the era deftly and never flinched when last-minute changes were needed. I couldn't have asked for better collaborators, and I do hope we find a way to tell more stories about the Lynx in the future.

Huge thanks to my superstar agent and friend Josh Getzler, who believed in this project from the moment I first mentioned it and didn't bat a lash at the complexities that came with it. HG Literary has proven to be the perfect home for my work, and I couldn't ask for a stronger advocate than Josh. Every author hopes for an agent that "gets" their work, and I'm blessed to have one.

I'll let you in on a secret about *Secret Identity:* In my heart of hearts, I wanted Zack Wagman to edit it before I'd written it. Years before I even put pen to paper on it, when it was just something I was researching and when he was working elsewhere, I knew Zack had to edit it. I try not to set myself up for disappointment in life, so my singular focus was uncharacteristic. But I just felt he'd get it. Our shared passion for comics, noir, and diverse and varied stories made this the ideal creative marriage, and every page is stronger, clearer, and better because of Zack's vision, thoughtful notes, and steady hand. He helped chip at and smooth over the story and bring out the characters in ways I couldn't have done alone, and I'm so grateful for his support, friendship, and mentoring. I'd also like to thank his superb assistant, Maxine Charles, and the entire team at Flatiron Books for making this a truly special experience.

I'm forever thankful to the book community at large—the booksellers and librarians who toiled through a year-plus of massive change, virtual events, and tumult. The readers who find ways to support us—spreading the word, reading our work, and always being there. They are the bedrock of what we do, and without them these books are just ink on paper. Readers, librarians, booksellers, and bookstores give our words life, and I can't thank them enough.

As noted, 2020 was a hard, brutal year. In many ways, the writing of this book helped keep me level and focused. It was a beacon of light during a time where there was very little anyone could control. I'm blessed to be surrounded by so many friends in life and in the comic book and mystery communities, and I'm forever humbled and grateful for my family, specifically my two beautiful children, Guillermo and Lucia, and my fearless, sharp, and lovely wife, Eva. They keep me hopeful, sane, and grateful, and I continue to relish living a life beyond my wildest dreams with them by my side.

ABOUT THE AUTHOR

Alex Segura is an acclaimed, award-winning writer of novels, comic books, short stories, and podcasts. He is the author of *Star Wars Poe Dameron: Free Fall,* the Pete Fernandez Mystery series (including the Anthony Award–nominated crime novels *Dangerous Ends, Blackout,* and *Miami Midnight*), and *Secret Identity.* His short story "Red Zone" won the 2020 Anthony Award for Best Short Story, and his border noir short story "90 Miles" will be included in *The Best American Mystery and Suspense 2021.* He has also written a number of comic books, most notably the superhero noir *The Black Ghost,* the YA music series *The Archies,* and the "Archie Meets" collection of crossovers, featuring real-life cameos from the Ramones, The B-52's, and more. He is also the cocreator and cowriter of the *Lethal Lit* crime/YA podcast from iHeartRadio, which was named one of the best podcasts of 2018 by *The New York Times.* By day he is the senior vice president of sales and marketing at Oni Press, with previous stints at Archie Comics and DC Comics. A Miami native, he lives in New York with his wife and children.